THE EIGHTH LION

TONY THOMPSON

THE EIGHTH LION

Copyright © 2020 Tony Thompson.

All rights reserved. No part of this book may be used or reproduced by any means, graphic, electronic, or mechanical, including photocopying, recording, taping or by any information storage retrieval system without the written permission of the author except in the case of brief quotations embodied in critical articles and reviews.

This is a work of fiction. All of the characters, names, incidents, organizations, and dialogue in this novel are either the products of the author's imagination or are used fictitiously.

iUniverse books may be ordered through booksellers or by contacting:

iUniverse
1663 Liberty Drive
Bloomington, IN 47403
www.iuniverse.com
844-349-9409

Because of the dynamic nature of the Internet, any web addresses or links contained in this book may have changed since publication and may no longer be valid. The views expressed in this work are solely those of the author and do not necessarily reflect the views of the publisher, and the publisher hereby disclaims any responsibility for them.

Any people depicted in stock imagery provided by Getty Images are models, and such images are being used for illustrative purposes only.
Certain stock imagery © Getty Images.

ISBN: 978-1-6632-0123-2 (sc)
ISBN: 978-1-6632-0124-9 (hc)
ISBN: 978-1-6632-0122-5 (e)

Library of Congress Control Number: 2020917019

Print information available on the last page.

iUniverse rev. date: 10/07/2020

I dedicate this book to Ron White, one of the Eighth Lions in my life. Ron started as a substitute teacher's assistant in my classroom. Hired to be my para-educator, he quickly became a fabulous co-teacher and Mentor. One of my favorite colleagues, he blossomed into one of my dearest friends. I look to Ron as an older (and much wiser) brother and the father figure I never had growing up.

Once, when I became upset about a mistake I had made, Ron looked to me and said, "Hey, it proves you are human." Words of Wisdom.

~MAP~
THE KNOWN WORLD

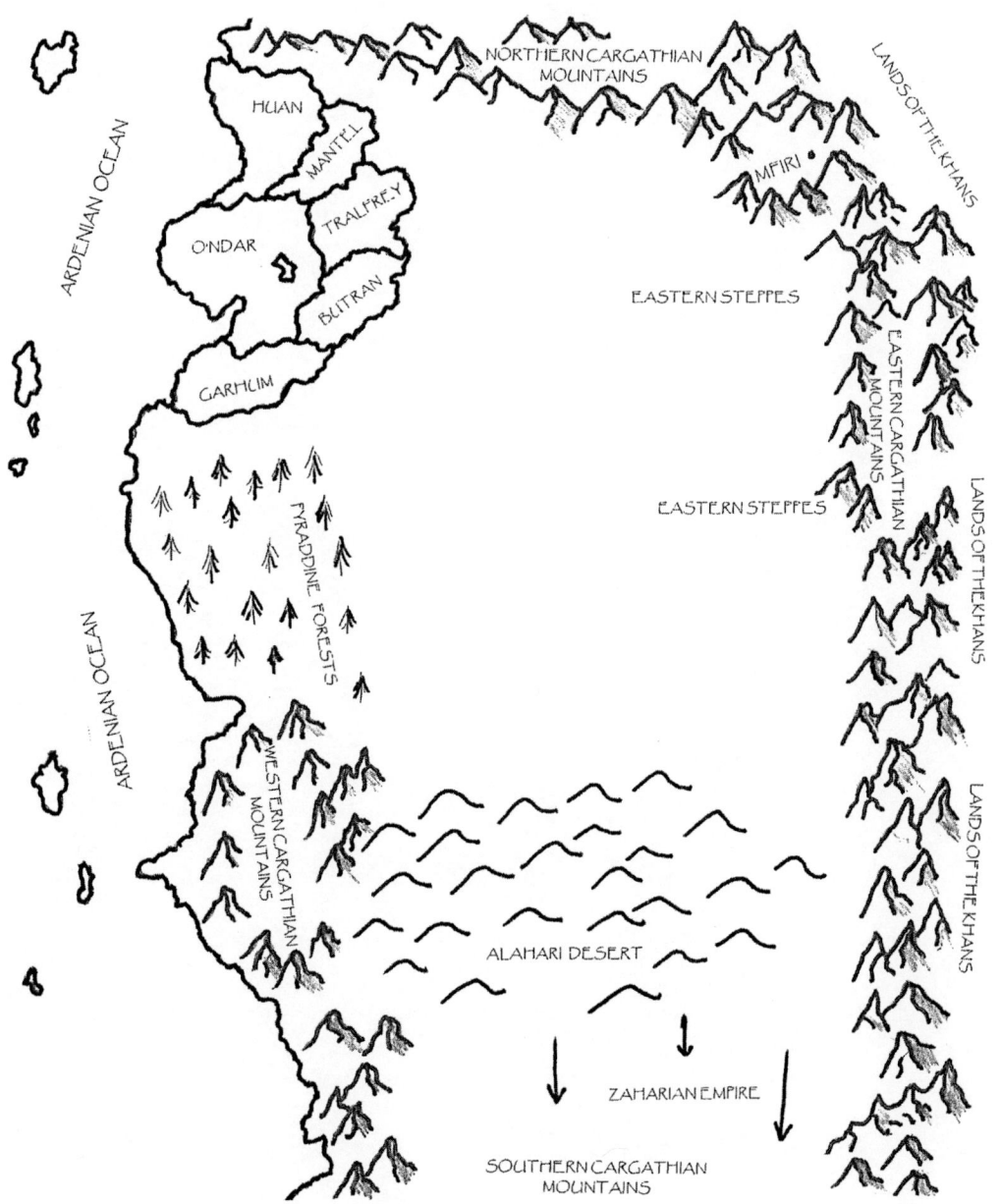

A BRIEF HISTORY OF DRAGONS

IN THE SPRING OF MY SEVENTEENTH YEAR, WHEN I WAS still a brash, young-man and much too clever for my own good, news of a large, emerald colored Dragon was brought to the Feasting Hall of my lord, Gheldari, leader of the clan, recently anointed King, and protector of us all. Witnesses reported the Dragon flying northward along the coast out of the Pyraddine Forests.

Gheldari was a large, powerful man. His strong, hawk-like nose, fiery green eyes, and muscular frame exuded strength and vitality. Very few could match his strength with the sword, the spear, or the fist. His intelligence was above reproach, proven by his ability to weld the clans together into a military force powerful enough to carve out a Kingdom for himself. His face, covered with a full, black beard, which only enhanced his grizzled features.

Yet, even with all of his strength and intelligence, my lord had learned, in order to be a practical King, wisdom was also an essential quality. This was true especially when it came to the issue of dragons. While he yearned to ride out and fight the dragon, Gheldari instead sent for advisors.

Immediately, Gheldari asked for their advice on how to deal with this potential threat. Fear of the Dragon coming closer to the newly created city-state of Chondar spread quickly through the group of terrified men.

Gheldari wanted to send five-thousand soldiers to meet the threat. It was clear his generals disagreed. There had never been a dragon killed by the weapons of man. The wrath and anger of the mighty King quickly dissipated, replaced with despair.

Seeing my lord distraught, brazenly I stepped forward and asked to be able to speak.

"My Lord, may I be of service in this matter?" I said, almost too timidly.

Many in the Great Hall wanted me whipped for my insolence. My courage began to wane and the heat from the roaring fire was stifling. I wavered for a few seconds. The long, oaken tables, placed close together for the morning meal, made it feel as if the room had shrunk, and was now very overcrowded. Within a few seconds, though, I regained my courage and held my head high.

Gheldari, on the other hand, seemed amused by my bravery and ordered me to step forward. I did so quickly and kneeled at the feet of my master.

I offered to travel south to speak with the Dragon in order to ask it to spare Chondar and its citizens.

The entire room erupted into chaos with curses yelled at me from all directions.

"Throw him out the window, My Lord."

"Lop of his head, the nerve."

The generals were strongly opposed to my plan. They yelled obscenities at me vehemently. A few of the warriors unsheathed their swords and offered to run me through on Gheldari's behalf.

Gheldari sat on his throne silently. He leaned forward, elbow on his thigh with his chin resting in his right hand. He smiled at me and seemed pleased.

"Are there any other ideas?" he demanded to those in the hall. Not one person answered.

My Lord, not having any other sage advice and any other viable options, patted me on the shoulder, ordered me loaded with provisions, and sent me immediately south. I am quite sure everyone, including Gheldari, surmised this would be the last time I set foot in our illustrious city.

Initially, I went to the harbor and sought passage on one of the longboats anchored there. Chondar, with its calm harbor nestled within a wide bay, had already become a trade route to many nations across the ocean. To my disappointment, none of the captains would agree to a voyage to the south. News of the dragon had reached their ears, as well. Thus, leaving Chondar one bright morning I traveled south slowly on foot. The realization of my brashness had settled in and I began to regret my offer to seek out the dragon. On foot, I travelled for twenty-three days.

While I travelled, I stayed as close to the coast as I could. Keeping the ocean to my right, I eventually made it to the northern reaches of the Pyraddine Forests. It was the furthest I had ever been from home. The beauty of the coast mesmerized me, as did the wonderment of the giant Red-Barked trees, thickly populating the forest. Some of the trees seemingly disappeared into the sky, blending with each other into a thick, luscious canopy.

Eventually I found a spot a mile or so inward from the coast, a spot where the forests blended into the foothills of the southern reaches of the Cargathian Mountains. I set up camp. Determined to have a splendid meal, even though it was a cold one, I sat down and enjoyed the finest fruit cakes baked in Gheldari's kitchens. This I complimented with a hardy block of cheese and some fine wine from My Lord's very own stock, a gift from my master.

I spent my last night alone along the edge of the forest refusing to light a fire for fear the Dragon might discover my location. Assured of my impending doom, I was determined not to bring the event on more quickly. My body shivering, I slept rolled up in my robe and lying on the damp ground. I lay on my back for hours listening to the sound of the waves crashing into the rocks and echoing through the nearby trees. I spent much of the night staring at the stars twinkling above. It was a most peaceful night. One, I have never forgotten. The moon was full and bright. The cascading light filtered through the trees making the Pyraddine Forests seem a magical place.

In the morning, the sun broke above the foothills, streaming its golden rays through the treetops and along the forests floor. I arose feeling refreshed and for the first time in my life, I felt truly alive. I sluffed off my robe, picked up my spear, also a gift from My Lord, and quietly stepped into the ocean of trees before me. It was time I met the emerald Dragon of the Pyraddines. I determined I would present myself as a brave warrior and issue the demands on behalf of my King.

Entering the nearby forest, I had been walking a mere fifteen minutes when I heard the awful sounds of an animal in distress. The bleating reminded me of a time when, as a little boy, I saw a bull that had fallen off the edge of a cliff and had broken its front legs. The pain and the distress of that bull still burned within me and I ran towards the sound.

What I found amazed me. Lying on its back, crushed beneath a large tree, was a small, black dragon. The weight of the giant Red-Barked tree had pinned the Dragon's large arms across its chest. It was smaller than I had expected. The description of the emerald dragon had put it at least five times as large as this one. In my assessment, the scaly, black lizard equaled the length of five horses. I approached cautiously; aware this might be an opportunity to rid my home of another potential threat.

The Dragon looked to my spear held in front of me, the tip pointed towards the very eyes of the beast. It stopped struggling, aware I held its life within my hands. The forest was deathly silent.

I cannot clearly speak as to why I spared the Dragon. It might have been pity. It might have been compassion. Either way, I lowered my spear and looked for a manner to roll the burdensome tree away from the giant lizard.

Working slowly, I started by carrying as many large boulders as I could and placed them a few feet away from the trunk of the massive tree. The Dragon watched in silence, enthralled by my actions. It no longer cried out in pain.

Once the boulders were in place, I stripped large branches from a nearby tree and placed them beneath the tree hoping to create a fulcrum. Finally, after believing I had done as much as I could do, I lifted and carried a large boulder over to the branches. I climbed onto the branches, adding my weight to the boulders. These efforts moved the broad trunk a sliver, allowing the Dragon to squirm and un-cross its arms. I was able to witness firsthand the terrible power of the beast. Pushing upward against the trunk, the large Red-Barked tree flew away from the dragon, crashing to the ground loudly. I was petrified.

Once free, the coal-black Dragon quickly rolled over onto its belly, stood up on its four powerful legs, and faced me. I was sure I would become this Dragon's first meal of the day.

The Dragon opened its mouth and hissed soothingly at me. The thick, black scales flattened out along its back sending a wave of gray and black down the length of its body. The Dragon was trying to communicate. My heart beat rapidly in my chest.

"She says thank you," a silky voice offered. The words floated out of the trees and down from the green canopy above. My eyes darted back and forth through the trees. The ebony Dragon and I were not alone.

Quietly and ever so slowly, a green-feathered dragon stepped forward out of the surrounding trees.

I wondered if it had been there, witnessing the events, the whole time.

The Emerald Dragon equaled the length of one-hundred horses. Intimidated, I fell to my knees.

"Rise, Pelinnedes, the Historian. You have no need to fear me," the Emerald Dragon intoned.

The voice was silky smooth, almost melodious. My fear left me. I stood and faced the Dragon. She turned, hissed something at the black dragon. It flew away.

"I thank you for saving the youngest of my brood. She recently hatched and was out strengthening her wings. She became careless becoming trapped beneath the falling tree." The eyes of the green Dragon bore into me, but I was at peace, ready to accept death if needed.

"I am glad I did not save her. It was much more fascinating to see a member of the race of man risking his life to save a Dragon. How did you know my daughter would not kill you once she was free?"

I swallowed hard, knowing the Dragon could sense any deception on my part and offered only the truth. "I did not." This response brought a gentle gleam into the bright yellow eyes. They twinkled at me in the morning light.

All my fear left me and I moved closer to the Dragon. I reached out my hand and touched her feathers. This dragon, a mosaic of bright and dark greens smiled when I caressed her emerald-colored feathers. Similar to a bird's, they were both soft and coarse to the touch. She waited patiently as I walked along her flanks, stroking the feathers, mumbling questions and offering answers to myself.

"You look confused, Pelinnedes," her velvety, soft voice offered. The cat-like eyes continued to offer nothing, but warmth and kindness.

"I must admit, I am My Lady?" I stood dumbfounded, completely self-absorbed in what I had discovered. It was only then I realized I had touched her without her permission. I dropped to my knees and lowered my head.

"Please forgive my rudeness," I responded. My words seemed to endear her to me more. She cooed softly to me.

"You are forgiven. Rise, friend of the Dragons. And why do you refer to me as My Lady?" the Dragon asked, intrigued.

"You are more majestic, more beautiful than any Queen I have ever seen." I blurted out. She seemed pleased with my statement.

"May I ask a question, My Lady?" I stammered. She nodded her enormously feathered head in the affirmative, causing wisps of my hair to lift in the gentle breeze.

"You called me the Historian. I must be honest with you and let you know I am no more than cup-filler in the castle of my lord. At night, I sit outside his door with a bottle of his favorite wine. He calls. I enter quietly, fill his cup, then leave. No more."

Her response echoed throughout the forest. "You were, Pelinnedes, until today. I have been waiting a long time for you. You enter this forest no more than a filler of cups and will leave a historian. I attest you will live a long life, grow old and die many, many years into the future. You are destined to become one of the world's greatest historians. Your books will become required readings for the children of most noble houses hundreds of years from now."

I stood frozen as the words of this majestic beast sunk in. I looked into her eyes and saw sincerity in its rawest form.

"Go back to your camp, bring yourself some food. We will sit for a while so I may answer your questions." I ran as quickly as I could and returned with food.

After gathering a few logs, I looked to her questioningly and looked at the logs. She waited patiently for me to ask.

"My Lady, could you blow on these logs to start a fire for me?" I asked.

I admit to disappointment when she responded, "I am sorry, Pelinnedes. I do not have the power to breathe fire."

I took her at her word, sat down, and ate my cold food in silence.

I asked how she knew I would come to the Pyradinne Forests. She responded, "I will admit to you, and to no one else, I have mastered one of my orbs and can see the future. All Dragons are magical and can see the past. Very few ever develop the power to see the future, though."

I continued to pry her with questions, some she would answer and some she would not. Finally, the mighty Dragon spoke. Her voice no longer smooth and silky. It harnessed a new strength and was powerful, iron-like, "Climb on my back, Historian." I looked down the length of the Dragon petrified with fear. "Do not fear. We are going to my cave high in the mountains. It is time for man to have an accurate understanding of the Dragon Race!"

Her powerful voice bellowed, "I am going to break a covenant as old as time itself. I am going to break the covenant of the Dragon race and tell you our History."

"But, I have no way of writing down what you tell me," I stammered. This response brought an even bigger chuckle.

"Write it down? My good Pelinnedes. You are not going to write it down! You are going to memorize it."

She waited patiently for me to scurry up along her flanks. I settled in at a spot directly behind her head, on the back of her neck, nestling deeply within the feathers. Grabbing ahold of the thickest feathers, I was petrified I might at some point fall off during the flight. The Dragon alleviated my fears quickly by smoothing out the surrounding feathers, locking me into place.

"You are about to experience something few humans ever will. Remember this moment forever. In your books, be sure to remind men Dragons are not mules! We are not meant to be ridden in the manner men ride a donkey."

She leaped into the air like a cat, carrying us up into the air, above the tops of the trees. Immediately she stretched out the giant, bird-like wings and we flew into the sky, soaring up to the highest mountain peak. It was snow-capped, and looking at it from above, I must admit to having a religious moment. I closed my eyes and thanked the gods for my life.

As we neared the peak, four black dragons approached. They circled us flying away. Landing at the mouth of the cave the Dragon kneeled down. I moved quickly around to her face.

"Sit down my dear Pelinnedes," she ordered.

I listened intently as the magnificent Dragon recounted the History of the Dragon Race. Her awe-inspiring words included the birth of the original three Titans: Norduir the Ice-Dragon, Pahaida the Lava-Dragon, and Bosque the Emerald Dragon.

For the next three years, I learned many previously unknown things about Dragons. There are no male Dragons in the world. All Dragons are born coal-black and will transform into one of the three Titan forms, once they hatch a clutch of orbs. Eventually I was able to memorize her words in order to put them into a book when I returned home. I settled on the title while living among the dragons. The book's title would be <u>A Brief History of Dragons.</u>

During the few years spent with her, Meeha demanded I recite, word for word, all she told to me. In the morning hours, just before the sun peaked out above the mountaintops, Meeha or one of her daughters would fly me to the forests far below to gather food and to bathe in the lakes. It was very awkward at first, having the young, black Dragons watch over me. Meeha explained she would be distraught if anything bad happened to me. There are many predators, in these forests, that would like an easy meal. My embarrassment soon left me and I came to appreciate their presence

Finally, after three years had passed I finished my task set by the Emerald Dragon. In time, I memorized the <u>Brief History of Dragons</u> as told by Meeha, third daughter of Bosque.

One morning, after I again recited word for word all she had imparted to me, Meeha smiled and nodded at me in approval.

"We are finished my young historian, or is it my young king? It is time you return to your home."

Confused, I asked the Dragon what she meant.

Meeha, third daughter of Bosque, rose to her full height and looked down on me. "You have been away from your lord for three years. In that time, his brothers have poisoned Gheldari and have taken control of Chondar. They rule the city with an iron fist. They have killed all of his children except for his youngest son. They have stayed his execution out of fear the soldiers would rise up against them. They have grown powerful enough and now hope to cement their power. This evening, they will take his life."

I shook my head saddened by the news of my lord, Gheldari. I frowned upon hearing that his youngest son, Ghardenne was imprisoned.

"But, how does that make me king?" Meeha's eyes twinkled, reminding me for the first time of a snake stalking its prey.

Once again, the Dragon rose up, but this time crossed her arms. She had a stern look upon her face and stated loudly, "It is time I returned you to the race of man. You may return as Pelinnedes the Historian. You may also fly with me into Chondar, and we will kill all of your lord's brethren. You may then pronounce yourself King. None living will oppose either."

Though tempted, I hardened to my original purpose. "May I ask your support if I choose to go as the Historian? I would like help to restore the true king to his throne," I stated.

She looked at me with affection, responding, "I knew I chose true Pelinnedes. You have found a place always in the hearts of the Dragons of the Forests."

She turned to one of her daughters, the one I had saved in the forest years before, and nodded.

Placed gently before me were three items. The first was a Dragon's tooth. The other two gifts were bright, green Dragon feathers. All three were almost as long as I am tall.

"For the king," she whispered.

Once again, Meeha instructed me to climb aboard her back. I did so both saddened and elated. I climbed onto her back feeling blessed.

We leaped down from the edge of her cave, springing out away from the mountains and falling for a few seconds down through the clouds before she spread her wings. Thus, we soared away from the mountains across the skies. Heading north along the coast, long before the setting of the evening sun, we spied Chondar.

I could see thousands of citizens gathered in the center of town, waiting for the execution.

A great roar arose the moment they spotted us. Many had rightfully guessed a Dragon was flying towards them from the cloudless sky. Meeha chuckled, enjoying the terror her presence struck into the hearts of humans. She screamed loudly. The high-pitched scream was not the paralyzing scream the Dragons of the Forests use as a weapon, but it was loud enough to freeze every person in the courtyard in their tracks.

We landed softly in the middle of the city, a few feet away from the wooden scaffold erected for Ghardenne's execution. Ringed in by guards and other people, Meeha crouched down in order to allow me to gently slide off her back. I quickly moved around to her face and placed both hands lovingly on her feather-covered cheek.

There was a murmur from those in the crowd the moment they recognized me. The brothers of my lord Gheldari walked slowly across the courtyard surrounded by many of the soldiers who had once served my lord.

Meekly, one of them spoke, hoping not to anger the great beast lording over all present.

"What is the meaning of this?" Gehark, the eldest brother of my lord, asked. He was a large, fully bearded man. He looked very powerful, though, compared to my original master, Gheldari, he looked weak and feeble.

He was very intimidated by Meeha's presence.

Loudly, before the people and the guards, I demanded, "Where is Ghardenne? Where is the son of my lord, Gheldari?"

Gehark, angered at the insolence in my question started to speak "Silence!" I yelled. The entire throng of people fell into a hush. "I will ask one more-time, where is Ghardenne? If I do not have an answer within a few seconds, I will unleash this Dragon and burn Chondar to ashes."

The citizens fell prostrate to the ground. The guards and soldiers dropped their weapons, holding their hands in the air. "They are bloodless," some of them mumbled. Within a few minutes, Ghardenne was placed before me, his clothing tattered and unwashed. Dirt and soot streaked across his tear-stained face.

I was angered beyond my faculties. Smiling, though, I gently waved him to me. Timidly, he walked towards me. Protectively, I put an arm around his shoulder and whispered, "My Lord, all is going to be made right. This I swear."

"I am Pelinnedes, the Historian, brought here by this Dragon to right a great wrong brought on the house of Gheldari by his kinsmen. The Dragon has sworn that as long as a son of Gheldari sits upon the throne she will stay north of the forests, in the mountains. She swears it now before all present."

All eyes turned towards the Emerald Dragon. Slowly, waiting for the silence to return, Meeha shocked everyone by responding with a booming voice, "This, I swear."

Immediately, the soldiers and the guards seized Gehark and the rest of the rebels, dragged them to the platforms and hanged them to death.

I turned and knelt before Ghardenne, the young boy still shocked by the events unfolding before him. I said, "My lord. Sent on a quest by your father to ask the Emerald Dragon to stay out of your realm, I return to you to say the Dragon has agreed."

Immediately, everyone knelt and swore loyalty to Ghardenne and the House of Gheldari. The young King accepted their fealty and ordered all to rise.

I walked to Meeha and pressed my forehead once more to her softly feathered face.

"Goodbye My Lady. You have done me a great honor and I will remember you for the rest of my life," I stated humbly. Once again, the twinkling in her eyes re-appeared. She smiled even more broadly than ever before.

"Goodbye, Pelinnedes. Humans will begin to rise and may someday gain dominion over the earth. Use the knowledge given about the Dragon Race wisely," she said loudly.

I watched her with sadness as she flew away, disappearing into the horizon.

Early the next morning I received a summons from Ghardenne, requesting my presence in the Great Hall. I dressed quickly and went before the newly crowned king.

In the presence of all the new King spoke, "I thank you Pelinnedes, the Historian. If it were not for your bravery I would not be here today."

"I would like you to immediately begin writing down your experiences."

"I have brought along some gifts from the Dragon for you," I responded.

The King, who was no more than a little boy, leaned up curious and excited.

I knelt and presented to him the gifts from Meeha, third daughter of Bosque, the Emerald Dragon, and Queen of the Pyraddine Forests.

NINE-HUNDRED YEARS LATER

LIZARD FROM THE MOUNTAINS

ONCE, THERE LIVED A BROTHER AND A SISTER WHO WERE the only children of the King and Queen of the country of O'ndar. The most powerful of the northern nations of the Known World had a bustling seaport, a well-trained army, and a history like no others.

Ringed in by the distant Cargathian Mountains, the Known World included a vast swath of trees known as the Pyraddine Forests, the Grasslands of the Eastern Steppes, and the Alahari Desert in the south.

O'ndar was a bustling country, vibrant with trade and full of wealth. Its bulging treasury provided it the wealth needed to build the most powerful army of the northern nation states. The other five nations, each ruled by a monarch who could claim a common ancestry with O'ndar's king and the the direct descendant of the House of Gheldari.

Placed on their thrones by the legendary Chardon I, more than six-hundred years prior, the ancestors to the kings owed their rise to O'ndar and its military. Chardon I had welded the northern countries together through a series of military battles, but had refused to make himself emperor.

With a long and distinguished history, O'ndar was at peace with all of its neighbors. Its well-trained army helped maintain a peaceful balance, especially with the large bands of Horsemen from the Eastern Steppes. The Known World had not seen war in hundreds of years and there was none on the horizon.

Lyssa, daughter of the king, was sixteen years of age and less than a month away from her birthday. She was tall for her age. She was almost as tall as the King. Her soft, blue eyes sat above a tiny button nose, rosy red cheeks, and full red lips. Inherited from her father, her pale skin was porcelain like, soft and smooth. Many people considered beautiful.

Landon was fourteen years of age and idolized his sister. He, as the only son, was next in line for the throne. While his sister was fair-skinned with sandy-blonde hair, he had inherited his looks from his mother, the Queen. Brought north many years ago from a country in the far south, it was easy to see where his dark eyes and coal, black hair came from. Olive-skinned, he was lean, already muscular and full of vigor.

With a strong, straight nose and high cheekbones, the young man seemed to be the exact opposite of the Princess, yet the two siblings loved each other dearly. They genuinely enjoyed each other's company and were never apart for more than a few hours.

On the dawn of the first day of spring, at the time when the flowers bloom forth with a bright array of colors, the two decided to spend the day fishing and kite flying. Both had always been their favorite activities and with the melting of the winter snow they planned their first spring outing.

Lyssa met her father early in the morning, which she always did whenever the two left the castle. After a light peck, the Princess stood facing the king. "Good day to you my King and father," she said, smiling.

She stepped back, curtsied to her father, and spun around to run down the hall.

"Good day to you my daughter," Ghardenne XVI responded. The princess had already bounded down the hallway and out of site.

"When do you want to fly the kites?" Prince Landon asked his sister, her nose jammed into a book.

The two rode in a carriage pulled by two horses and accompanied by five of the Royal Guard. The carriage would wind its way through the Sleeping Hills Forests eventually stopping at Lake Windain.

"Let's fish first," she said, not looking up from her book.

Prince Landon laughed at her response. His sister had grown into a woman. Soon, she would head south, forced to marry a Prince in order to fulfill the Treaty that had brought his mother north. He frowned, but decided to shake off the gloomy thoughts.

Lyssa smiled and said, "If you are bored, brother, you could read a book to pass the time. Do you see the ones I brought for you to read?" She pointed to a stack of three books sitting on the seat next to him.

He held up a book the first book, a green-leather bound book titled, *The Languages of Nobility*. Landon feigned yawning. He tossed the book back onto the seat. The second book with a red cover and gold lettering brought a smile to his face. It was *Big Cats of the World*. He had read the book when he was younger. The book, a gift from his mother, included drawings and description of all of the known big cats of the world. There were Mountain Lions, Cheetahs, Leopards, and even Tigers. He had not looked at the book in more than three years. Landon opened his hands to show he was passing on her offer.

"Maybe another time," he responded.

"I better enjoy this while it lasts," he thought. Turning from his sister, Landon watched the castle disappear from site the moment the carriage entered the Sleeping Hills Forest. Swallowed by the large Oaks, the carriage slowly picked its way along the patch of dirt carved through the trees.

He had always wondered about the name given to this forest. There were no hills for miles around.

Each time he traveled through the woods he thought back to his first conversation with his mother about this very topic. He had been preparing for bed and she leaned in to tuck the blanket up around his neck. The Queen, Lenali, had smiled. She repeated the story told to her on her first day in O'ndar.

The Queen told him the forests lacked hills because they had fallen asleep and were now resting blissfully beneath the trees. The hills were snuggled beneath the forests, warmed by the roots of the trees.

"But how can hills fall asleep, mother?"

He remembered her smile, gentle and caring. She leaned in, finished tucking him into his bed, and bent forward slightly to give him a peck on the forehead.

"They can if you believe they can," she whispered. She added, "You just have to have faith."

"*I shall tell my children the same tale. Will my sister tell her children?*"

A gentle bump in the road lifted Lyssa off her seat. She almost dropped her book into her lap. Landon snickered a little, realized she was still ignoring him, and decided it was probably best to leave her to her book.

"*She has made me a better person,*" he thought to himself.

Landon had always been a difficult child to handle. He was boisterous, demanding, and childish. He often spent his waking moments harassing the soldiers of the Royal Guard. The Prince thought of the soldiers as nothing more than playthings.

Once, when he was eight years old he had yelled at one of the Captains of the Guard. In a burst of fury, Prince Landon took his riding crop and struck the man on the backside. The moment the riding crop struck, Lyssa had rounded the corner. Appalled by his actions, she apologized to the Captain for the treatment he had received. The man accepted her expressions of sorrow and went on about his business. Landon had never seen her so mortified.

After the Captain left, Lyssa turned to her younger brother with a look of sadness. It was clear she was embarrassed. Landon almost melted into the ground. He never wanted his sister to see him in such a negative light.

"Dear brother, I love you very much. As a Prince it is very important to me you grow into a kind, loving ruler. Please, please, do not behave in this manner ever again."

She leaned down and hugged Landon. He promised her he would do better. Landon immediately sought out the Captain and offered his apologies.

"Please tell all the men Captain, from this moment forward I will always behave towards each of them with utmost respect." He meant what he had said and within a few years, he noticed the admiration of the Guards as they interacted with him.

In the carriage, Landon yawned, looked to his sister once, then leaned his head back and closed his eyes. The gentle chirping of crickets floated into the carriage. Mixed with the call of the Cicadas it was the perfect music for taking a nap. Slowly, rocked by the swaying of the carriage and the sound of the insects, he fell asleep.

~

Once they arrived at the lake, the five guards remained with the carriage while Landon and Lyssa walked the remaining distance to the crystal blue lake.

When they were unpacked, Landon helped his sister put the bait on the hook. He enjoyed laughing at the way her face contorted each time he picked up a worm. The two sat near each other on the bank laughing and talking about the past, the present, and the future.

"You will come visit me, won't you?" asked Lyssa. Landon's heart felt the tug of his sister's words.

Landon smiled at her gently, "Of course, dear sister."

After three hours of fishing, which turned out to be very fruitful, and a light lunch, the Prince turned towards his sister and asked, "Are you ready to fly the kites?"

She smiled and nodded.

"This has been the perfect day," he thought.

"Great, pull in the lines and I will see to the kites."

The Prince began sorting out the two kites and unrolling the string. He hummed to himself softly, turning periodically towards his sister to watch her work. It had been a grand day, thus far, and the idea of flying kites in the gentle breeze seemed to be perfect.

Once the kites were prepared, Landon looked to his sister and asked, "Ready?"

Kite flying had always been her favorite activity. She loved her brother even more every time he offered to bring them.

"I'll get it aloft for you," he said with a broad smile.

Turning, he began running in the opposite direction. The kite trailed him slowly. The green and white cloth tail dragged along the ground. Lyssa did her best to let out the string to keep up with her brother's pace. The faster Landon ran, the more the kite lifted, and soon he let the kite jump from his hands into the air.

Lyssa laughed aloud. Her kite leapt and soared high into the sky.

It took Landon a few minutes to get his own orange-red kite into the bright, sunny sky. Soon the Prince and Princess were laughing, watching the kites dance back and forth.

"They are beautiful, are they not?" Lyssa called to Landon, her soft voice carried over the wind by the growing distance between them.

"*You are beautiful, my dear sister,*" he thought.

"Yes," he replied, not wanting her to see the sorrow on his face.

Landon took his eyes off his sister to watch his own kite twist and turn. It lifted higher and higher into the sky. Grudgingly he admitted he enjoyed kite flying.

"It's majestic," he said quietly, "Magical." He did not hear her first question.

"What's that?" Lyssa repeated.

On the horizon, soaring high within the vast ocean of blue, a tiny speck changed direction and flew directly at them. Landon thought it might be an Eagle, though it was not the season for the Eagles to come to the coast of O'ndar.

"*A hawk?*" he thought. The bird, slowly growing in size, headed in their direction, from the other side of Lake Windain.

"What's that?" she asked, a little bit louder than the first time.

Lyssa turned towards her brother with her finger pointing into the sky in the opposite direction.

She turned to look at the large bird and had to spin her head back in his direction the moment he yelled at the top of his lungs.

Landon had drawn his sword, pointed it towards the sky, and charged in her direction. "Dragon!"

Landon felt the hairs stand on the back of his neck the moment he realized the speck in the sky was not a bird, but a dragon. The fear he felt quickly over-rode by the worry he had for his sister. She was a great distance away, and by the time he had yelled, "Dragon!" the great beast had already begun to swoop down out of the cloudless sky.

The coal-black dragon pulled in its mighty wings. It tucked them close to its body and dove from the sky towards the lake like a giant meteorite. Its keen sense of hearing had captured the brother's alarm to the sister, but the wind had muffled his yell. The Princess was the Dragon's for the taking.

As she turned to flee, the dragon changed its trajectory by spreading its wings. It used the air current to swoop in over the waters, quickly closing the distance between them. She had taken only a few steps when the dragon opened the talons wide on its right foot, reached out, and snatched her from the earth. It glided ten to fifteen feet above the approaching Prince. For a few seconds the eyes of the dragon locked with Landon's own. The Dragon smiled before turning and gliding back across the lake.

Beating its wings ferociously, the ebony beast climbed into the sky. The cold, dark claws circled the body of the wailing princess. The moment they disappeared into the depths of the sky, Lyssa passed out. Slowly, with each flap of its wings, the Dragon climbed higher and higher until it disappeared into the horizon, heading east toward the Cargathian Mountains.

FERLYNNE

"I FORBID IT!" GHARDENNE XVI YELLED, HIS BOOMING voice echoed off the walls of the great chamber startling his counselors.

The King and Queen sat stoically on the Emerald Thrones looking down at their son, Prince Landon and their most trusted advisors. The Royal Guard standing sentry in their famed emerald green chainmail listened intently to the heated debated. The rest of the onlookers waited for the heated argument between the King and the Prince to run its course. Tension filled the air. The Princess Lyssa was loved by all and her abduction weighed heavily on all their faces.

The argument between father and son, King and Prince, had raged on for at least an hour.

"Father," Landon responded, almost as forcefully. He had been in a rage since being summoned to the Great Hall. The King continued to demand his counselors offer viable options, which were then discussed and debated, almost without end. When one of the counselors stepped forward to offer another idea, Landon's eyes roamed to the walls of the majestic room, stopping to gaze into the eyes of the previous kings forever captured in the royal paintings. Seventeen faces stared back. Gheldari, the original King, had been the first painting added to the collection less than a year after his son Ghardenne I assumed the throne. The history in the seventeen faces stretched back more than nine-hundred years.

Landon's eyes were drawn like a magnet to one painting in particular. Without failure, his gaze fell upon the painting of Chardon I, his great, great grandfather a few times removed. The likeness of Chardon I, originally named Ghardenne VII, sent shivers up Landon's spine. The man in the painting was muscular and powerful, broad shouldered with a long-flowing mane of blonde hair cascading to his shoulders. Hawk-like features and a chiseled face embodied power.

"*He would not have hesitated,*" thought Landon.

The legend of Chardon I and his military exploits were well-known to all the inhabitants of O'ndar and equally known in the nearby kingdoms. Looking at the painting, Landon's eyes admired *Wynde Ryder*, the famous dragon-toothed sword created for the House of Gheldari, a little less than one-thousand years ago. The artist who had painted Chardon I had captured the man's ferocity, his raw strength, and unending vitality. He had also captured the beauty of the jeweled hilt and the smoothness of the blade. The milky-whiteness of the dragon-toothed blade leaped off the painting, swallowing all attention, even though it was adorned with diamonds, rubies, sapphires, and emeralds. It was a shame the sword had been stolen years ago, lost to the House of Gheldari forever.

As a descendent of Gheldari, Landon knew the story behind the making of *Wynde Ryder*. A master sword maker from a country in the southeast had been paid a King's ransom to travel to O'ndar. The man had taken more than five years to hone the dragon-toothed blade into a weapon. It had been, as he had described it, his finest sword. Ghardenne I immediately named the sword *Wynde Ryder* in honor of Meeha, the Emerald Dragon of the Forests.

Looking at the painting, Landon could not overlook the famous green-feathered shield, also a gift from a Dragon to his House.

Briefly, while the King and his counselors continued to discuss an appropriate course of action, Landon thought about the legend of Chardon I, whose exploits had elevated Ghardenne VII into a living legend.

More than six-hundred years ago, Norfuir, one of the daughters of Norduir, the eldest Dragon of the north, had swooped into the kingdom searching for her mother. Enraged by the loss of three Dragon orbs, Norfuir blamed Chondar, swooping from the clouds seeking vengeance.

The ferocious Ice-Dragon demanded the return of the orbs and information about the whereabouts of Norduir. The populace was oblivious to either, but the Dragon would not be swayed from her demands. She screamed loudly to the heavens declaring the citizens of Chondar had three days to appease her demands or face complete destruction.

When the three days came and went, the Ice-Dragon began attacking outlying villages in the north, destroying four of them in less than a day. Eventually, she arrived at gates of the city-state of Chondar.

Rather than hide or flee, a strategy recommended by his most trusted advisors, Ghardenne VII sent a messenger to the Dragon challenging the beast to battle. He offered to meet the giant lizard on the Plains of Mandar at sunrise. Norfuir agreed to the challenge, promptly ate the messenger, and flew to the Plains to await the arrival of the King.

That evening Ghardenne VII mounted Pelin, his favorite horse and rode out of the castle determined to be on the field the moment the sun peaked over the horizon. Pelin, covered in emerald green chain-mail and trained since birth for war with Dragons, seemed as eager for the battle as the King.

With *Wynde Ryder* at his side and the Dragon-feathered shield mounted on the side of his horse, the muscular King meant to turn back the Dragon or die in the attempt. Riding all night, accompanied by three of his most trusted Generals as witnesses, the King waited for the coming of dawn.

The Plains of Mandar, a grassy area between the Cargathian Mountains in the north and Chondar were a part of the House of Gheldari lore. His soldiers had won a decisive battle on the Plains of Mandar more than nine-hundred ago, placing him on the newly created throne of Chondar. His military exploits helped the city-state grow in power and stature.

Gazing at the painting and reflecting on its significance, Landon was convinced the Dragon Norfuir must have been shocked to see the King standing before her, unafraid.

The two adversaries attacked each other with a thundering ferocity never before witnessed.

The battle between Dragon and King raged for hours, with neither gaining the upper hand. Realizing this human would not to be cowed into submission, the Dragon targeted Pelin the horse. Standing over the body of his favorite steed, the King became more enraged and energized, re-engaging the beast on foot. The green-feathered shield had protected him from the dragon's icy flames. Norfuir's ability to freeze the mighty King had depleted quickly.

During the battle, Norfuir repeatedly cursed the family of Bosque, the Emerald Dragons of the Forests, and Ghardenne VII.

After three hours of battle, Ghardenne VII, in an act of desperation, charged the snow-white Dragon. She swiped at his head with one of her massive claws, but he ducked, sliding beneath the mighty Dragon. Using *Wynde Ryder*, Ghardenne opened up a giant gash the length of her body.

Norfuir, knowing she had been mortally wounded bellowed to the skies, "Mother, I have been slain by the warrior-king Chardon."

Whether it had been difficult for her to correctly pronounce his name, or whether she had done so intentionally did not matter. Ghardenne VII rode into his Kingdom and proclaimed he was now Chardon I, a title to be given to future Kings for legendary exploits.

The King immediately ordered Chondar to be renamed O'ndar. Since that day, more than six-hundred years ago, no other King had earned the title of Chardon. Each time he looked at the painting, Landon dreamed of the day he might be elevated to the status of Chardon II.

Landon brought himself out of his reverie when a counselor announced that without *Wynde Ryder* there would be simply no way to save the princess.

Four years after the famous battle between Chardon I and Norfuir, *Wynde Ryder* had been stolen while the King slept in his tent. He had used the sword and his military genius to challenge the other northern nations, placing his cousins on each of the thrones. After the final battle, his servant reported seeing a *Shadow* enter the King's tent while he slept. Gathering both *Wynde Ryder* and the green-feathered shield into its arms, the *Shadow* had disappeared.

He had been in the Great Hall for more than an hour and it was clear the King intended to prevent him from going after Lyssa.

"Father, the longer we wait, the longer we dally, the greater the chance she will be harmed," he yelled.

"The army will be too slow. I can ride a horse quickly and change mounts at every village," Landon said, frustrated.

"Yes, I am aware an army will move slower than one man," the King responded. He was willing to concede this point. He was not willing, though, to acknowledge it would be the Prince to make the journey.

"The heir to the throne should not be the one to go," the King stated firmly.

Prince Landon shook his head violently. He turned and paced back and forth in front of his parents, each passing second agonizingly painful.

"She's in danger and all they are worried about is the throne!"

He knew he was arguing against the will of the King.

The Prince stopped in front of the Emerald Thrones and looked into his mother's eyes. Landon turned, faced her, and their eyes locked onto one another. The way to change his father's mind rested on her ability to influence the King. Slowly, a faint smile grew across her face.

The King started to stand, but paused when the Queen reached out with her slender hand and gently placed it on his forearm. He looked at her with anguish on his face, but his frustration had melted away.

"My Queen," the King whispered. Tears streamed down his face.

"I know my dear. The pain is almost too much. If she is to be brought back alive, I feel it will need to be by the hands of our valiant son," the Queen said.

The counselors stopped talking amongst themselves. The Queen had sided with the Prince.

"But," the King's voice trailed off. He turned to face the Prince.

The King paused, stood up from the throne, and said loudly, "Go swiftly my son and bring her back to us alive."

Landon was over-joyed. His mother had faith in him. He knelt before them, and then bounded up the steps to the thrones.

"Thank you, father! Thank you, mother! I will not let you down," he said excitedly. He bent down and kissed his mother on the cheek.

As he turned to leave, the King asked, "My son, I insist you take five soldiers with you. They will have orders not to hinder you in any way. If there are not enough horses for all, those who can will continue with you. Remember, though, if the Dragon has taken your sister into the Cargathian Mountains it may take weeks for you to get there. It will take even longer to find her."

The unspoken words of, "*She will most-likely be dead by then,*" floated in the air between the two.

"Yes, My Lord," Landon said.

"Are there no other options?" he asked, looking to his parents with panic in his eyes.

"*It's impossible. She will be dead before I can get there to save her,*" he thought.

Landon scanned the faces of the counselors wishing one of them would offer a suggestion. He paused as his eyes once again locked onto the painting of Chardon I.

Most of the counselors had been shaking their heads when a gentle voice responded.

"Perhaps I can be of service, My Lord."

Shocked, the King's counselors turned in unison to see who had made the statement. Twenty-three men parted, opening a path for a frail looking man leaning against an oaken staff. The man hobbled slowly over to the steps, looking as if he might fall at any second.

The King's elated voice asked, "Ferlynne, old friend, is it truly you?" He met the elderly man at the bottom of the steps, embracing him gently.

The old man wore a pea-green robe that seemed to swallow his entire frame from head to toe. Slowly, when the King released his embrace the old man stepped back to remove the hood. His scalp was almost completely bald. Soft flecks of grey hair grew in light patches, the rest bare. The lean face smiled warmly.

Landon, standing next to the Queen, leaned in and asked, "Who is that man, mother?"

The Queen whispered to him quietly, "Hush, let's see what he has to say, then I will explain."

The King and Ferlynne whispered to each other, pausing frequently to look at Landon.

After a few minutes Ferlynne spoke loud enough for all to hear.

"It is agreed then, my King," the elderly man said.

Ghardenne XVI responded, "Yes, old friend, it is agreed."

Without speaking another word, Ferlynne lifted his hood, turned, and walked slowly out of the Great Hall. Once again, like the waves of an ocean, the counselors parted to let him pass.

The Queen motioned for Landon to follow her. Ghardenne XVI remained to speak with his counselors.

The Queen gestured for Landon to sit with her on a divan. "The man you just saw, the one called Ferlynne, is owed a great debt by your mother and father. It is one which can never be repaid," the Queen said, waiting for Landon to ask.

"What did he do?" Landon asked.

"He saved our lives," she responded.

The Queen spent the next few minutes explaining to Landon what had happened during his childbirth. There had been a moment when both of them were in serious peril. The best midwives and doctors of the land were summoned, but the bleeding could not be stopped and their breathing had become more shallow with each breath.

In haste, the King finally called for a hermit, a man who had come to O'ndar only a few years before. News of his ability to work with potions and healing had not gone unnoticed, so Ghardenne sent a group of soldiers to bring the terrified man to the castle. They placed him, shivering in fear, in front of the dying Queen. His fear quickly left him when he realized the danger to the life of the woman and the infant.

It had taken a miracle, but Ferlynne had saved their lives, nursing both of them back to full health. The King and Queen were so grateful they offered to have him moved into the castle and to make him a Royal Doctor. He gratefully refused, wishing to be returned to his cave to live his life in solitude.

Landon sat stunned. "Why haven't I heard of him?" he asked. She explained they had agreed to respect Ferlynne wishes to live out his years in peace.

Landon sat for a few minutes then asked quickly, "Who is he? Where did he come from?"

The Queen raised a hand to her lips as if to hush her son. She stood, walked over to a bookshelf and took a green colored book from the top.

"After your first birthday we sent the Royal Scribe into the Sleeping Hills Forest to speak with Ferlynne. We requested, for posterity, he tell us his story."

Landon looked at the book in his lap. His mother continued, "It's a quick read, but it does give you the information about Ferlynne which you were just seeking."

Landon picked up the book and opened the pages. Silently, he began to read.

Ferlynne

So you say you have been ordered by the King and Queen to write down everything I say about my life? Did you just write that? Oh never mind.

They want to know about the life of an old hermit, living alone in the middle of a forest. I am not sure there is much to tell, but since it is ordered by the King and Queen I will comply. I honor our Father and Mother above all. It is because of them I finally have a home. Because of them I have a full belly. I swear to protect their lives, always.

Not ordered? Oh, I see, requested by the King and Queen. Where to begin? Oh yes, I guess at the beginning. I hope you understand as an old man it is difficult to remember things. I forget names of people and names of places, but can remember clearly almost every moment of my life.

My name is Ferlynne.

I see by your pause you are waiting for my surname. Well, I do not have one. It is just Ferlynne, the old man named after a cat. I see the chuckle. I guess I would do the same in your place.

My parents were poor farmers, who lived in a country far to the southeast, beyond the Steppes. In the far south, there are a few unconquered territories each free from the rule of feudal lords. I happened to live in one of with a lord.

We all know the Eastern Steppes are a hostile place. The tribes of horsemen roam unhindered. They are ferocious and live life on the frontier the way it was meant to be lived. One day at a time. My country, if that is what it can be called, was at that time one of the few parts of the frontier welded together by a strong hetman.

My parents settled near a small village on the eastern side of our lands, near the foothills of the Cargathian Mountains. There were no more than five or six crudely built huts in the village. I remember it was southeast of the Alahari Desert. Yes, the wretched desert that has been the death of many an unlucky soul.

Each hut was made of mud and thatch. They were constantly in need of repair as they wore down during the heavy rains or during the thick snow in winter. We lived a mile or so away and always seemed to be battling with the elements or the animals of the forests.

The villagers made their best efforts at trying to raise crops in order to survive. I am the ninth of thirteen children. My father once told me; when I was a young man, about the circumstances surrounding my birth. My mother had been working in the fields all the way up until the time of my birth. When her water broke, she walked almost a half mile, opened the door to the cabin, walked in, squatted down, and I popped out onto the floor like a dropped melon.

When I hit the floor, the big, yellow tomcat walked over curious. I am sure he thought he was going to get a free meal. My mother took one look at him, looked back at me, and said, "Ferlynne." She handed me to an older sister, walked back to the fields, and went back to work.

In my family, all of the children were named after something which happened to catch the eye of my mother at the moment of birth. In our house, the cat had a name that started with an F, but beyond that, I do not know how I ended up with the name Ferlynne. To this day it still escapes me. Why do you chuckle?

I was born more than seventy-three summers ago in a land far to the southeast of O'ndar. My home was even further south than the country that sent us our beloved Queen. Bless the Queen mother, by the way, if you do not mind me saying so. Did you write that down? Good.

I venture to guess I might be the one person who may have travelled a little further from their home to O'ndar. It is interesting to note the limitations of our maps, in these northern lands. Many do not include the uncivilized countries to the southeast or the civilized countries to the southwest.

Where was I? Oh, that is right, my birth.

I had twelve siblings. We were given all kinds of unique names. In our family, as is true of most agrarian families, the moment a child is capable of working they go to work. By the age of four, I was assisting my parents in the fields, around the house, and anywhere I was needed. The only thing is, and it took me many years to figure this out, I must not have been a good worker since I was eventually sold.

In the kingdoms to the southeast, especially those living on the edge of the wilderness, battling for life on the Steppes to survive requires every member to work hard. One day, I guess I would have been ten years of age, a traveling doctor arrived in the nearby village looking for a helper. His ward had just died from a stomach illness and he was looking to purchase a new one.

My father sold me, without asking my mother, though I am not sure she would have put up much of an argument. I was taken by my father to the village and left with a complete stranger. I had not been able to say goodbye to anyone in my family. I did not have time to be sad about my plight. From the moment I was sold I was expected to work long hours for my new master.

The doctor, to whom I was sold, spent his days traveling from village to village offering potions to heal ailments of all kinds. I would like to say the years I spent with him were good, but I cannot do such a thing. He beat me with a cane to wake me up and beat me with a cane to get me to sleep. Often-times I fell asleep exhausted and did not care where I slept.

While the years were not good, I did learn about plants and medicines and healing. He did have a knack for curing people and we found it was a skill in which I was more than proficient.

Finally, when I turned fourteen, after being beaten with a cane for not cleaning the wagon properly, I stole his medicine bag and ran off, disappearing into the night.

In my younger years I would wander from village to village working for food and shelter when I could and stealing both when I could not. Do not look shocked. You would be amazed at what you would do to stay alive, my friend.

At some point, in the winter of my fifteenth or sixteenth year, I offered a tonic to help an old farmer laid up in bed with a headache. The potion worked so well he allowed me to sleep in his barn free of charge.

He must have been impressed because he told a local merchant who passed the story on to a nearby lord. Eventually the lord offered to allow me to apprentice with the Royal Doctor. The thought of full-time employment and the opportunity to have steady meals was exciting. I readily accepted. I do not recall the name of the lord, though I do remember he was not a king. His castle was a large, log-cabin located in the eastern part of the country. I have often wondered if it is still there today. No, I have no intention of travelling to find out.

I spent the next seven to eight years in the service of this Lord. Eventually I mastered the healing arts. My master, the Doctor was so amazed with my skill he arranged for me to take his place when he retired. Thus, I was promoted to the rank of Senior Royal Doctor.

Working in the castle, I looked after the servants, the ladies and lords of the castle, and any of wealthy merchants requesting my services. It was a good life.

Being the son of a poor farmer, I did not realize life in a castle a dangerous competition between those who serve their lords. I do not mean any disrespect to our King and Queen. I do not believe this is the case in O'ndar.

But, in the less sophisticated Kingdoms to the southeast life in a castle can be challenging. The son of this merchant or the nephew of that lord may covet a position and will take the necessary steps to gain their prize.

At some point, a few coins must have passed hands and before I knew it I was accused of trying to poison the niece of the lady of the castle. Without a trial I was arrested, beaten, tortured, and thrown into the lower dungeons.

In solitude, for most of my thirty years in those dungeons, I would often sit in darkness for hours mumbling or signing to myself to pass the time. It was dark, musty, and I sat alone for the vast majority of my life. To pass the time I would repeat over and over the recipes used to cure most of life's illnesses. I did not want to lose the knowledge of medicine.

This is why I prefer to be left alone in my cave. I prefer to sit in the back of my cave in total darkness.

Once or twice a week I would be taken out into the sun by the guards.

To be honest, I would have preferred not to have seen the sun at all. Each time I longed for what I was missing. When forced back into the dungeons my heart would ache and my thoughts would scream in my head.

Yet, I held on. In the thirtieth year of my imprisonment they came to my cell and I was set free. No explanation was offered. They just took me out to see the sun and when I turned to go back into the dungeon they pointed me in the other direction.

It took them beating me with sticks before I would leave. I kept trying to run down into the dungeon. I waited in the same spot outside for more than a week. I waited for them to bring another prisoner up to see the sun. When they did I tried to run back down into the dungeon.

Finally, two guards with wooden canes beat me ruthlessly. They followed behind me, laughing and hitting me harshly until I was more than a mile away from the castle.

I was lost. I had lived in a dungeon for what turned out to be forty years. I went in a young man and came out feeble and old. But, freedom has a way of bringing back vitality, and though hobbled when I walked, I took the opportunity to walk right out of my country. I never looked back. I did not go to look for my parents. I was free.

Can you imagine being locked in a dungeon for forty years? I had lost track of ten years. But, Ferlynne the Healer was finally free.

Once free, and probably because I had been locked in one place for so long, I made up my mind to spend the rest of my life visiting every kingdom in the known world. I roamed the south, repeating what I had done as a young man. I healed when I could. I traded these services for food, and stole when I could not. It was a glorious time. My back ached from my life in the dungeons, which is why I have my staff. In one village, a staff-maker was suffering from a toothache. It was a fair trade and this well-made staff has been with me for many years.

I roamed to the southern part of the Cargathian Mountains in the west, traveled across the Alahari Desert, and eventually settled in the

Eastern Steppes. I have found that as a Healer, most people are very accepting. I ended up living among the Horsemen, the great tribes of the Steppes. I eventually grew restless and longed to go west to the oceans. Once there I decided to spend a few years along the coast. The vastness of the ocean had called to my soul.

During that time in the wilds, and in the cities I walked, rode, begged, practiced medicine, stole, fought, killed, ran, laughed, and cried while moving from one country to the next.

Eventually, I headed north along the coast. After many years of travel, I walked into O'ndar looking for food and a place to rest. I was told by an old barkeep there was an abandoned cave deep in the Sleeping Hills Forest. I sat out at once, found the cave, and have been living here ever since.

I was shocked when our Majesties sent the guards to bring me to the castle. I was sure I was going to be thrown into the dungeon. When I saw the Queen in pain and her health failing I lost all my fear and did what I was trained to do.

She and the noble Prince lay dying. It was by some divine intervention I am sure, not these worthless old hands, both were able to make a full recovery. I brought all I knew about the healing arts into my mind and did my best to save them.

I was happy to do so and would have done so without any expectation of a reward. Yet, as you well know, the King and Queen are beloved for a reason. Both are gracious, caring, and giving. They have been my benefactors since and I thank them.

And that is the end of my story.

So, my friend, tell the King and the Queen I honor them, I revere them, I wish them many years of happiness. This feeble old man will always be at their service.

~

Prince Landon quietly shut the book and looked at his mother. The King had entered the chambers. He had sat down, waiting for Landon to finish reading.

The Queen responded, "Ferlynne, is solely responsible for the two of us being alive." She waited for her words to sink in and then moved over to sit next to Landon. The King walked over and sat in the spot previously occupied by the Queen.

"This is true. He was unknown to us and by happenstance I was told about his skills. It turned out to be the best decision I have ever made," the King offered. He looked at his wife, "My apologies. The second best decision." The two smiled at each other with genuine affection.

Landon said, restlessly, "Father this is all good and I realize I owe this man my life. But, how can he help?"

"In one of his stops in the Pyrradine Forests Ferlynne happened to winter with another hermit. The two agreed to teach each other their arts."

Landon asked the question, "And how does this help get us to Lyssa faster?"

The King responded quickly, "This other hermit practiced in the art of wizardry."

The Queen leaned up startling the two of them. She asked, quickly, "Who was this wizard? Why did Ferlynne not put this in his story?"

"Yes, father?" Landon asked, wanting the King to continue.

The King turned to the Queen, realizing he had ignored her questions. He said, "He is a forgetful, old man. He told me he happened to be near the castle today seeking some herbs, when he heard the news about the Princess. News travels fast. He came as quickly as he could."

The King turned back to Landon before continuing, "Ferlynne has once again offered his services to his King and Queen." The Queen had gone quiet. Landon looked at her, puzzled by the expression on her face.

"And how could he help us father?" asked Landon.

"Ferlynne was taught a spell that allows a person to be sent from one place to another," the King said.

Landon leaped to his feet, saying, "That's wonderful. He can send us immediately."

The King hesitated and said, "There are a few things which we must consider."

"First," the King said, "Ferlynne can send only one person." Landon nodded, understanding he would be the only person sent after Lyssa.

"Father, there must be something else causing you to hesitate."

The King sighed, looked to his wife and said, "There can be only one person sent and whoever casts the spell must give his own life in order for it to work."

Instead of being upset the Queen looked to her husband and son. A look of relief flowed across her features. She turned to both of them and said, "Poor Ferlynne, but if this is what will bring our beloved Lyssa back to us, it is a price I am happy to pay."

The King agreed Landon would meet Ferlynne, in his cave, at midnight. Once Landon entered, the cave would be sealed. "It was Ferlynne's request to be entombed in his home after his death."

Landon thanked his father, kissed his mother, and turned to leave. He intended on gathering some soldiers for the journey to Ferlynne's cave.

THE CELESTIAL PLANE

FOR LANDON, THE WAIT WAS FILLED WITH ANXIOUS moments and hectic plans. He took the time to speak personally with each of the ten soldiers chosen to escort him through the Sleeping Hills Forest.

The stress wreaked havoc on his emotions. *"I've been such a fool,"* he thought, thinking about how petulant he had been all his life. Lyssa's abduction had placed a heavy burden on his heart.

"We are to be immediately entombed, sealed within the cave," he stated matter-of-factly when letting them know of his plans. They resisted his orders, confused, until his father came along and affirmed the command. Landon did not mind. He would be King, someday, but he was not King currently.

An hour before mid-night, eleven men quietly exited the castle heading for the passage into the Sleeping Hills Forest.

The darkness of the Sleeping Hills Forest amazed Landon. The flickering torches cast long shadows which seemed to dance away up into the branches. Landon was certain he saw three or four pair of red eyes glaring back at them. The wolves were out, but they avoided the light and the heavily armed soldiers. The Prince, once again, had a new appreciation about how dangerous things could be without his father's men for protection.

"Never again will I take them for granted."

An hour into the forest, Landon spotted a torch burning brightly through the darkness. The men followed the winding path until they stopped in front of a tiny cave nestled in the side of an outcropping of rock.

"*He chose to live here rather than in the castle?*" Landon shook his head quietly.

Ferlynne stood statue still beside the flickering torch, waiting patiently for Prince Landon to arrive. He still had on his pea-green robe, but the hood was pulled back away from his face and draped over the back of his shoulders. With the torch stuck in the ground held by his left hand and the staff planted in the ground held by his right hand, Ferlynne waited in silence for the wagon to come to a halt.

"Welcome, My Lord," Ferlynne said, his voice raspy and dry. The old man attempted a bow, but it was obvious he could bend no further. He stepped forward, placing both hands on Landon's shoulders. The piercing green eyes bore into Landon forcing him to look away.

Landon stood quietly confused about how to respond. He knew he owed this man his life, but he did not know if he could show gratitude to someone he had only recently met.

Ferlynne laughed quietly. He grabbed the torch, walked into the cave, and waived for Landon to follow.

Landon looked at the Captain and ordered, "Seal up the cave. Neither of us will be leaving this tomb."

The soldiers began to remove stones from the wagon. Once he and Ferlynne had entered, they started to pile them at the mouth of the cave. Inside the dimly lit cave, Ferlynne lit two more torches and sat down on a rickety old chair waiting for the soldiers to finish. Landon felt uneasy once the cave was completely blocked by stone. The torches were not as bright as he would have liked.

"*There is no going back now,*" he thought.

"Exactly Prince. We are approaching the point of no return," Ferlynne responded with a knowing smile.

He motioned for Landon to follow him deeper into the cave. Based on the size of the entrance, Landon expected to find a small cave with barely enough room to move around. The cave was quite spacious.

"Would you care for some water?" Ferlynne asked. He gestured to a natural basin nearby. Landon shook his head.

The walk to the back of the cave offered more surprises. Each time Ferlynne approached an unlit torch it would burst into flames, snuffing out just as quickly when the two passed. Landon looked back into darkness, tempted to ask about the magic behind the self-lighting torches.

"I would say Ferlynne knows more than a little magic," he thought.

Ferlynne chuckled to himself and said, "Yes, indeed. I do at that." Landon started to ask if the old man read minds, but decided to keep his questions to himself, for now. He was anxious to get to his sister.

When they arrived at his sleeping area, Ferlynne offered Prince Landon a chair. The chair was of high quality, quite sturdy, and lined with velvet-covered cushions. Ferlynne noticed Landon's expression and responded with, "A gift from our mother and father." He bowed to Landon.

Ferlynne walked over to a table and reached into a worn-leather pouch. Pulling out a block of aged-cheese, the old man used a small knife to cut a slice. He handed it to the Prince, saying, "Eat something Majesty. The spell I am about the cast can take a heavy toll on the body. Eating will help alleviate some of the symptoms." The old man found another chair which he dragged over to Landon. He watched while Landon ate the slice of cheese.

Landon looked around the cave, noticing a shield and a sword leaning against a nearby wall. The two weapons looked worn and well-used.

Ferlynne guessed correctly where his attention had fallen. "Yes, it is true, they are mine, used quite often in my younger years."

"I must admit to confusion," Landon started. "I was under the impression you were a healer with potions. Not a warrior."

The old man chuckled. He amusingly offered, "Sometimes, we are all more than we seem." The shield, emblazoned with a purple cobra wrapped around a tree, looked ominous. Speckled with silver flakes, the gilded edges of the cobra's hood looked sinister. The shield, which did not belong to any of the northern nations, had to have belonged to a Lord at some point. It was far too expensive to be in the hands of a feeble, old man. The hood of the purple cobra flared open and the bright yellow eyes signified the owner was ready to strike at any moment. *Beware!*

Landon imagined a field of a thousand or ten thousand similarly equipped soldiers. The shiver he felt earlier returned.

The finely made sword shined brightly in the flickering light. Ferlynne went to the shield, patted it with affection, and returned to Landon.

Landon had difficulty gauging the old man. Ferlynne sat quietly enjoying the silence. Finally, after a few slices of cheese and a few swallows of wine, Landon spoke, "I thank you for helping me get to my sister."

Ferlynne's eyebrows raised and his lips smiled with delight. He offered, "It's the least I can do. Your father and your mother, especially the Queen, have already done far too much for me and mine. They truly have been wonderful masters,"

Landon detected sarcasm, but chose to ignore it.

Ferlynne continued, "Years ago, when I was rather young, I had a son. The last time I saw him he was a little older than you are now." This tidbit of information captured the Prince's interest.

"What's that?" Landon asked. The old man ignored Landon's question. He gestured for Landon to move to the center of the cave.

After a few seconds pause, he continued, "My Lord, I feel obligated to say the journey you are about to take is perilous. You may never return. Are you willing to sacrifice yourself for your sister?"

Landon responded with force, "I would not be here otherwise."

"I find myself wanting to be honest with you before I cast the spell. I imagine your parents offered you a chance to read the story of my life. Some of what I told them is not true. I was raised in a country far to the south. In my previous country I was a warrior. I worked diligently to protect the life of my Sultan and expand his empire," the old man said.

Landon stared intently at the old man. He mind raced with questions. *"Why is he choosing to tell me this now?"*

"I tell you this so there is honesty between us. You do remind me of my son. He went on a journey to the north never to be seen again. I am telling you this so your choice is not made lightly. Do you still wish to go?"

Landon did not hesitate. He nodded.

"Good, let us begin," Ferlynne said. "Did you bring the item I requested?"

Landon reached into his leather tunic to remove a white-lace kerchief. It had belonged to his sister. Quietly, he cursed himself for thinking of her in the past-tense. He handed it to the old man.

Ferlynne took the kerchief, smelled it, and nodded mumbling, "That's nice. Lavender I believe. It is an intoxicating scent and a bold, vibrant color."

He knelt down, placing the kerchief on the floor of the cave. The hermit spoke a few inaudible words before throwing a pinch of powder onto the kerchief. The powder sparked. A hint of bluish smoke rose a few feet above the kerchief, hovering, and then formed into a cloud, rolling back and forth.

"It should take a few minutes and then we will be ready," Ferlynne started. "My Lord, we are about to do what I call the Stretching of the Soul." He seemed pleased Landon did not ask questions.

"The body, the mind, and the spirit are all connected by a thread. It is, for lack of a better phrase, what I like to call the life-thread. Through this spell, a man may offer his life in order to stretch the soul of another across great distances. Once the soul has travelled to a specific location away from its body there are two options in order to re-connect them. Either the soul and the mind must be pulled back to the body or the body is pulled outwards to the soul."

"I'm not quite sure I understand," offered Landon, though he was genuinely intrigued.

Ferlynne looked at Landon, his eyes piercing. He responded, "Once, when I was a very young man we rescued a man who had fallen into a patch of quick-sand." His smile showed he was impressed with the inquisitive nature of the Prince.

"Quick Sand?" asked Landon.

"Yes. In my country there are small patches of bottomless sand. If not careful, a man can be swallowed by them the way water swallows a man who jumps into a lake." He watched Landon's face to make sure the Prince understood.

Ferlynne continued, "When the man was revived, he described seeing a bright light ahead of him. He also described floating towards bliss. When he looked backward he could see his body lying motionless in the middle of the sand. He described everyone present including what each of us wore. At some point, based on the efforts of those who saved him, his soul was pulled back into his body."

Ferlynne waited to see if his statements were understood. "I did not truly understand his tale until I met the hermit in the mountains near the Pyraddine Forests. The hermit told me of a spell that could separate the body and the soul. He sent me to the northeast, near the base of the Cargathian Mountains, to find a village in which the spell could be found."

Once again, the hairs on the back of Landon's neck stood on end.

Landon was tempted to abort his mission. Things were not as they seemed.

"But, if he really does know this magic, he is my only hope," he thought. He decided there was no going back. The old man was Lyssa's only hope.

"What was the name of that village?" Landon asked.

"Mfiri. It's Mfiri, my friend. Be aware though, Mfiri is not a place for a Prince. It is full of dark magic. I do not recommend anyone go to Mfiri. Once there, it is nearly impossible to leave."

After an awkward pause Ferlynne continued, "I hope you understand what I mean by the Stretching of the Soul."

Landon was still confused.

Ferlynne said, "Put your hands together, like this."

When Landon complied Ferlynne directed him again, "Leave your right hand in the same spot and move the other one away from it. Yes, that is it. Now, imagine the hand that did not move is the body. The other hand is the soul. If you want the soul to come back to the body, what do you do?"

Landon clapped both hands together. His facial expression showed elation. He understood what Ferlynne meant by the Stretching of the Soul.

"Repeat the steps. If a person decided to bring the body to the soul what would you do?"

Landon moved the right hand towards the left. Ferlynne clapped loudly and said, "Wonderful."

"If this spell separates the soul from the body we will send the body back to the soul. By doing so a person can be transported, across what we call the Celestial Plane, back to the soul."

Landon started to speak, but stopped the moment Ferlynne raised a forefinger on his right hand. The Prince could not help himself and asked the question, anyway.

"The Celestial Plane?" he asked. "I must know what it is."

"It's best we not delve into questions about the Plane. Just be assured, it does exist," the old man responded.

The old man chuckled, once again impressed by the inquisitiveness of the Prince.

"The best way I can explain it is this. We live in a physical world, one in which our bodies reside. We also are surrounded by the Celestial Plane, one in which only souls may reside. The Celestial Plane is used by the dead so their souls might find a final resting place. It is also used by wizards, Dragons, and demons to ply their trade, which is magic."

Ferlynne understood Landon's startled face and added, "No, my Prince, I am not a wizard. I am an old man who happened upon a spell. Where was I? Oh yes."

"Think of your hands. If we reverse the steps we are able to pull the body back to the soul. It explains quite well the Stretching of the Soul, and the re-connecting to the body."

Landon nodded, understanding the concept behind the spell. He said, "I am ready to begin."

"You will need to remove your sword," Ferlynne gestured to Landon's weapon.

He glared at Ferlynne, hesitating to go any further. His father had said nothing about going unarmed.

Ferlynne shrugged and said, "Sorry, I did not make the rules."

Landon disarmed himself, stepping toward the rolling cloud, which still hovered above the kerchief. Ferlynne raised his hand to stop him.

"I am sorry. It will need to include anything made of metal." He pointed to Landon's belt buckle, his ring, and his knife. Once all of the metal was removed from his body, Ferlynne nodded at Landon. He said, "If there is any other metal on your body, I can assure you, the spell will fail."

Landon bent over and removed a small blade tucked in his boot. Ferlynne laughed gleefully.

"Sit directly on top of the Princess's kerchief. Ignore the vapor swirling around your face and close your eyes. Once I begin the incantation do not move no matter what you see or hear."

The old man paused and then continued, "You may open your eyes only when the Stretching of the Soul has ended. Do not move though. Do not fight what you witness. Allow the soul to be stretched. When you are near the Princess you may open your eyes. I will finish the spell. Your body will be drawn across the Celestial Plane and back to your soul."

"How close will I be to her? How will I know when I am done?" Landon asked.

The old man shrugged once again and stated, "I have never used the spell. I would guess close enough. You will know when it is okay to open your eyes. You will have stopped moving for more than a minute. Be aware, though, if you open them before the soul has been stretched far enough, that is the where you will be when the two are re-connected. I will be dead and will not be able to re-try the spell."

He chuckled, thought about how it must have sounded, and shrugged again for the third time.

Landon softly walked over and sat down on top of the kerchief, he said, "I am ready."

"Good luck with your Quest mighty Prince," Ferlynne said. He sat in front of Landon, opened up a scrolled parchment, and held it out in front of him.

Before he started to speak Landon blurted out, "Wait." The old man paused, confused by the interruption. "I....I wanted to say thank you. My father informed me you would have to sacrifice your life." He looked introspectively at the old man.

Ferlynne was touched. He had not expected this response from the Prince. Tears welled up in his eyes. He responded, "It is with honor I do this, your majesty. I have lost one son and understand the unbearable pain caused by such a loss. This poor, old man's life is worth risking if it brings back the Princess."

Once again, Ferlynne instructed the Prince to close his eyes. After a few breaths he began to read from the parchment.

"*Frathma ark Frathman. Eriden a frathma. Frathma ark Frathman er Lyssa. Eriden a frathma tu Lyssa,*" he read. Slowly, he lifted his right hand to the swirling cloud floating around Landon's face. Turning his palm upward, he blew onto his hand causing a white powder to lift up and mix into the blue cloud. Some of the powder struck Landon in the face, the rest fused itself into the vapor. Sparkles of red, blue, yellow, and green filled the cave.

Landon felt the gentle tug on his body, as if an invisible rope had been wrapped around his waist. He began floating backwards, keeping his eyes closed. Landon felt the dampness of the cave wall when he passed through it. He felt the brush of the dew covered leaves outside the cave, and he felt the cool night air when he floated away from Ferlynne. Landon heard the soldiers working with rocks to seal up the mouth of the cave.

"*They should have returned to the castle by now,*" he thought when he floated past them.

He resisted the urge to open his eyes, remembering the warning from the fragile, old man. Landon began weaving back and forth, tugged gently one way and then another. He could feel the gentle brush of the bushes or the soft scrape of the leaves against his skin. Landon floated backward for hours, smelling the forests and then the grassland along the way. His passage was smooth and quiet. Eventually, as the pulling on his waist lightened, he began to slow. At some point it felt as if he moved at a snail's pace, but the tugging sensation continued, so he kept his eyes closed tightly.

Quietly, softly, he landed gently upon the earth. The floating sensation ended. He waited for a few more seconds and opened his eyes.

Landon gasped aloud into the darkness. Stretched out in front of him, only a few feet apart from each other, were thousands of him. The semitransparent versions of him sat cross-legged, hands on thighs, mimicking his posture. Each Landon remained connected to the one in front of him by a glowing, red string. Landon believed if he followed the red twine far enough, it would lead him straight back to the old man and his body.

"But how far is that?" he wondered. He had been floating for hours. It could be hundreds of miles.

The thousands of Landons wound back and forth into the distance, disappearing into the horizon. Some avoided the trees while others were embedded into the large trunks. Some blended into boulders, while others floated above the grass. Landon remained motionless, not wanting the break the spell before its fruition.

He heard a gentle clap and heard Ferlynne's voice clearly, *"Be safe my young Prince. It is with a heavy heart I sent you on this journey. Please remember, I personally meant you no ill will."*

"How is this possible?" he wondered.

Once the final words had been spoken by the old man, the Prince's body began to make the leap across the Celestial Plane. He felt the gentle tug on his soul, but remained grounded in his current spot. Starting in Ferlynne's cave, his body slammed backward into his first soul, then into his second, and then into his third. The process continued across the Celestial Plan as his body leaped to rejoin the separated soul. Landon sat, eyes open, waiting for the spell to run its course. He waited patiently, not knowing how long it would take for the thousands of him to re-connect in order to make him whole again.

He was shocked to see, far ahead of him, the inner-connected souls, thousands of them collapsing backwards into each other.

With a final snap his body finished its journey across the Celestial Plane, slamming forcefully into the last of his souls, knocking him backward a few feet. Breathing was difficult. Landon felt as if his lungs were on fire. Eventually, he blacked out.

He awoke in the dead of night, lying on his back, looking up at the thousands of stars in the cloudless sky. It took him a few minutes to remember where he had been and what Ferlynne had done. Sitting up, Landon quietly praised the old man. He had thought it impossible.

"But where am I?" he thought. Landon tried to stand, but found himself dizzy. Eventually, he bent over and threw up the cheese.

After a few minutes, the dizziness wore off and Landon was able to stand. He looked around. The Cargathian Mountains ran north and south less than a mile away to the east. He followed the rise of the mountains trying to find the peaks, but the heights were dizzying. He shook his head hoping the effects of the spell would wear off.

Remembering his lessons on maps, Landon praised his tutors for insisting he learn about the constellations. They explained it would help someday, if he were ever lost in a distant land. Looking around, he found the familiar *Tea Cup* to the north and the *Bowman* in the south.

"*If I make it back, those three old men are going to be rewarded.*" Once again, he felt childish about the way he had treated them when he was younger.

Feeling better, Landon started the long walk up the side of the mountain, drawn in that direction. The branches of the sparsely growing trees were slimy with dew, the ground slippery. He made his way well enough, though.

Landon was well-beyond tired. He paused a few moments to sit on a boulder. He froze. He could hear, though only faintly, further up the mountain, a female voice singing. He stood up and ran quickly to the sound. The song grew in volume. He mumbled, "Is it her?"

A large outcropping of boulders forced him to stop, go back about a fourth of a mile, and try a new path. He fought against the urge to call out to her. Landon hoped the Dragon had not heard his passage through the rocky terrain. He rounded the same outcropping, though from the south, and stopped dead in his tracks.

Lyssa was sitting on the ground humming softly and singing. She looked peaceful and happy. The black dragon was lying next to her, fast asleep. The massive head rested near her legs. She patted the beast, caressing it tenderly.

He walked to her slowly, without saying a word. Landon did not want to startle the beast.

"*Maybe it doesn't know I'm here*," he thought.

Lyssa smiled when she saw her brother. She did not stand and run to him in terror. She spoke to him the moment he drew close. The Dragon's eyes popped open. It lifted its head to look in his direction. Lyssa kept her hand on the side of its face, caressing it. She smiled and cooed to the giant lizard.

"Hello dear brother. We have been waiting for you."

QUEEN LENALI

IMMEDIATELY AFTER LANDON LEFT THE KING AND QUEEN to prepare for the night's journey to Ferlynne's cave, Queen Lenali secretly sent a message to Ryden, the Captain of the Royal Guard. As Captain of the Guard, he would be in charge of the soldiers assigned to accompany Landon. The message ordered him to her chambers for a quick discussion. If he had not been planning on being a part of the mission, her note changed his mind for him. He would be expected to be there to represent the Queen and her interests. While she waited for Captain Ryden, Lenali spent most of this time with Ghardenne, hoping to keep him from changing his mind.

"We have no other choice," she thought. *"All of my plans rest upon having Lyssa here. Without her, changes will have to be made."*

Captain Ryden arrived a few minutes before the scheduled appointment. He was ushered in by one of the Queen's servants. He had been puzzled by the Queen's order, but was a good soldier and would ensure that her wishes were followed.

Lenali went straight to the point, saying, "Captain, my son is going on a quest to save the Princess." The Captain acknowledged the Queen, though he had already met with the King.

"You are aware our dear friend Ferlynne is going to sacrifice his life in order to make this happen?" she continued. The Captain nodded in the affirmative.

"In my country, when someone passes, it is customary for the family of the deceased to place two gold coins over the eyes of the departed. I fear unless this happens Ferlynne will not be escorted properly to the Afterworld," Lenali added.

The Queen continued, "I cannot imagine our dear friend's soul condemned to walk endlessly without a safe harbor. I know you understand."

Captain Ryden looked to his tunic, noticed the wrinkled bottom and smoothed out the fabric. He responded with, "I understand, My Queen. In my youth I spent some time in the east with our military. I met tribes that held a similar belief." The Queen looked pleased.

"I also know you have orders to seal up the cave once they have entered. I would like you, though, to wait a few hours and then unseal the cave. Find Ferlynne's body and place these two coins over his closed eyes," she held up the two coins. He held his hands out to take them while the Queen spoke, "Once you have finished your task, seal the cave back up and report to me once you have returned."

The Captain affirmed her faith in him by acknowledging her wishes without asking questions.

"Only part of my faith," she thought. The Queen had watched the Captain's eyes widen momentarily when she displayed the two gold coins.

"We both know, Captain, neither of these coins will find their way over Ferlynne's eyes."

She did not care. The Queen wanted proof the hermit had died.

"It will be done, my Queen," Captain Ryden promised. He stood, bowing to her.

"One more thing, Captain," Lenali said. "Our conversation is to remain private. I rely on your discretion and confidence. No others will find out about the task given you. In my native-country funeral rites were very private matters."

The Captain nodded, bowed again, and left.

The Queen went to find the King so the two of them might wave goodbye to their son. They did so, watching Landon walk with the soldiers into the darkness. The torches showed their progress as they wound their way along the well-worn path and to the edge of the forest.

Many hours later, Queen Lenali waited impatiently, standing in front of an expansive tapestry mounted on the northern wall of her private room. Often, when she was anxious, the Queen would stop at the tapestry and stare at the patterns for hours. It soothed her worries. It had been sent with her on her journey north, years ago. If she stared long enough at the lavender and violet threading, glimpses of a person would flash through her mind. She often wondered if he had been the one who sent the tapestry. She felt he was powerful, and foreboding.

The heavy, thick cloth, hanging along the walls, helped keep the drafts out of her sitting room on chilly evenings. Each wall was adorned with similar pieces of cloth, but this one in particular fascinated her the most.

"What is it about this piece?" she thought. It was ten feet long and at least twenty feet in height. The thick, plum-colored fabric ringed with golden threads along each edge was a masterpiece. The portrait of a man in a diamond-crusted crown dominated tapestry. His likeness superimposed over the top of an ivory-colored oval-shaped background. He was clean-shaven, olive-skinned and very exotic. Deep-blue eyes popped out at the observer. The piercing gaze exuded power and grace.

"That was someone who was born to rule," she thought, captivated by the designs woven into the massive tapestry.

"It will be fascinating to be a part of that empire," she mused. *"Maybe, I will rule it as Queen."* Everything depended on Landon and his efforts to recover Lyssa from the clutches of the dragon. Her eyes drifted slowly, once again, over the cloth.

The corners of the fabric each housed another pearl-white oval imprinted with a chariot drawn by two, purple horses.

"Why that color? I have never seen a purple horse?"

The charioteer and a spearman, both bedecked in amethyst-colored tunics, populated each of the four corners, their heads crowned with golden helmets. Each standing spearman held a golden spear. The silver-tipped spears, pointed toward the heavens, looked menacing. Beneath the Lord of the tapestry, Lenali decided to think of him as a Lord or a King, was a majestic looking Date Palm tree, full of fruit and life. Curled around the bottom of the tree, winding its way up the trunk until it turned to face the observer just below the leaves, was a noble King

Cobra. Its skin had been dyed bright purple. Hood open, with yellow, piercing eyes, the imposing lavender-colored snake projected grace and power, just like the Lord of the tapestry.

Once again, Lenali became frustrated. She could not remember who had provided her with this rich, pomegranate-colored fabric. It had been more than seventeen years since she had made the journey. Much of her younger life seemed hazy and forgotten. All she could remember was the second half of the journey across the desert, which did not surprise her. She had never been able remember any of her other pasts.

The King and the citizens had welcomed her arrival enthusiastically. She was immediately ordained a citizen of O'ndar. Lenali had been very pleased with these years of her life. The *'desert flower'* had become the flower of Ghardenne and the people of O'ndar. Her exotic skin, dark hair and mesmerizing eyes captured the spirits of everyone who came into contact with her.

"Hopefully, the next sixteen will be just as fantastic," she thought.

Even though she could remember little of her life before the journey across the desert, bits and pieces of her childhood often flashed into her mind. Lenali had grown accustomed to this over the years. There were always left over memories.

Lenali forced herself to move away from the tapestry; otherwise she would remain there for hours. She moved to the divan and picked up the book once again. She had read and re-read the story of Ferlynne a number of times since Captain Ryden had left. She hoped each time to find other pieces of information about the reclusive man. Nothing new was discovered. Every few minutes she would stand, pace back and forth, and then return to the book. Nothing seemed to help alleviate her frustration.

"Where is that damned Captain?"

It was nearly four hours past midnight. She had talked to the King for an hour after the soldiers and the Prince had walked into the forest. She recalled the earlier conversation.

"Do you think he will succeed?" the King asked. The pain in his voice stung the Queen to her core. If Ferlynne succeeded, Landon could end up hundreds, if not thousands of miles away.

"He will be successful, my husband," Lenali said demurely. She patted his hand hoping the contact would alleviate some of his concerns. She spent some time sitting quietly with the King. She started to read a book about life in Istanabad, while she waited. Those who grew up in the semi-barbaric lands far to the south were accustomed to believe in 'es shala,' which translated into, *"What will be will be?"* While she had not really understood what this meant, she used the phrase to help control her fear.

She had arrived from the Deep South years ago, sent by her father, the Sultan, to fulfill an arranged marriage to the King Ghardenne XVI. Though he was more than ten years older, she accepted the order from her father with grace, according to the diplomats from O'ndar. She had grown to love the King, bearing him two children, both of whom now faced the possibility, if not the absolute certainness, of death.

"I am capable of love," she thought. She continued to argue the thought with herself, quietly. *"Yes, this I know."*

Lenali brought herself back to the present and found she was once again standing in front of the tapestry.

She often wondered if the man in the fabric was her father, the Sultan. She did not know for sure, having forgotten the earlier part of her life.

The Sultan rules the most powerful nation in the south while Ghardenne rules the most powerful nation in the north. The two countries were separated by rugged mountains, a vast desert, and the Eastern Steppes. Both men hoped to create an alliance sealed with the marriage of the Sultan's son and the King's first born daughter. In the north a King took one wife. In the south, the Sultan had more than fifty wives, each bearing him children. The Sultan used these children as pawns to consolidate and strengthen his hold on the vast empire.

The first half of the agreement had been fulfilled. If she bore a daughter, once the daughter came of age she would be sent south to be married to one of the Sultan's sons, most likely the heir to the Zaharian Empire. Thus, two powerful nations, one in the north and one in the south would have an alliance welded by blood.

"I was very much looking forward to the journey south," she thought.

Lenali started to pick up the book, but placed it quickly back on the couch. Quietly, she went back into the bedroom and checked on the King. He was sleeping soundly. She had ground a pinch of Sleeping Nightshade into his drink and had given him the tonic. He thought it warmed, spice-wine and happily sipped it for a few minutes. The Queen helped him lay his head on his pillow, happy he would be out of the way for the rest of the evening.

Walking over to the window, the Queen looked down hoping to catch a glimpse of torches returning to the Castle. It had been four hours.

"Maybe they have returned while I was reading?" A few minutes later there was a quiet knock at the door. The Captain entered quickly.

He bowed to her and said, "My Queen."

"Please, Captain, sit down so we may talk for a few minutes." The Captain moved to a wooden chair in the corner. He looked fatigued. It had been a long night and she too was ready for sleep. He turned to face the Queen.

"So, did you do as I commanded, Captain?" she asked. He nodded.

Lenali said, "Tell me everything you observed. Please do not leave anything out."

"My Lady. We sealed up the Prince and the hermit, my apologies, Ferlynne the Healer, as we were instructed to do by the King. Once we were finished the other guards were ready to leave, but I informed them we had other orders to follow before departing. I did not tell them who the additional orders had come from."

The Queen smiled and nodded for him to continue.

"We waited for two hours and I had them unseal the cave. They grumbled, but did so quickly. I ordered the men to remain outside. I entered the cave, moving quickly until I made it to the back of the cavern. I found the old man. His body lay upon his bed, eyes shut, his arms crossed upon his chest. He was dead. The spell must have worked for there was no sign of the Prince."

"You are sure he was dead?" the Queen asked. She stared at him, breathing rapidly in anticipation.

"Yes, My Queen," the Captain continued, "it was him. His body seemed to have aged many years. It had shriveled up and dried out. But there was no mistaking Ferlynne. I examined him closely. He wore the same green robe. He had the same clean-shaven scalp. The spell took a heavy toll on the body, draining all the vitality out of him, leaving his body a shell of its previous self." He paused and then said, "It was a shame to see him in this state."

The Queen seemed relieved and stood up. She asked, "And then?"

"Once I identified it was Ferlynne, I placed a gold coin over each of his eyes. I performed the ceremonial rites in the manner you instructed." Lenali followed Captain Ryden's gestures. He used his hands to replay his actions in the cave.

The Queen nodded towards the Captain, but her thoughts belied her good will. *"I do not care about the coins Captain. Otherwise, I would have you searched and would no doubt find them hidden somewhere deep inside a pouch."*

"Good. Ferlynne was such a dear friend. I could not bear to think he died without the proper observances," the Queen said.

"Once the rites were observed, I exited the cave, had the others re-seal it as instructed, and returned to the Castle." The Captain looked weary.

"Thank you Captain. You and your men have done very well. Once again, I do not wish this to be discussed with anyone. Not the King, nor any of the other soldiers. Do you understand?"

The Captain nodded in agreement. Lenali said, "Go get some rest Captain. You have done very well this evening." He smiled. Lenali dismissed him and he exited quietly.

"Dear Ferlynne, our faithful friend. Thank you for your sacrifice. You will be missed." The Queen had spoken the words aloud, happy to hear herself.

"Now, if my son can bring the Princess back, maybe I will be able to make that journey south."

Walking over to the couch she picked up the book and replaced it on the shelf. She stopped once more in front of the tapestry, mesmerized by the colors, the designs, and the hidden stories behind its pictures. She forced herself to look away, realizing she was exhausted from the long day.

Quietly, she went to bed.

WE HAVE BEEN WAITING FOR YOU

EVEN IN THE LIGHT PROVIDED BY THE ILLUMINATION OF A thousand stars, Landon was sure his sister could easily see the look of shock on his face.

"We have been waiting for you brother," she had said. The numbing words whirled through his mind. Landon looked at his sister puzzled.

"Is she mad?" he wondered.

Landon, frightened by the presence of the mighty beast, raised his right forefinger to his lips. He did not want to do anything to cause it to react violently.

Whispering, he asked, "What do you mean we have been waiting for you? Who are we?" He looked around searching for others. They were alone. The air was chilly. Landon's teeth chattered.

Lyssa smiled, patted the dragon on the head, and gestured towards it with her head.

"She can't be serious?" he thought. The yellow, cat-like eyes stared at Landon. The beast seemed to enjoy his sister's caresses. That at least was a positive.

Once again the beast looked at Lyssa. It startled Landon, when it raised its massive head and yawned. White fangs glistened brightly in the starlight. Two were at as long as Landon's forearm. Once finished, the beast lowered its head near his sister's thighs, closed its eyes and fell back asleep. Landon knew Dragons were highly intelligent. It had to know he was here to rescue his sister. He burned with fury, remembering the smile offered by the flying lizard as it flew overhead with his sister in its clutches.

"Do not make the mistake of underestimating its intelligence," Landon's reminded himself. His stomach churned. He felt he might vomit, again.

Lyssa stood and walked over to her brother. She reached up, mussed up his hair, and leaned in to hug him. "I was afraid you would not come," she said. Landon returned the hug. Her statement made him tear up.

She smiled broadly and said, "He said you would. I was afraid of the great distance separating us. I cried hysterically. My tears stopped when he made a promise." She pointed to the sleeping dragon and said again, "He said you would come."

Landon looked at her incredulously, "He said I would come?"

"He promised me you would be along quickly." He refused to tell me how it would be possible. He just smiled at me, if you can imagine such a thing."

"You should never have doubted for a minute," he said. They hugged each other, once again.

Landon asked, "Would you please tell me what is going on? When you say we have been waiting for you, what do you mean? I see no one else here with us."

She seemed not to hear his question and continued, "It was his idea to meet you here on the side of the mountain. It was also his idea we meet you like this. In a non-threatening manner." She looked approvingly at the coal-black dragon. "I explained to him nothing could keep you from finding me. I explained you can be hot-headed and would be ferocious if you thought I had been harmed. So we decided to meet you here. Otherwise, I was afraid you would end up killed or worse…eaten."

Lyssa had spoken too quickly. The excitement winded her.

"I meant what I said. We have been waiting," she said turning to point to the dragon. The beast remained asleep.

Landon flustered by Lyssa's comment, asked, "We…you mean you and this giant lizard?"

"Please don't," she responded. She looked sympathetically at the dragon before adding, "Please don't call him that." Tears welled up in her eyes, reminding Landon of why he loved his sister so much. She was compassionate even in the face of certain doom.

"Dear sister, it is a Dragon. It is an animal, no more, no less. Besides, we both have read the Brief History of Dragons and the two other lesser-known volumes by Pelinnedes. All Dragons are female."

"The History books are wrong," Lyssa said firmly. She said it so matter-of-factly, without any hesitation Landon decided it best not to argue.

"Pelinnedes was told the truth. All Dragons are born female. That much, I still believe is the case. But, this is only biologically. This Dragon, though born a female, is now…" she hesitated, trying to figure out the correct wording to explain her thoughts, "a male."

Landon stared at her in disbelief. *"How could a dragon be both male and female?"*

"It's not possible?" he thought. His thoughts were racing more quickly than his words could be formed.

"I know it is a lot to take in. Believe me, I know. But, I have had hours to process everything he has shown me. I can say firmly, without hesitation, this Dragon, which was once a female, is now a male," she added.

Landon opened his mouth to speak and quickly closed it. He decided to wait rather than ask the myriad of questions flying around in his head.

"Sit dear brother," Lyssa directed. She moved back over to the dragon and sat beside him. Gently, the Princess placed her delicate fingers upon his head and began to caress him once again. Landon was amazed the beast was allowing the two of them to sit so closely without attacking.

"I will start at the beginning," she started, "first by saying thank you for your bravery. I know your love for me transcends even the most innate fear most have when facing a Dragon." She smiled at Landon until he acknowledged her words with a nod.

"I will admit to you that I passed out while flying to Captain Arem's cave." It bothered Landon to hear her refer to the dragon with a name.

"When I awoke, I was in the cave lying on a bed of grass thick enough to fill a mattress. Cold water in a golden cup and a few ripe, red apples had been placed near me. Arem, the Dragon was awake, watching me intently. My initial reaction was fear, though quickly replaced with curiosity. The Dragon did not attack me. He made no efforts to devour me. After a few minutes my fear overcame me and I gulped the water and ate the apples. The two of us watched each other. I was sure any minute I would be eaten," she said.

"I understand why Pelinnedes, the Historian, was tempted to stay in the mountains with the Dragons. Their power and grace is magnificent. Even more, I agree with Pelinnedes, knowing they are caring and compassionate. At least the Dragon Arem is all of these things."

Landon looked at her shocked.

"Once I finished eating Arem beckoned me over with one of his giant paws, the talons scaring me. I was sure I would be eaten. Yet, when I came closer to him he gestured for me to sit. The mighty Dragon brought an orb to me."

Landon gasped. He had read the history books. The orbs were used by Dragons in magical ways. Fascinated, he leaned forward to hear his sister's words more clearly.

"Now we are getting somewhere," he thought.

"When placed before me, the orb shined bright blue. It was luminous. The emanating light filled the cave. It was as if I was standing in front of a tiny sun. I looked into the Dragon's eyes and he gestured for me to put my two hands on the orb. I did so."

Landon watched his sister as she used her hands to replay for him what she had done.

"What happened?" he asked, truly curious. For the first time in his life, one of the history books, a foundation of his education, was coming to life. Fascinated, he was absorbed in the story and was like an expectant child. There were moments in the conversation when he caught himself holding his breath.

Lyssa smiled, "I can see by your reaction brother, you are as excited as I was." She laughed aloud and then continued, "I placed my hands upon the glowing orb. Immediately, words flowed into my mind. At first they flowed quickly, almost too quickly for me to comprehend. I could tell by Arem's expression he was frustrated. After a few minutes the speed and the cadence of the words decreased so that I could understand them better."

Landon looked from his sister to the Dragon. He had not realized it had opened its eyes again and was watching the two of them intently. The Dragon seemed passive, though he knew it could unleash its power at any moment.

"I understand," Landon said. "The orbs can be used by Dragons to communicate with humans. But what did the beas…" He stopped, catching himself. "What did this dragon say?" He could not bring himself to call the beast Arem.

"Well. He told me about his life," she responded. "We talked for a few hours and he explained to me everything I needed to know about him, including why he abducted me."

Landon was awed by his sister's words. She had communicated with a dragon. She had been abducted and he was sure she would be dead by the time he had arrived. Yet, here she was, sitting quietly in the foothills in the chilly night air waiting for him to come to her rescue.

Lyssa continued, "After answering all of my questions he showed me parts of his life, using the orb of course."

"What do you mean he showed you?" Landon asked.

"Well, Arem used the magic of the orb to show me his past. I was there, standing nearby, watching, listening, and observing everything that happened to him. It was amazing. The others in his past could not see me, but I could see them clearly. I was there with them. Amazed, I had even reached out to touch one of them as he passed me. My hand swept through him without making any contact."

Landon sat quietly trying to process everything his sister had told him.

"He is in pain my brother. An evil curse has been placed upon him. This Dragon is in pain and his time is running out. If the curse cannot be broken all will be lost."

Landon did not attempt to understand everything she told him. She had been given more information and more time to process everything.

She offered, "It is a lot to take in. I realize it. It was almost more than I could comprehend, but when he spoke to me, through the orb and then showed me, I now understand why he sought us out."

"He did not seek us out," Landon blurted. He was angry. "He abducted you. It was only through the magic of some poor old man, who is dead now." With these words the Dragon lifted its head and growled at Landon. The Prince leaned backward. The growl echoed through the mountains like rolling thunder on a stormy night.

"Please, brother, for all our sakes, remain calm. While Captain Arem is inside this Dragon, you should be aware the Dragon is there, also. Try not to say or do anything that will push it beyond Arem's control."

Landon wondered, *"What did I say? What angered him?"*

She said, "It is a lot to take in. The best way to help you understand is to show you." She looked at the Dragon the massive head nodded in agreement.

The two of them began walking side by side, up the mountain. Landon hesitated and then followed.

The two walked ten to fifteen feet ahead of him. The size of the Dragon was immense compared to his sister. She barely reached the height of the Dragon's knees. While they walked in silence Landon watched the two of them and marveled at last twenty-four hours.

He smiled the moment they reached a part of the hill too steep for his sister to climb. The Dragon reached down, picked her up in its clawed paws and place her gently ahead fifteen to twenty feet. She then waited for the Dragon to catch up.

Lyssa called back to her brother, "Would you like some assistance, dear brother?" Landon shook his head briskly. He was too proud, and stubborn, to be helped up the side of a hill by this beast. He clawed his way up the steep slope, falling backward a few times.

The three of them walked in silence for more than an hour. Finally, up ahead, he saw his sister and the Dragon standing atop a rocky ledge. They had stopped to watch him climb. Fifteen minutes later, as he pulled himself up over a ledge, Landon stood and gasped.

"Dear brother, this is Captain Arem's cave."

INTO THE SULTAN'S HOUSE

THE THREE OF THEM STOOD FOR A MINUTE OUTSIDE THE large entrance to the rocky cave. It surprised Landon to find the cave big enough to house the Dragon.

"It could house ten dragons, easily," he thought. Exhausted from the climb, he looked at his sister and the dragon, both waiting patiently for him to catch his breath.

"You will be happy to be in the cave. The heat generated by Arem's body, by the orbs, and by the eggs will help keep the night's chilly air at bay," she said. Lyssa turned and entered the cave. Landon was again awed by her actions. She was not fearful in the least.

"I must think of the dragon as it, not him," he reminded himself.

While the journey up the side of the mountain had been difficult, it had given Landon time to figure out an escape plan. For now, he would have to play along, but at the moment an opportunity presented itself he would grab his sister and flee.

"She will come to her senses when she is away from its grasp. She has been hypnotized and does not realize the danger she is in."

The black dragon turned and followed Lyssa. Once past the entrance it turned and looked back at Landon. It bowed to him, acknowledging his royalty. The dragon gestured with its left paw for Landon to follow. Even in the darkness of the cave's entrance, the ivory fangs glistened. Landon walked into the cave happy to feel its warmth. The rush to find his sister and the scramble to follow the two of them up the side of this mountain had kept the chill at bay, barely. Standing inside the coziness and warmth of the dragon's lair, he realized how cold it was outside.

He was also surprised to find the cave well lit. Landon had been expecting a cold, dark cavern filled with the bones of other men. Instead, the cave was clean. The light provided from the radiating orbs filled the massive cavern. Landon counted more than twenty eggs toward the back of the cave.

His sister moved over to a rock near the glowing orbs and sat down. She looked back at him smiling, gesturing for him to join her. The dragon sauntered over to her, moved a few feet past, spun around, and faced the mouth of the cave. It lowered its massive body onto the rocky floor. Crossing its front paws, the ebony beast watched Landon with a twinkle in its eyes. Landon was reminded of the royal hounds, the large Mastiffs that roamed the castle.

"Maybe it's time I trust her judgement," he thought. Landon shook his head quickly trying to drive the thought from his mind. *"Careful."*

She offered, excitedly, "Do you see, brother? Do you see the beautiful orbs?" Landon looked to where she had pointed. There were three egg shaped globes from which all of the light within the cave seemed to flow. The soft-blue light was both calming and mesmerizing.

He acknowledged his sister with a nod, lifting his gaze from the orbs, to the dragon, and then back to his sister's face. Her eyes shined with the excitement he had seen many times in their lives.

"It is as I said. Arem has a large clutch of eggs," she said. She pointed beyond the orbs at a pile of eggs, each the size of a watermelon. "These are the orbs, used by Captain Arem to communicate. Those are the eggs destined to become Dragons."

"Why do you refer to him as Captain Arem, dear sister?" he asked.

"Before he was a Dragon, Arem was a Captain. He was a soldier in the mightiest army in the south. He was the son of a great general. Because of his abilities, and because the Sultan trusted his family above all others in his realm, Captain Arem was chosen to go north to O'ndar.

"Once he was on this mission, certain events unfolded placing him into the body of this Dragon." Lyssa smiled when she heard Landon gasp in disbelief.

"Impossible! What you say is impossible," he stammered.

"I know you think it's impossible. Arem told me you would think it a mad fantasy. He also reminded me it might be best to show you. Then, we can answer any of your questions."

She motioned for Landon to come closer, scooting over to make room for him on the large, flat rock. When he sat down they both looked up at the dragon. The coal-colored lizard lifted both front paws and gestured downward.

Lisa explained, "Captain Arem would like the two of us to place our hands like so; on the top of the orb. We will be transported into the past, his past, using something called the Celestial Plane."

Landon looked at her sideways and said, "I am familiar with the Celestial Plane." Lyssa was full of questions.

"How? We never learned about it in our studies."

Landon smiled at the turning of the tables. He said, "My journey here dear Lyss. How do you think I covered all of those miles so quickly? The old man, the one I told you about, I believe he was a wizard and used the Celestial Plane to send me to you." Landon looked at the dragon, deciding it would be wise not to mention Ferlynne's plight, again.

"It looks like we both have reason to be amazed," Lyssa responded. "Captain Arem uses the orb to show us the past and to speak with us in the present. He does this by sending us across the Celestial Plane. Not our bodies," she started to finish her sentence, but Landon blurted out.

"But our souls." Things were beginning to make more sense to Landon, though doubts still assailed him.

"Remember what I said before. We will be observers in Captain Arem's past. We will see events as he saw them. No one will be able to see us, or hear us, do you understand?" Lyssa turned and looked at her brother with conviction. "We will hear everything in our language, thanks to Captain Arem."

"Yes, I understand," he answered. He raised both his hands, spread his fingers and held them above the orb. Lyssa stood, moved to the opposite side of the orb and knelt down. She raised her hands and placed her fingers a few inches away from the top of the melon shaped orb.

"Ready?" she asked.

"Yes," Landon said.

"One, two, three, now." The two of them placed their hands fully on the bright glowing orb. Landon felt the familiar tug as his soul pulled away from his body.

He tried to look at his sister, but the cave had become infused with bright, fluorescent blue light. It forced him to squeeze his eyes shut. This sensation lasted for only a few seconds. When the radiance dissipated, Landon was standing next to his sister in a long, spectacular hallway. It was ornately furnished, with a white-marbled floor. The floor stretched a great distance in both directions. Each ivory tile had been inlaid with flecks of gold, splattered like tiny droplets of rain.

"If those are real gold flecks, there is great wealth here." Landon thought.

The length of the hallway was awe-inspiring. Landon felt the richness of this citadel and knew the master of this place was wealthy beyond anything imagined in the northern states.

Slowly, he walked away from Lyssa and stopped in front of the tapestries hanging on the walls. Each finely-woven fabric vividly depicted a scene of some great battle. Each successive one seemed more colorful and spectacular than the one before. Midway down the hallway Landon was drawn to the largest tapestry, a pomegranate-colored one. A purple hooded cobra dominated the tapestry its powerful body wrapped around the trunk of a majestic tree. The hood spread wide, the bright, yellow eyes of the snake stared back at him. Above the cobra and the tree, towered a King. His body was covered in fine, lavender-colored silk. Both the breeches and the tunic complimented each other nicely. His ice blue eyes pierced through Landon. The chin was lean and masculine. Landon caught himself staring into the eyes, fixated.

"A King? An Emperor?" he thought.

"It is the history of our Nation's Military victories," a booming voice said, excitedly.

Landon stepped back shocked. He looked to his sister puzzled.

"Do not be frightened brother. It is the voice of Captain Arem," she said shrugging her shoulders.

"He is here with us, but I do not see him," Landon responded.

Lyssa giggled, offering, "He is here with us as an unseen guide."

Landon looked back to the original tapestry. The commanding voice offered, "My apologies Prince Landon. I should have prepared you before I spoke. I was excited to see you drawn to the tapestries on the walls of the royal hallway."

Landon paused and then said, "No apologies necessary. I have never communicated with a dragon before and should have prepared myself. As you were saying, these tapestries are depictions of battles?"

"Yes, they include the Sultan and the General representing the Sultan in battle," Arem answered.

Even without seeing Captain Arem's face, Landon could hear the excitement in his voice as he explained the wall-fabrics and their importance.

Landon asked, "What is the significance of the purple cobra in the middle of each tapestry?"

"The cobra is Elzahari, the Chosen One. Your sister told me about Meeha, the Emerald Dragon of the Forests whose image is used on the Coat of Arms for O'ndar. It is significant because of its role in the creation of the most powerful nation of the north. Elzahari holds the same significance to the Zaharian Empire. While our nation is wealthy, our capital is only a tiny fraction of the Sultan's domains. When we are finished I can show you the history of the birth of our great nation, if you like."

Landon was still looking at the tapestry, drawn to the strength of the man in the middle and the power of the cobra. He hardly noticed his sister when she spoke.

"Let's go dear brother. He should be along any minute," she said. Lyssa reached out and tugged on Landon's arm.

"How are you able to touch me?" he asked.

She responded quickly, "I do not know. Now let's go. He will be along any minute."

Almost on cue, a small boy no more than eleven years of age came running around the corner up ahead. He almost fell to the floor, laughed aloud at his own antics, then scurried down the hallway. He passed the two of them never noticing their presence. It was clear he was excited and in a hurry. He had black hair, olive-colored skin, and laughed as he ran. Landon was reminded of his mother and her own exotic features.

A small woman with the same complexion followed behind. "Arem, slow down. You must not run in the Royal Hall," she scolded in a whisper. The little boy was too excited to listen. He continued running.

"Hurry mother or we will be late." Panting, the young boy waited for his mother to catch up.

"We will not be late. And as your father's son, it is not right for you to run. He is being promoted to General today and his son cannot be seen running through the Sultan's castle."

The little boy nodded, grabbed his mother by the hand, and tried to drag her more quickly along with him.

They reached two massive oak doors, each gilded with more flecks of Platinum and Silver. Two heavily armed guards, their armor dyed deep purple, saluted the pair and lifted their scimitars allowing the mother and son to enter. They shut the doors leaving Landon and Lyssa on the outside.

"Now what do we do?" Landon asked.

Laughing, Lyssa stepped forward, passing through the guards and the doors as if they were made of smoke.

Looking around, the Prince was again astonished at the size and elaborateness of this palace. Hundreds of onlookers had gathered in the Ceremonial Hall of the Lord, clustering together on the white-marbled floor. The nobles wore fine clothing made of purple silk, each man and woman covered in diamond crusted rings or gold necklaces.

There were more than thirty armed guards, each bedecked in the deep, purple armor. The first guard on either side held their scimitars, unsheathed. The heavy swords a warning to the observers they would be dealt with severely should anything get out of control. Ten of the guards were armed with a bow and arrows.

His sister reached out and grabbed him by the elbow. Landon did not resist and allowed Lyssa to drag him along behind the boy and his mother. He continued to look around at the ornately decorated hall. A finely dressed man, one covered in richly-woven silk stepped forward halting at the bottom of the steps. He looked up to the large, diamond throne, covered by a lavender-colored bearskin rug.

The man looked to someone standing along the walls near the guards and nodded. With this cue, a row of trumpets began to blare loudly. A few seconds later the Sultan Muraffe III, the Emperor of the Zaharian Empire entered from the back of the Great Hall. Everyone in the room immediately kneeled in supplication. Landon noticed the guards remained standing, watching those who prostrated themselves before the Sultan.

Landon stepped away from his sister moving closer. This was the man on many of the tapestries hanging on the walls of the Great Hall. The Sultan entered slowly, scanning the room to ensure everyone had kneeled quickly and appropriately.

Though his eyes were fixed on this powerful man, a flash of purple along the floor behind the Sultan caught Landon's attention. Looking down, he gasped. Slithering behind Muraffe III was a large, purple cobra.

The Emperor picked up his pace and moved quickly over to the crystal throne. Stopping behind it, he placed his left arm on the back and rested his right arm on the hilt of his jewel crusted sword. While the cat-like movements of the emperor were on full display as he panned his supplicants with his piercing stare, the cobra stopped behind him and slowly glided its way up his back. The snake swirled its body around his torso slithering up to his shoulders. The large cobra stopped and rested its head on his right shoulder. Slowly, almost lovingly, both the snake and the man leaned in rubbing their faces against each other.

Lyssa whispered to Landon, "Fascinating, isn't it."

This was a man who ruled his empire with an iron hand. He demanded his subjects bend to his every whim and was willing to enforce his will, with violence, if needed. The Sultan waited a few more seconds and bellowed loudly to his subjects, "You may rise."

He reached up and patted the snake on the head. He caressed it gently, humming to it. Pointing to the cushion on the throne he said, "There." The snake slithered over his shoulder and down his stomach. Landon watched the tail of the snake as it wound its way up and down the Sultan's body, stopping only when it was coiled up on the cushion of the throne, its body blending in to the lavender-colored bear skin rug.

"That snake has to be at least ten feet long," he said.

She looked back at him and responded with, "It's fifteen."

Following his command, every head lifted. Landon looked to their faces and saw smiles and adoration.

Landon brought his attention back to the throne. He found it difficult to pull his eyes away from the cobra lounging comfortably on the luxurious bear-skin. The throne was a magnificently carved diamond, the largest Landon had ever seen in his life. If carved by a master diamond cutter, it would yield as many diamonds currently held in the treasuries of most of the northern countries combined. It had a tall back and two meticulously carved armrests, each sculpted into the head of a cobra.

The small, elderly man stepped forward again and bowed to the Sultan. He waited for the Sultan to nod in approval and turned to face the onlookers. His leathery fingers slowly unrolled the parchment. He paused and then read aloud for all in the hall to hear.

"By the order of the Sultan Muraffe III, our exalted Lord and the Emperor of all he surveys, it has been decreed, which is his Divine right to do, that from this day forward, Colonel Faron of the Third Legion will be promoted to the rank of General. His bravery in the Battle of Ishmanenin against the invading horde of Tartir horsemen, and his leadership upon the unfortunate death of General Hydaenate, led to the repulsion of the raiders. Additionally, General Faron immediately assumed control of the Legion following the death of his lord and General. He rallied the soldiers, ordered a counter-attack and followed the retreating horde for two days until every last one of the devils was slaughtered. As a soldier in the Sultan's military, General Faron has exemplified the greatness of the Sultan's army. General Faron, please step forward."

Landon looked at the little boy who was beaming with admiration.

The elderly man turned and looked at Muraffe III, who sat quietly on the edge of his throne. The cobra was still curled up, lying behind the Sultan. He scowled at the elderly man and waived him back. The old man bowed low and backed into the crowd of onlookers. No one had stepped forward.

The Sultan stood and said, "General Faron. Please step forward." His powerful voice echoed throughout the hall. Landon tried to stand on his toes to see the man being promoted to a General for his bravery. He noticed the General had not moved when directed to do so by the Royal Messenger. He had waited for his lord, the Sultan, to command him.

Lyssa whispered to him, "It is Arem's father, do you understand?" Landon nodded realizing the importance of the event. The throng of onlookers parted and a large, powerfully built man walked through them. He moved slowly, his scimitar hanging at his side. Landon appreciated the trust the Sultan placed in his Generals, allowing them this close to his person while armed. Other than the guards and the Sultan, there were no others with swords in the room. General Faron walked to the bottom of the stairs leading up to the throne. He bowed.

The Sultan stepped forward, walked four steps down to the man, and grasped him by his shoulders. He kissed him gently on both cheeks saying, "My friend, our children have always been playmates together and for this I thank you."

"Trained by the best minds in the art of war, you have risen through the ranks of our military. You have always been in front of the battle with our soldiers. You have been ready to wage war for me and the Empire. And for this I thank you." The Sultan once again kissed the General on both cheeks.

"For your bravery, for your honor, and for your courage I promote you to the rank of General, a rank attained by your father and your father's father." He kissed the General on both cheeks one more time, patted the man on the shoulders and turned him around to face the crowd.

Landon inhaled loudly. His sister looked at him sideways without turning from the ceremony.

"It's Ferlynne," he whispered.

GENERAL FARON

"FERLYNNE?" HE WHISPERED. THIS MAN, STANDING AT THE bottom of the steps before the Sultan, was much younger than the hermit, but Landon was sure it was the same man. He said as much to his sister. "He is the wizard who sent me to you."

Lyssa responded, "But how can that be? This is Arem's father, promoted to the rank of General in Arem's eleventh year." She started to speak again, but stopped herself, "Watch dear brother, important events are about to happen."

"None of this makes any sense. Ferlynne was much, much older than the man standing before him," Landon thought.

Both Ferlynne the hermit and General Faron had piercing green eyes and hawk-like features. Ferlynne though was wrinkled and gray, having aged much beyond his years.

The Dragon Arem's voice said, "Do not doubt, my Prince. It is my father. The man you call Ferlynne was known to me in my youth as father and in my brief military career as General."

"If this is true, I now have many doubts about your intentions," Landon responded.

A helpless feeling swept over him. *"Are we puppets in some sort of game?"*

Landon returned his attention to the ceremony. The Cobra, lounging on the lavender cushions, had lifted its head off the cushions, watching with intensity.

General Faron graciously thanked the Sultan for his support, for the promotion, and pledged his life to the empire. He turned to the Sultan and proclaimed loudly, "My Lord, it would be an honor if my son Arem, my first born, could be adopted into the Sultan's house, to be trained in the art of warfare by his majesty's best minds."

The Sultan smiled broadly, his white teeth shining brightly. Landon was reminded of the cobra. He expected Muraffe's tongue to flick out between his teeth testing the air.

The Sultan nodded and graciously accepted the offer.

General Faron turned to his wife and son. He gestured for Arem to come forward. The young man remained in place, refusing his father's commands.

Landon waited for the General to yell at his son for having embarrassed him in front of his master. Instead, the General smiled, pleased.

The boy looked first to his father and then slowly turned to look into the eyes of the Sultan. The Sultan smiled, gesturing for Arem to come forward. The boy did so timidly. When he reached his father he kneeled.

"Rise young Arem, my new son," the Sultan bellowed. He continued proudly, "It seems both your father and mother have taught you well. It would be an honor to adopt you into my household as my son. With the proper training and conviction, someday you may even earn the distinction bestowed upon your father." He turned to his assistant and said, "Let it be known throughout Istanabad and throughout the Zaharian Empire." He looked at Arem and nodded with warmth and affection.

Arem stood, looked to his father and mother once more, bowed to both, and left the hall with the elderly man. He did not look back.

Landon started to ask a question, but stopped as the blinding brightness returned. When the illumination faded they were standing a few feet behind the boy, who sat patiently on a thick rug in the middle of a marble-tiled room. Sunlight beamed in through a window. Dark-purple curtains had been parted to allow sunlight to pour into the room.

Landon looked to the door and wondered who this young boy was waiting patiently to see. A few minutes later the door opened. General Faron and Arem's mother entered. Arem rose quickly and ran to hug the both of them.

"Father, how did I do?" he asked. General Faron spread his arms wide, scooped the young boy up into his arms, and twirled him around in the air. He hugged him closely for a few seconds before placing him back down on the ground.

"You were absolutely perfect," he said. Arem ran to hug his smiling mother. She had pulled her auburn hair back into a coif, her dark brown eyes twinkling. She was beautiful.

"Are you prepared for this?" the woman whispered. She placed her cheek against his cheek. A tear ran down her face.

"Do not be a silly woman," General Faron said. He added, "He has been given the greatest honor bestowed on someone in our kingdom." His words did not match the look of sadness on his face.

Lyssa broke in, "There are watchers in the next room. They listen and watch everything in this palace."

"Yes mother, I am," Arem responded. "My father was adopted into the house of our exalted Lord and it has allowed him to become a great General. It is my goal to follow in his footsteps and some day to surpass him. I will become the greatest general of all-time." He laughed lightly, looking up with admiration into his father's eyes.

"And you shall young one. Remember, after this moment you may no longer refer to me as father. To you I am General, nor more, no less. Be aware though, both your mother and I love you above all in this world. The love you would have shown to us must now be shown to our beloved Sultan. Do you understand?"

Arem nodded, the reality of the moment sinking in. He had been prepared for this moment, as had both of his parents. Yet, the moment was here and now all three regretted the finality of what was about to happen.

"Yes, father. I mean yes General," he said. He frowned at his father and mother, but held back the tears.

"It is time," General Faron said. He looked to his wife and gestured at the door with his head. Quietly, Arem's mother leaned down one more time, kissed her son on his cheek, and walked over to the door.

Arem looked into her eyes and mouthed the words, "I love you, mother." She returned the sentiment and left.

"I am proud of you Arem," his father said, solemnly. He leaned down to hug him and whispered, "Remember, though, I will always be your one and only father." Arem watched in silence while General Faron followed his mother out the door.

The blinding luminosity returned. Once again, Landon and Lyssa closed their eyes waiting for the light to disappear. When Landon opened his eyes they were back inside the cave.

"Do you see, brother?" his sister asked. "Arem's father was promoted to General. In the Zaharian Empire, every General must offer up their firstborn son to the Sultan. Considered an honor, it is also a way for the Sultan to ensure their loyalty."

Landon had been trained in the art of warfare by the best minds in O'ndar. He was awed, though, by the prospect of forcing a father to give up his son. He loved his father dearly and did not know if he would have been able to do it.

"The Sultan has the loyalty of his minions and his army. Many of the leaders of the military are raised as his children, taught to follow his command without hesitating. From birth until death, the armies of Muraffe III are filled with soldiers fanatically loyal. For one reason, or another, the Sultan has their allegiance."

Lyssa paused, waiting for Landon's response.

Landon stared at the Dragon, looking into the yellow eyes, hoping to see the little boy.

ELZAHARI: THE CHOSEN ONE

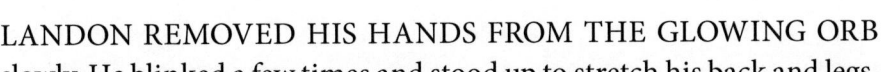

LANDON REMOVED HIS HANDS FROM THE GLOWING ORB slowly. He blinked a few times and stood up to stretch his back and legs.

The blue glow of the orbs continued casting heavy shadows against the rocky walls. The shadows danced back and forth, flickering the way a shadow dances when cast by the flames of a campfire. Landon blinked a few times trying to avoid focusing on the hypnotic flames.

"How long were we inside the orb?" he asked. He expected Lyssa to say an hour, maybe two.

"We were inside the castle and the Ceremonial Hall for a little more than an hour, but in our world no more than ten seconds has elapsed. The Celestial Plane is not affected by time as we are," she responded. She looked at the Dragon with affection. It bothered Landon to see her do so.

Landon found it hard to believe he his back had become stiff from sitting for only a few seconds. Maybe his mind had convinced his body he had been sitting on the rock for an hour.

Standing up, the Dragon looked at Lyssa, nodded, and walked carefully over to the mouth of the cave. He looked back at the two of them, bowing his head deeply. Once upright, the mighty beast turned to the mouth of the cave, hopped a few feet until his body cleared the opening, spread his massive wings and flew up into the clouds.

"Where is he going?" Landon asked. The orbs continued to pulsate even without the Dragon present.

"He has flown from his cave to give us the chance to talk and to give us a chance to leave if it is what we choose to do."

Landon was dumbfounded, "He's giving us a chance to escape?" Once again, he was bewildered. With a chance to leave, they must act quickly.

"Is this real? He is just waiting to snatch us up in his claws," he thought. Landon was unaware he had referred to the Dragon as him.

"It is no trick brother. Arem is in need of our help. More specifically, he is in need of your help. Despite the monster you claim to see before you, he has feelings and emotions. He came from a loving family. He does not want to see either of us harmed. If we are to continue it has to be by our own volition. He will not put us in harm's way unless we are committed," she said.

"I admit sister, when I arrived and found you I have been thinking about a way to escape," he declared, lifting his hand to stop her from responding.

"These have been strange events," he said. "I need more information before I can truly understand what is happening. We may be puppets controlled by some unknown hand. We may be pawns in a game. Arem may be a victim of treachery or he may be a villain using us for some vile purpose." His sister shook her head.

Lyssa's abduction helped him realize they had sheltered lives. Their world, which had been their castle and the surrounding forests and lakes, suddenly seemed very tiny. It was a major change in his perception and he hoped his sister could appreciate the magnitude. Their lives would never be the same.

"When I woke yesterday morning I never imagined any of these things possible. It both saddens me and excites me to know the world is far bigger than O'ndar. We are not the center of the universe, dear Lyss. Yet, I have to admit I am happy to learn about new lands and not just from a textbook.

"There are creatures, and nations, and dragons, and a wide array of adventures far beyond our understanding. As I have stated to you a few seconds ago, it saddens and frightens me. So I will stay for now, but I have a few demands," he stated matter-of-factly. "I have questions and will go no further until some of them have been answered."

"So you agree to stay?" she asked. He could feel her excitement. Her attitude helped to placate his fears.

"For now dear sister, I will stay. If I do not receive satisfactory answers, we will leave. Make no mistake, if I choose to leave and you resist, I will take you with me by force. Even if it means death for the both of us," he declared. He still distrusted the Dragon's intentions.

Landon wondered, *"Did Meeha foresee this?"* He could not help but think of Pelinnedes and the Emerald Dragon Meeha. *"Did Meeha know his sister would be abducted almost a thousand years later? Did she know Landon would travel across the Celestial Plane, hundreds of miles, to find his sister waiting on the side of a mountain with a Dragon?"* Meeha had claimed the power to tell the future. Reading the stories and the histories of the past, Landon had always doubted. Now, though, he was forced to believe. Dragons were mysterious creatures.

Once again, Landon looked at the flickering shadows cast by the glowing orbs. A shiver of fear ran up his back. The rocky cave offered sanctuary from the cold, but those shadows foretold of an evil to come. Landon wished he could seek the advice of his father, a man who ruled with wisdom and confidence.

Taking his hands in hers, Lyssa kissed him on the forehead the way she used to when they were younger. He enjoyed the kiss, grateful she had not argued about his demands. Looking over to the mouth of the cave Landon was surprised to see the Dragon had returned.

The large Dragon moved gingerly past the two of them, swirled around and once again sat down facing the mouth of the cave. Landon was sure Arem did so for protection. He wondered what a dragon would fear. *"He would fear a larger dragon,"* Landon thought. Arem gestured for the two of them to join him. When they were sitting, once again he gestured for them to place their hands on top of the glowing orb. Landon expected another blinding flash of light, but nothing happened.

"I thought I should answer any questions you might have before we go any further," Arem said, his voice echoing inside their minds.

Landon looked into the Dragon's eyes and thought he saw sincerity. He asked, "Was it really you as a little boy?" The Dragon responded by nodding his head.

"I must admit to being a bit skeptical," Landon said.

The Dragon said, "I would have expected nothing less from a future king."

Landon chose to ignore the compliment. He did not want to be thrown off-course by mere words.

"I have a lot of questions," Landon said again. He paused and then said something, which shocked the other two.

"I will not ask my questions until you have shown me everything. When I was younger, I learned the best way to understand something is to watch and observe closely. Once I have seen everything then I will ask my questions. Otherwise, we could spend hours talking and I would still have more questions once we returned to this cave."

"I must admit I am pleasantly surprised, young Prince," Arem offered. Landon could see admiration on both of their faces.

"Where would you like to begin?" the Dragon asked.

"I would like to begin at the beginning. Where else should a person start?" he asked. "Show me the history of the Zaharian Empire. Show me more about the Cobra Elzahari; the Chosen One."

The brilliant light returned, forcing them to shut their eyes tightly. After a few seconds, while the light was still blinding, the Dragon Arem spoke, "In a few seconds, you may open your eyes, but remember you are in no danger."

They opened their eyes and Lyssa screamed loudly. Landon wanted to reach out to comfort her, but was too fascinated.

The two of them were floating thousands of feet above the ground. White clouds swirled around them, gathering above and below. Slowly, they began floating downward.

"Below us is Istanabad, the cradle of civilization as it was three-thousand years ago," Arem said.

Landon looked at Lyssa. She had stopped panicking. Her eyes betrayed the fear she felt, but at least she was breathing normally. He looked back to the ground, appreciating the perspective. Looking to the north, Landon could see a vast desert stretching away into the horizon.

"This must be what it is like to fly. It is exhilarating," Landon thought.

"Exactly!" the Dragon's voice responded.

Once again Landon had the suspicion Arem, in his Dragon form, could read minds.

"The Danztuke River is below," Arem said. "It flows from the Cargathian Mountains in the east, bringing much needed water to this bustling city and the future capital of the Zaharian Empire."

Landon gasped at the implication. Three-thousand years ago, the city of Istanabad was almost as large as the entire nation of O'ndar.

"Three thousand years ago," Landon said. Landon watched the thin clouds barreling past them as they slowly descended.

"Yes. The city as it was in the reign of Xerxes the Terrible. The Sultan ruled Istanabad with an iron hand for more than fifty years. There have been none more horrible in the three-thousand years since. Muraffe comes close."

Lyssa blurted out, "Was he truly that terrible?"

Arem continued, "Yes. We are about to witness the fruition of his evil reign, though. After more than fifty years of torturing his friends, torturing his enemies, torturing those he suspected of treachery, after more than fifty years of forcing his counselors and generals to slay their first born children to show their loyalty, the reign of Xerxes the Terrible is about to come to an end."

"Look!" Lyssa yelled. Far below them, Istanabad glowed brightly in the coming dawn. A vast number of fires pocketed the city. Some were small, while others engulfed entire buildings. The smoke billowed up into the sky trailing off with the wind in thick, black rows.

Arem explained, "It started out as a slave revolt and blossomed into much more. Two-thousand city slaves, raging against the oppression of a madman, rose up in an attempt to throw off the yoke of servitude. They have been joined by angry citizens, burdened by high taxes and a crushing tyranny. All have turned against Xerxes. The city guard has joined the revolution. The violent mob has become a coordinated movement, moving unopposed through the city. The violence of the previous night has abated, but you are witnessing the terrible price the city has had to pay for the maltreatment of its citizens."

Landon identified more than fifty fires burning in various parts of the city, maybe a hundred. They continued to float downward giving him more time to look at the city walls. Massive in width and height, the white-sand walls surrounded the great city. The westward flowing river wound south a few miles outside Istanabad. The river flowed into the city from the north, through part of a northern wall. Landon noticed giant metal portcullises built to allow only the water of the Danztuke River into the city. Massive walls built outwardly from this point of the city stretched along the river for more than a mile. While the portcullises offered a strategic way into the city, the extra fortifications along the river would cause an invading army to have second thoughts about this point of entrance. The river wound its way through Istanabad eventually exiting through a similar array of portcullises along another wall to the south. The fortifications, intricately built, allowed water to flow through the city, while at the same time keeping the city safe from an invasion.

The two of them were now less than five-hundred feet above the city. Thousands of men, women, and children ran through the city streets screaming in anger. The rule of Xerxes the terrible had unleashed deep resentments. Only the death of some in the ruling class would help extinguish the years of anger. Landon had read about similar events in his history books. He was well-versed about the power of an oppressed mob pushed by many years of frustration to desperation. These people were at the point of no return. He could hear the screams of the people in the crowds as they marched towards the castle. Landon knew there would soon be blood on the steps of the Sultan's castle.

The two of them landed gently directly in the center of the crowd that numbered in the hundreds of thousands. They walked quickly, trying to catch up with the mixture of rebellious slaves, oppressed merchantmen, and soldiers. Rather than walk around, Landon stepped through the mob, passing through various people like an apparition.

The Dragon said, "You are witnessing the culmination of more than five-hundred years of an oppressive Sultanate. Xerxes was the final catalyst after years of torture, high taxes, and mistreatment. If it had only been the slaves, the rebellion would not have taken hold. If the Sultan had been less cruel the citizenry would have never taken up arms against him.

"Xerxes had been raised to believe he was divine in nature and above the laws of man. Eventually, though, it is man who finally throws off the yoke of oppression, especially when pushed beyond all reason."

Landon shook with nervousness at the display of anger and hatred by this mob. Even though he knew he was not in danger, the power of this unruly horde shook him to his core.

"What could this man have done for fifty years that led to this?" He vowed to rule gracefully and with an even-hand.

The light flashed again, but dissipated just as quickly.

Landon and Lyssa were standing in front of the large castle. Massive walls of stone, more than thirty feet in height, and more than six feet thick, towered above them. Landon was sure the Sultan would be safe behind these walls. The castle was a fortress inside the white-walled city. The anger of the mob, armed with sticks and pitchforks, was no match for the thick walls.

Suddenly, the large, metal portcullis lifted. A small bridge was lowered across the surrounding castle moat. This act of betrayal shocked Landon. His house guards would never do such a thing.

"Would they?" he thought. Landon thought back to the time when Lyssa had scolded him for their mistreatment. He shuddered, looking at this mass of people entering the sacred home of their lord. Thousands of people poured in through the opening. They charged the castle stopping a few feet below steps leading up to the main doors. All of the soldiers stood aside watching. Some even joined the ranks of the mob. Landon could see them distinctly in their sand-colored uniforms, interspersed throughout the crowd.

Standing on the top step, waiting for the mob to approach, stood Xerxes the Terrible. He seemed oblivious to the events unfolding before him. The large man stood more than six feet in height. His shoulders were broad and muscular. The look of contempt on Xerxes face froze Landon in his tracks. The Sultan had unsheathed his sword, a large scimitar, which glistened in the morning light.

"He is either mad or truly believes he has some divine protection!" Landon thought. Looking at the crowd, the look of rage on all of the faces, Landon quivered with fear.

The mob stopped at the bottom step. Generations of citizens had been educated to fear the Sultan, raised from birth to believe in his divineness. Many viewed the Sultan as a god and feared his wrath.

"INFIDELS!" Xerxes the Terrible yelled at the top of his lungs. The entire crowd fell silent. Landon gasped at the power this man held over his subjects. He had quieted a horde of more than three thousand people.

To the left of Xerxes, a few steps below, a group of priests bowed low hoping to avoid the outrage and fury of the Sultan. These bearded men had gathered to witness the events, hoping their presence would be appreciated by whichever side came out on top.

Xerxes, bedecked in an ivory-colored, silk tunic stepped forward a half step. He raised the scimitar above his head with both hands. Those in the crowd, though they outnumbered him three-thousand to one stepped backward in fear.

"INFIDELS! You dare to enter the house of the Sultan! I will have your heads…"

The thrown sword caught Xerxes unaware, driving him backward. The blade, thrown from a soldier in the crowd, sunk deeply into his chest. The Sultan collapsed to the ground grasping at the sword. He made feeble attempts to pull it from his chest, but died quickly.

"Let me take you inside the castle," Arem said. The blinding flash returned.

When they opened their eyes they were in a giant room, filled with large cisterns. The room was empty. Each large vat was more than fifteen feet tall and made of smooth concrete. Ladders had been mounted on the sides of each tank, allowing access to the top. Landon quickly walked around one of the cisterns returning from the other direction.

"Climb one of the ladders and tell me what you see," Arem directed.

Slowly, Landon climbed the ladder and looked down into the cistern. "It is filled with some kind of dye," Landon called out. He was tempted to reach out and touch the dye, but was afraid the stain would cover his finger.

Landon returned to the floor and asked, "Is each cistern filled with a dye?"

Arem answered, "Yes. More than three-thousand years ago craftsmen in Istanabad perfected the art of dyeing textile materials. The dyes are coveted by many of the nearby tribes and burgeoning nations. It is the largest source of trade for our country. At least it was three-thousand years ago. It is a secret process guarded closely by our Sultan and our military,"

Landon had never considered something like this strategic enough to protect. *"The art of dyeing cloth fibers a closely guarded secret?"*

"Each cistern is filled with a colored-pigment. There are many rooms like this with hundreds of various colors," Arem continued. "What color did you see when you looked into the vat?" he asked.

Landon answered, "It looked to be violet."

"The dye is lavender, also called orchid, grape, or pomegranate. Used correctly, it can offer a wide-variety of shades of this color. It can be dark and rich in its depth while offering numerous hues."

"Look to the edges of the room, what do you see?" the Dragon asked.

Both Lyssa and Landon looked to the nearest corner and noticed three, large, fiber baskets. They were three feet tall and had a circumference of about four feet. They walked over to the baskets.

Arem explained, "The four corners of this room each have three similar baskets. It is the same in all the rooms of dye. Each basket contains a cobra. The snakes are bred for their size and aggressiveness."

Landon remembered the size of the cobra sitting on the Sultan's throne.

"Look at the vents above the baskets," Arem directed.

Landon had not noticed them until now, but there were three small vents above the baskets. He wondered at their purpose.

"At night, prior to the workers going home, the lids of the baskets are removed using a hook. The cobras, twelve of them, have free-reign of the rooms until morning. Each morning priests trained to handle the cobras enter the room and place them back in the baskets. They sing to the cobras using a flute. Obediently, the cobras will return to the baskets at dawn to sleep out the remainder of the day."

Landon blurted out, "And each room has twelve cobras?"

"Yes. The doors are guarded, on the outside at night, while the dye is guarded on the inside by the cobras. A great deterrent to someone attempting to steal one of Istanabad's many secrets," the Dragon said.

He paused and then added, "Each cobra is stained the color of the dye that they guard. The cobras in this room are purple in color. After many, many years, the cobras no longer have to be dyed. The pigmentation in the skin has been passed down from one cobra to its young,"

Landon nodded to no one in particular. He listened attentively, looking at the three baskets, happy they had lids.

"One last thing before we move on," Arem said. "The cobras in this room, the purple ones, are referred to as Elzahari. Each room and those cobras guarding it have a different name."

The hairs on Landon's neck felt as if they were standing on end. While he knew it not physically possible, goosebumps developed on his arms. He could seem them clearly.

Arem continued, "I would like the two of you to walk to the next corner at the far end of this room. Remember you are in no danger, I promise you."

Landon began walking. He stopped to look back at Lyssa. She had not moved from her spot. Landon walked back over to her and said, "Are you okay, sister?"

"I am not," she responded. "I am terrified. I do not know if I can continue this part of the journey, brother." Landon frowned at her, but nodded.

"Would you like to return to the cave?" Arem asked.

"I would, most definitely, captain. But, I also know I will regret not knowing what you need to show us." She took a deep-breath. "I will continue. I promise not to let fear get the best of me. I am in good hands with the two of you and will be well-protected."

She walked past Landon heading to the far corner of the large room. A minute later, the two arrived at the corner, finding two baskets with lids and the third knocked over. The lid was lying on the floor a few feet away.

Lyssa stayed close to Landon. He leaned over to look into the basket, expecting to find a large, purple cobra coiled up inside.

"Empty," he said aloud. He saw Lyssa look around, her eyes wide-open.

"Do not worry, princess," Arem stated calmly. "Elzahari is not here. He has fled this room."

The two of them exhaled with relief. The blinding flash of light returned. When it dissipated, they were standing in a large hallway in front of two doors. A large group of people walked towards them, each armed with a sword.

Followed closely by guards, four priests led the group of men to the doors.

Landon recognized one of the Priests. He had been in the group standing near Xerxes when he challenged the mob.

"Are they here, in these rooms?" asked a large man.

He gestured furiously, with his sword, towards the two doors. This man wore a blood stained shirt, covered in grime and filth. His smoothly shaven face was pocked-marked and wrinkly.

The Priest nodded quickly in response, too shaken with fear to protest.

Landon counted twelve men in the group. Three priests, seven armed guards, and three men whose clothing reminded him of those in the mob outside. The large man seemed to be the leader of all of them.

The man looked back at the guards, glowering. They made no effort to dissuade him. He turned towards the door on his right, lifted his heavy boot, and kicked it inward. The door crashed against the wall and bounced back almost slamming shut in their faces. The men rushed into the room with swords raised. Lyssa and Landon followed, expecting to find some of the Sultan's personal guards on the other side. Instead, they were greeted by the wailing of a small child in a crib.

"Why are these men in this room?" Lyssa asked. Before Arem could answer the twelve men rushed the crib, raised their swords and brought them crashing downward onto the child. Death was instantaneous.

"Stop!" Lyssa yelled. The men were oblivious to her pleas. Landon wanted to vomit. He tried to piece together why these armed men would kill an innocent baby.

"Is this the son of the Sultan?" Landon asked.

"That is very astute of you, my prince. Yes, this is one of two twins, born in the year of the great rebellion. Less than four month's old, this baby boy was slain by a group representing the rebellion," the Dragon answered.

Lyssa responded, "It's horrible. They have slain an innocent child. They are beasts." She bit her lip trying to hold back her tears.

The large, dirt-covered man turned back to the three priests. He demanded, "Where is the other one?"

Once again, the lead Priest cowered and answered, "In the room across the hallway."

Without hesitation, the large man elbowed his way past the others and exited the room. He moved to the other door and kicked it in. The wood splintered and cracked. The door flung off its hinges. Landon quickly entered, walking through the men untouched and unseen. He moved over to the crib where a baby lay quiet. He found what he expected to find.

The twelve men entered the room quickly. Some moved toward the crib. The Priests yelled, "Stop!" Eleven of the men stopped. The twelfth man, the large, filth-covered man refused to heed the warning. He continued walking to the crib, but had looked back at the other men when he passed them.

When he turned to look into the crib, he froze. A massive, purple hooded cobra raised its head up a few feet, meeting the man face-to-face.

The Cobra struck without hesitation, sinking its fangs into the man's cheek. Dropping his sword the man recoiled. He grabbed his face in both hands, moaning. He crumpled to the floor dead.

Landon watched the snake lower its body, coiling around the sleeping infant once more.

The remaining eleven men hesitated for a few seconds. One of the plainly dressed men insisted the guards kill the snake. The Priests disagreed.

"This is Elzahari, the Chosen One," the Lead Priest said firmly. "Elzahari has chosen to protect Arsames, son of Xerxes." The other priests nodded. The guards looked fearfully from the Priests to the other armed men.

"We have not come this far to allow one of Xerxes heirs to live," an older, plainly dressed man said demanded. He raised his sword and moved to the crib, saying, "I will kill them both."

Before he could get any closer, the Cobra once again raised its body. Instead of striking, it spat venom into the man's eyes. The man dropped his sword screaming in pain. He rubbed his eyes trying to remove the poison.

"Help me, please!" No one moved to help him. Within two minutes, he too lay dead on the floor.

"Do you see?" the elder Priest exclaimed. "Elzahari, the Chosen One has killed the unbelievers." He pointed to the bodies of the two men lying prostrate on the floor. Leaving his sword on the floor, the Priest took a few steps closer to the Cobra. It swayed back and forth watching those left in the room.

Kneeling, the Priests exclaimed loudly, "Elzahari, we ask for your forgiveness. The Purple Cobra slithered down out of the crib over to the Priest. The old man quivered with fear waiting for the strike, which did not come. Circling around the Priest, the snake returned to the front of him. Lifting its head to his eye level, the snake leaned in and touched the tip of its face to his nose.

The others in the room stared transfixed. The snake turned and slithered its way back up the crib. Once again it coiled itself, gently, around the sleeping baby.

The blinding flash of light returned. Landon had begun to grow accustomed to the bright light and almost did not shut his eyes. When his normal vision returned the three of them were back in the cave.

They kept their hands on the glowing orb.

"The Zaharian Empire owes its creation to Elzahari, the Chosen One. The House of Xerxes was going to be obliterated, but the Cobra prevented Arsames from being slaughtered. Elzahari, the Chosen Ones, are revered as demi-gods in Istanabad. The priests and the other witnesses reported what happened."

The Dragon continued, "Arsames was raised and protected for the rest of his life by Elzahari. The rebellion died almost as quickly as it had begun. The descendants to the House of Xerxes sit on the throne, revered and feared by the people because of Elzahari."

Landon asked, "But how did I see the Sultan Muraffe with a Purple Cobra? How is that possible?"

"When Elzahari protected Arsames it set off a chain of events that still impact the Zaharian Empire to this day. All of the purple cobras are protected. They have been removed from guarding the dyes. They continue to be well-fed, and sheltered deep within the Sultan's castle.

When a concubine of the Sultan gives birth to a male child the child is placed in a room to spend the night with one of the Elzahari."

Arem continued, "Most are killed by the cobra. Yet, every so often, a cobra refuses to kill the child in the crib. From that day forward it becomes the guardian and protector of the heir to the throne. A son may not ascend to the throne unless he has been chosen by Elzahari."

"Are you telling me every male child born to the Sultan is killed by snakes?" Landon could not believe Arem's claim.

"Yes, except for the Chosen One. The ones, who are not killed, have developed an unnatural bond with Elzahari. The cobra develops an inseparable bond with the heir. Most sultans live many years longer than other citizens of Istanabad. It is believed that as long as there is an Elzahari, the House of Arsames will live forever."

"But what keeps the Cobra from killing others who are around?" Lyssa asked.

"There is a bond between the Sultan and the Elzahari. If the Sultan is happy and does not feel threatened, the snake is docile. I have witnessed other children playing with the future Sultan. The snake ignores everyone around. I have also witnessed children bitten after they anger the future Sultan."

The Dragon added, "It is important for the both of you to understand. The House of Ghardenne has its dragon. The House of Arsames has its cobra. Think of Elzahari as the dragon of the desert."

There was a long pause. The three of them stared at each other. Landon looked up into Arem's eyes, cleared his throat and said, "Thank you Captain. Now show us the rest of what you need us to know."

CAPTAIN AREM

"AS YOU WISH," THE DRAGON RESPONDED. HIS YELLOW EYES sparkled in the pulsating light. A winged shadow flickered along the wall opposite Lyssa. Landon found himself caught up in the illusion.

"Brother?" Lyssa's concerned voice brought him out of the hallucination. They placed their hands once more onto the glowing orb and were transported back in time, across the Celestial Plane, and into the world of Istanabad.

The Dragon began, "I would like to show you three things. The first is my promotion to the rank of captain. The second is a war-counsel I was allowed to observe when I became a captain. The third is my assignment to deliver a princess to the north," Arem's voice held a note of sadness with the final words.

Landon ignored the tone. He was looking forward to seeing his mother's journey north through someone else's eyes.

When he opened his eyes, they were once again standing inside Muraffe's fortress. Landon recognized the large tapestry fastened to the top of a wall.

Landon had stopped to stare at the tapestry when a young man, no more than sixteen years of age, rounded the corner walking briskly. He passed through the two of them. Olive-skinned with dark eyes and dark hair, his looks complemented his lavender tunic. The military insignia was unrecognizable to Landon, but the military dress of the empire was not. The young man walked with a purpose. He used his left hand to keep the long sword, dangling beside him, from bouncing while he walked. When the two of them had last seen this young man, he was a boy recently adopted into the house of Muraffe III.

"You have grown a bit," Landon said.

Lyssa added, "I have seen this part before and admit it is my favorite part of this story. You were happy while you were on your way to the ceremony. Were you not?"

Captain Arem responded, "Indeed. I was happy. I am almost seventeen years old. I have been trained in the art of warfare by the Sultan's best minds. I have fought in four battles and five times as many skirmishes. Recently, I led a squad to a remote village in the east. It was a hotbed of rebellion. Though outnumbered, two to one, my squad defeated the rebels. I am to be promoted to the rank of Captain."

Arem entered the Ceremonial Hall proudly. Four generals, each armed, stood together at the bottom of the steps leading up to the Diamond Throne. General Faron watched passively as Arem entered. Landon looked into his face trying to read his emotions.

Slowly, the door located behind the Diamond Throne opened.

Landon gasped. Elzahari slithered into the Great Hall, unaccompanied. Everyone in the room quickly kneeled. The snake made its way to the throne, but did not stop. It glided past the throne, down the stairs to the kneeling generals. Stopping in front of General Faron the snake froze in its place. Yellow eyes wavered back and forth but never looked away from the General. Landon felt goosebumps return to his forearms.

Tension filled the Great Hall, though everyone remained silent, kneeling with their eyes lowered to the floor. Muraffe III entered the room quietly, gliding as silently as the cobra. He walked over to the throne and surveyed the room. A look of disdain swept across his features until his eyes fell upon Arem. Disdain was replaced with pride.

Finally, after scanning the room, Muraffe III walked slowly down the steps and stopped behind the giant snake. The cobra turned and looked at the Sultan. The Emperor pointed to the throne. The snake slithered up the stairs, taking its place on the bear-skin cushions. Once coiled into place, the yellow eyes turned to the Sultan and to General Faron. The cobra nodded to Muraffe.

Muraffe III looked down at General Faron with disgust, lifted his left boot, and kicked the general in the side of the head. Faron knocked backwards from the kick rolled over, and quickly resumed his kneeling position.

"You may rise," the Sultan commanded. Everyone in the room stood. No one spoke. The wrath of the Sultan was on full display.

The Sultan's movements once again reminded Landon of the snake. Landon watched, mesmerized.

Muraffe pointed to Arem and asked, "Whose son is that?"

General Faron looked at Muraffe and responded without hesitation, "That is the son of my lord and protector."

"Exactly general. He is my son. MY SON!" Muraffe III bellowed.

The Sultan seemed pleased by the exchange. He smiled, looking at Arem with pride. The young man remained motionless during the exchange. His features betrayed no emotion. The Sultan waved Arem forward.

Arem took two steps forward and stopped at the bottom of the steps. He lowered his eyes and knelt down onto one knee.

"Rise my son. There is no need to bow to me today. As your father, it is a day filled with pride and joy," the Sultan exclaimed. "You have done well. I remember years ago adopting you as my own so you might be raised properly in the house of your true father, your Sultan, your Emperor. You have listened to all I have commanded and in doing so have excelled in leading troops in our military."

A look of pride spread across Arem's face. He beamed with the compliment.

"Because of this success I am promoting you, my son, to the rank of Captain," Muraffe proclaimed. He looked to the generals below, and one of them stepped forward to pin the rank of Captain onto Arem's lapel.

Arem looked to the Sultan and bowed.

Muraffe seemed very pleased. He looked from face to face and saw nothing, but admiration. Landon watched a look of joy spread across Muraffe's face. The Sultan turned to Captain Arem and spoke firmly, but gently. "Captain, I praise you as my son and as one of the future leaders in our illustrious military. But, there is one in this room who has offended your father. This man hesitated to kneel when Elzahari entered the room. Muraffe and Elzahari are one and the same. We are the Chosen One! Would you not agree?" the Sultan asked.

Arem responded without hesitation, "Absolutely, My Lord." He started to kneel to both Muraffe and the Cobra, but Muraffe stopped him.

"My son, I was not referring to you, of course. You have been faithful in your service and as my son I admire and adore you. I was referring to General Faron," the Sultan said.

General Faron dropped to his knees immediately and bowed to Muraffe, "My apologies, my Lord. I did not mean to…."

"SILENCE!" Muraffe exploded. Landon watched the spittle fly from the Sultan's mouth.

Muraffe shoved a finger in the direction of the General, but continued to look at Arem. He exploded, "Do you see? Once again, he insults me. He dares to interrupt me while I talk to my son."

Muraffe trembled, his hands shaking violently. The Cobra, had remained on the throne, but lifted its head a few feet. It was looking at Faron intently. Landon shuddered, unsure about what was happening. He had never before seen a king treat one of his favored generals with such callousness.

"My son?" Muraffe asked.

Arem responded, "Yes, My Lord and father."

"This man needs to be punished for his insolence. Would you not agree?" He looked into Arem's eyes.

"I agree and it will be done, my Lord," Arem answered. He turned to call to the guards, but was stopped by Muraffe.

"No, my son. The guards should not be the ones to punish the General for his insolence. I would like you to do it. Take him into the courtyard and give him twenty lashes. Do not kill him, though. But, make sure the lesson is well-learned," the Sultan ordered. Arem marched over to the four generals, grabbed General Faron by the left elbow, and led him away.

Landon looked at Lyssa's face. She was saddened. The Sultan turned and left the hall, escorted by Elzahari. The moment they left the scene froze.

"Did you do it?" Landon asked. He knew the answer, but wanted to hear it from Arem.

The Dragon answered, "I stripped my father's shirt off and gave him twenty lashes with a whip. He nearly died. The look he gave me when I finished, as he lay there bleeding, the look he gave me was one of love. I nearly whipped my only father to death."

The anguish in his words tugged at Landon's heart. He thought about having to whip his own father. He did not know if he would have been able to carry out that order.

Landon could hear the pain in Arem's voice. He imagined large tears streaming down the Dragon's face, back in the cave, and onto the rocky floor.

"You did not have a choice," Lyssa said. Her words hung hollow in the air.

"We all have choices Princess. Please remember I did not show you this to invoke sympathy," the Dragon's voice hardened.

Arem continued, "Living in the Sultan's house I had come to view him as my father. I had been raised in his house, had learned his customs, and had come to value his beliefs as my own. When I tied General Faron to the whipping post, I did it in anger, furious since he had insulted the Sultan."

Landon questioned Arem's statement, "You were furious, but why?"

"I agreed with the Sultan. General Faron had hesitated. He deserved to be punished. If the Sultan was angered, then I was angered," Arem answered. "The first strike was the cruelest. I laid it across Faron's back with the force of pent up anger. The second was nearly just as bad."

Lyssa gasped.

The Dragon ignored her surprise, continuing, "Halfway through the twenty lashes I became exhausted. I walked to the post to check on General Faron. My Sultan ordered twenty lashes, but he also ordered me not to kill the general. I was well aware the watchers were there, unseen. I am convinced they would have stopped me if they thought General Faron was going to die."

Landon asked, "You do not think the Sultan secretly wished for the General's death?" Landon asked, intrigued.

The booming voice responded, "I leaned in to check on General Faron and froze. The look on his face, which I expected to be one of pain, was one of love and admiration. The General whispered to me softly."

Landon watched Lyssa's reaction. She could not contain herself and yelled, "What? What did he say?" They were still in the Great Hall, the scene frozen before them.

"The general had collapsed, half-dead, against the whipping pole. The skin on his back shredded bare by the whip. He looked into my eyes and whispered….always my son. The moment he said those words I knew he was still my father. I moved quickly back into place, aware the watchers would report to Muraffe all they witnessed. I immediately began the final ten lashes," Arem said.

Lyssa yelled, "No! You did not stop. Why? He is your father."

Landon looked to her, aware he was now defending Arem, "He could not stop, dear Lyss. To do so would have meant death for the both of them."

Arem continued, "True. Yet, as I whipped General Faron I realized he had always been my only father. His words spoken to me when I was eleven years old rang clear in my head. Each time I brought the lash down upon his back I remembered my father's words."

Landon nodded. He understood why Arem had chosen to show the two of them this part of his past. He appreciated the emotional anguish this event must have caused. Faron had taken the twenty lashes without complaint to protect his son. Arem had given the twenty lashes without complaint to protect his father. Muraffe's goal of teaching a lesson to the both of them had backfired, but the Sultan would never know the truth. Each man had chosen to love the other regardless of the pain the Sultan demanded.

"I thank the two of you for not judging me too harshly," Arem said.

Lyssa whispered, "We would never."

Landon smiled at his sister, appreciating her genuineness at this moment.

The Dragon said, "Let us move to the second part of my story, the war-counsel."

The light flashed briefly, dissipating quickly. The two of them were standing behind a group of men sitting around a large, circular table. Made of carved marble, the massive table had enough space for more than forty people. Thickly cushioned and meticulously carved, each armrest of the oaken chairs resembled the head of a cobra. More than thirty officers sat in the chairs.

Landon looked from face to face. He was shocked to see General Faron sitting among them.

"Is this before or after the promotional ceremony?" he asked.

"It is less than a year after. The Sultan may be cruel, but he is wise enough to realize my father is one of the most brilliant military tacticians in the empire," Arem answered.

The Sultan sat in the largest chair listening attentively to one of the generals. A giant map of the Known World, intricate in the minute details, had been placed on the table for all to see. Landon looked at the map, recognizing the Alahari Desert and the Cargathian Mountains. He looked along the coast and followed the mountains as they wound their way north. The northern countries, including O'ndar, were accurately portrayed. He was unfamiliar with many of the nations of the south. Most seemed to be a part of the Zaharian Empire, though there did appear to be some independent nations.

He was shocked to see the northern nations included on the map. The northern maps, which did not include any of the names of the countries of the south, always ended with the desert. In the east, beyond the mountains, Landon recognized the mysterious Lands of the Khans.

Landon lifted his eyes from the map and looked at those sitting around the table. He had assumed the four generals in the promotional ceremony would be all of the generals of the Sultan's army. He counted thirty generals at the table.

"Just how large is this army?" he wondered. The O'ndarian military, if the cavalry were included, had ten generals.

"The Sultan's army is at least four times as large as the military of O'ndar. Additionally, if he chose to conscript men from all of the nations within the empire, Zaharian armies could muster ten times the number of men it has currently," Arem said.

Landon realized why his father had chosen to form an alliance with the Zaharian Empire. Even though the two countries had a vast desert between them, this alliance someday might help prevent an invasion from the Horsemen of the Eastern Steppes. The wild tribesmen had been pillaging villages along the frontier for thousands of years. Someday, the hordes might gather together, lashing out to spread terror throughout the world. It comforted him to know the Zaharian Empire could send troops north and east if needed.

Muraffe asked, "General Tisdon. How are preparations coming along for the invasion?" The Sultan nodded to the man sitting a few chairs to the left of General Faron. The General was small in stature, but Landon was not fooled. The man had a quick-witted mind.

"Very well, my Lord. The provisions for the army continue to be stockpiled, per your orders. We are on pace with the manufacturing of our weapons. It was gracious of our Lord to give us many years to build up our arsenal. By the time we are ready to invade, the entire army will have the necessary weapons it requires," General Tisdon answered.

Landon noticed the Sultan was much different in this room with his generals. He carried the same air of superiority, but seemed more relaxed than he had been in the two ceremonies. Landon knew the Sultan ultimately relied on his generals to spread the reaches of his empire. These highly trained men were needed to fulfill his wishes. The Sultan spoke politely, even respectfully to each of them.

"That is good to hear," Muraffe said, smiling. He turned to another General and asked, "General Hurrte. How about the passageway?"

The general cleared his throat before answering, "My lord, carving the passageway through the Cargathian Mountains is going slowly, but progresses according to your wishes. The twenty year window you have given us should allow us time to complete the highway." He paused before continuing, "We have four thousand slaves working day and night. We will be ready. Do you require me to speed up the process?"

Muraffe waited a few seconds before responding, "No General. Do not push the slaves too much. We need every able-bodied man, and therefore must proceed cautiously. When we invade the northern countries our vast army must be well-equipped. Those provisions will need to be stockpiled in the mountains, ahead of the arrival of our troops. We will need to be able keep an army on the field for at least three years. Though with General Faron leading our invasion we will most likely not need much time." Muraffe smiled at General Faron.

"You are most gracious, My Lord," Faron responded.

Muraffe nodded, pleased. He turned to General Faron and said, "General, we have a few new captains in our ranks. Please explain so they are brought up to speed."

General Faron stood and pointed to the map, "Our planned invasion of the north is a multi-faceted, almost twenty year plan. Our illustrious Sultan would like to make the nations of the north a part of the Zaharian Empire. Step one of our plan will begin in less than a year. Ambassadors from O'ndar have agreed to an alliance, on behalf of their king. One of our Lord's daughters will travel north to marry the King of O'ndar. While O'ndar accepts this overture as friendly, it is only a feint, a distraction."

Faron looked at a few of the Captains. He kept his eyes away from Captain Arem. He continued, "Our engineers have begun secretly carving a passageway through the Cargathian Mountains. The goal is to slowly bring up provisions and eventually stockpile weapons as far to the north as possible. Once the passageway is complete our military will invade with more than two-hundred thousand soldiers. The combined forces of the northern nations will not be enough to stop us."

The Sultan looked pleased. He leaned forward and spoke, "Generals, you have done well. Once this highway is completed, and the stockpiles have been put in place, we will launch an invasion. Even the most powerful nation in the north, O'ndar, will swear fealty to the Zaharian Empire."

Landon was shocked. Lyssa gasped. Captain Arem stood quietly against the wall, listening to the war plans.

The Zaharian Empire had signed a treaty with O'ndar, but it was obvious the treaty was a ruse.

"But, why through the mountains?" Landon asked.

Arem's voice boomed inside his head, "Muraffe has longed for an invasion of the north so our military might prove it is the mightiest on earth. Crossing the desert is not an option. Getting an army this size across the desert has proven too difficult. Even with years of preparation there would be no guarantee the military would be in any shape once it arrived."

"But why not circle to the east and north?" Landon asked. He responded to his own question saying, "The Horsemen of the Steppes."

"Repelling invaders is completely different from attempting to cross through the Steppes. While it is tempting to the Sultan to sweep into the northern nations from the east, the pesky horse tribes would unite against any attempt to cross their lands. The Zaharian forces would defeat them, yet the loss of men, horses, equipment, and provisions might prove too costly. The Sultan has chosen a plan which will take longer to accomplish, but will allow his forces to invade unscathed," the Dragon said.

"That plan involves using a pathway carved through the Cargathian Mountains from the south," Lyssa added.

Landon smiled at his sister and then responded, "They are carving a passageway through the mountains. Hoping the army can launch an invasion of the northern countries. The goal is to add the northern countries to the Zaharian Empire."

"Yes! The Sultan wants to be the ruler of the Known World," the Dragon's voice exclaimed.

"Does his plan include invading the Lands of the Khans?" Landon asked, referring to the lands east of the Cargathian Mountains. The lands had long since fallen into legend. The Eastern Cargathian Mountain range separated the Steppes and the rest of the Known World from the Lands of the Khans.

The eastern warriors, beyond the mountains, were legendary for their ferocity and fighting skill. Proficient with sword, with bow and arrow, on horseback, or on the ground, the warriors of the Lands of the Khans had no equal. It had been many years, though, since anyone from the Lands of the Khans had braved the mountain passes.

"I do not know. I am sure if Muraffe could find a way he would," Arem answered.

"Why do you show us this, Captain Arem? You are violating one of the most sacred oaths an officer can make in the service of his Lord," Landon said.

"I understand your question and concern. As a leader of soldiers, and a lord, you want the absolute loyalty of those who serve you. A sickness has once again infected Istanabad. Muraffe has come to believe himself a god, reminding me of Xerxes. I came to this belief as I whipped my father. An evil has taken hold of Muraffe. I do not know if it is Elzahari or if it is Muraffe who now rules," Arem proclaimed.

Landon started to speak, but was stopped by Arem, "Let me continue, please. What I have shown you has nothing to do with why you are here. I chose to show you this to prove I have nothing to hide. As the future king of O'ndar it is imperative you understand what is coming. Your sister is almost seventeen."

"Are you telling us the mountain passage is almost complete?" Landon asked, mortified. The countries of the north would respond to the invasion by unifying their forces. Their combined military forces would be no match for the size of the Zaharian military. He wished he could get this information to his father.

"Have Zaharian forces begun moving into the mountains?" Landon asked.

Arem responded, "No. The passageway is not complete, but the work has gone more quickly than originally planned. The highway is only three months away from completion. A garrison of three thousand soldiers keeps the slaves working day and night. When finished, other slaves will bring the stockpiles of weapons and provisions north, ahead of the army. Moving two-hundred thousand men will be much easier if the armaments are already in place before they get there."

Lyssa looked to Arem, "Is O'ndar doomed?"

Landon looked at her and asked, "Had he shown you any of this prior to my arriving?" She shook her head in response. Landon's mind raced. He would have to figure out a way to stop them. Turning away from Lyssa, Landon looked to the Generals in the room. He also looked to where Captain Arem was standing.

"You have stated this was not all you had to show us," he said, sternly. His anger boiled.

The Dragon said, "I want to take you to my audience with Muraffe the day before we left for O'ndar. I have been ordered to escort Princess Lenali, the desert flower."

Lyssa smiled, "The desert flower?" She enjoyed hearing her mother referred to in this manner.

"Your mother's name was chosen because it means desert flower. There are beautiful flowers which bloom deep in the desert, every night. Lenali is one such flower," Arem said.

"We are ready," Landon blurted out. He was ready to be away from the war-counsel.

"I advise we wait for the remainder of the conversation. Listen once more," Arem directed.

General Faron looked to his Sultan and asked, "Should I offer the remainder, My Lord?" The Sultan nodded.

Faron continued, "Princess Lenali has been ordered by the Sultan to bear a daughter within a year to King Ghardenne. If it is a son, she is to abort the child. Our plans rely on her eldest child being a daughter. Once the daughter is of age, she will be sent south just before her seventeenth birthday. The King will suspect nothing. If needed, though, spies will poison the King and Princess Lenali. She does not know of our plans, but she will not be allowed to interfere, even inadvertently."

Lyssa said, "I am ready to leave this place. Please."

Once again, the dazzling flash appeared. They were transported into a small, lavishly decorated room, with spectacularly colored, silk curtains. The marble floor was richly covered with flecks of gold and silver. Elzahari and the Sultan lounged with each other on a divan.

Captain Arem was kneeling in front of him, head bowed, listening to the Sultan's directions.

"You will be wary Captain, of all the perils the desert has to offer," Muraffe said.

"Yes, My Lord and father," the Captain responded.

"Repeat them to me, Captain," the Sultan ordered. Elzahari lifted its head off the cushions.

"I will take ten guards and escort Princess Lenali across the Alahari Desert. The journey will take more than three months. I will ensure she is guarded at all times. Once she has been delivered to the King of O'ndar, I will return with the guards and report immediately to you," Captain Arem offered.

The Sultan smiled, "You have been chosen because you are one of my sons I trust the most."

"I thank you father," Arem continued to looking at the marbled floor.

Muraffe smiled. He said, "Perfect. Remember, Lenali has no idea of our future plans. She is not to be made aware. Tomorrow you begin your slow and arduous journey across the desert. Do not take any unnecessary chances. Speed is not important. Arriving safely is. Do you understand me?"

"Yes, My Lord. Thank you once again for choosing me with this task," Arem said. He stood, ignored the stiffness in his knees, and left the room.

Light flashed and the three of them were back in the cave. Landon looked up into the Dragon's eyes.

"If you were chosen to escort our mother and we know she made it to O'ndar, how did you end up in the body of a Dragon?" the Prince asked.

"It is the final part of my tale. Look back into the orb. I would like to show you the journey of Lenali, the desert flower."

Landon paused, waiting for the Dragon Arem to lift his head and make eye-contact. He found the warmth of the cave re-assuring. He was no longer afraid of the ebony beast. The long claws, the thick scales, the yellow eyes, and the ivory fangs no longer instilled fear into his heart.

The moment Landon's hands touched the orb Arem's voice rang loudly in his head.

"It seems I have tried to rush things. I apologize. I agreed to answer all of your questions," the Dragon intoned.

"I thank you for showing us everything. Yet, I cannot go on any further unless you answer a question."

"Ask the question, please," the Dragon said.

Landon looked to his sister. She had a puzzled look on her face. He scanned the walls, watching three shadows waver back and forth in the pulsating light. This quest had been full of surprises. His cushioned life had been turned upside down. He was excited, fearful, and nervous at the same time.

"Why?" he asked.

"Your majesty?" Arem responded, puzzled.

"You heard my question, Captain Arem. Why? Why did you abduct my sister?" Landon demanded.

The Dragon's yellow eyes bore into Landon, yet the Prince did not flinch. A day earlier, Landon might have broken off his gaze. He might have fainted or run away in fear. Now though, since he had come to know the Captain behind the eyes, instead of flinching and looking away he locked his eyes onto those of the Dragon and held the gaze.

"Why not abduct me? She could have remained safe in O'ndar. You have put my sister in danger." The anger bubbled up and spilled out of Landon before he could contain it.

"All of this could have been shown to me without putting her in harm's way. So again, I ask, why her?" He did not try to hide his anger.

"If it had been you, your majesty, two things would have happened. First, I would have had to kill you at some point. You are stubborn," the Dragon explained.

Landon listened intently. He acknowledged he may not have given the Dragon Arem time to explain why he had been abducted.

"What is the second thing?" Landon asked.

"Your sister would have tried to follow, even if it meant across the Celestial Plane. This could have caused some issues since she would not have been allowed to do so," the Dragon said.

Landon admitted Lyssa would have been adamant about following him. She would have argued the same point and might have convinced her parents to allow her to follow. If they had not agreed, she would have snuck out of the castle, riding a horse to the ends of the earth trying to find him.

"My sister is very tenacious. She might have convinced the King and Queen to allow her to attempt it," Landon responded. He looked at his sister.

Arem's next words startled Landon, "She would have convinced the King, but not the Queen."

Lyssa was the one who responded, "Brother, do not be angry. Watch the rest and you will understand. I promise you."

Landon shook his head. He did not take his eyes away from the Dragon, saying, "Dear sister, I vowed I would go no further until my questions were answered. I want Arem to provide the answers."

Landon watched her looking back and forth to each of them, puzzled about how to continue. She had recognized the sternness in his voice, which said, "*I will accept nothing less than an answer.*" For the first time the Dragon seemed indecisive.

Lyssa looked to her brother and said, "Why me? You ask why me? I will answer for the Captain." She raised her hand when Landon started to speak and said, "Please."

It was his turn to be surprised. Her posture and tone said it all. She said, "Captain Arem had no choice. There are moments when choices are limited. We make them driven out of a necessity to survive. The Captain made his choice, whether it was right or wrong, good or evil, it was a choice. He had his reasons and I trust him with all my heart." Lyssa stood and walked over to the Dragon, leaned in and hugged him. The Dragon Arem returned the sentiment, lifting his right paw to completely encircle her body with his claws.

"That still does not answer my question. Why did he abduct you? Why did he have his father send me halfway across the Known World? Why show us his Sultan's sinister plans? Why show us the journey north with our mother?" he asked his questions quickly.

Lyssa leaned away from Arem, turned to Landon and responded, "What if she is not our mother?" She leaned back in and hugged the Dragon once more. She finished the hug, pushing against the massive chest of the Dragon, turned away, and moved back over to the rock near her brother.

"What do you mean what if she is not our mother?" Landon asked, her words confusing him. "That is not possible. Of course she is our mother. Otherwise, we would not be here."

Lyssa's words had the desired effect. He no longer demanded an answer from the Dragon. He looked at her and she smiled slightly.

She whispered, "Place your hands back onto the orb. Let us observe the journey north, across the Alahari Desert."

THE DESERT FLOWER

LANDON REGRETTED ASKING THE QUESTION. HE HAD NOT expected his sister to come to the Dragon's defense so forcefully, though it did not shock him. He was quite sure he would regret opening his eyes once the light dispersed. *"Maybe, she is not our mother,"* Lyssa's words rang in his ears.

"Once again, before your sight is restored, I must warn the two of you," Arem warned.

Lyssa asked breathlessly, "Are we falling from the sky again?"

The Dragon answered, "No, Princess. I wanted your brother to be aware of the sensation he is about to experience. Our journey across the desert was slow and tedious, even on horseback. Our pace, though, is faster than a person walking."

Landon responded for the two of them, "If we are traveling across the desert we would be hard pressed to keep up unless we were on horseback or…"

"…floating alongside our group," the Dragon finished Landon's sentence.

The light evaporated like a gentle fog in the morning sun. Landon looked back and forth to the guards and the rest of those in this group. The two of them floated a few feet above the ground, keeping pace with the plodding horses. Lyssa had already seen this part of the tale. She smiled at the human version of Captain Arem, riding beside a younger version of his mother.

The Captain rode a beautiful white stallion. "That is Imferion, my horse," the Dragon's voice boomed with pride. Landon also heard sadness in Arem's voice, but refrained from asking about it.

"Captain, may I ask a favor?" Landon queried.

Arem responded, "Absolutely, Prince Landon."

"Until yesterday, Lyssa and I have never travelled very far beyond the walls of my father's castle. While we have read about it, we have never seen the desert. Would it be possible to raise me up high enough? I would like to have a look around?" he asked, hopeful.

Landon heard Arem's chuckle, "You are your sister's brother."

Before he could ask, Lyssa chimed in, "It is the first question I asked when shown this part of our mother's journey." Landon looked at her and smiled. He began floating higher, lifted more than one-hundred feet into the air. He gasped. Landon's eyes widened and his heart raced. At this distance, the riders were smaller, yet there were sixteen of them in a row. Looking ahead, Landon could see a rider in a lavender uniform. He looked back and saw a rider trailing the group. He spun around slowly taking in the vastness of this place.

The Alahari Desert extended in every direction as far as his eyes could see. The signs of morning were starting even though sunrise was more than an hour away, the light cascading across the dunes, which stretched for hundreds of miles.

The scene reminded Landon of the calmness of the Ardenian Ocean along the coast of O'ndar. Once, when he was younger, and no more than nine years old, his father insisted he take a boat out with a local fisherman. It was a calm, sunny day and the vastness of the ocean troubled him. He had the same sensation now, spinning around and looking at waves of sand. There were no trees, no grass, and no life in this part of the Alahari. *"Much different from the ocean, though. Beneath those waves, life was abundant. Beneath these dunes only more sand,"* he thought. He began floating downward to his original position.

When he stopped descending Lyssa reached out, touched her brother on the arm, and said, "Listen brother. It is fascinating to hear our mother, when she was just fourteen years of age, engaging in a conversation with Captain Arem." Landon turned his attention to the two of them.

"It is true, Princess," Captain Arem was saying, "out in the desert, we must avoid the singing dunes at all cost." Princess Lenali sighed, disappointed with the response.

Landon asked, "The Singing Dunes? I fear we have come into the middle of a conversation. What is a Singing Dune?"

It was the Dragon Arem, who responded, "In the desert, when the sand piles high into giant dunes, strong winds will often blow causing the sand to shift. This cascading sand can become an avalanche. The noise of these avalanches can be heard up to ten miles away on a quiet day. A traveler of the desert, who is not wary of the danger of the singing dunes, may be smothered by this barrage of sand before they realize what is happening."

Princess Lenali kept up the conversation with Captain Arem. Her horse was a smaller mare, chocolate brown in color. She asked, "Is there no way to get close enough to see it in person? The noise we heard last night frightened me, yet I am most curious to witness it firsthand."

Lenali looked with admiration at the Captain, "Is there no way?"

"I wish there was a safe way my Princess. The rule of thumb, when traveling in the desert lords over us all. If a person can hear the singing dunes then they are too close," he countered.

"Years ago, I was sent into the desert by our father to train with some of the nomadic tribes. I witnessed twenty-three men swallowed by the singing dunes. My guide made no attempt to save them. He knew they were doomed the moment the collapse had begun. Instead, he grabbed my arm, pointing out the mistakes the men had made."

"Mistakes?" the fourteen-year-old Princess replied. Landon could see the fascination in his mother's eyes. She was eager for Captain Arem to share what he knew about the desert. Kept in the safety of her father's castle for her entire life, Lenali had a developed a curiosity about the rest of the world.

The Captain continued, "Yes. First, when traveling in the desert, never travel from the bottom to the top of a dune unless the goal is to look around. Travel only at the top or at the bottom. This allows the desert traveler to avoid the shifting dunes. If an avalanche occurs and one is at the bottom, there is time to flee. If the avalanche occurs and one is at the top, the person may avoid beings swept away."

"Second?" his mother asked.

Landon was impressed by his mother's inquisitive mind. The stories she had told him about the voyage across the desert never included this discussion with Captain Arem. He wondered why she might have chosen to leave this moment out. Landon promised to ask her about it when he returned to O'ndar.

"The twenty-three men were trying to impress me, since I was an officer in the Sultan's army. Or, they were trying to prove they were better than me. In doing so, they lost their lives because of a misguided sense of pride. I was worried the leader of the tribe, the *Yafi*, would be angered since I might have been the cause," the Captain continued.

"So what happened?" Lenali asked. Captain Arem's story had captivated her attention.

He answered, "The opposite happened, my Princess. The *Yafi,* who was a great leader, used the loss of the men as a teachable moment. He expressed anger. His men had forgotten the lessons taught to them as children. Out in the desert there are forces more powerful than any man. The desert will be respected or it will exact punishment."

Landon admitted he was enthralled by the conversation between this younger version of his mother and the human version of Captain Arem. He wanted to ask multiple questions about life in the desert, but refrained.

"Is there a third lesson in the desert, Captain?" The young Princess smiled, enraptured by the handsome Captain and his tales.

His response spoke of wisdom, "The third lesson is to never hurry. The sand shifts too quickly under foot. A running man will move no faster than a walking man, especially in the desert. The only difference is the running man will be winded. If battle is to be joined the running fool will be at a disadvantage."

Landon watched Princess Lenali smile. It was obvious she was excited about the prospect of traveling to unknown lands. Life in the palace was quite boring especially, for a Princess. The look on her face told Landon everything he needed to know about her feelings at being given away to a stranger. She was eager to meet her new King and husband. Landon felt warmth towards his mother, watching her ride on horseback across this vast desert. She was unafraid and unworried, her vitality apparent out here exposed to the elements.

Caught deep in his thoughts, Landon almost missed his mother's next statement.

"You know Captain; there was a time when I was in love with you."

Lyssa giggled. Landon inhaled deeply, holding his breath. Their responses were mild compared to that of Captain Arem. His face darkened into a scowl. He was not amused in the least. Landon looked to Lenali, thinking, *"That was rather bold."*

"You should not say such things, Princess. Do you see the guards ahead of us? Do you see those behind? All of those soldiers would be obligated to slay me immediately should something like this ever be mentioned in their presence? Just as I would slay one of them should you say this about them in front of me," the Captain said, looking deeply into Lenali's eyes.

"Yes Captain, I do understand the predicament I put us in by uttering those words. Yet, I do not say that I am in love with you. I wanted you to know there was a time in which I was in love with you. You were and always will be my first love. The love I had for you, can never be assuaged, and I will never regret having had you as my first love. My biggest regret in my life would have been if I failed to tell you," the Princess said, softly.

Captain Arem was clearly uncomfortable with the turn in the conversation. Lenali had caught all of them off-guard by shifting the conversation away from the singing dunes. The horses continued to trudge along, oblivious.

Captain Arem asked, "How should I respond to this statement, my Princess?" His serious demeanor showed he was not amused. He added, "I apologize for having misled you in any capacity, but fail to see how you would have or could have fallen in love with me since we have never talked prior to this journey."

"When I was a young girl, I watched General Faron's promotion and your adoption into the Sultan's house. I was not in love with you then. I was too young. Yet, I was able to watch the ceremony and saw the excitement in your eyes when the Sultan promoted your father. Do you remember the day it happened? I do. I can close my eyes see your eyes sparkle with pride." The Princess closed her eyes and her smile widened. Seeing his mother smile brought a smile to Landon's face, even if the conversation was about her loving someone other than his father.

Captain Arem listened to her, fully aware the others were too far away to hear. His shoulders relaxed. The light of the approaching sun warned the travelers of the oncoming day's heat.

"I must say this to you Captain. I must. I am traveling north, and most-likely will never return to my homeland. When I was young and infatuated with you, I thought it would only be an infatuation. Yet, on the day the Sultan ordered you to whip General Faron, I watched your face while hidden from your view," she proclaimed.

"I was ordered by our father," Captain Arem blurted out.

"No, Captain. Not our father. Yes, mine, to be sure. But, though you were adopted into Muraffe's house, you are no more his son than one of the guards who travel with us now."

"Why do you say such a thing?" Captain Arem demanded. Landon watched Arem's face redden. The conversation had taken a turn for the worst.

"I say such things because the two of us know they are true. Captain, I fell in love with you when I watched you whipping General Faron. Do you know why?" she asked. It was clear to Landon his mother enjoyed making Captain Arem uncomfortable.

Landon was caught off-guard, once more, when Lenali changed the direction of the conversation. She said, "When I was much younger, one of my many mothers told me I was very inquisitive."

Landon asked his sister, "One of her many mothers?"

"Yes. Our mother was born to a concubine. She was taken from her birth mother to be raised by a wet-nurse. It seems she may have had more than one," Lyssa said. She gestured back to Lenali, encouraging Landon to watch.

Lenali continued, "One of my many mothers told me she was very impressed with my mind and my intellect. In my father's house, women are to be silent, not heard. One of my mothers had seen what I have always felt. I have a brain. I am intelligent. She leaned over and put her left hand onto Captain Arem's shoulder. Landon noticed the Captain did not attempt to remove it. He too was absorbed by the aura of Princess Lenali.

Lenali went back to her original statement, "While others who witnessed the whipping saw anger and hatred towards General Faron, I saw nothing but love. You hid it well Captain and your secret has always been safe with me. Do you know why?"

Landon asked, even though the fourteen-year old Princess could not hear him, "Why?"

Captain Arem did not respond for a few seconds. Landon had begun to suspect he had not heard the Princess. "Why?" he whispered. Landon leaned in towards them in anticipation.

"It is because you were my first love. I loved you then and I will admit something else. I have changed my mind. I am still in love with you," Lenali said, laughing.

Captain Arem started to respond, but was cut off by the blowing of a horn. The soldier ranging ahead had returned. He had blown his horn to warn the travelers of the coming sun. The group stopped on a flattened surface of sand, safely away from any large dunes. Quickly the servants hurried to set up camp. Captain Arem left the Princess with this group and went to speak with the soldiers.

Landon looked to his sister to gauge her response. She had already seen this part of the tale. She looked back to him and shrugged her delicate shoulders.

"You travel only at night?" Landon asked. He realized the wisdom of traveling this way across the desert. Watching the guards set up the perimeter security, Landon did not hear the question Lyssa asked the Dragon Arem.

"Did you ever tell her?" Lyssa asked.

The Dragon did not respond to Lyssa's question. She asked it again, louder. "Captain Arem, did you ever tell our mother?"

Landon turned and scowled at his sister.

Before he could express his frustration with her for interrupting his chance to watch a desert camp being set up, Lyssa yelled, a little too forcefully, "Captain Arem, take us up higher please. Now!"

The two of them floated up quickly into the air. The bustling camp was well out of earshot. Landon turned to look at his sister. She had a look of sadness on her face.

"Did you ever tell her?" she asked again.

It was Landon, who responded, "Tell her what dear sister?" She had seen these events twice now. He must be missing something. He waited for the Dragon Arem to respond.

"No. I did not and never would. My duty as a soldier kept me from saying it."

Landon felt excluded and blurted out, "What is it I do not understand?"

Lyssa turned to Landon and said, "He never told her. Captain Arem never told our mother his true feelings. He loved her more than life itself. He ached to tell her the truth when she rode away to watch the servants set up camp."

"Is this true?" Landon asked. *"But how did Lyssa know? I saw nothing indicating the Captain was anything other than vigilante with his duties,"* he thought.

"I must confess to feeling awkwardness with your question. The feeling is similar to how I felt when talking with Princess Lenali on the open desert," the Dragon Arem said.

"I had not planned on showing you this part of the journey. Your sister talked me into it. I now know why," Arem continued.

"Do not be angry Captain Arem," Lyssa said. "I suspected, but needed verification. The signs are there if one is to look close enough." She looked around, still fascinated by the vastness of the dunes sweeping away into the horizon.

He said, "I am not angry. I am only embarrassed. As a soldier, I should have kept my emotions well-hidden."

Landon was speechless. The Captain had not intended on showing him this part of the journey. They had only witnessed this scene based on his sister's wishes.

Landon watched with fascination as the sun sped up, crossing the sky quickly. It now lay at the edge of the desert in the West. In a few minutes it would dip below the dunes. Slowly, Lyssa and he began their descent, floating downwards until they were once again waiting beside the Captain and Lenali.

"I have sped up this day so we might continue to what I need you to see," the Dragon offered.

The soldiers, and the servants, dismantled the camp. The group began the slow and arduous trip one more time. There was no more discussion between the two about love. Captain Arem had ordered the group to travel near the top of the dunes, wanting to have a view of their surroundings now that they were clear of the singing dunes.

A few hours before sunrise the soldier assigned to range ahead returned to the group to report an oddity.

Captain Arem listened intently while the man explained, "Less than a mile ahead, yes Captain. A lone child is standing, atop a dune, clearly in our path."

Lenali chimed in, "Are you sure Sergeant? A child?" The Sergeant nodded deferentially to the Princess, but returned his attention to the Captain.

Captain Arem seemed uneasy at the Sergeant's report.

"Change directions, Sergeant. Ride to the front and shift our direction there," he said pointing towards the West. "We will travel at the bottom of the dunes for a few miles and then will return to the tops on the morrow." The Sergeant turned his horse away to carry out his orders.

"Wait," Lenali demanded. The Sergeant paused, confused. He looked to the Captain for further direction. Captain Arem raised his left hand and waved the Sergeant on.

The Sergeant started to turn away again, but once again had to stop. "I said wait, Sergeant," Lenali repeated.

The look of anger on her face forced him to stop. He again looked to his Captain for guidance.

Lenali moved her horse closer to Captain Arem, "Captain, we cannot abandon a child out here in this desert," she said, her eyes pleading with him.

"Princess, I am charged with taking you safely to the north. The orders from our father were to be safe and cautious. I am doing both. It is a bad omen to find a naked child abandoned in the desert. It is an even more of a bad omen to take such a child into our group," Captain Arem countered.

Lenali started to protest, but was stopped by the Captain's raised hand.

Landon watched as his mother's lips pouted into sadness. The younger version of Lenali was stubborn, to a fault. Even at fourteen, the Princess was not used to being told no, especially by one of her father's soldiers.

Agitated, the Captain turned to speak to the Sergeant, but was cut short by Lenali, "Captain, I will not allow you to abandon a child in this desert. Sunrise is coming in less than a few hours. If we do not at least go see why the child is alone I will ride there on my own."

Her abrasiveness shocked the Sergeant. Captain Arem, though, seemed slightly amused. He turned to look at the Sergeant and said, "Very well, we will go meet this desert waif. If I deem the child dangerous to our party, we will abandon it. Even if it means I must have you tied to your horse and carted away like baggage. Are we clear?" The Captain unbuckled the leather strap holding his scimitar in the scabbard.

Lenali smiled, oblivious about Captain Arem's actions. Happy at the small victory she answered, "Crystal clear Captain."

Captain Arem looked to the Sergeant who listened passively. He ordered, "Take us to within a few dunes of this child Sergeant. Then halt the party. I would like two men armed with bows and arrows to accompany for my visit with this child of the desert."

"Captain, are you seriously concerned about the danger posed by a lone child?" she asked. Lenali's smile melted away at the sternness in his voice.

"Princess. You are not of the desert. Neither am I. Any person, alone in the desert, is someone no one should trust. My years among the desert tribes taught me to respect and suspect what I do not know. Right now, all we know is there could be a child alone in the desert." His voice raised in pitch and volume. The concrete firmness of a Captain accustomed to leadership rang across the dunes. The travelers in the back halted their horses listening.

"It might also be a distraction. It could be a rogue party of bandits, hoping to catch us unaware. I do not fear the nomadic tribes. Muraffe's standard has always afforded our military protection. Yet, there are rogues even among the tribes. Cast out warriors who have banded together. They have allegiance to no one. No allegiance to tribes, no allegiance to families, not even an allegiance to each other," the Captain said, loudly.

Captain Arem looked at Lenali, the scowl returning to his face. Her demeanor had also changed. She sat demurely upon her horse, realizing she had pushed the Captain too far.

"So you wish for me to see why there is a naked child standing alone in the middle of this god-forsaken desert," he demanded. Landon held his breath mesmerized by the strength Captain Arem was now projecting. His mother had insisted the Captain go against his military training and instinct. He had agreed, though Landon did not understand his reason.

Captain Arem raised his voice, yelling loudly for all in his group to hear. The mighty warrior was on full display when he looked to and spoke to the Sergeant, "Let us go Sergeant. I would like to have a conversation with this desert waif.

THE DESERT WAIF

THE LONE CHILD, A TINY GIRL, STOOD NAKED AND shivering atop a tall dune about two-hundred feet away from the group. The coldness of the desert at night shocked Landon in the same manner the searing heat of the day had done. It was unimaginable that two extremes of temperature could be present in the same place.

"I am allowing the two of you to feel the sensation," Arem explained. "I want you to appreciate the journey your mother took all those years ago."

Landon had noticed the cold after midnight as the horses trekked along silently across the dunes. Their mighty breath blew wisps of steam that trailed along their faces into the night air.

Landon could see the little girl standing silently on the sand. Her matted hair tangled with knots had pressed against her grime-covered face. Alone in the vastness of the desert, she was a sight to behold. Landon guessed her age at nine years.

Her presence alarmed him. This group had been on the desert for days and had seen no other signs of life. Yet, here she was, this Desert Waif. *"Why did Captain Arem call her the Desert Waif?"* he wondered.

The child did not cry out in fear when the group of travelers crested the nearby dunes. She stood facing them, a quiet sentry in this lonely and desolate wasteland. Landon and Lyssa continued to float alongside the horses, buoyed by the Dragon Arem's magic. Landon looked into the Captain's face while he rode his ivory-colored Stallion, Imferion. The Captain, with an intensified look about him, had earned Landon's appreciation. He was not taking this girl on the dunes lightly.

"Sergeant. You have my orders?" the Captain said.

"Yes, Captain. These two will go with you while you talk to the Desert Waif. They will remain thirty paces away with arrows notched and bows ready. If this is a trap, they will guard your retreat after you have killed the girl," the Sergeant responded, nodding at the two archers. They dismounted and waited for the Captain to do the same.

Captain Arem looked at Princess Lenali, jumped off his horse, and unsheathed his sword. He held the blade away from his body, firmly in his right hand. He turned to lead the two soldiers across the top of the dune. His dark, purple cape draped down his back. Captain Arem reached up to his neck and unclasped it. He let it drop behind him, onto the sand. The thick cape, worn for protection against the cold, night air, would be a hindrance should he need to fight.

His blade held out before him, pointed slightly downward, the Captain walked with a sense of purpose. His piercing stare unsettled Landon, but he was acutely aware the Captain was in his element. This is what the soldier been trained to do.

The three men walked slowly, keeping the little girl in sight. She made no attempt to run. Landon watched her intently. *"Why? Why is she here?"* he thought.

"Is this a trap?" He doubted attackers would be able to sneak up and ambush the soldiers.

"They should not have come here," Landon said. Lyssa looked back at him, silent. They floated along listening to the exertions of Captain Arem as he walked across the sand, his pace slow and steady.

"Wait here," Captain Arem said, gesturing for the two archers to take up a position less than fifty feet away from the child. Landon looked at the two soldiers, both held their bows notched with arrows. The tail of their lavender tunics swayed gently in the light breeze.

These two were well-trained and could impale this child with their eyes closed. Landon noticed Captain Arem made sure not to place himself between his archers and this little girl.

"He is a cautious one," Landon thought.

She was a tiny child, her long, unkempt hair sandy-brown. Deep, green eyes peered back at Captain Arem.

Landon, shocked to see her frailty, felt a pang of sympathy. "She looks like she has not eaten in weeks. But, how could that be possible? If she has been out here for more than a day she should have died!"

Captain Arem spoke softly, but firmly to the little girl, asking, "How did you come to be here, my Desert Waif?" He hoped not to sound harsh, but his distrust of the appearance of this pathetic looking child, could not be hidden. His stern voice sounded uncaring.

The girl's skin had begun to blister from the heat of the previous day's sun. Small pustules had filled with water pocketing her dusty skin. Landon was sure she had been here for more than a day. Parched lips, cracked by the lack of water, fluttered. The little girl started to cry. The Captain took a step backward, unsure about how to respond.

"Stop!" he demanded. "That is not helpful to our situation," Captain Arem blurted out, once again, a little too forcefully. His words had the opposite effect. The little girl's shoulders bounced up and down as she sobbed. Large tears streaked their way down her chest, leaving trails in the layer of dust, covering her body. "I said enough!"

"That will do Captain," a soft voice said. Arem spun around quickly, surprised to find the Princess approaching the two of them. She explained she had defied the Sergeant and the others when they tried to stop her from leaving the group. She passed the archers, ordering them to lower their bows. They complied, but quickly raised them again when she made it to Captain Arem.

Landon watched the anger spread across Captain Arem's face. He too, would have been furious. The Captain turned back to the little girl. She continued to sob uncontrollably.

Princess Lenali slowly approached the little girl cooing to her softly. She offered, "Don't be afraid my child. No one is going to hurt you. This I promise."

"Princess!" Captain Arem said, loudly. He raised his sword.

The little girl, startled by his sword and the harsh tone in his voice, wrapped her arms around Lenali. She begged, "Please don't let him hurt me. Please." Lenali returned the hug and assured the little girl she would be safe.

"Do not worry. He looks scary, but really is just a big…a big…." Lenali seemed at a loss about how to refer to Captain Arem. She looked at Arem over the little girl's shoulder and waved him back.

"Scary Tiger?" the little girl replied. They both giggled.

"Yes, that is correct. Captain Arem is just a big, fluffy, scruffy, scary Tiger. But this Tiger will not hurt you. He is here to protect us all. Isn't that right, Captain?" Lenali asked, soothingly.

Landon turned to watch the emotions play out on Captain Arem's face. He had defied his Sultan and changed his course to appease the Princess. She had defied her Captain and had approached this unknown child, putting herself into harm's way. She had broken her promise to remain with the other soldiers. Captain Arem was at a loss.

Landon turned to his sister, saying, "That was a mistake. Mother should have listened to the Captain." Lyssa nodded.

Once the girl stopped sobbing, Princess Lenali stood and looked at her gently. "You must understand, though, my Desert Waif, I have already angered the Captain enough. Unless we are told how you came to be in this desert, I must confess we may need to leave you here unattended. Do you understand me?" the Princess asked. Lenali looked to Captain Arem hoping her words had earned his forgiveness. He was still angry.

The girl stopped crying and looked from the Princess to the Captain. His sword still in his right hand pointed in her direction. "Will he hurt me?" she asked. She pointed to his scimitar, the blade shining brightly in the morning light.

"Captain, please put your blade away," Lenali directed. He refused.

"I will not. Princess, please step away from her," he commanded. Lenali complied. Her hands broke contact with the young girl's fingertips. The girl looked confused.

"Thank you," the Captain stated coldly.

"You. What is your name?" he asked. Captain Arem paused, softened his tone, and asked again, "What is your name?"

"I am named Opuntia, My Lord," the girl responded fearfully. She understood her life was in his hands.

"I am no lord so there is no reason to refer to me as such, Opuntia," he said.

Arem spoke softly to her, "I must admit I am confused. How does the prickly pear come to rest upon the dunes of the Alahari desert?"

Opuntia giggled.

Lenali looked from the girl to the Captain, confused. The Captain smiled at the girl's response. He had seen an Opuntia, many years ago, on the edge of the desert when training with one of the desert tribes. The prickly cactus, with a thick skin and large thorns, held water should it be needed in an emergency.

"Yes, that is my name. It means prickly pear, the cactus of the desert. Though, I must admit I have never seen one before," Opuntia said.

Captain Arem pointed to the rising sun and said, "Opuntia. The light of day is almost upon us. Tell us your story, quickly. If I deem it true we may allow you to travel with us. We still have more than a month to cross this desert. Yet, if I have any concerns, we will either ride away leaving you to die or slay you out of compassion."

The Captain finished his sentence, watching the little girl absorb his words. She lifted her chin in defiance without responding. Lenali covered her mouth, shocked by the finality of his words.

"My name is Opuntia, the prickly pear. I was born to the lord of our desert tribe. My father is the most powerful man of the tribe, but to me the most hated. He keeps more than thirty concubines," she said, her voice floating across the desert in a silky smooth contralto.

Landon watched the words affect Princess Lenali. She was the daughter of a concubine.

"Please continue," Captain Arem responded. He seemed indifferent to her words.

"I was told my father became angry when I was born. He had been told by some priests my mother would bear him a son. Out of anger he had the priests drawn and quartered and staked to the ground on the open desert. He left them alive so the desert vultures might feast upon their living flesh," the little girl said, her face offering no emotion.

Lenali was shocked at the child's description.

Opuntia started to continue, but was stopped by Captain Arem's raised hand. She paused confused. The Captain turned to the two archers and signaled to one of them. The man saluted and returned to the group of soldiers.

Lenali asked, "What is happening?"

"The light of the day is almost upon us. I have ordered the servants and soldiers to set up camp," the Captain responded, ignoring Lenali's smile.

"Does this mean Opuntia will be allowed to camp with us?" she asked. She turned to the little girl and smiled. Opuntia smiled back.

"Not at all, my Princess. It just means we are now down to two options. Either she camps with us, which has not been decided. Or I will kill her here on the open sands. We no longer have the option of abandoning her. She is a Desert Waif; the child who has been abandoned. Yet, she will not be abandoned again," Arem said, sternly.

Opuntia's smile disappeared. The Captain had not granted her a reprieve. He waited patiently for her to continue her story. Her death waited in his hands. The blade well-honed to cut deeply, should it come to that.

"Please continue," Captain Arem ordered. Landon heard the grit in his voice. Princess Lenali had placed them all in danger.

Opuntia shuddered beneath his gaze and started again, "My mother was a favorite of my father. I was not. When I was five years old I was cast out of her tent and raised among the dogs. In the evenings, after those in the camp had eaten, I would be given scraps periodically in order to survive. When I turned nine years old I caught the eye of one of my father's generals. He was a slimy man, one who reminded me of the giant salamanders living on the eastern edge of this desert. They eat any who wonder into their domain."

Lenali covered her mouth again. Captain Arem seemed less impressed, but nodded for Opuntia to continue.

"The man ordered me brought to his tent one night. I did not understand why he had done so. I, Opuntia, the prickly pear who fought with dogs for food and lived on the scraps provided by my tribe had been ordered by a slimy, old man into his tent. Barely clothed, infested with sand fleas, and with hair that had never been combed in all of my life, I tried to flee. Running away quickly across the sand, I was lassoed by his warriors, brought back and dropped into his tent. He laughed at my fear making me very angry."

Opuntia looked directly at Captain Arem and said, "When they placed me in his tent, I was afraid. His warriors made the mistake of untying me. The gleam in his eye made me angrier. When he touched me on the shoulder, I remembered the fights I had with the feral dogs that followed our camp. Too often, I had been bitten and scratched by these mangy animals over a scrap of bone. I learned ferocity, which I used to my advantage. I turned quickly and bit off his little finger."

Lenali laughed and clapped at Opuntia's description.

Landon looked to his mother. Sadness swept over him. *Her life in the Sultan's castle was more of a struggle than I realized*, he thought. Opuntia's words had hit a nerve with Lenali.

"The General was angered and ordered me bound and taken deep into the desert, if there is such a thing. Once here, they dropped me off at the top of this dune. I was stripped of my clothing and left to die a slow, painful death," Opuntia finished.

"My poor girl," Lenali whispered. Landon looked to Lyssa hoping to gauge her reaction. She was passive. She was not exposing what she already knew.

"Well Captain?" asked Lenali. Captain Arem stood statue still, atop the dune, seeming to wait for something more. Opuntia offered nothing. The little girl looked from the Princess to the Captain waiting for his decision.

"If we allow you to come into our camp you have to work as a servant. Do you understand me?" he asked. "We will have no one with us who does not work for her keep." He looked sternly at the little girl. Opuntia did not smile in response, but nodded.

"Princess Lenali," he said.

Lenali turned to look at the Captain, "My recommendation is we kill her and get back to camp to wait out the heat of the day. Yet, I know you will be opposed. Therefore, though it is against my intuition, I will leave the decision to you."

Lenali smiled, relieved. She had been expecting the Captain to step forward and drive his sword through Opuntia's body. She looked to the little girl and said, "You can be my servant. How does this sound?" Opuntia smiled in return and walked over to the Princess. They took each other by the hand and began walking across the dune towards the camp.

Landon turned to follow, but was once again shocked when Captain Arem turned to face the two of them.

He looked at and spoke directly to Landon, "I should have listened to my intuition."

Landon asked, "How?"

"I have decided to use this version of me to explain my mistake. Do not be alarmed. I want the both of you to see my face. I want you to be able to look into my eyes," Captain Arem explained.

The Captain looked distraught. He asked, "Do you understand? I should have never allowed this Desert Waif into our camp."

"But, you could not have known," Lyssa responded, her voice anguished.

"As a soldier, as a leader of men, I should have followed my own voice. I should have been stronger and more assertive. I did not do what I was trained to do," the Captain countered.

"It is because you loved her. Deep down you did not want to disappoint her because of love," Lyssa argued.

The Captain waited a few seconds and said, "I should have driven this blade into that little girl's heart. If I had only done so, all would have been avoided. I am sorry to the both of you, I am sorry to your mother for my failure."

Captain Arem fell to his knees dropping his sword. He leaned forward placing his hands onto the sand. "Please forgive me," he said.

Landon, shocked to see tears streaming down Captain Arem's face, looked at backs of the retreating figures.

Lyssa floated over to the Captain and leaned down. She took him into her arms and let him cry into her shoulder. Landon watched as his sister caressed Arem's hair. She crooned to him soothingly, hoping to alleviate some of his agony.

Flustered, Landon said, "Captain, I do not know what requires my forgiveness." He waited for more than five seconds before Captain Arem responded.

Captain Arem lifted his head away from Lyssa's shoulders and looked directly into Landon's eyes.

"It is because of what happens next to Lenali, the Desert flower."

QUI OTO

LANDON WATCHED IN SILENCE WHILE HIS SISTER AND THE human version of Captain Arem followed the Princess and the child across the dunes to the encampment. His mind was in turmoil after witnessing the anguish on Captain Arem's face.

"She is just a child. How could she be a danger to anyone?" Landon thought. He remembered his sense of foreboding, though.

Watching Opuntia walk hand-in-hand with Princess Lenali, it was difficult to fathom the danger this child represented. *"Would Captain Arem have preferred to run the little girl through with his sword?"*

Quietly, without calling out, Landon tried to catch Lyssa and Arem before they reached the tents. Just outside the perimeter of the campsite Captain Arem turned one more time and looked directly at Prince Landon.

"My apologies for my outburst back there on the dunes, Prince Landon," Arem offered.

Landon nodded acceptance.

"Re-living this part of the tale has driven me to the point of emotional exhaustion. There were so many missteps," he said, pausing briefly. "I should have followed my intuition. My years in the military were no match for a young, beautiful princess determined to have her way. Yet, I cannot use this as an excuse. She was never trained against the dangers this world has to offer." He waited for Landon to speak, adding, "I ask for atonement when none can be given. I ask her children to forgive the unforgiveable. Do you understand?"

Lyssa responded quickly, "We forgive you." Tears trickled down her cheeks.

"I do not know if I can forgive what I have not seen," Landon responded. Lyssa frowned at his words, looking at him disapprovingly.

"His words, though harsh, ring true, Princess. How can I ask for his pardon if he does not know how he was wronged?" Captain Arem said.

He looked at both of them explaining, "We will now move forward in time. I am taking you to the final part of the tale."

"Once we added Opuntia to our group the journey across the desert continued for more than a month. The princess grew fond of Opuntia and the child returned her fondness in kind. Her hair was cut, combed, and she blossomed from the prickly cactus into another beautiful flower of the desert," the Captain said.

The Captain looked directly into Landon's eyes and spoke softly, "This is the last time that I will look at you directly in my current form. I will no longer be able to see you. I will once again be an actor in a tragedy and you will be an unseen spectator." The Captain entered his tent to wait out the heat of the day.

The moment Captain Arem entered the tent Landon and Lyssa shot up quickly into the sky, hovering more than two-hundred feet above the tents. Landon, accustomed to the sensation, hardly took notice.

"Look," Lyssa said. She pointed to the sun the moment it emerged from beneath the sands. It started slowly, at first, and then began to pick up speed. Blistering with brightness, the sun crossed the entire sky in less than a minute. The moment it dipped out of sight in the west it was quickly replaced by the glowing moon.

Landon felt the familiar tug he had experienced when crossing the Celestial Plane. The two of them began floating along quickly heading north. Landon watched, fascinated, to see the encampment set up and broken down numerous times, quickly. The group traversed more of the desert moving in fast-motion.

It would have been a dizzying sensation had he continued to look down at those trekking across this vast desert. Instead, he kept his eyes up and focused ahead of them. He enjoyed the sensation of flying. Landon reached out and held Lyssa's hand. They floated along in silence both deep in their own thoughts.

Landon counted the number of times the sun and the moon replaced each other in this fast-forwarded version. *"Twenty-one, twenty-two, twenty-three,"* he counted quietly.

By the time he reached *"Twenty-eight,"* Landon and Lyssa had come to a complete stop. The sun, now less than an hour away from dipping below the horizon, showered the land in golden rays.

Lyssa grabbed Landon by the shoulder and spun him around so he faced the edge of the desert. "Do you see brother? We are less than a day away from leaving these sands," she said. Lyssa pointed far ahead, to a spot on the horizon where the sand melted into the sky.

Landon's eyes squinted in the fading light. He could see the outline of the greenery ahead. Behind them the sand went on forever. Ahead, though, Landon knew would be the grasslands and the lower edges of the Pyraddine Forests. He knew by experience the thickly populated, giant Red-barked trees that skirted beside and into the western range of the Cargathian Mountains.

"The edge of the desert. Finally!" he whispered to himself.

They landed just outside one of the tents. It was flannel, the sandy-brown fabric pulled taught with ropes and secured by stakes pounded deep into the sand. A few seconds later Captain Arem emerged. He looked around, checking on everyone's progress.

"Sergeant," Captain Arem called. The Sergeant looked up and Arem asked, "Why are Princess Lenali's servants out here?" He gestured to the women.

Before the Sergeant could respond one of the women answered, "We were ordered out of the tent, Captain. Princess Lenali told us she wanted to be left alone so she might meet with Opuntia in private." The Captain looked towards the Princess's tent. He started to walk in its direction.

"That is odd," Landon said to his sister.

The voice of the Dragon echoed in Landon's head. He said, "I had the same feeling."

Landon watched the look of puzzlement on Captain Arem's face. There was no movement, not even from the guard stationed inside her tent's vestibule. Once again, the Princess had chosen to break his orders. He had warned the servants to never leave her alone.

The Princess's tent had been the largest. Sandy-brown, and made of the same flannel material, she had complained to him about it on their first night in the desert. Captain Arem assured her the quarters would be most comfortable.

Captain Arem stopped outside her tent and called out softly, "Private."

The Private on duty did not respond. Frustrated, Captain Arem called out again, "Private." Lifting the flap to the vestibule, he entered. He lowered the flap behind him and waited a few seconds in order to give his eyes time to adjust.

The Private was lying on his back, unconscious. Captain Arem's initial reaction was to kick the man, angered to find him shirking his duties. He lifted his boot to kick the Private, but noticed the man was not asleep. Leaning down, Captain Arem shook the man by the shoulders. The Private moaned in response. The unconscious man's sword was still in its sheath.

Landon looked sideways to his sister, "Has he been attacked?" Before she could answer they watched Captain Arem lean in closer to the prostrate man.

Captain Arem smelled the Private's breath. There was no hint of alcohol, yet there was a hint of a fruity smell. He asked aloud, "Drugged?"

Removing his sword, Arem lifted the inner flap to the Princess's tent and entered. His concern for her safety overrode concern for her privacy.

Lyssa said, "Brother, watch in silence. Otherwise you may miss something." They followed Captain Arem into the tent.

The exterior of the tent had matched the color of the surrounding dunes, but the interior walls, were grape colored, the hue light and pleasing to the eye. It was very spacious. Large, thick rugs had been laid in an interlocking fashion on top of the sand. While the Princess had been forced to take a journey across the Alahari Desert, the Sultan had spared no expense. Every effort had been made to allow her to do so in comfort. Heavy, purple cushions, with large silk-covered pillows had been scattered around the inside the tent.

The Captain scanned the tent looking for signs of Princess Lenali. He held his sword at the ready.

Arem's eyes focused on something lying on the floor, on the other side of the tent. The Princess and Opuntia lay unmoving between crumpled up blankets.

Captain Arem bounded, cat-like, over to them. He looked down at the Princess and then over to the child. Both were unconscious. Leaning down, he placed his left hand on one of Lenali's shoulders and shook her gently, whispering, "Princess. Princess." He kept his eyes up, looking around the tent, but could not see any sign of an intruder.

Opuntia moaned softly. The Captain turned to the little girl hoping to 'rouse her to get some answers. The little girl moaned once again and tried to speak, "Captain." Opuntia mouthed a few inaudible words.

Landon watched, horrified the moment Captain Arem put his sword onto the ground next to the semi-conscious girl. The Captain placed his hands down on the rugs and leaned in more closely. Captain Arem turned his head to the right, placing his left ear next to Opuntia's mouth.

To Landon, the next few seconds happened in slow motion. The moment Captain Arem's head rested near her lips, Opuntia slowly lifted her right hand and brought it up to the back of his head. The movement was subtle, going unnoticed.

Landon's eyes widened. Opuntia's nails had grown into sharpened claws extending more than an inch from her fingertips.

Landon wanted to scream, "Beware!"

Opuntia's hand grasped Captain Arem's hair into a tight grip, pressing his head against her face. Her left hand jerked up simultaneously gripping Captain Arem beneath his right armpit. When he attempted to fling himself backwards, away from her, the little girl wrapped her legs around his waist. The battle between the Captain, completely caught off-guard, and Opuntia was brief and violent. Jerking his head to her left, she squeezed his body closer to her own. Opuntia lifted her head and sank two, long fangs deep into Captain Arem's neck.

The scene reminded Landon of a spider he had seen once seen in his childhood. He had watched it closely, fascinated to see it catch its prey by injecting venom to immobilize the insect. The battle between the arachnid and the bug had been brief. The outcome was never in doubt. Landon watched, petrified, knowing Opuntia was going to overpower the Captain.

Captain Arem struggled in vain. The scuffle lasted a few seconds. His body grew rigid and jerked. It convulsed, while the poison worked its deadly magic. Slowly, Opuntia released her vice-like grip on his head. She gently rolled the paralyzed Captain onto his back, rolling with him. The girl ended up sitting astride his chest, looking down into his wide-open eyes.

Landon, appalled to see the Captain wide-awake, thought once again about the Spider and its prey. He remembered watching the spider devour the still living prey. Landon wanted to turn away, fearing Opuntia might begin to devour Captain Arem. He forced himself to watch.

"There, there, Captain. Do not try to struggle. My poison has done what it was designed to do. It has rendered you immobile," she smirked with satisfaction.

"I like my prey to remain alive after I inject them. It would not do to kill you. Otherwise you would be of no use to me." The little girl stood up. Her feet remained on both sides of Captain Arem's chest. She lifted her arms above her head, interlocked her fingers and stretched. Without saying another word she plopped back down onto Captain Arem's chest. The thud sounded like a melon slapped by someone's hand. The Captain's arms and legs remained rigid and unmoving. His eyes, though, watched Opuntia with fear.

His eyes showed recognition that he comprehended Opuntia's words. The moment Opuntia sat squarely back onto Captain Arem's chest she leaned in closely. Landon watched a tear stream down Captain Arem's cheek.

"Look at me, Captain. No. Do not look over to her. Look at me," Opuntia demanded.

Captain Arem's eyes darted away from the unconscious Princess and met the desert waif's gaze. His face twitched as the poison continued to work its way more deeply into his system.

"Do you see me, Captain? Do you see a helpless little girl alone on the sand? Or do you see me for the one who now has your life in her hands?" she asked. She waited for an answer, which she knew he was unable to give. Her wicked smile displayed two razor sharp fangs.

"Imagine it. Opuntia, known as the prickly cactus of the desert. I have defeated a mighty Captain from the Zaharian army. Are you not impressed?" she asked, giggling.

Landon watched, frightened. The little girl leaned her face in more closely to Arem and sniffed him the way a wolf might sniff the rotting remains of a deer. "You should have killed me on the sands Captain," she whispered. "I could tell you wanted kill me."

She looked back to where Lenali lay unconscious. "You should have listened to your instinct. I spoke truth when I described being abandoned by the nomadic tribe. Yet, I had been abandoned because they had figured out who I am."

"I was caught unaware. Before I could act they bound me tightly. Their priests were immune to the myriad of curses and spells I yelled at them. I spoke truth when I said they placed me on those dunes to die," she said. Her eyes bore into Captain Arem, piercing.

She smiled and continued, "Can you imagine the surprise I had when your scout found me? I have lived in this world for almost six-thousand years. I had been resigned to my impending death on the open dunes. But I was saved. I only had to pass your test. Which I did! Are you not impressed?"

"W...W...Why?" Arem whispered. He could barely move his lips. The effort to do so required the utmost concentration and will-power. Speaking was very difficult. He tried to look over again to Lenali, but could not turn his head. Opuntia smiled when he moved his eyeballs to their corners.

Landon knew the Captain's fear for the Princess outweighed concern for himself.

"Why? Dear Captain. Surely, you might have guessed. You are an inquisitive soldier. Very intelligent," she said. The little girl sat up away from his face and pointed to the Princess. "I am here so I might continue to live. I hope to remain immortal." She smiled and asked again, "Are you not impressed?"

Landon almost recoiled at her words. He had not expected this from the desert waif. Her sharpened talons told him she was something unnatural. Yet here she was, sitting on Captain Arem's motionless body, moments after having injected him with some toxin. Her two, ivory fangs protruded from beneath her upper lip. Each time she spoke the fangs glimmered in the faint light.

"I must admit to a hatred of you Captain," Opuntia said, quietly. Her eyes flared, angrily. She continued, "It is a hatred born out of anger. You, a mere mortal, held my life in your hands. You were to be my executioner. You did not want to allow me to live and only gave my life back to me out of a compassion forced on you by her." She gestured over her shoulder to Princess Lenali.

"You alone determined whether I lived or died. I am offended that a mortal had the audacity to claim the power over my life. And now, I seek my revenge."

Opuntia spoke more quickly, "Yes, I have a hatred for you Captain. Even with this hatred, I have an internal obligation to speak truth, at the moment of your death, and so must tell you who I am.

"I am cursed to tell all of my hosts and all of my victims my truth, whenever possible. You see, I am Qui Oto, the immortal one. I live in the bodies of others and in doing so have remained immortal. I have lived in more than two-hundred bodies in my life-time," the little girl smiled, enjoying the torment her words were putting him through.

"I have lived among the human race long enough to know what you call me. I am called a human parasite by those of your race who have figured out how I survive. The nomads have figured it out and are always looking for signs that I might be living in their tribes," she said.

Landon's eyes widened in amazement the moment she finished. He shook his head not believing what she had said.

Opuntia waited for her words to sink in and added, "I have wandered this world, feeding off the body of a human host for as many years as possible. Once my host has withered with age or is no longer valuable I will switch bodies. I must admit, though, I prefer to stay young."

She paused and continued. "My sisters and I live on the edge of mankind's existence, unknown and unseen for thousands of years," Opuntia sighed. She leaned forward and placed her elbows onto Captain Arem's chest. She brought her face to within inches of his and softly planted a kiss onto his lips.

"In other places and other cultures we are referred to as vampires. Yet, it's an unfair comparison. The vampires are savages who kill their prey outright. The comparison is almost insulting. We do not feed off the blood of our prey. That would be uncivilized," she exclaimed.

The little girl seemed pleased with her words, saying, "Make no mistake Captain, I am Qui Oto. There are no more than a handful of us left in this world and I plan on living for an eternity." She leaned up and clapped her hands in front of his face.

"Are you not impressed?"

Captain Arem focused his efforts and responded, "Kill…me…. Leave her." His words a soft whisper. He could not turn his head, but Landon saw the Captain's eyes dart again towards Lenali.

Opuntia complimented the Captain, "Admirable, my dear Captain, but I do not accept your offer. As Qui Oto, I can only reside in a female host. So, you are not an option. Additionally, I have changed my mind. I was going to kill you, but now do not plan on killing either of you." The little girl turned her head and looked over to the Princess.

She looked back and spoke again, "Though, you would prefer death to the other option. In order to reside in my host, I must remove her soul. As Qui Oto, I must remove all of it except for a tiny sliver. The remaining amount is so small, but is necessary to keep the body from dying." She looked at Captain Arem to see if he understood.

The little girl lowered her voice and said, "If a soul is completely removed from a body for a long period of time, the body dies. The Qui Oto need a host in order to survive. This little girl's body has allowed me to live long enough to find the Princess. I will remove almost all of her soul and in doing so will be able to take over her body."

The little girl stood, walked over to Lenali, and bent down to pick up an item. She returned and plopped down again onto Captain Arem's chest.

"Do you see this? It is a perfume jar, but one on which I will place a spell. It will be the vessel housing the soul of your Princess. I will leave a tiny pearl of her soul in her body. The rest will be placed into this jar. It is too difficult for your mind to comprehend, just know she will still be alive.

"Because she is alive, your Princess's soul will feel and experience everything I feel and experience. I will be in control of the body, though, making decisions for the both of us. As long as I am alive, inside her body, she will remain living. It's the least I can do as a repayment for the use of her body. The moment I move to a new host, the remainder of her soul will attempt to travel across the Celestial Plane to find this bottle. The two portions, though, will be unable to re-connect with Lenali's soul housed safely away. My victims all live forever, inside these containers."

"Are you not impressed?" she asked, again.

Opuntia stood once more and walked over slowly to Captain Arem's sword. It shocked Landon to see the little girl easily pick up the sword and carry it back over to the Captain. The wicked smile returned.

She said, gruffly, "When you wielded this sword you held my life in your hands." Opuntia whirled the sword around her head with one arm. She raised it high above her head, placed both hands firmly onto the hilt and brought it crashing down towards Captain Arem. The sword stopped inches from the Captain's face.

"I was going to kill you Captain, but as I said before I have changed my mind. I have decided to allow you to fulfill the Sultan's orders and guard Princess Lenali until death brings an end to your oath. The two of you will be able to live, side-by-side.

"Your existence will be a never ending agony knowing you are trapped forever. The two of you will be completely aware," she said. She stood up, walked over to Lenali's perfume case, and picked up another jar of perfume. Opening the lid, Opuntia emptied its contents onto a rug. She moved over to Captain Arem and held the jar in front of his face.

"Do you see Captain, I am going to be compassionate and allow the two of you to spend eternity together? Now, watch as I, Qui Oto, do what is in my nature to do. Your Princess will make it to the north to meet her new King. Only, instead of a Desert Flower he will marry a Desert Waif," she said laughing.

Opuntia placed both hands on Captain Arem's head and gently turned his head to face the Princess. She whispered, "I want you to be able to watch, Captain. Do not worry. She will not suffer, until her soul is locked inside this glass container."

Landon was gripped with fear. He watched horrified. Opuntia walked over to the unconscious Princess. Standing over Lenali, the little girl began reciting words in an unknown language.

"*Fretha n Onleqdt, menalin su tfrathk. Mafwfira un Lenali.*" Straddling Lenali's chest, the same way she had done with Captain Arem, the little girl sat down softly. Leaning in, she slowly opened her mouth a few inches above Lenali's face.

Landon gasped the moment the first proboscis uncurled from an opening in the little girl's forehead. The hair-like tube grew out of Opuntia's skin, unfurled, and straightened out. The thin tube caressed the unconscious Princess before attaching itself to her forehead.

More hair-like tubes grew and extended out from Opuntia's face. Landon counted more than fifty of the hair-like structures, each of which quickly attached to Princess Lenali.

Leaning down, Landon looked into Opuntia's eyes. He re-coiled. Her eyes had filmed over. Slowly, the little girl's mouth opened wider and two larger proboscis, both at least a half-an inch thick slithered out of her mouth. They parted and each wormed their way across Lenali's face to her ears. They entered the side of the Princess's head.

Lenali's body began to shiver. Her body convulsed once, twice, and her mouth opened. A thin white cloud mixed with a green vapor escaped from between her lips. It swirled a little above her.

"That is her soul," Lyssa said to Landon. He did not turn to look at his sister.

A few seconds later, Opuntia brought the empty perfume jar up to her face. One of the proboscis curled out and away from Princess Lenali's ear. The end wormed its way over to the glass container. The moment the tube entered the jar, the greenish liquid squirted out and into the empty jar. The little girl used her other hand to put a glass cap onto the jar. The moment the jar was filled, Opuntia's body convulsed. The hair-like tubes quickly retreated into her body and she collapsed onto the Princess.

Landon and Lyssa watched for more than a minute as neither Opuntia nor Lenali moved. Slowly, Lenali lifted her hands and rolled the little girl off of her. Landon looked at Opuntia and saw no signs of life. She was dead.

Sitting up, Lenali looked over to Captain Arem. Tears streamed down his cheeks. She smiled at him and spoke.

"It is finished Captain. Your precious Princess is now housed inside this perfume jar. I have placed a spell that will allow her to remain alive, inside this jar forever. A tiny part remains in my body, but none of consequence. Qui Oto was Opuntia and now has become Princess Lenali. Do not fret, I will do the same for you and allow the two of you to spend eternity side-by-side. You may guard her forever, knowing you are responsible for putting her into harm's way."

Princess Lenali stood and walked over to the prostrate Captain. She leaned down and turned his head to look into her eyes.

She kneeled gently beside him and placed the jar holding Lenali's soul onto the rug. Princess Lenali picked up another empty jar. She said, *"Fretha n Onleqdt, menalin su tfrathk. Mafwfirag."*

Landon watched in horror as Princess Lenali leaned in and looked into Arem's eyes. The two, large proboscis extended from Lenali's mouth. Both wormed their way along Captain Arem's face and entered his ears.

A few seconds later a greenish-white mist exited his mouth floating away into the air. Lenali brought the perfume jar up to her face and the proboscis exited one ear. It expelled the liquid into the glass container.

Landon looked to Arem. His chest had become motionless. Princess Lenali smiled and held the jar up to her face.

"I know you can hear me Captain," she said to the jar.

Princess Lenali looked at the dead, little girl, who lay motionless on the rug. She walked back over to the body of Captain Arem and held the jar up to her face once more.

Speaking to the jar she asked, "Are you not impressed?"

THE BLACK DRAGON

THE PRINCESS SMILED EVILLY AT THE JAR HELD OUT BEFORE her. She picked up the jar containing Lenali's soul and put the two of them together. The glass containers clanked softly. She muttered, "You will be able to guard her for an eternity." She turned, walked quickly across the rug-covered sand, and placed the both of them next to an ornately carved wooden container.

Landon suspected the finely made wooden box, inlaid with polished gold threading, contained all of Lenali's favorite jewelry. His sister owned a similar one, though not as ornately designed. He looked down twice, wishing the bodies of Captain Arem and Opuntia would spring to life.

Princess Lenali moved quickly. *"Qui Oto is a demon!"* he thought, terror-stricken to learn his mother's body was controlled by a demon.

Landon followed Princess Lenali to the opening of her tent. She paused to look, lifted the flap, and exited. Inside the vestibule, the Princess kneeled down beside the unconscious Private. She caressed his right cheek with her forefinger and then repeated the movement on his left cheek. She leaned down whispering into his ear, *"Ina dag'e n me ana."*

Startled, the Private's eyes flashed open.

Lenali stood above him, her nostrils flaring with anger. She barked, "Private, you have fallen asleep on duty. In doing so, you have placed your Captain in danger. More importantly your actions have placed me in harm's way." The confused Private kneeled quickly. He knew the penalty for falling asleep on duty.

Lenali spoke again, "Do you understand what you have done Private? Go look inside my tent and return quickly. Do not touch anything!"

He hesitated at first and then did as ordered. He returned, his face ashen white, the look of fear on his face evident.

The Princess exclaimed, "Yes Private! Your Captain is dead! The little girl brought a disease into our camp. You failed in your duties, as did the Captain by allowing her to travel with us, in the first place. Luckily, I was on the other side of the tent when the convulsions struck Opuntia. She died, expelling her poison into Captain Arem's face. He died quickly, the victim of some unknown infection."

The Private listened quietly to the Princess's explanation. He had already foreseen his own impending doom. Her next words gave him hope.

"Private, I would be willing to forgive your dereliction if we can reach an understanding. It is not in my nature to harm others. I would rather find a way to keep you alive. It would shameful if they had to execute you, out here in this vast wasteland. I do not want to see you staked to the ground and your entrails drawn out while you still are living. It is horrible to think of vultures feeding on your body, while you scream in agony unable to stop them." Lenali said. The Princess's facial expression softened.

"I would be willing to do anything Princess," he responded, looking into her eyes, pleading for her to accept it as a promise.

She smiled in return and ordered, "Good. Go to your Sergeant and report the death of Captain Arem and Opuntia. Do not allow anyone to enter this tent. The danger to them is too great. No one is to enter the tent and no one is to examine the two bodies. Is that understood?"

The Private blurted out, "The Sergeant may insist on seeing Captain Arem's body Princess. How do we prevent this?"

She countered, "It is not my responsibility to help you figure out how to keep this from happening. Just know, if the Sergeant or anyone else enters the tent, two things will happen. One, that person will become infected by the disease brought into our camp by Opuntia. Secondly, I will report to the others that you had fallen asleep on duty. Is that clear?"

"Rest assured, I examined the Captain's body from a safe distance and he is dead," she said, hoping to assuage his concerns.

THE EIGHTH LION

The Private nodded he understood, but continued to hesitate. Princess Lenali added, "Bring the Sergeant to me. Once I have gathered a few things I will meet with the two of you outside my tent. If he accepts our explanation, I will not mention your failure."

Before he could leave, Lenali put her hand on his forearm. She said, softly, "In exchange for my kindness, I will need you to carry out a task for me. It involves a long journey to the north. I have two items that I need taken to an old friend. I will explain later. Agreed?"

He agreed and left to find the Sergeant. Princess Lenali re-entered the tent and moved across the rugs to pick up the wooden container housing her jewelry. Before exiting, she opened the box lid and placed the two liquid-filled jars inside.

Within a few minutes, the Sergeant was standing in front of her, with the Private in tow. He was breathing heavily. The look of shock evident in his eyes, told Lenali his response to the news.

He bowed to her and said, "The Private has just told me what happened. Are you in good health?" The fear of an infection spreading to the others apparent on his face.

Princess Lenali nodded responding, "I am fine Sergeant. I am saddened, though, by the death of Captain Arem. He was a good man. I must admit to confusion about his inability to foresee the dangers offered by Opuntia. It forces me to question his leadership abilities. I am hoping the Private has explained how you may avoid making the same mistakes." She looked sternly at the Sergeant, then softened her features and smiled.

"He has Princess and I am in complete agreement," the Sergeant answered. "There is no need to put everyone else in danger. We will collapse the tent onto their bodies and leave it to be buried by the desert."

Lenali accepted the Sergeant's words and said, "A true leader makes tough decisions. I expect you, Sergeant, to get me to my future husband safely. Can you do this?"

The Sergeant paused for a second, bowed to her, and responded with a nod.

The Sergeant turned to speak to the Private, but Lenali cut him off, "Sergeant, I have just decided it most-wise for you to assist the Private with a task. I would like the both you to deliver some items for the Sultan." The Sergeant's eyes-widened, confused.

Landon looked to Lyssa floating beside him, but remained silent. *"Why would she want the Sergeant to go with the Private?"* It did not make sense. The man, unaware of the events inside the tent, should not have been a danger to her plans. *"Had Qui Oto noticed something in the Sergeants eyes that she did not like?"*

Before the Sergeant could respond Lenali continued, "Do not worry. I know I will be in safe hands during your absence. I witnessed firsthand the Sultan's orders to Captain Arem. He instructed me to write a letter when Captain Arem had finished completing his mission. The Captain was to meet me, afterwards, in O'ndar. I am sure the Sultan would be most furious to find out his orders were not carried out."

At those words, Landon watched the Sergeant and the Private both swallow convulsively. Everyone in the Sultan's army knew the penalty for disobeying his wishes.

Princess Lenali continued, "I must add Sergeant, Captain Arem mentioned something to me two nights ago, during one of our conversations. It was his wish, should something ever happen to him, that you take ownership of his favorite horse. What is its name again?"

"Imferion?" his words were both a statement and a question. The horse was a prized possession. The Sultan had personally given it to Captain Arem. The Sergeant's mind raced, caught up in receiving this illustrious gift by his dead Captain. "I have no words Princess." Any questions he had about the secretive mission had already been forgotten. The Sergeant waited patiently for her orders.

"You and the Private should leave immediately. You are to head northeast to a remote village located along the foothills of the Cargathian Mountain range," she directed, opening her jewelry box and handing him a small parchment of yellowed-paper. "Here is a map to follow. Once there, you will find the village. The Sultan wishes you to give the guardian of this village these two jars."

The Private and the Sergeant looked closely at the two perfume jars. The Sergeant took both, holding one up to his face to look at the greenish liquid inside.

She continued, "Once there, give these jars to the guardian who stands on the bridge. Do not leave them anywhere. Do not ever leave them unattended. Place them into her hands. Give her this message. Your master wishes you to know these are for the Seven."

Lenali paused waiting for questions. When there were none forthcoming she said, "Please repeat what I have said." She listened closely while the Sergeant did so. When he finished she looked to the Private and insisted he do the same. Satisfied, Lenali smiled at the both of them, her happiness put them at ease. "One other thing, the Guardian may request a word, a secret code to be used to show the message and the contents really are from her master. If she does, simply respond, *Mfiri*. This will assuage any of her concerns."

"Now Sergeant, go give your orders to the remaining soldiers about what they need to do to get me safely to O'ndar. The two of you should leave immediately. I leave it to you whether to join me in O'ndar, at the completion of your mission, or whether you return to Istanabad to await the return of the others." The Sergeant left to speak to the other men.

The Private turned to follow, but was stopped by the Princess. She held her hand up for silence, waiting until the Sergeant had moved away from the two of them. "Private, I expect you to follow my orders. Do not allow anything to happen to those jars until placed into her hands. Do you understand? If anything happens to either jar, I will hold you personally responsible, as will the Sultan."

He raised his eyebrows at her next statement, "If the Sergeant should not make it back, neither the Sultan, nor I would be displeased." She did not wait for a response and waived him away.

Landon was again shocked. *"She uses them as pawns. She does not care whether they live or die."*

Fifteen minutes later, the Sergeant and the Private broke away from the rest of the group heading northeast. The Sergeant seemed pleased to be riding the white stallion, Imferion. Eventually, the sands of the desert disappeared. The ground smoothed out into a flat, hardened-surface, quickly replaced by miles of prairie grass. The two men talked sporadically. Each hoped to complete the journey to the village as quickly as possible.

Landon expected to follow Princess Lenali for the remainder of her journey. He was surprised when they changed course to follow Imferion.

"I am assuming we are following your soul?" Landon asked.

"Yes!" Captain Arem's booming voice responded. "Let me take you to the fifth day of their journey north." The light flashed quickly.

Landon and Lyssa were out of the desert, floating above a sparsely wooded terrain covered with thick clumps of prairie grass. Landon could see the slope of the foothills of the mountains, the ground interspersed with rocks and stone. The travel on horseback had slowed considerably, though the Sergeant and the Private made better time than they did in the desert.

The two men had struck up a conversation. Landon floated next to them listening intently.

"I wish the Captain had confided in me about this secret mission," the Sergeant said. He looked sideways at the Private.

"I understand, though I expect the Sultan had sworn him to secrecy," the Private responded. "I am curious about the contents of the two jars. Why does the Sultan insist they be taken to a remote village far in the north?" He did not like to question the Sultan's wishes, but felt safe to do so since the Sergeant had opened up the conversation.

They had been skirting along the edge of a group of trees growing along the banks of a small stream. The two had crossed the crystal-clear waters, three times, as it wound back and forth for the last few miles. Up ahead, both the stream and the thick grouping of trees forced them to make a sharp turn to the left.

The Sergeant leaned down and reached into the Private's saddlebag. He pulled out one of the jars, lifting it to his face. He shook the contents, watching them splash and swirl within the jar. He started to lean down to put the container back into the Private's saddlebag when Imferion let out a screech, reared up on its hind legs, and threw him from its back. He crashed harshly to the ground, a sharp pain shooting up his left elbow. He had landed on it awkwardly. Ignoring the pain, the Sergeant leaped to his feet, drew his sword, and looked for an attacker. The jar had not fallen from his right hand.

The moment Imferion had screamed in fear, the Private's horse bolted away in the other direction, carrying with it the startled Private.

The Sergeant leaned to his right and peered around the horse. Imferion remained frozen in fear. A large, black dragon squatted on its hind legs near the stream. It was eating a small deer, but stopped as the yellow eyes gleefully locked onto the horse. The dragon completely ignored the man.

The beast dropped the deer carcass, jumped up, bounded over to, and pounced onto the horse. Imferion cried out in pain, collapsing beneath the dragon's weight. The massive jaws opened and snapped shut, clamping down onto the horse's neck.

The presence of the black dragon startled Landon. He cringed at the sound of Imferion's neck-bones snapping. Landon averted his eyes the moment the dragon's jaws snapped shut. He turned to look at the Sergeant, the petrified man had not moved. Landon saw the man's facial features contort into anger the moment the ebony beast clamped its jaws onto Imferion's neck.

The warrior in the Sergeant rose with a fury the moment he heard the horse cry out in pain. Rather than flee, the Sergeant raised his right arm and threw the only item he held. The glass jar flew from his right hand and shattered against the dragon's scales.

Landon watched the perfume jar sparkle, the moment it left the Sergeant's hand. It moved in slow motion, traveling through the air. It smashed into the thick scales, shattering into a thousand pieces. The green liquid splattered onto the side of the beast, flowing into and beneath the hardened chinks. Before the furious dragon could turn to lash out at the Sergeant, the beast collapsed unconscious to the ground.

Landon and Lyssa watched silently while the Sergeant checked the horse. He shook his head from side-to-side. It was clear the animal was dead. The Sergeant turned and ran off in the same direction the Private's horse had bolted. Landon and Lyssa remained with the dragon, floating a few feet above the unconscious beast. Landon examined it closely. Though the Dragon was a little smaller than the one in the cave it was the same one.

"Is it you Captain?" Landon asked. "Is this you?"

The Dragon's voice, stern and sad, answered, "Yes. Somehow, when the sergeant threw the jar containing my soul, it flowed beneath the scales into her skin. I was absorbed into her body. I woke up..." He paused, noticing Lyssa's worried look. "Do not worry. We will not be here to witness that part of the story. I eventually flew back to my cave."

Landon asked quickly, "Why do we not want to be here for that moment?"

"I think you already know," the Dragon responded. "When I wake up, I will devour Imferion, my favorite horse."

"I am sorry, Captain. It was a mere curiosity," Landon offered. He stared down at the unconscious dragon.

"None is needed," the voice answered. "I too would have been curious about what happened next. When I woke I took leave of this place and flew back to my cave, located due east of here. It took a couple of years for me to become fully aware of my situation and remember who I used to be." Arem's voice flowed with excitement and frustration. "I remember it quite well. The moment I became fully aware of my past. Without knowing why, I had developed an urge to fly northward, along the Cargathian Mountains.

Captain Arem waited a few seconds before continuing, "At some point, my soul began to battle with the essence of the dragon for supremacy. It felt as if I lived only in a dream. In my madness, since there is no other way to describe it, I even dreamed my father had found me. We talked in my cave, hugging each other closely, one last time. Eventually, the dragon won control, at least for the next few years. Before becoming aware I had been a human, I remained in my cave, caring for my orbs and trying to master their magic."

Landon listened to the Dragon's explanation, fascinated. The Dragon added, "Slowly, though, my human memories began to return. I felt a compulsion to fly further north again. I spent a month or so moving from cave to cave, until my orbs, my eggs, and I ended up in this cave. I had become fully aware of who I had been, made possible once I mastered the power of an orb. It was then I realized why I had chosen my current home."

Lyssa responded before the Captain could, "It is to be near her, isn't it?" She looked at her brother hoping he would understand.

"Yes Princess. We are within a few miles of Mfiri. I found a cave a few miles away from the jar that contains the soul of Princess Lenali."

WHAT DRAGONS FEAR

THE FINAL FLASH OF LIGHT BURNED AND FADED QUICKLY, before Landon needed to shut his eyes. The moment his eyes re-focused Landon laughed out loud. They had returned to the cave. The Dragon's yellow eyes were staring into his own, the ebony face only a few inches away. Prior to traveling across the Celestial Plane, the water in Landon's blood would have frozen in his veins if a dragon had stared at him, thus. He was no longer afraid of the Dragon Arem. Instead, he leaned forward, almost touching his nose to that of the Dragon.

Confused about why the Dragon Arem leaned in so closely to her brother's face, Lyssa asked the purpose. The Dragon Arem looked from her, then back to the Prince.

Landon answered for the Dragon, "He wanted to look into my eyes hoping he could ascertain my thoughts. In the Celestial Plane, he can read our minds. Out here, in the physical world, it is much more difficult. Dragons are very powerful creatures, my apologies. Dragons are very powerful. To read thoughts in the physical world requires reading the facial and body expressions of others. Captain Arem was hoping to look into my eyes and gather my thoughts."

Lyssa looked at the Dragon, "Is this true, Captain Arem?"

"It is true princess. I have shown the two of you the past and hoped to use my power of observation to figure out your brother's thoughts," he answered. "I admit he is very tough to read. I am unable to guess his thoughts."

Landon accepted the Dragon's words as a compliment. He was proud he had been able to keep his thoughts hidden from the powers of a mighty dragon. He looked to the two of them and said, "I would like a few minutes to consider everything I have been shown." The Dragon started to stand, but was stopped by Landon's raised hand.

The Prince said, "There is no need to leave, Captain. I will step out to the ledge of the cave." He stood, but stopped Lyssa. She had risen in order to accompany him. "I need to be alone, sister." She started to protest, but stopped. Landon turned away and exited the mouth of the cave. He was grateful for the coolness of the night's air. The waves of cold air helped awaken his senses. Inhaling deeply, Landon exhaled and watched his breath curl up and float away, a wisp of steam trailing away into the night. It felt like he had been inside the orb for hours, days, even months, though he knew here, in the physical world it had been no more than an hour. Pacing back and forth along the ledge, Landon considered everything he had witnessed. The events of the past had unfolded before him and now there was no going back.

"But where do I go from here? Even if all of it is the truth, what do I do next?" he thought. He admitted he was in a quandary. There would be no easy answer to this puzzle. No easy solution to this question. Once again, he found himself wishing he could seek the counsel of his father. The King had an impressive quality about him. Landon's father could listen to all sides of an argument, patiently. Then, with an almost uncanny intuition, he would offer the solution. He was rarely wrong. *"Never when it was important."*

Landon shivered. The coolness outside the cave no longer felt refreshing. He returned to the warmth of the cave, pausing inside a few seconds to allow his eyes to adjust. The moment reminded him of the time Captain Arem had paused inside Princess Lenali's tent. The outcome had not been a good one.

Moving back over to the orb, Landon sat down without speaking, and placed his hands back onto the orb. Lyssa did the same. She looked to Landon. He looked directly into the Dragon's yellow eyes.

"First, how was your soul transported into the body of this dragon?" Landon asked.

"My only guess, Prince Landon, is a dragon does not have a soul. It has an essence, which is similar, yet not the same. A dragon's essence comes directly from Ea. I know the stories passed on to Pelinnedes about mankind and the power to reason. Yet, having once been human and now a dragon, I can only say they are nearly the same, though are slightly different," the Dragon explained.

Landon accepted the answer. He did not want to engage in a philosophical debate about a Dragon's essence versus a person's soul. He nodded he understood and continued, "How does your father play into all of this?" Lyssa wanted to protest his directness, but decided it would be best to listen.

"I do not know for sure. I can conjecture, but may not be correct," Arem answered.

"Please do, Captain," Landon responded. He had his own thoughts about how Ferlynne or General Faron had come to O'ndar.

"I can only guess the Sergeant and the Private completed their journey to the north. When they returned to Istanabad, they must have presented their findings to the Sultan or to my father," the Dragon intoned. "He did not believe the story of my death and decided to come north to investigate it."

Landon agreed with Captain Arem's explanation. It could be the only reason why General Faron fled Istanabad and traveled to O'ndar. Yet, it did not explain the ruse. It also did not explain the spell he had learned. Ferlynne had mentioned a village far in the north, one in which he had learned the Stretching of the Soul spell. *"Could it be the same village?"* There were many unanswered questions.

The yellow eyes fixated on Landon's face, "My father is a very intelligent man. At some point, if he were able to ascertain the truth, it would make sense for him to try to send you to me. Yet his reasons for wanting you to face me would have been different from mine."

Landon was puzzled, *"Could Ferlynne have figured this all out? How would it have been possible?"* He decided to ask, "What would have been his reason for me to face you?"

"He wanted me to kill you out of revenge?" the Dragon said.

"Captain!" Lyssa responded, shocked at his words. She had not expected this level of truth from the Dragon.

Landon did not ask him to elaborate on the point. "And what was your reason?"

"To save them!" the Dragon responded, gesturing with his head to Lyssa. Once again, she was shocked, but this time decided to remain silent. Landon suspected he knew why Captain Arem felt she needed saving, but he wanted the explanation nonetheless. The Dragon did not offer one.

"Your goal was to save my sister from the Queen. Correct?" Landon asked. He watched as the Dragon's head nodded in the affirmative. Lyssa looked at Landon for an explanation. "Dear sister, in less than a year you were going to be sent to the south in order to fulfill the treaty. You would not have gone south. At least, your soul would not have made the trip. Qui Oto planned to take over your body. She planned to send your soul to Mfiri. You were destined to spend an eternity locked in a glass container, sitting on a shelf, next to our real mother. Spending all time with the seven, whoever they are."

Landon finished speaking and looked at his sister, the realization visible on her face.

Lyssa blurted out, "It is almost too much to think about." Tears streaked down her face again. Landon wanted to reach out to comfort her, but decided it would have to wait.

He looked back at the Dragon asking, "What do you mean save them?" He saw doubt in the Dragon's eyes.

Yet Captain Arem spoke with a full conviction, "I meant both Princesses."

Lyssa did not respond this time. This told Landon she had been privy to Captain Arem's plan to save their mother from the fate forced on her by Qui Oto. He knew Arem continued to carry the guilt of what happened in the desert. Even in the form of a dragon, the Captain's thoughts of saving the Princess reigned supreme.

"I am listening, Captain," Landon said. "The fact that I am still alive means you did not agree with your father's plan. It also means you believe there is a way to rescue my mother's soul." He looked at the Dragon pleased to know he had been correct in his assessment.

"You are a powerful Dragon, Captain," Landon said. "If the Princess is housed somewhere in Mfiri, why haven't you gone to save her?"

Landon's question brought Lyssa out of her own thoughts. She nodded back to the Captain. She had not thought of this before. As a Dragon, feared by all others, he could fly into Mfiri and save their mother.

"I must admit, I am very impressed with the speed and depth of your intelligence. I also suspect you know the answer to your own question," the Dragon responded, leaning his face in closely, once again, their noses almost touching.

Lyssa looked at the two of them and asked, "Do you know Landon?" She was surprised when he nodded.

Landon turned to Lyssa and said, "My dear sister, the Dragon Race is the oldest race on the face of the planet. There is only one thing on this planet capable of causing fear in a Dragon." He paused and waited for her to ask.

"And what is that brother?" Lyssa asked.

Landon responded without turning back to her, "Another Dragon."

MFIRI

"ARE YOU SAYING OUR MOTHER'S SOUL IS BEING GUARDED by a dragon?" Lyssa asked, clearly shaken by the revelation. Landon shrugged his shoulders, without removing his hands from the orb. He did not know for sure what he meant. He waited for the Dragon Arem to respond.

"I have gone as close to Mfiri as I can, but my instinct or call it my dragon sense, forces me to turn back. Otherwise, I would have used all of my strength and powers to invade the village. I would have torn everything apart to find her," the Dragon proclaimed. "You must believe me when I say I would have stopped at nothing to rescue your mother."

A strange feeling washed over Landon the moment Arem referred to the Princess as their mother. Landon, well aware the Dragon was referring to a different person, different from the woman he knew. Queen Lenali had raised, loved, and cared for him as much as any mother could. Yet, he was expected to reject that woman and accept another person as his mother. The two had inhabited the same body, at different times. They would have to be different, though, because of their souls. It was another philosophical question that he did not feel he had enough time to contemplate.

"Is it a bigger Dragon or an older Dragon?" Landon asked. Lyssa turned to him again, puzzled.

"What do you mean, brother?" she asked.

Landon looked to the Dragon Arem for an explanation. The Dragon answered, "You are mostly correct in your assumption about dragons. There are other things which invoke fear in a dragon's heart. But, for the most part, our trepidation is usually caused by the presence of other dragons." Arem paused. "I do not know if it is an older, more powerful dragon or a larger, more powerful dragon. I do know there is a dragon in Mfiri. Her presence prevents me from going any closer. This is why I am in need of your assistance."

It was Landon's turn to change the subject. Captivated by Captain Arem's statement about what Dragons feared, he asked, "I must know, Captain, more so out of curiosity, what else could instill apprehension in a Dragon?"

The possibilities absorbed Lyssa's attention. She had been holding her breath through parts of the conversation. Now, listening to her brother's questions and to Captain Arem's responses, her excitement grew.

The Dragon said, "We fear older dragons. Many have mastered a lifetime of orbs and have enhanced magical powers. We also fear larger dragons because of their size and increased physical strength." He turned his head to look at Lyssa. "Dragons also fear powerful wizards, though there have been no more than a handful of them throughout our history. Most who claim the power of wizards are mere magicians…tricksters. They use illusion, but those spells make them no more than frauds. Their spells work on the race of men, but any dragon who masters a single orb can see through the subterfuge.

"We also fear men who have mastered orbs, whether they are wizards or not. A wizard who has mastered an orb can be as powerful as a dragon, depending on the power the orb offers. We also fear some of the demons residing inside the Celestial Plane. They are as old as the Dragon Race and therefore have as much knowledge. These beings have instilled fear into some dragons. An example of a demon that has crossed over is the Wendigo."

Lyssa quickly interrupted, "A Wendigo? What is that?"

"It is a human possessed by a demon that has crossed into our world. It feeds on the flesh of other humans. Living in the darkness of caves, it will devour any humans who stray away from their homes at night," Arem offered, he watched her shudder at his words.

He continued, "The dragons though, do not fear the creature as much as we fear the demon spirit. Most of the demons cannot cross over into the physical realm. They are of no consequence. I suspect Qui Oto was a demon that did cross over."

Landon held his breath, captivated by the discussion. He spoke, "I did not know wizards existed. We assumed they were made up stories to excite children about their studies." He looked to Lyssa, who nodded in agreement.

The Dragon Arem responded, "More than five hundred years ago, an evil wizard named Jochi found a pass through the Cargathian Mountains. He used it to cross over from the Lands of the Khans. He was already very powerful when he arrived. He stole an orb, mastered its power, and used it to capture a few dragons. He then used their orbs to enhance his already mighty powers. Ultimately, though, he was not after the dragons, only their orbs. Before he could grow too powerful and enslave the Dragon Race the three Titans united and used their combined strength to defeat him. The battle raged for seven days and seven nights before the might of the Titans won the day. Jochi mortally wounded, his body shriveled and broken, fled quickly back across the mountains never to be seen or heard from again."

Landon listened fascinated. He nodded hoping Arem would continue.

"Pahaida used her flames to seal up the breach in the mountains." Arem said. "The thunderous battle took a toll on the three Titans. Each returned to their homelands. None of the three has been seen since that battle. It was also was the last time anyone from the Lands of the Khans crossed into the Known World."

Landon was mesmerized by what the Dragon Arem shared with him. This brief look into the life of a Dragon seemed almost as important as the meeting between Pelinnedes and Meeha nearly a thousand years ago.

"I thank you Captain, for showing us everything. I also thank you for your honesty. I am assuming you have brought me here hoping I would travel to Mfiri and try to recover the soul of Princess Lenali."

Landon could not bring himself to say, *'The soul of my mother.'* He waited for the Dragon Arem's response.

It was Lyssa, though who spoke first, "Yes, this is the reason brother. Captain Arem also brought the two of us here at this time because he is afraid the human part of him is slipping away. If this happened before he was able to show us her past, our mother could never be saved from the eternity of imprisonment."

"What do you mean?" Landon asked, intrigued by his sister's words. It was hard enough to imagine a Zaharian Captain trapped inside the body of a female dragon. Just when he had come to grips with this, he learned the Captain within might fade away. *"Could the Dragon truly return and be master of the body?"*

"Captain Arem's time-line has been sped up by the realities of being a dragon," she explained. "Brother, look around you at the orbs and the eggs." She watched while Landon scanned the cave. "What do you notice about all of them and the light they are emanating?" Their shadows still flickered along the walls of the cave.

Landon answered, "The light is pulsating. Is that not normal?" They had been pulsating since he had walked into the cave.

"No," she responded. "They begin pulsating when they are getting nearer to hatching."

Landon looked more closely, amazed. *"When will they hatch? Will it be possible for me to hold a dragon hatchling?"* The sober look on Lyssa's face told him there was more here than his eyes were telling him. He waited patiently for her to explain.

"Remember the lessons from our books brother. Especially, the Brief History of Dragons by Pelinnedes. Once a dragon hatches its first clutch of eggs," she said, pausing to give him time to respond.

Landon leaped to his feet, "It changes to one of the three Titan Dragon forms." He looked at the Dragon Arem more closely. "Are you saying Captain Arem is going to change into an Ice-Dragon, a Lava-Dragon, or a Forest Dragon?"

"Yes," she answered. "Captain, tell him your biggest fear, other than Dragons." Landon thought he heard a hint of sarcasm in his sister's question.

The Dragon offered, "I do not know when I will mature into the next stage of a dragon. I also do not know whether I will retain my human memories. Some of my memories are already dissipating. Only the orb has allowed me to continue to remember my past. It is imperative, to me, that we save Princess Lenali, before my eggs hatch." The Dragon fell silent for a few seconds.

"Show him Captain," Lyssa demanded.

Landon watched, amazed. The Dragon stood and turned slowly to his right, exposing his left side to the two of them. The scales lifted in unison. Without removing his hands from the orb, Landon leaned in and saw the glowing Dragon skin beneath. The skin pulsated with radiance, reminding Landon of the orbs.

He asked, "Do you know the type of Dragon you will become?"

The ebony Dragon turned back and looked into Landon's eyes, "I suspect I am a descendent of Pahaida. I was drawn to the mountains, initially, when first absorbed into this Dragon's body."

Landon understood the seriousness of why Captain Arem wanted him to go to Mfiri, immediately. Once the Dragon eggs hatched, the Captain would evolve into a newer type of Dragon. There would be no guarantee the Captain would retain his human memories. The Dragon might take control again and Captain Arem would be destined to live out his life with the awareness that he was a part of, but not in control of the Dragon. The fate was similar to that of Princess Lenali, prisoner in the container housing her soul.

On the other hand, he might finally die, completely. The Captain was prepared to die, but was not prepared to let the Princess's soul stay locked in a jar, without trying to save her.

"Captain, if your hatchlings come before I get back from Mfiri, what is to become of my sister?" he asked, looking at her. "I would prefer she not be harmed." Landon smiled at her with all of the love and affection he could muster.

"I have thought of this, young prince. I have no wish to devour your sister, either. Yet, if I sense my hatchlings will arrive before you return, I will send her across the Celestial Plane, back to my father's cave. At least there, she will be safe from me," the Dragon answered.

"And if I fail to return?" Landon asked.

Captain Arem promised, "I swear, no harm will befall your sister on account of my actions. Whether by human or dragon design."

Landon thought for a few seconds then nodded in agreement. He accepted Captain Arem's word. His sister would be safe from harm. That was what mattered.

He stood up and removed his hands from the top of the orb. Lyssa looked up and asked quickly, "What are you doing, brother?"

Landon smiled and leaned over to kiss her on the forehead, "I am leaving sister. I am going to Mfiri." He turned away from the two of them, walked over to the mouth of the cave, and looked back once more. The light of the day started to peer through the mountain peaks. There was just enough light for Landon to look down through the mountains. He looked closely and spotted a tiny village a few miles away.

"Mfiri," he whispered to himself. Without looking back, Landon left the cave.

―

Years ago, when Landon had turned twelve years old, his father ordered him to go on a bivouac with a group of soldiers who had just finished their three months of training required by the O'ndarian army. Originally, he argued with his father about having to sleep out in the woods, without the comforts of a tent or a warm fire. His mother tried to intervene on his behalf, but the King refused to change his mind. He rode out of the castle angry with his father, but returned with admiration and thankfulness for the experience.

The training, rigorous and harsh, gave Landon a new appreciation for the army and the men he might someday command in battle. Landon returned to the castle a different person. Once again, his father had shown an ability to make a wise decision. The Prince's respect for the soldiers in the army increased tenfold, once he realized all of them were capable of living off the land and surviving on their own. The experience humbled him.

The first step Landon took away from the ledge ended with him tumbling down the side of the mountain for fifteen to twenty feet. Even while falling down the slope, Landon hoped Lyssa had been looking the other way. When he stopped falling, he was very sore on his left side. A sharp pain, which felt like a knife stabbing into his hip, worried him. He lay on his back for a few minutes, breathing heavily, looking into the sky at the fading stars.

"We are all in trouble if I am already falling. I have only been away from the cave for a few seconds," he thought, chuckling. Landon sat up

and took a few deep breaths. He reminded himself to slow down, to think about each step before taking the next. Getting to Mfiri quickly was very important. It was more important to get there alive.

"I do not know what awaits me when I get there," he said aloud. It did not surprise him when he spoke to himself. When he was younger, he often spoke to himself, especially when alone. He was surprised, in the quietness of the mountains, to hear his voice echo away and bounce back to his location. He found the mountain peaks mesmerizing.

Slowly, Landon pushed himself upright, making sure of his footing before walking. He slowed his pace, scanning ahead for any signs of danger.

He lifted his right hand and pointed. *"If I climb this slope, walk along the top of that ridge and follow it until I reach that ledge."* He mapped out his direction, the speed at which he should walk, and the best path to follow before starting again. The rocky surface was initially difficult to traverse. Dew had moistened many of the rocks. As the morning wore on, though, the dew evaporated and Landon's footing became less perilous. He continued for about an hour and a half before deciding to take a short break. His stomach growled at him, complaining about the morning's exertion. Landon had nothing with him to eat.

"I am hungry. I should have eaten one of Captain Arem's eggs," he chortled. He wondered how Lyssa and the Dragon would have responded to such a request. *"Lyssa would have been mortified. Arem? He might have eaten me instead."* He laughed again. With his short break over, Landon started to get to his feet, but froze. A shiver of fear ran up his spine.

A catamount, muscular and sleek crouched a few feet away, ready to pounce. The large snow-white mountain lion looked at Landon, hungrily. It was the most powerful looking animal he had ever seen. Hunched close to the ground, muscles rippled along the beast's flanks. The large cat had moved stealthily towards him, unnoticed. It had glided across the rocky surface without making any noise. If he had not stood up to continue his journey, it might have sprung on him, while he was completely unaware. The triangular ears perked up once it realized he was aware of its presence. Grey-blue eyes shone brightly behind the large, white whiskers covering its face. Landon glanced down at the sharpened claws extending from each paw. Even at this distance, he was certain they were razor sharp, each capable of slicing him open. The two of them stared at each other, neither moved. Landon decided to act quickly, before the cat regained its nerve.

Slowly, without taking his eyes off the mountain lion, Landon reached down and grabbed a few hand-sized rocks. He stood back to his full height and waved his hands back and forth over his head. Landon took one quick step towards the massive cat, yelling loudly.

"EEEEIIYaaaww!" he screamed at the top of his lungs while throwing the first rock. It landed less than a foot away from the cat. Startled, the snow-white leopard leaped back away from the rock. It paused, started to turn back towards him, but froze at the motion of his arm when he threw another rock. Landon threw the second rock with more precision and more force. The fist-sized rock struck the cat in the shoulder. Shrieking in pain the cat turned and loped away as quickly as possible. Landon reached down picking up two more rocks. He looked around, but the cougar was already gone. It had disappeared into the jagged outcroppings of rock. The Prince waited for a few seconds, allowing his breathing to return to normal. The surge of adrenaline helped sharpen his senses, yet it came with a price. His stomach growled in hunger, again.

"I do not have time to worry about food."

For the rest of his journey, Landon kept two rocks ready, one in each of his hands. It made climbing cumbersome, but he needed something to defend himself, should the big cat return. The cats, which lived in the mountains, were solitary animals. They hunted animals with stealth and speed. The quietness, with which the mountain lion had snuck up to him, left him shaken. He would not be caught off-guard anymore.

Landon continued along the ridge he had previously chosen as his path. He scanned up ahead looking for his next route, deciding to climb up and over two smaller sloping hills hoping it would bring him near the bottom of a ravine. According to his calculations, he should be able to follow the ravine and would wind up on the outskirts of the village. The village seemed closer than it did when he looked at it from the ledge of the cave. It would still take a few hours to reach, though.

He reached the edge of the ridge, knowing he would have to descend a steep decline. Landon sat down and slid slowly, climbing his way down in some spots, sliding down in others. Less than a half an hour later he was at the bottom between two hills. Without pausing, he began the climb up the second hill. It was slower going. Landon dropped one of his rocks, went back down a few feet to retrieve it and began climbing again. Having them with him put his mind at ease. He made it to the bottom of the second hill, turned to his right, and began following the ravine.

Landon walked along the ravine, hoping he was heading in the right direction. The rocky outcroppings continued to be obstacles. He had to crawl over, slide under, or walk around them in order to make headway. A few hours later, he walked around part of the mountain and came out into a flattened plain surrounded by small hills. The mountain peaks loomed above, reaching high into the sky.

Landon sighed, cursing aloud. From his previous calculations, he should have been standing in front of the village. He had walked, climbed, scurried, slid, and belly-crawled his way through these mountains and the village was nowhere in sight. Refusing to entertain any negative thoughts, the Prince shrugged off the frustration. He had come too far to stop. He was confident he would find this mysterious mountain village, eventually.

Landon decided to climb one of the nearby hills. He chose the smaller one, no more than sixty feet in height.

"I will get to the top and get my bearings," he thought.

Landon climbed gingerly. The first half was easy going. He had to lean in slightly in order keep standing while walking slowly up the steep slope. Patches of grass, some brown and some green, sporadically covered the side of the hill. Leaning forward, further, he ended up crawling his way to the top. The moment he made the crest, Landon laughed aloud.

There, in front of him, at the bottom of the hill, wrapped in a dense, blue fog, was a village. The light from the sun disappeared into the blanket of mist surrounding it. Up here, away from the haziness below, the sun shone brightly. Its energy brightened everything it touched. Yet, looking down at the murkiness encircling the village filled Landon with a sense of gloom. He paused for a few minutes to look around.

The thickness of the blue-haze prevented him from making an accurate assessment of the size of the village. At this distance, he could barely see the tops of many of the houses. There were hundreds, if not thousands. He could not be sure. Mfiri, nestled in a small valley, stretched away for miles, in both directions.

"*This village is far larger than I assumed,*" he thought.

"*How is it, that a village of this size has never been seen on any of the maps?*" Landon determined to have it explored by the O'ndarian army when he made it back to his homeland.

"*If I make it back,*" he thought. The mysterious village worried him.

After a few minutes, Landon took a deep breath. He exhaled, slowly. Head up, he began walking down the hill towards the fog-covered village.

GAMAYUN

LANDON MADE IT TO THE BOTTOM OF THE HILL WITHOUT slipping and falling, which he counted as a small victory. He kept the two, fist-sized rocks with him, but was sure they would be no match should a soldier from the village ride out and challenge his presence. At this elevation, in the Cargathian Mountains, the dense fog condensed together thickly, forming into greyish-white wall completely enveloping the village.

Previously, when on the hilltop looking down from above, he could almost see over the wall of fog. At the bottom of the hill, though, he thought he could move closer for a better look. It was not. The unnaturally thick haze surrounding the village looked foreboding. Landon shook his head in dismay after looking in both directions. The heavy mist surrounding the village extended as far as his eyes could see. He looked once-more to his right and then back to his left.

"Which way do I go?" he asked himself. Applying what he knew about the villages in his country, Landon thought it best practice to announce his arrival, to whoever guarded the village. *"But where do I find such a person?"*

Landon turned to his right and started walking at a brisk pace. His legs were relieved to be walking on a flat surface. The aches and pains he had experienced on his journey tested his endurance. Looking again at the gloominess, Landon felt fear of the unknown slither into his heart. He moved away from the fog, but continued walking forward. The possibility of an ambush, without enough time to mount a defense, made him wary and nervous.

He spoke aloud again, urging himself to be cautious. Landon knew he had spoken louder than he needed. His nerves were on end. Silence hung in the air. He wished Lyssa were here to talk with him.

"I wish Arem were here." The Dragon had been afraid to come closer to Mfiri, but having Arem nearby would have alleviated Landon's concerns. *"Who would dare attack a Dragon?"*

The fast pace, even on the flat surface, began to wear him down. His whole body began to tire. He had been searching for a way into the village for more than an hour. His legs ached. His calves screamed at him, with each step. He refused to stop, though, knowing he was close to the village and the answers he needed.

Landon halted. Up ahead, less than a fourth of a mile away, both the village and the dense wall of fog curved slightly away to the left. *"This is no ordinary fog."*

At the spot where the village and the fog curved away, the end of a wooden bridge jutted out from the mist. Landon approached the bridge from the side, but maintained his distance. He stopped less than fifty feet away and looked it over. Landon could only see half the bridge, the other half swallowed by the wall of fog.

He kneeled down to inspect the underside of the arched bridge. He was impressed by the solid, wooden structure. There were four massive oak beams, spaced equally apart from one another. They formed the foundation of the bridge. Landon lost count adding the number of abutments, caps, and other components. This was a solidly built, wooden structure. The beams, logs, planks, and boards were freshly cut. Thick wooden nails had been driven deep into the logs connecting the planks, reinforcing everything with thickly cut interlocking timber. Landon did not expect to find a well-kept structure this high in the mountains. Even the sides of the decks, the wooden railings, were solid.

"I could cross this bridge with an entire army, including the heavy wagons, and it would be sturdy enough to hold."

Landon looked down below the Bridge. Down in the gorge, which trailed off hundreds of feet below, Landon could see jagged rocks. He whistled aloud.

"Falling in would mean instant death," he thought. He sighed. The Bridge offered the only access to the village. *"The only way into Mfiri."*

The other half of the gorge disappeared from eyesight, swallowed by the massive wall of fog surrounding the village. Landon swallowed nervously, fighting the urge to run away. He was wary of this bridge. Landon looked around wanting to be sure he was alone.

Landon stood up and said a prayer of thanks. He was happy he had not tried to cross into Mfiri by walking through the fog. The thick mist had completely covered the treacherous ravine in every other spot surrounding the village. He would have fallen to his death.

Landon turned to walk around to the front of the bridge, moving slightly away from it as he did. He decided to give the bridge opening a wide-berth, hoping he would be able to look to the other side. Once again he froze. A large animal crouched in the middle of the bridge, less than ten feet away from the opening. He had been caught up inspecting the bridge and had not noticed the animal.

Landon stepped a few feet closer, but remained at the ready. He hoped it was not another mountain lion or one of the bears that sometimes frequented the mountains hunting for goats. Thankful he had kept the two rocks, he weighed them in his hand. He knew they would not stop a bear.

Slowly, he inched closer hoping to see what kind of animal it might be. Landon was prepared to run and dive into the ravine, if needed. If it were a bear, turning and running would be a bad idea. The bear could easily run him down.

"Is it an animal? A bird, maybe?" Landon spied a mass of large, black feathers covering its entire body.

Weighing the two rocks in his hands, Landon walked forward a few steps. He stopped less than a foot away from the bridge. The hairs on his neck stood up on end. Two large, white eyes peered back at him from a small opening between the large pile of feathers. They were the size of his fists. The pupils were a mixture of blue and green. It was a large bird. The ball of feathers was taller than Landon. The saucer-sized eyes watched him unblinking. Landon looked up and down the long black feathers, each tipped with white. They encircled the giant bird completely. Two large feet stuck out from beneath the feathers at the bottom. Its three-toed feet, dark grey, bulbous and leathery, each had long ivory claws extending from the wrinkled toes. It was the largest bird Landon had ever seen.

Landon's eyes darted from the eyes, to the toes, and back. His nervousness returned.

He had been tempted to throw one of his rocks at the bird to scare it away. Landon hated to give up his only weapons, though. He decided to yell loudly, instead. Holding the rocks at his sides, Landon moved to step onto the bridge. Landon lifted his right foot and started to place it down onto the bridge. The bird shook its feathers furiously. The eyes glared at him with hatred. He lowered his foot back onto the ground stunned by its response. He repeated the gesture, only to have the feathers shake harshly, once again. The bird glared at him angrily, once more.

"What an odd bird," he thought. *"I will just go around it and run into the village."*

Landon kept his eyes on the bird, slowly side-stepping to his left. Once, twice, three times. He stood in front of the left side of the bridge, the wooden railing less than a foot away. Lifting his right foot, Landon started to step onto the bridge. The animal shook its feathers ferociously, hopped two steps to its right, and blocked his path. The feathers shook savagely once more, the two eyes wicked in their countenance. The black plumage stood on end, but the body of the bird remained completely hidden. Landon began to have doubts about it being a bird. A bird would not have behaved this way.

Landon decided to move slowly to his right, crossing the width of the bridge. This time, the animal hopped with him, staying in front of him. The menacing eyes remained locked onto his eyes. By the time he made it to the railing on the right, the large, feathered bird once again squatted in his way.

Slowly, Landon and the bird moved back to the middle of the bridge. They were back to where they had started, before this awkward dance had begun. Landon was frustrated. The large, saucer-sized eyes continued to glare at him with hatred.

"Fine, I have no choice then."

Landon stepped back, raised his right arm holding the rock near his shoulder. He lifted his left foot to step onto the Bridge. He intended to throw the rock. When it hit the target he would run by as quickly as possible. He could charge through the fog and into Mfiri.

The movement of the bird caught his attention. The feathers shook furiously, again. Landon paused.

The group of feathers on the right wing opened a tiny fraction. A large, four-fingered hand crept out from beneath. The grey, leathery fingers were long and wrinkled. A large talon grew out of one of the fingers. Its razor sharp end pointed towards Landon. The finger shook back and forth. The bird lowered the claw to the bridge, placed the tip onto the wooden planks, and scraped it along the board, leaving a deep scratch. The hand returned into the thick plumage, the feathers closing once again.

Landon swallowed convulsively. He lowered his hand back to his side and placed his foot back onto the ground. He still had not touched the bridge. He did not know what kind of bird it was, but the razor sharp talon instilled fear. Landon jumped, startled. A voice emanated from within the mass of feathers.

"Tell me young human, why do you come to my village?" it asked. The scratchy voice sounded almost human, though Landon doubted the bird had vocal cords. The voice reminded him of a time when Lyssa had taken to the flu. She had lost her ability to speak. When her voice had returned, it was raspy and dry. He teased her about it for days until she fully recovered.

Landon watched and waited in silence. The animal's eyes, wide and uncaring, continued to glare at him.

"I am sorry," Landon responded. "Could you repeat the question?"

The feathers shook one more time, ferociously. They opened slightly. Landon leaped a step backward. The giant legs and body of the animal exposed to Landon made him shudder. The feathers opened and the bird stood up, stretching its body to its full height. Landon looked up into the face of a woman towering above him. The bird-like creature, with the woman's face, was more than fifteen feet tall.

"Beware young human, for I am Gamayun, the Guardian of this place. I will ask you only one more time, why do you come to my village?" she demanded.

The woman's face was enormous. Her head was wider than Landon's body. It was disproportionate, in size, to the thin birdlike-body. The large, saucer-sized eyeballs stared at him, unblinking. Other than the large eyes, the woman was pleasing to look at. She was not ugly, though her oversized features made her seem grotesque. Her skin was porcelain white, smooth and silky. Her nose straight and fair wore well on her pale skin. Two high cheekbones complimented full, voluptuous lips. Large, white canines flashed at Landon, when she spoke, but when she was silent, Landon counted her as one of the most beautiful women he had ever seen. Supported by a thin neck, her face looked at him sternly with disapproval. Her impatience, at his lack of a response, wore heavily on her features.

This was too much for Landon's mind to comprehend. His head ached and his eyes became blurry. The whole world seemed to spin for a few seconds. He released the rocks. They dropped to the ground with a soft thud. Landon backed up another step, stumbled over his own feet and fell onto his backside.

He lay there looking upward into the large eyes. The pupils of each the size of the rocks he had just dropped. Landon sat up and looked at his feet. He was bewildered. The events of the last twenty-four hours piled up, stacked up like bricks in his mind. His thoughts raced back to the moment the Dragon had swooped in and taken his sister. He thought about the trip across the Celestial Plane that had him up into the Cargathian Mountains. Somehow, through a magic he did not understand, Landon had been transported into the past of a country far to the south, across the vast expanse of a great desert. Placed on a journey to an unknown village high in these mountains, Landon had been excited to find the village. Now, just when he had found the village after walking for hours, an animal with the face of a woman and the body of a bird blocked his path.

"*Gamayun?*" he thought. "*Did this animal speak and offer me its name?*" He leaned backwards and looked up into her eyes. She was tall and menacing, yet her face soft and bewitching. He tried to mouth an answer, but his words would not come out.

Landon cleared his throat and tried to swallow. The image of his sister, soaring away into the cloudless sky, flooded into his mind. It was an image that filled him with fury. The anger bubbled up into his consciousness like a pot of boiling water. He remembered her body dangling limply beneath the Dragon.

He allowed the anger to boil up quickly, unchecked. In the last few years, as he matured, he made it his goal to keep this anger locked away, under control. He learned to keep his anger in check, knowing his hot-headedness might get him into trouble one day.

Now though, with this long-legged, bird-like creature blocking his path, he decided it was time to allow the anger to bubble up to the top and spill out. Landon stood, picked up the two rocks and stepped towards the creature.

Clearly agitated, he looked up into its eyes and said sternly, "Gamayun, I demand passage into Mfiri!"

BEGGAR, THIEF, OR KING

AFTER GAMAYUN PREVENTED HIM FROM CROSSING INTO Mfiri Landon's anger flared. His response had the correct effect on the creature towering over him. Rather than reacting with threats, Gamayun leaned her head back and cackled loudly into the air. The sinister laugh did not match the graceful beauty of her face.

The razor, sharp talons extending from her wrinkled fingers retracted slowly. Though angry, Landon was acutely aware his life still hung in the balance. The creature seemed pleased when he had spoken to her forcefully. When he had acted timidly, moving slowly to the side of the bridge, Gamayun had glared at him with hatred. Now, her eyes twinkled with affection.

Landon decided to test it once more, "You dare laugh! I demand you provide me passage into Mfiri." He made the forceful statement with as much anger as he could muster. He stepped forward once more, halting less than a foot from the bridge. He kept his eyes locked onto Gamayun's face. The bird-like feathers bounced up and down as the beast shook with laughter.

She stopped, smiled at Landon, and bowed to him, "Finally, I have someone before me who is not afraid to speak his mind." Her raspy voice, infused with affection caused Landon to smile. She stood back up to her full height and asked Landon. "Tell me young human, is it the beggar, the Prince, the King, or the Emperor who stands before Gamayun?"

Landon's mind raced. The soft, lady-like features of the creature's face did not fool him. This creature was powerful, quick-witted, intelligent, and dangerous. He had only split seconds with which to answer. If he paused too long, he might lose the upper-hand he had gained by his boldness. That advantage might not last long.

Looking into her eyes, he thought, *"She wants me to speak my mind. She does not want me to be afraid of who she is or what she looks like. She wants honesty."*

Landon said without hesitation, "All of them, My Lady. I come as a beggar asking passage into Mfiri. I come as a thief with plans to sneak into Mfiri and steal an item I need if passage is not granted. I come as a Prince, born into the House of Gheldari, the first king of Chondar. I come as a future King, heir to my father's throne of O'ndar. And with luck, someday far into the future, I may become the next Emperor, Chardon II." He smiled widely at her, genuinely happy with his response.

"Well said, young human. May I ask your name?" The hoarse voice had softened, becoming pleasing to Landon's ears.

Landon listened to the huskiness in Gamayun's voice, enthralled. It was not unpleasant. While initially startled, he listened attentively to her every word. He reminded himself once more to be careful with his responses. He considered telling her a different name, but remembered her words about speaking his mind. Landon was sure lying would not be helpful.

"I am Landon," he said, looking into her unblinking eyes once more. The claws remained retracted, which the Prince took as a good sign.

"Aah. Prince Landon, how pleasant it is to have one of the chosen ones standing before me," she said smiling. The twinkle in her eyes offered a genuine fondness. Landon wanted to inquire about her words, but decided to push his question aside. All that mattered was safe-passage into Mfiri.

He looked around Gamayun at the wall of fog. He bowed to Gamayun and said softly, "At your service, My Lady."

Her guttural voice asked, "What is your business in Mfiri?"

Gamayun spread her wings widely, catching the sun's rays. Landon noticed a soft glow beneath the right wing. She saw his eyes and lowered that wing, sheltering whatever it held from his view. She remained fixated, though, on Landon, who remained just outside the bridge.

Landon misunderstood the creature's intentions the moment she spread her wings, saying, "There is no need to block my passage, Gamayun. While I came as a thief I give you my word I will not try to cross the bridge without your permission."

The wide-mouth smiled, exposing sharpened canines. The eyes flickered with delight and Gamayun responded, "It is good you did not try to cross this bridge without my permission. I would have had to pluck out your eyeballs and toss you over the rails into the ravine below. Now, tell me the purpose of your travels to my village."

Landon paused for a few seconds. He was glad he had not tried to enter without Gamayun's permission. She would have done exactly what she threatened. He looked back into her eyes and said, "I am here to see the seven."

Landon decided the best response would be a direct one, getting straight to the point. Qui Oto had directed the Private to give the bottle to the Guardian at the bridge. She must have been referring to Gamayun.

He held his breath. If she reacted angrily, Landon was prepared to run away with the hopes of finding another bridge. If another path happened to be available, he would find it. Otherwise, he would return here and try to kill her before she could slice him in half with her sharpened talons.

He looked up at her trying to examine her face more closely. The large eyes locked onto his face. He knew she was examining him in kind. Gamayun's facial features betrayed no emotions. Earlier, when hidden behind the ball feathers, her eyes had glared at him with anger and hatred. He decided to watch her eyes.

"They will show me how she feels. If angered, her eyes will tell me first."

"The seven is it? And what makes you think you are worthy of meeting the seven?"

"How does a person show worthiness to another?" Landon asked quickly. He froze. The look of anger flashed again in her eyes. *"That was a misstep."*

"I humbly offer my deepest apologies to you beautiful lady. I was rather rash with my question," he offered, smiling at her once again. The anger slowly disappeared from her eyes. Landon exhaled. He had been nervous before, but his anger and his assertive response had won him her affection. When he stated his business to Gamayun, she did not react angrily, even when he told her his plan to sneak into the village to steal. She only became incensed when he had asked his question. *"I wonder?"* he thought.

"May I ask you a question, Gamayun?" Landon asked, watching her eyes closely.

The razor, sharp talons extended quickly from each finger-tip. The hatred and anger flooded back into her eyeballs. Gamayun leaned down closely and said, "I think it is time I…"

Landon mustered all of the displeasure and frustration he could and threw it into his voice. "SILENCE!" he yelled. Gamayun's smile returned and she relaxed. The eyeballs showed no signs of outrage with the way he had spoken. The claws retracted and Gamayun's calm demeanor returned. He had been prepared to make his escape if she tried to snatch him up in her claws.

"Finally, I have someone before me who is not afraid to speak his mind," she responded again. She looked down at Landon and smiled. Her next words were surprising.

"Will you become my husband?" Gamayun asked. The question had come out of nowhere. Landon wore the shock on his face, honestly. He was afraid to answer her. *"I do not want to offend."*

Gamayun chuckled gently the moment Landon's eyes looked into her face and then traveled down the length of her body.

Landon admitted to being caught off-guard. That might have been her intention. He also admitted to himself he was intrigued by her offer. *"How could we be husband and wife?"*

"Shame on you Prince Landon," she said. "There are more ways to consummate a marriage, other than the physical." Gamayun smiled at his discomfort.

"You read my thoughts, Gamayun," Landon responded, making sure to state it matter-of-factly, rather than posing it as a question.

"The males of all species are all alike, especially the humans. Your thoughts mostly are venereal in nature, which makes you the most easily manipulated. Even so, I understand the limitations that would be placed on our relationship, but there are far more pleasures available than those experienced by physical love. I do not say it lightly, young Prince. I want you to know I find you intoxicating and…" she paused, searching for a word, "exotic."

Landon admitted to her, "And I you, Gamayun." The two smiled in unison. "You may be one of the most beautiful women I have ever seen." He offered the words candidly, knowing he did find her beautiful.

Landon thought about her question for a few minutes. He realized he had not given an answer to her offer.

"I will not, My Lady. The offer is most gracious and I must admit I am tempted," Landon responded, forcefully. There was no hint of sarcasm in his voice. *"Why am I tempted?"*

He admitted to being tempted. He continued with his answer, "I am on a quest and must get into Mfiri in order to see the seven." He waited to see if she would be angry with being turned down.

Once again, his assessment and response had been the correct one. Gamayun leaned her head back and laughed aloud. She raised her wings once again, then lowered her them back to her sides. Squatting, she leaned down onto her massive elbows and looked into his eyes. Keeping her body on the bridge, she extended her neck to get closer to him. Landon did not flinch. He kept his eyes locked onto Gamayun's. Her face halted a few inches from his own.

"It would have been a wonderful union, Prince Landon. We could have spent an eternity enjoying each other's company. The discussions we would have had. I admit I am drawn to your dark features. I am captivated by your coal-black eyes, your straight and powerful nose, and your olive hued skin.

"As a wedding gift to you I would have given two things. The first would have been the gift of power. The second would have been the gift of immortality. These are two things which all humans covet, but are always held just beyond your reach. But for you, my love, I would have given them freely," she said. Gamayun smiled once more. At this distance, Landon could see the auburn hair flowing down her face. He smelled her skin, the fragrance intoxicating. He had mistaken the hair on her head for feathers. He felt a pang of guilt for having made the mistake.

Landon wondered if he had made the correct decision. Years ago, he had studied the concept of power and its hidden nature. It was a relative construct, difficult to understand and always elusive. It was difficult to grasp and even more difficult to gain. Power, once gained, inevitably would clash with greater power. Power, for those who sought it, seemed to be elusive even when held in one's hands. Sought after by millions, power always remained evasive. It was intangible, not easily grasped. Though one might have it, or perceive power had finally been achieved, it had its limitations. Some limitations were forced onto those with power by others with more power. Yet, even those with power were constrained to use that power with limited amounts of time. Power was intangible, but the laws of nature were not. Within these laws even those who gained power eventually died. Those with absolute power were never satisfied. Deep down they understood having all the power in the world could never prevent their own death. In the end, those with power paid the final price demanded of all living things. Those with power had the same fate as those without. A man with power always feared death. In fearing death, a man with power ultimately feared life.

Landon looked into her face entranced, *"Has she bewitched me?"* His mind raced. He continued thinking about her offer of power and immorality. The attraction to gaining power was too inviting. In the wrong hands power was dangerous *"It's why the Dragons were angered with Ea's decision to give humans the ability to reason. It gave humans power."*

Gamayun's offer was exciting and enticing. *"Too enticing,"* Landon thought. Power was seductive to all humans, but Landon had come to the belief it was too difficult to hold.

Immortality, though, was a different matter. Out of the two offers, Gamayun's marriage would mean Landon could live forever. He admitted he found her invigorating. His attraction went far beyond a physical one. He had only looked to her body out of curiosity. Nothing more. Nothing less. They would never be able to consummate their marriage. Not in the traditional sense. Yet, as Gamayun had stated, their love would transcend a physical one. They would be soul-mates.

"Maybe I should reconsider. It would be so easy to say yes." His mind raced about the implications of living forever. Gamayun's offer of

immortality tugged at his heart. He was most tempted to look into her large, beautiful blue-green eyes and change his mind.

Landon remembered an argument from his past. He had disagreed, vehemently, with one of his elder tutors when he was just ten years old. The grey-haired man had recently celebrated his day of birth. He entered his nineties, happily. He smiled when off-handedly mentioning to Landon he had earned his rest. It had taken Landon a few minutes to realize the man was saying he looked forward to the day when he lay down and did not wake up.

The Prince was shocked. The thought of losing his tutor, one of his favorites, made Landon cry at the thought of the man passing away. Finally, the young Prince blurted out, "Don't you wish you could live forever?"

"Good lord no, My Prince!" the man responded. Confused, Landon asked him to explain.

Looking into Gamayun's eyes, Landon remembered his teacher's response, and said, "Gamayun, humans are destined to live for no more than one-hundred thirty years. If I were immortal, I would have to live without my family and my friends. I do not want to watch everyone I love die." Thinking of the old man's response had forced Landon to think about Lyssa and his father.

"I could not watch everyone die while I lived forever. Not Lyssa. Not my father." He was puzzled that he had left his mother out of his thoughts. Frowning to himself, Landon looked back at Gamayun. He waited patiently for her to continue.

"So it's the seven you are seeking. An audience with the seven comes with a high price, Prince Landon," she said, pausing to gather her thoughts. "Yes, I have it now. In order to see the seven you must spend the night with the four." The large head bobbed up and down happy with her response. The smile widened.

"Do you understand me? To see the seven you must spend the night with the four," she repeated. She watched Landon closely, waiting for his response. It was clear she would speak no more until he answered her. Landon wanted to ask some clarifying questions. Her words were confusing. He had never been into Mfiri and had no idea who the seven might be. Now, he was being told he could only see them if he spent a night with the four.

"Who are the four? Who are the seven? How do I get into Mfiri?" his thoughts clouded with confusion. He could not ask, otherwise he risked Gamayun's anger. The talons were currently retracted into her fingers, but could flick out in a split second. The sharpened claws could disembowel him more quickly than he could react.

"Would she really kill me just after having professed her love for me?"
"Yes she would."

The large eyes looked at him still inches from his own. Gamayun placed her nose almost against Landon's forehead and inhaled. She smelled him and smiled once more. He looked upward once more into her eyes.

"I accept your conditions," he responded angrily. The bird-like creature, with the face of a beautiful woman, smiled once more.

"Finally," she responded, "a person who is not afraid to speak his mind."

Landon looked up and said, "Let's begin."

PASSAGE

"LET US BEGIN, INDEED," THE BIRD-LIKE CREATURE responded. She chuckled loudly again, stood up to her full height, and spread her wings once more.

"The price of admittance into Mfiri is high. Passage into Mfiri is not. Which would you like to pay first?"

Landon started to respond, but stopped himself. *"There is trickery here. I must be wary. Gamayun is the Guardian. She is the one tasked with guarding this bridge. She is also in charge of refusing admittance to those she determines unworthy. Once inside, how does one leave?"*

"Gamayun," Landon said, angrily, "Tell me the rules of Mfiri." He scowled at her.

The woman's facial features softened for a moment and then hardened, "Your countenance will no longer work on me Young Prince. That part of the game is over. I will tell you what you must know, not because you demand it, but because I am required to do it.

"The passage onto this bridge, across it, and into Mfiri comes with a price. The price across the bridge is set by the Guardian. The price into Mfiri is set by Mfiri. The way out of Mfiri is never a guarantee. It may be too difficult to find, even for a chosen one."

Gamayun continued, "Be warned Prince Landon. Mfiri stands at the threshold to the other worlds. It is a weigh station of sorts. It is a gateway across the Celestial Plane, an entryway into the underworld, and a connection to other dimensions.

"Those who enter Mfiri never leave. They either cross over to the Land of the Dead or remain prisoner, trapped between both worlds.

Mfiri has always been and will always be. Only once has someone escaped from Mfiri without earning his release. He left without my permission.

"An old man tricked Gamayun into giving him passage across this very bridge. He found a witch who had died a hundred years before, but whose soul refused to cross over into the Underworld. In her desperation, she unknowingly gave the old man the spell of freedom. Or she gave it purposefully, hoping to gain some sort of revenge against Gamayun and Mfiri." The Guardian frowned when she saw Landon think about everything he had just been told.

"Do not consider this as an option, though. Gamayun threw the witch into the Underworld, replacing her with another just as wicked. The book of spells has been removed from anyone's control. That way out of Mfiri is eternally blocked."

"Could that have been Ferlynne?" Landon thought. He did not dare broach the subject. Gamayun had been angered when she told him about an escape from Mfiri. Maye she had been hoping to scare him into reconsidering her offer of marriage.

"Why am I going in if there is no way out?" Landon wondered.

"Do you accept these conditions?" she asked.

"I accept your rules," he grumbled. "Tell me the rest."

"Once in Mfiri, you must follow the path. Do not step away from it for any reason or for any moment. Do not stop for anything. Do not touch anyone? If you do you will be trapped in Mfiri, forever," Gamayun explained.

"How will I know how to find my destination?" Landon asked. Gamayun looked at him without responding.

"There is a way out," Landon said.

Gamayun nodded and responded, "All who enter Mfiri have a chance to gain an exit. None, other than the one I mentioned before, have ever done so. Mfiri keeps what it catches."

"I go then Gamayun, to spend the night with the four so I might seek an audience with the seven," Landon said.

"First," she responded, "you must get onto the Bridge. Then you must get across the Bridge, and then you must get off the Bridge. Do you understand?"

Landon nodded.

She continued, "For you *My Love*, the price onto the bridge is the same as the price to cross the bridge. The price off the bridge is a different matter."

He waited patiently. She continued, "Remember one thing, above all. All who enter Mfiri must do so in the same manner they entered this world." She smiled, pleased with her cleverness.

"There is a price to step onto my bridge," Gamayun said. "Are you willing to pay?" Her voice continued to be melodic, deep, husky, and hypnotic.

Landon nodded and said, "Tell me the price to step onto your Bridge, Guardian."

Gamayun's smile broadened. She looked into Landon's eyes and said, "My price for admittance onto Gamayun's Bridge is a sweet kiss from the only man I have ever loved."

Landon returned the smile. Gamayun leaned down closer to Landon's face.

Placing his hands on both sides of her face Landon looked deeply into her eyes. He moved in closely and gave her a gentle, but loving kiss. Her lips were soft and flowery.

The two remained locked in the kiss for more than fifteen seconds. When they parted, Gamayun leaned back and stood up to her full height. She stepped backward three steps allowing Landon to step onto the bridge.

He did so with a little trepidation. He expected the long claws to sweep out from beneath her feathers and slice him in half. Gamayun was true to her word and offered no violence. Landon looked up to her and said, "Come here." He raised his hands, placing them once again on her cheeks. This time, when they kissed, Landon closed his eyes and locked his lips onto hers for more than a full minute. He lovingly caressed her cheeks enjoying the kiss as much as Gamayun.

"I truly am in love with her," Landon thought. The kiss was deep and loving. He mustered all of his emotions and put them into his lips. He smoothed her hair away from her cheeks, tucking the strands behind her ears. Landon felt her happiness. She too, enjoyed the moment. When their lips parted, Landon opened his eyes and looked at her. Gamayun

had shut her eyes during the kiss. They remained shut. Her lips fluttered, pouted, and then she opened her eyes.

"You are my only love," she whispered. "If I could change into human form I would do so in a moment. I would give up all this power. I would give up immortality just to hold you."

"My love," Landon whispered in return. "My love." A tear trickled down his cheek stopping for a moment on his upper lip.

Gamayun shook her head breaking the spell of the second kiss. She took three more steps, backward, disappearing into the fog. "You may cross into the fog. Do not be afraid."

Landon took ten steps and walked into the fog. He almost bumped into Gamayun's large face. She had crouched, waiting for him to walk through the fog. Similar to the second one, it was a full-minute before the lips of the two parted. Once more she backed up three steps. Once more it took Landon ten steps before he caught up to her.

His final step brought him to the end of the bridge. He tried to walk forward, but was met by some invisible barrier. He bounced backward, almost falling. Landon looked to Gamayun confused. She smiled and shrugged her feathered shoulders.

Landon looked at her sternly remembering her words, "The price into Mfiri is set by Mfiri."

"Gamayun, tell me the price into Mfiri," he spoke sternly, but without raising his voice. It saddened him to know they were soul mates, yet they would not spend eternity, together.

"There is a price, my love, for Gamayun to give you that answer." She smiled, leaned in, and closed her eyes once more. Landon was not angered at her response. He felt the love they shared when their lips met. In another time, in another place, they might have become the world's greatest lovers.

Slowly, he reached up and caressed her hair gently. Gamayun opened her eyes and looked into his.

"I do love you, Gamayun," he thought. He leaned in once more, before she could respond, and gave her a final kiss.

Gamayun reminded him, the moment their lips broke contact, "You may only enter Mfiri in the manner in which you entered this world."

She had whispered the last words, still caught up in the euphoria of their kiss.

"In the manner I entered this world? What does it mean?" Landon thought back to his birth, looked at her, and smiled. A wicked smile spread across Gamayun's face. She enjoyed his embarrassment at having figured out the price into Mfiri.

"It is not my rule, young Prince," she said, her features looked mischievous.

It was Landon's turn to shrug. He had decided he would not allow himself to be embarrassed. *"She is a bird, at least most of her. I will not be embarrassed."*

Slowly, he began to undress. After he had taken off all of his clothes and was standing in front of her naked, it was Landon's turn to chastise her. "Remember, Gamayun," he started, noticing her eyes traveling up and down his body, "remember your words about love being more than physical in nature." Gamayun smiled.

"Well said, young Prince. If only I could become human…know I would, in a heartbeat."

Landon waived goodbye to her, turned to step off the bridge, and walked forward. Once again he was met by an invisible barrier. This time he had been walking briskly, hoping to get away from her since he was naked. He bounced off the barrier and fell backwards onto the ground. His legs flew upward into the air as he rolled onto his back.

Gamayun cackled loudly.

"Now I am embarrassed and angry." Landon stood up glowering at Gamayun. She leaned her head back and laughed, enjoying both his embarrassment and his discomfort.

"I have paid the price, Gamayun. I demand you allow me into Mfiri," he said sternly.

"I told you, Prince Landon, the only way into Mfiri is to enter it in the same manner in which you entered this world," she responded. She batted her eyes at him, flirtatiously. He was not amused.

"I know you see me standing naked in front of you. This is the manner in which I entered this world? Tell me where I am mistaken," Landon demanded.

"For a price young Prince. For a price." Landon did not notice Gamayun's facial features harden with her last words. He did not notice that she had become a bird of prey. He closed his eyes waiting for another kiss. He did not look up into the hardened eyes, gleaming at him with wild abandon and hunger.

Gamayun stood up to her full height, leaning over the top of Landon. Eyes closed, he remained oblivious to the change in her demeanor. Stretching her lips open wide, Gamayun's neck extended. She placed her face directly over the top of him. She leaned down and sucked him into her mouth. Startled, Landon struggled, but to no avail. Gamayun stood back up, tilted her head to the sky, and swallowed him whole.

HOLD ME, I'M COLD

LANDON SHUDDERED WITH FEAR THE MOMENT HE realized Gamayun was swallowing him. He tried to grab onto her teeth, but this was difficult since his head and upper torso were inside her mouth, almost touching the back of her throat. He felt the sharpened edge of the tooth cut into his hands, the blood making them slippery.

Landon struggled to prevent himself from sliding down the giant bird's throat. The image of a stork eating a frog flashed in his mind. He had watched the event, when younger, on one of his visits to Lake Windain. He could see the image of the green frog, grasped tightly in the yellow beak. The poor amphibian had squirmed, thrashing its body back and forth hoping to break free. Ultimately, though, despite the best resistance the frog could muster it was only a matter of time before it became the meal. He watched the head of the stork tilt upwards to the sky. The beak darted forward and backward in the air. The bird opened its beak wider, the frog's legs dangling outside its beak. Within seconds, the bird had swallowed the frog.

"I am not a frog!" Landon yelled. His voice echoed down into Gamayun's throat.

"*Please, don't eat me,*" he begged, silently, his body thrashing violently.

Landon's feet squirmed back and forth. He planted them widely on the ground and tried to use them to pull himself out of her mouth. It did not work. Gamayun stood up to her full height and tipped her head backwards. She lifted Landon off the ground, turning him upside down in the process. Both feet stuck upwards pointing towards the sky, he kicked with futility. The rest of his body remained locked inside darkness. Her mouth opened wider, preventing his blood covered hands from holding onto her teeth. Gamayun opened her mouth wider and swallowed. Landon screamed in fear the moment he slid down her throat into complete darkness.

Gamayun's neck muscles contracted forcefully, shoving Landon into her stomach. He gasped for air while screaming in panic. The little amount of available air smelled putrid, and of death and decay. Landon settled into Gamayun's belly with a splash. He landed in a mixture of slime and moisture, the lining of her stomach slippery. Landon rolled over back and forth desperate to stand. His hands and feet thrashed and kicked ferociously. Afraid he would drown in the contents of Gamayun's stomach, he decided to climb his way back up and out of the bird's mouth. He needed to find something he could grab. Shortly though, the lack of oxygen in the cramped space began to take its toll. His nostrils burned with the putrid gases floating around his face. Landon's eyes squinted. The reaction was instinctual. Covered with rancid ooze, he struggled to see anything in the darkness. Slowly, the exertion to keep his mouth and nose above the liquid contents in her stomach took its toll. Landon tried to stand a few times, lost his footing, and sank deep into the muck.

"This is how it ends?" Landon thought. He screamed one last time at the top of his lungs. "Gamayun!" She must have heard his screams since she hopped up and down excitedly, bouncing him up and down, along with the contents of her stomach.

Landon hurriedly gasped for air, became drowsy, and a few seconds later passed out.

Gamayun, patted her belly the moment Landon slid down her throat and landed in her stomach. Like a devoted mother pregnant with child, she caressed her now rounded belly. She smiled lovingly, looking down at her now protruding gut.

Even though Landon could not hear her response, Gamayun said, "You may only enter Mfiri in the manner in which you entered this world." She leaned her head back once more and cawed vociferously.

Keeping her right wing tucked next to her body, Gamayun hopped three times landing away from the bridge. The last hop brought her to the edge of Mfiri. She squatted down, her face grimaced in pain. Gamayun took a few quick breaths, cawed loudly again, pushed, and birthed Landon out naked and cold, onto the hardened ground.

The moment he struck the ground, covered by the slimy contents of Gamayun's gullet, Landon gasped for air. The impact forced him to take a deep breath. He rolled back and forth struggling to get enough oxygen. Eventually, flipping over onto his hands and knees Landon opened his mouth and vomited.

"I hate that god-forsaken bird," he thought. The unchecked fury rose in him again. Landon, still gasping for breath, sat back up on his knees and yelled, "Gamayun, you ate me!" He looked at the creature with hatred. "You ate me!" He repeated, loudly.

Gamayun laughed once more. The glee in her eyes infuriated Landon. "Damn it you wretched bird! I am not some worm to be plucked out of the ground and eaten whole." He spat a raw chunk from his mouth. It tasted of decaying fish.

Gamayun's face grew serious, for a split second, and then she smiled wickedly once more. "You…are a petulant little man," she responded, softly. The silkiness in her voice still soothing when she spoke.

"You wanted to go into Mfiri. You are now in Mfiri. Now you want to complain about the manner in which you entered. You are an ungrateful…a thoughtless… a spoiled little Prince. This is no way to speak to your birth mother," she said, smiling scornfully at him.

"No matter now. Mfiri owns you. There is no escape. There is no reprieve. Only Mfiri will decide if you ever leave Mfiri. Do you understand?" she asked, standing up to her full height.

She hopped back onto the bridge and turned back to look at Landon. He was still on his knees. He glared at her with his hands on his hips. The slime continued to run into his eyes, sliding down from his forehead.

Landon thought about her words. They seemed sincere and alleviated the anger he felt boiling inside. Only a little, though.

"You ate me," he said once more, though more conciliatory.

"Only temporarily, My Love. Besides, you should be thankful I did not do so with the intention of feeding you to my children. Otherwise, you would not have come out in one piece."

Landon, his eyes squinting from the ooze trickling down his cheeks, looked into her face. He found it hideous and revolting. *"How could I have ever been in love with her?"*

"I hate you Gamayun," Landon shouted. "Do you hear? I…hate…you!"

He stood up slowly, his legs shaking from the exertion. The struggle to prevent her from eating him and the effort to survive had made him queasy. Landon feared he might pass out once more. He looked at the Guardian. She frowned back at him shaking her head disapprovingly.

"I am sorry to hear those words my love. For you will always be the love of my life. Go forward now and follow the path leading you to the four. If you survive them, you might get to see the seven. If the four do not choose to kill you or the seven do not choose to eat you, it will be a miracle. They, unlike Gamayun, will not allow you out once you are inside their bellies. Even if you survive, I fear you are destined to remain inside Mfiri for the rest of eternity. My offer of marriage is now rescinded." Gamayun brought her left wing tip up to her mouth, blew Landon a final kiss, turned away, and hobbled back across the bridge, disappearing into the fog.

He spent the next few minutes wiping the remaining residue from his face. He scraped his fingers along his cheeks, shaking them quickly to remove the sticky slime. Without a shirt to wipe off his hands, the process took some effort. Finally, with his eyes clear and his sight returned, Landon looked around at the mysterious village.

Though it was only a few hours past noon, Mfiri was eerily shrouded in the paleness of the evening, when the last moments of light remain just before the arrival of nighttime. It was a gloomy place. The nearby houses were devoid of light. In O'ndar, thousands of candles would have already provided light through the windows a village of this size. Hundreds of lit torches would have already lined the streets.

Earlier, when he stood outside the wall of fog the sun shone brightly. Looking up, Landon could see the same sun, though it was not bright and yellow, but dull and blue. It appeared void of color. The light of Mfiri seemed to be absorbed upward into the sun, rather than the rays shining down into the village. The sun above Mfiri provided little illumination.

The houses in Mfiri were tiny and ill kept. The nearby houses made of sticks and logs had been crammed together haphazardly. Up ahead, some of the houses looked to be more solidly constructed. Some were made of sod bricks and covered with a darkened moss. There were thousands of houses, extending as far as he could see.

Landon had seen the tops of thousands of houses when standing on the hill and looking down into Mfiri. At ground level, he admitted to himself, he had undercounted. There might be tens of thousands of houses.

"Where are all the people?"

Landon whistled. The rows of huts and mud houses went on forever, disappearing into the horizon. The nearest houses were small and looked empty. The village seemed desolate, though Landon doubted it to be the case. Mfiri was dark and foreboding.

Once again, Landon shivered with nervousness. He felt the same apprehension he had felt when meeting the Dragon Arem. This village disquieted him. Mfiri was strange. It was also a place of sadness. He could feel its gloomy aura settling deep inside his bones. The village on the edge of the world would be a lonely place to spend eternity.

"This is the gateway to the Underworld," Landon reminded himself.

If the things Gamayun said were true then Mfiri lived up to its billing. Landon regretted agreeing to travel to this village. *"I do not want to be trapped here forever."*

Landon spotted the only path into the town, off to his right. It was at least four to five feet wide and dark. The glass surface was made of finely crushed obsidian. The surface had been shined to a smooth perfection. He could see his reflection in the surface.

Landon had learned about obsidian, the lava rock, years ago. A tutor had captivated his interest by showing him how to polish the small, black pebble given as a present. It had become one of his most prized possessions.

Though he feigned indifference, the tutor had been patient with him. The man spent a few days showing the Prince how to smooth over the darkened, lava stone. With care and hard work, polished obsidian turned into glass. Landon had been fascinated with the process. The rock had travelled hundreds of miles, from the northern range of the Cargathian Mountains, to find its way into his hands. Slowly, he buffed and smoothed the rock into a shiny bead. Because of his efforts, it became very precious to him. He placed it upon his dresser inside a glass case, back at the castle.

The causeway into Mfiri had been crafted carefully and with care.

"By whom?" he wondered. The pathway would have taken hundreds of years to complete. The obsidian had to be ground into fine pea gravel and then slowly, meticulously, smoothed by hand. The blackness of the obsidian stone stretched as far into the horizon as his eyes could see. He stepped gingerly onto the path expecting the obsidian to be slippery beneath his bare feet. It was not. He enjoyed the coolness of the smoothed, lava rock on his bare feet. Landon sighed with relief. Obsidian, if not polished, could be jagged. Landon felt relief knowing he would not cut his feet.

Up ahead, Landon saw the blackened path split and diverge into three directions, all of which were lined with rows of huts. One direction looked as good as the other.

"Gamayun told me the path would get me to the four. But which direction should I go?"

He decided to follow his gut instinct. He turned right making sure to stay on the path. Knowing Gamayun would not allow him back across the bridge, he decided to quit worrying about its location.

Landon passed between another row of huts made of branches and mud. They were tiny, single-story houses, each dark grey and covered with a layer of dark, green moss. They all had two openings for windows, but no glass. There was a doorway in each, without a door.

Mfiri was a ghost town.

Landon felt eyes peering back at him when he tried to look into the darkened huts. He could not be sure the eyes were human. Once or twice, he saw a set of red eyes in the darkness of the doorways. These eyes disappeared the moment he walked past. Landon refused to look backwards, hoping the owners of the eyes would not follow.

Once again, the path divided. Faced with the same choice as before, Landon refused to go back to where he had already been. Up ahead, the obsidian path continued for more than a mile before coming to a dead end. The end of the pathway stopped directly in front of a large, two-story house made of mud and sticks.

"*Am I going to have to go back?*" he asked himself. It took a few more steps before he realized the path was not a dead end. He had been walking on a slight, uphill slope.

The change in the elevation had been imperceptible. The path also slanted to the left, causing him to see the illusion of a dead end. Landon turned left and picked up his pace, though the hairs on his neck stood on end. Looking into the nearby houses, Landon could see the outlines of hairy creatures in the doorway. Some were human like. Others were not. It was hard to discern what they were. He hoped they would let him pass, unmolested.

When he turned to look away from the creatures, Landon had to slow his pace considerably. A small, round face, chubby child stood beside the right side of the path, less than a hundred feet away. In the semi-darkness, Landon had wrongly thought him a small animal. He continued walking, shortening the distance between the two of them. Landon almost stopped to speak to the child when Gamayun's warning flooded back into his mind. He slowed his pace considerably, though determined he would never completely stop.

"*Keep moving. No matter what happens,*" he thought.

He continued walking, but looked down into the face of the little boy. The child was pitiful. He was no more than four years old, and stood shivering in the cold. His clothing was torn and ragged. His brown hair was dirty and unkempt. His skin was pale-white, almost pasty. The sad looking child covered his eyes with his balled up hands, crying. The child's eyeless sockets looked up at him sobbing. The empty spaces, where the child's eyes should have been, looked sinister. The child looked directly at Landon.

"*How can he see me?*" Landon thought.

"I've lost my mommy and my daddy. Can you help me find them?" the little boy pleaded. He looked miserable. Tears streaked down his face. He took a step closer to Landon, raised his hands up in the air, and gestured for Landon to pick him up. Landon noticed the child avoided stepping onto the path.

"Hold me. I'm cold," the little boy said, sadly. He wrapped his arms around his shoulders for warmth.

Landon's heart melted with pity. Here was the first person he had met in Mfiri. A lost, little boy, standing in the cold and alone. He started to reach down to pick up the little boy, but Gamayun's warning came rushing back to him, once again. Landon lowered his hands back to his sides and said, "I am sorry, I cannot help you." He continued walking, moving past the little boy.

The child wailed louder crying out in despair, "Please Mister, please help me. I am lost and cold. Hold me, please."

Landon looked back to see the little boy walking behind him. The eyeless sockets bore into him. He turned away, picking up his pace. His goosebumps reminded Landon how frightened he was of the little boy.

Up ahead the path branched in two directions. Landon quickly turned to the left. He needed to rid himself of the little boy. He walked a few steps, but almost stopped to turn around to walk back in the other direction. The same little boy stood beside the path, up ahead of him.

"How is this possible?" When Landon had moved to within arms distance the two of them made eye contact. *"He does not have eyes! How can he look at me?"*

Once again, the little boy lifted his hands and said, "My mommy and daddy are dead. Please hold me. I'm cold." This time Landon did not pause. He kept his hands at his sides, forcing his eyes away from the child.

Rather than cry out, the little boy turned and walked beside Landon, keeping pace. His little feet running furiously in order to keep up.

"I said hold me, I am cold!" the four year old bellowed. His yell startled Landon. He almost stepped off the path. Landon refused to look down into the little boy's empty eyes. He kept walking and then started to run.

"He's a demon," Landon thought. He ran for more than two blocks to be sure he had left the little boy far behind. Landon slowed to a walk. He turned at the next right taking the path in a new direction. Landon cursed aloud. The little boy stood, up ahead, waiting for Landon. This time, though, instead of crying, the little boy pointed excitedly at Landon.

"Momma! Momma! This is the mean man who won't hold me!" the boy shrieked, his voice shrill and icy.

Landon looked around to see where the little boy was pointing. A wrinkled, old woman stepped out of one of the darkened doorways, a few houses ahead. She wore a night-blue scarf around her matted down gray hair. He skin too was pale and white. Landon could clearly make out her features even in the dim light. Her nose was long and pointed. Landon could see the warts pocketing her nose and cheeks.

"*She's a witch!*" Landon thought. She was the embodiment of every fairy-tale he had read as a child. Landon was sure this witch gathered, each evening, around a boiling cauldron stirring the contents with her broom.

She glared at Landon, raised a long, bony finger, and pointed at him. Landon shuddered. He saw the two large fangs in her mouth the moment she screeched, "You dare to refuse to hold my son!"

The old woman moved away from her house walking quickly toward the path ahead of Landon. He feared she would try to block his way and force him to stop. Just before she stepped onto the pathway, though, she stopped and turned to stare at Landon.

The moment she stopped beside the path, Landon spotted more movement in the doorways of the next few houses. Tiny figures darted out of the houses and ran quickly to the woman.

"*Five, six, seven.*" Identical copies of the first little boy ran from the houses. "*Eight, nine, ten.*" Landon stopped counting at ten. He was sure there was at least twice that number. They surrounded the woman. All of them stood quietly next to the darkened path. Each of them glared at Landon with hatred the moment he started to pass by them.

They all raised their hands in unison and yelled, "Hold me, I'm cold." Landon moved away from the group to the far side of the path. He avoided stepping off the path, but wanted to avoid accidentally touching them. He continued walking.

One of the little boys hollered loudly at the woman, "Eat him mummy. Can we eat him?" All of them clapped loudly, at the same time, at this suggestion.

Landon refused to make eye contact with any of them. The soulless eye sockets on more than twenty little faces glowered at him from behind. Fearful, he almost turned back to look once more, but then heard her respond. He was glad he had not looked.

"We can't eat him he's poisonous. Let's eat..." She paused for a second and then pointed into the mob of little boys, "Tandro."

The little boy named Tandro squealed, "Noooo!"

He started to run away, trying feverishly to push his way out of the group, but was quickly seized by the other little boys. Laughing in unison at his fear, they picked up Tandro holding him over their heads.

They were all chanting loudly, "Eat him! Eat him!" They carried a screaming Tandro into a darkened house. A few seconds later the screaming stopped.

Landon heard the old woman curse at him once more, but was too far away to know what she had said.

"None of them tried to touch me," he thought. Landon vowed he would never leave the path until he reached his destination.

He walked quickly away, distraught by what he had witnessed. *"What kind of mother eats her own child? Was she the mother?"* Landon doubted it. When the path branched once more to the left, Landon turned and continued walking.

"If I had touched any of them my journey would have ended here. I would have wound up supper in one of those dark houses." Landon hated the guardian for having swallowed him. However, he was grateful for her words of warning. Had he fallen off the path, when startled, the little boys would have pounced, and would have devoured him. They would have carried him kicking and screaming into the darkened house to have him for supper.

Landon walked silently for more than half an hour. His eyes darted into the houses on both sides of the path. They were still dark, but there were no more red eyes peering at him from the blackness. It took a few minutes before Landon noticed the houses had changed.

"When did they change?"

The previous houses had been made of thatch, sticks, and mud. Built of a sturdier material, these solidly built houses had been constructed using clay bricks. The windows and doors were still barren and open. The interior of each house was still dark and menacing.

Once again, when the path branched off in three directions, Landon did not hesitate. He continued straight ahead. After passing another three blocks, Landon once again almost stopped. Up ahead, on the left side of the pathway, walking slowly towards him, was a soldier.

SERGEANT

LANDON IMMEDIATELY RECOGNIZED THE PURPLE UNIFORM worn by the approaching soldier. The man looked angry, his scimitar swaying back and forth which each step. The lavender tunic, distinct to the Zaharian army, was wrinkled and dirty. The shirt neatly tucked into a belt that held both the sword's sheath and the trousers. This large man looked furious. His darkened features contorted into a snarl. Years of living in the southern countries had given his skin a suntanned complexion. He walked quickly towards Landon, cursing silently under his breath.

The distance between the two men closed quickly. The man stopped, but looked startled when he realized Landon was not going to do likewise. Gamayun warned Landon not to stop for anything. He meant to heed her words.

"Greetings to you Sergeant," Landon offered the moment they made eye contact. "It is nice to see a familiar face in this gloomy village." Landon nodded and smiled. He did not feel gleeful, but hoped his mannerisms would help dissuade the angry man from doing anything rash.

"Do I know you?" the Sergeant asked, confused. He turned towards Landon, stepped onto the darkened path, and walked alongside Landon. His broad shoulders spoke of strength and power. His features were those of a man who had spent his life in the military.

It was Landon's turn to be confused. The *demon* children and the witch avoided stepping onto the path. Yet, the Sergeant stepped onto the walkway without hesitating.

"I know of you, indirectly," Landon responded. He watched the man's countenance, closely. The anger and confusion still simmering, but his facial features softened at Landon's greeting.

"Really. How so?" the Sergeant asked. "I have never met you before in my life."

Landon answered, "I know of you, Sergeant, through an old Comrade of yours." He waited for his words to sink in and have an effect. Landon chose his words carefully, not wanting to startle or anger the soldier. The scimitar the man carried at his side could deal death and destruction. Landon, un-armed and naked, did not wish to engage in a fight.

"I am a friend of Captain Arem," Landon continued, looking sideways at the man.

"This man is a warrior. A soldier. He has seen death inflicted in its most barbaric form."

"I am sorry to inform you, sir, Captain Arem is dead. He died on the edge of the Alahari Desert less than ten days ago," The Sergeant looked distraught. "He died and by now has been buried beneath the sands of the desert."

"Less than ten days ago?" thought Landon. Captain Arem had died more than sixteen years ago. The man carried a fresh look of anguish on his face. He was still grieving for his Captain, as if he had recently departed.

Landon thought to cheer the man up, by saying, "He is not dead, Sergeant." He waited for a response, but received none. The Sergeant turned towards Landon, placing his right hand on the hilt of his sword. He slowed for a second, but started walking quickly to catch up when Landon did not stop.

"He is dead, sir. We left him inside a tent, along with the body of a little girl. By now sand covers their corpses. I gave the orders myself less than two weeks ago." He removed his hand from his hilt, but his annoyance returned.

Slowing his pace, Landon offered once again, "I assure you the Captain is alive. I spoke to him two days ago, less than five miles from this spot. Please, walk with me. I cannot stop, but would like to continue our conversation." He gestured with his right hand for the Sergeant to keep pace.

"That is not possible," the Sergeant countered, angrily. "Are you sure it was him?"

"Be assured, Sergeant. Captain Arem is alive. He told me his tale. He also spoke of holding no grudge for the decision to leave him in the desert. The little girl...what was her name again....Opuntia had died, certainly. The Captain had only...passed out." Landon did not feel it a good idea to tell the Sergeant the entire story. "The Captain followed you here, but has been unable to physically enter this village. He asked me to do so, on his behalf."

"The Captain bears no bitterness towards you for your decision," Landon stated honestly. He watched the shoulders of the Sergeant sag in disbelief.

"Alive! He was alive. I should have checked the bodies," the man said, distraught. The agony in his voice cut into Landon deeply. He felt the Sergeant's sadness. Landon purposely slowed his pace hoping the two could talk for a while. He had tired of being alone in this place. The two men walked in silence for more than a minute.

"Where are you from?" the Sergeant asked. "And why are you naked?"

Landon chuckled at the question. He wondered how long it would take the Sergeant to get around to asking. He said, "I am from O'ndar." He looked sideways at the Sergeant, trying to gauge the man's thoughts.

"We were escorting Princess Lenali to your country," the Sergeant exclaimed. He looked excitedly at Landon. "If I find my way out of here I am to re-join the Princess. Otherwise, I can travel back to Istanabad and report to the Sultan. I have always wanted to see the northern countries. I am of a mind to join her." It was the first time he had shown any sign of emotion, other than rage. Landon smiled.

"But, this place is cursed. I have been wandering these streets for hours. There seems to be no way out." The man's statement alarmed Landon.

"Hours! He believes he has been in Mfiri for hours." Landon pointed up ahead to let the Sergeant know which direction they would take.

The Sergeant nodded, but kept talking, "I must admit to some confusion. I am from Istanabad. I am a soldier in the Zaharian military. You are from O'ndar, a country far to the north. How is it we both understand each other? I do not know how to speak your language. Only our officers are trained to speak other languages."

Landon thought about the Sergeant's question. He had not pondered why the two men, from different parts of the world, would be able to understand each other. When he was in the Celestial Plane, observing Captain Arem's past, he was able to understand the Zaharian language because of the magic of the orb. He was no longer in the past, but was sure Mfiri remained connected to the Celestial Plane, somehow.

"My best guess," Landon responded, "is this place holds some type of deep magic. All languages are one, in Mfiri." The Sergeant accepted his words, without argument.

Landon realized he had avoided the question about being naked. There was no acceptable explanation for being gawked at by a lustful, overgrown bird. He did not want to recount the tale.

"How did you come to be in this place, Sergeant?" Landon asked. When Arem had last shown him the Sergeant, the man had thrown the jar containing the Captain's soul. The trooper had run off in search of the Private, whose own horse fled in panic.

"I should not tell you, but I was ordered by the Princess to carry out orders given by the Sultan. As a military man, I am committing treason by divulging my mission. Yet, the strangeness of this place surpasses anything I have ever seen. I will tell you and then maybe, with your help, the two of us can leave this god-forsaken village, once and for all," he said. He looked at Landon and asked, "Is this the reason the Captain has followed me to Mfiri? To ensure I completed the mission?" It was clear the Sergeant had accepted Landon's assurances that Captain Arem was alive.

"My mission takes me in another direction, Sergeant," Landon thought. He thought it better not to divulge the news, just yet. The Sergeant believed his mission had been ordered by the Sultan. Landon, though, was curious about the Sergeant's presence in Mfiri.

According to Gamayun, Mfiri was the gateway to other worlds. Landon was starting to believe it true.

"Please continue," Landon said. He wondered if the Sergeant would include his brief interaction with the black dragon. The Sergeant did not.

"Five days ago, I found a pass up through the mountains. It led the two of us to Mfiri. The journey had been uneventful, for the most part," the Sergeant began.

"The two of you?" Landon asked. He knew the Private had come along, but assumed the man had died since he was not here with the Sergeant. Now he was intrigued.

"Yes. I brought a Private with me. And when I find him, I am going to personally strangle the life out of the coward!" he growled.

"Please continue," Landon said calmly. He looked to the Sergeant. The man lifted both hands, imagining them around someone's neck. The Sergeant lowered his hands and continued.

"We followed a giant wall of fog for a day and a half before finding the only bridge into Mfiri. The bridge, though, is guarded by a giant bird with the face of a woman."

"Gamayun," Landon whispered. The Sergeant nodded in agreement.

"The Private was too frightened and asked me to present a jar to the Guardian. It contained a green-colored liquid. We had been ordered by the Sultan to take it to the creature."

The Sergeant looked into Landon's eyes and looked away. He seemed to be in a daze when he continued, "I stepped forward, bravely stating our purpose. The damned-thing cawed loudly into the air, scaring both of us immensely. I had been tempted to run, but the creature made no overtures against either of us. She offered her outstretched wing, in order to take the container from my hands."

"Why? Why did he do it?" the Sergeant whispered. He mumbled to himself a few other words, which Landon could not hear.

"What did he do, Sergeant?" Landon asked. He could feel the sadness in the Sergeant's voice. He looked back at the man's face hoping to find the answers.

"I need to be patient. The man has been through some trauma," Landon thought.

"When she reached out to take the container from my hands, the Private shoved me from behind and onto the bridge. I stumbled forward into her grasp," he said sadly. His face contorted with anger. "The coward shoved me into the giant bird's clutches. I turned to flee, but she grabbed me from behind and cawed again, loudly. The noise was deafening." The

Sergeant placed his hands over his ears trying to block out the sound of Gamayun's cawing.

He continued with the anguish apparent, "I squirmed to escape her clutches. When she looked into my eyes, I froze in terror. I could not move. Immobile, I watched in horror when the lone claw slowly extended from the tip of a bony finger. She put it against my chest and stabbed me with the razor sharp nail." The Sergeant turned towards Landon and pointed to the hole in his uniform.

It had gone unnoticed by Landon, but he could clearly see the hole in the tunic. Gamayun's talon had poked through the Sergeant's chest, above his heart. Landon was shocked.

"Could it be?" Landon was now certain he understood why the Sergeant had been able to step onto the walkway with him.

"The moment before I was stabbed, I yelled to the Private for help. I pleaded for his assistance. The coward, though, had already mounted his horse and was riding away. The moment the beast skewered me with her talon me I passed out. It must have carried me through the wall of fog and into the village. Eventually, I woke up and have been wandering around this village for more than three hours looking for a way out, every turn more confusing than the one before. I have seen unimaginable creatures and beasts. I have witnessed specters walking on two legs and four. I have heard shrieks of anger and cries of pain. There is agony and suffering in this village. Yet, none of these beings has dared to attack me. My scimitar has kept me safe." The Sergeant patted his hip for assurance.

Landon put his hands to his mouth and gasped aloud. Without stopping, he turned to look into the Sergeant's eyes, *"How do I tell him? It makes sense. The others could not walk the path, but the Sergeant can because he is dead."*

"Sergeant, I met the Guardian at the same bridge. She told me a number of things about this village, which I find useful. Mfiri is a gateway to other worlds," he offered, watching the Sergeant's face.

"It does not surprise me," the Sergeant responded. "This is a strange place. I can feel its aura. I can feel the magic it holds."

"I do not know how to say this delicately, Sergeant, but feel I owe you an explanation because of your allegiance to Captain Arem. I feel I need to be direct and to the point," Landon said, relieved when the Sergeant nodded in agreement.

"Would you be offended if I am blatantly direct and to the point, no matter how shocking it might be?"

The Sergeant seemed relieved, saying, "I would prefer it. Three hours in this place is long enough. If being direct helps me leave here more quickly, please be direct."

Landon thought for a few seconds and began, "Sergeant, time in Mfiri is not the same as time outside Mfiri. Mfiri is a gateway to other worlds. It is also a gateway to the Underworld. It is a gateway to the Afterlife. Time in Mfiri is just not the same." He saw a look of puzzlement on the Sergeant's face and realized he had taken the wrong approach.

"I am afraid to tell him the truth. Would I want someone to tell me?"

"Let me try again," Landon offered. "Sergeant, you feel you have been in Mfiri for three to four hours. However, it is not the case. You have been walking inside Mfiri for almost seventeen years."

This time the Sergeant did stop. Landon continued walking, but slowed his pace. The distance between the two had grown to almost one-hundred feet before the Sergeant began walking again. Landon looked back to see the Sergeant trotting to catch up. The man held his hand on his sword to keep it from bouncing while he ran. He did not look angry. He did not look confused.

When he was once again walking beside Landon, he responded, "What you say is not possible. I have been here for only a few hours. If I have been here for more than sixteen years, how is it you know of Captain Arem? Also, how would you and I be speaking together if this were the case?" The Sergeant glared at him. The anger had returned.

Landon shrugged, "Sergeant, when you were pushed into Gamayun by the Private you said she stabbed you with one of her claws. Correct?"

The Sergeant answered, "Yes. She must have carried me into this village, afterwards, and dropped me." He looked to Landon for acknowledgement.

"She never brought you into Mfiri, Sergeant. I believe Gamayun ate you and fed you to her children." He remembered her admonition about Landon needing to show gratitude.

"I am grateful," he thought.

Landon expected the man to scream at him. He expected an argument from the Sergeant, but received neither.

"You are wrong," the Sergeant responded. "The hideous creature carried me into the middle of this god-forsaken village and left me here. I have been here for hours trying to find my way out. It has been to no avail." He shook his head.

The Sergeant continued, speaking softly, "I am sorry we ever met. I mean no offense, but I regret I agreed to walk beside you. This has been a waste of time and effort. I do not believe you have met Captain Arem." He paused to collect his thoughts. "I think maybe you are the ghost. You are some type of apparition sent to torture and harangue me."

The Sergeant turned away, and without saying another word, began walking in the opposite direction.

Landon's mind reeled with pity, *"That poor man. He is lost. A forgotten soul. I wanted to suggest he try to make it to the gateway to the Underworld. At least there, he would not wander eternity in solitude. I fear the Sergeant is destined to range the streets of Mfiri until the end of time."*

Landon did not look back to see if the Sergeant had changed his mind. He had not noticed the houses of Mfiri once again had changed. They were now more solidly constructed. They reminded him of the houses of the merchants of O'ndar, though not as large. Each constructed of sturdy materials, lacked windows and doors, with the interiors dark and desolate.

Before meeting the Sergeant, the Prince was sure he had been walking the darkened path for more than two hours. The Sergeant's lack of an understanding of time made Landon second-guess his own time in Mfiri.

"Maybe I have been here for years. Am I dead? Did I die in Gamayun's stomach? Did she feed me to her children? Am I now a lost soul destined to search for a way out until the end of time?"

Turning left, Landon's fears heightened. A darkened castle loomed on the horizon. It was nestled at the end of Mfiri, carved into the mountainside. Even at this distance, more than a mile away, the massive castle towered above the houses of the village. The blackened-stone, formed into giant bricks and mortared into thick walls absorbed all the light emanating from the bluish sun. There were massive stained-glass windows, each well lit. Hundreds of flickering torches lined the ramparts.

Even at this distance, Landon could see the people walking into the castle. He was too far away to make an accurate assessment of them. There were hundreds of them. Each person moved slowly, plodding along in silence. No one spoke. No one turned to look at the others. Each walked towards the raised portcullis. As they entered, none looked back. Each person glided across the pathway in solitude. Landon became afraid.

"*That is a dangerous place,*" Landon assured himself. His gut told him to avoid the castle. He decided to circumvent it at all costs, even if it meant turning around and going back.

"The Lord of this dark castle would never let me leave," he thought. The hairs on Landon's neck stood on end. He shivered with fear, but continued along the path leading to the castle. He made a commitment earlier to follow his instinct. Landon knew he needed to turn away. When the next opportunity came, he changed direction, moving off to the right. Landon's new direction ran him parallel to the giant citadel, but turned him back east. He was less than a fourth of a mile away from the fortress, happy to be heading in another direction.

At this distance, Landon could hear horrible screams emanating from the black fortress. Someone within was being tortured. It took a few seconds to realize the screams were coming from many voices. There were hundreds, if not thousands of voices, screaming in pain. Landon shuddered once again. He covered his ears with the palms of his hands and walked onward. Picking up his pace, he hoped to put some distance between himself and the pitch-black castle. After a few blocks, the castle finally disappeared from his sight. The shrieks of agony no longer carried to his ears.

"*I will not turn in its direction, again! The castle has to be the gateway to the Underworld. It is no wonder the Sergeant has walked these streets, refusing to find the Gateway. Entering it would be tragic. There is no way back from that place.*"

Landon asked himself, "What is on the other side?" He pushed the question aside and continued walking. He felt temptation tugging at his heart. A small part of him wanted to return and enter the castle.

"*Maybe I am truly dead.*"

The path branched off, once again, into two directions. Landon turned to the right, hoping to put more distance between himself and the Stygian Castle.

"*I will not be prisoner to the Lord of the Black Castle,*" he thought. He might have mumbled it aloud, but could not be sure.

When he came out of his reverie, Landon reacted, completely startled.

This time, Landon almost made the mistake of dropping to one knee, out of instinct, in supplication. Had he done so, he would have stopped, resulting in his being trapped forever in this cursed place.

Standing before him and blocking his path, less than fifty feet away, was a white Dragon.

THE ORIGINAL TITAN

"YOUR MAJESTY," LANDON SAID AS DEFERENTIALLY AS possible. He bowed low, keeping his head and eyes up to maintain his footing on the path. He continued walking, fully aware he would, in less than a minute, walk into the Dragon, straddling the pathway. Its large talons glistened in the waning light. Her massive paws placed on either side of the causeway, the majestic looking dragon with the ice-blue eyes waited for Landon to approach.

He felt foolish bowing to the Dragon, since it was no more than ten feet tall. Yet, instinct told him this was no ordinary Dragon. *"Nothing in Mfiri is ordinary."*

Landon sized her up quickly. The beast was an armored-plated weapon, with thick, plate-like scales fastened in rows like chinks of armor down its back and sides. Long, ivory teeth poked out from between its upper and lower jaws.

"But how is this possible?" he wondered. He knew, from his readings, that all dragons were born the same ebony color. Newly hatched Dragons retained this color until they were much older. The Dragons would change color once they were able to hatch their first clutch of eggs. Yet, standing before him was an ivory-white Dragon, no taller than the height of two horses. It could be no more than five years of age.

The ice-blue eyes bore into him with a wild ferocity. Even with its diminished size, Landon was well aware the Dragon could destroy him at whim. Here was a danger against which he was powerless. He had never seen a Northern Ice-Dragon. Yet the power and grace of the animal, even at this diminished size, was apparent. The Dragon

Arem had been coal-black, sleek though athletic in nature. The Dragon standing in front of him had a muscular, thick frame. It was robust and solid.

"*Until recently, I have never seen any Dragon,*" he reminded himself. The sketches of Dragons, drawn by the greatest artists in the lands did a dis-service to the thunderous vitality these beasts held when viewed in person.

Landon slowed his pace, wanting to avoid coming to a halt. The distance between the two was shrinking and unless it moved away from the path, he would have to crawl beneath it. The Prince did not relish the idea of placing himself beneath this snow-white beast.

When less than ten feet from the Dragon Landon called out, "Excuse me, My Lady. I am on a quest and am not allowed to stop." He was pleasantly surprised when the Dragon moved out of his way to let him pass. He suspected the Dragon would reach out and snatch him away from the pathway the moment he tried to pass, but instead she turned to walk beside him.

The deep, resonating voice spoke, "Welcome to Mfiri, Prince Landon of the House Gheldari." The voice was intoxicating. It reminded Landon of rumbling thunder following bolts of lightning during a storm. Her voice was compelling. Here was a voice accustomed to command. It was vigorous and forceful, yet calming and warm.

The Dragon had called him by name. In another place, Landon might have been caught off-guard by this. In Mfiri, it did not surprise Landon to have the Dragon refer to him by name.

"*I will never again be surprised by anything,*" Landon thought.

He asked the Dragon, "May I have your name, My Lady?" Pelinnedes used the same approach, a thousand years ago, when conversing with the Dragon Meeha.

"I am Norduir," the Dragon replied. Her powerful frame sauntered alongside Landon.

Landon had not been expecting this response. He declared, "I must confess to being somewhat surprised to hear this, My Lady." Landon looked deeply into the ice-blue eyes, but could not hold the gaze long. He had no way of knowing if the Dragon offered her name truthfully.

"Norduir is the original Titan. She is one of the three daughters of Ea. If you are Norduir, how is it you are here, My Lady?" Landon added the 'My Lady' only after realizing he had questioned the Dragon's veracity.

"Careful," he thought.

"It is the truth I speak to you Prince Landon. While humans peddle honesty and lies without a care about the difference between each, the Dragon Race places a value on one over the other. Rest assured, a Dragon always speaks truthfully to man. When a man lies, he does so out of fear. Dragons have nothing to fear from man and therefore have no reason to be dishonest," she proclaimed.

Landon responded, without thinking, "Is this why the Dragon Race warred on each other? Stealing orbs from one another as if they were candy to be taken from a babe?" Without thinking, the words had flown from his lips, like a bird in flight. Her words angered him. She judged humankind too harshly. He should have thought out his words, though, before responding. He regretted his impulsiveness, but knew he could not take back his statement.

The Dragon roared with laughter at Landon's insult, "Well said, my young Prince. Well said." Landon expected anger, but instead the Dragon seemed pleased.

"I am Norduir; of this you can be assured," she promised. The Dragon looked down at Landon, watching as he sized her up with his eyes. His puzzled expression was clear to read.

Landon spoke, "I must admit to confusion, My Lady. Norduir, who is the original Titan, has always been described as a massive, almost castle-sized Dragon. If the legends are true and are to be believed." He looked once more to her feet and shrugged. His gesture was not lost on her.

"I am Norduir, Prince Landon. The magic of this evil place has bound me into the size and form, you see before you. Mfiri's magic is powerful. It is more powerful than I had suspected. Had I known this, even I would have avoided traveling to Mfiri," she explained with a look of sadness in her blue eyes.

Landon was shocked to think Mfiri held magic more powerful than an original Titan. He apologized saying, "I am sorry, My Lady. I should have never doubted." Landon looked up ahead to see the obsidian pathway branching into three directions. He wanted to turn left, but the Dragon stopped him.

"The place you seek is on the edge of the village of Mfiri, directly to the north," she said. "It is nestled against the Cargathian Mountains and lies straight ahead. If we keep walking, you should arrive within the hour. The Dragon's sincerity well received, Landon nodded his thanks.

The white beast said, "I have scoured this entire village and have traversed every pathway hundreds of times. The darkened citadel is located at the western edge. The Lord of the Castle and I have had words numerous times. I have threatened to tear down his walls, but to no avail. He will not let me pass through. The blackened towers carved into the mountains stand as a beacon to the dead. The Master of that place is Sentinel to the Underworld and to the Afterlife. Its purpose is very different for Dragons, though.

"The area you seek is the furthest point north of the village. It lies just before the highest peaks found in all of the Cargathian Mountains. The bridge, the one guarded by a cursed bird lies on the eastern edge. The southern border has a ravine bounded by a wall of fog." Norduir finished her explanation and listened patiently to Landon's questions.

"How did you come to be here, mighty Norduir?" Landon asked. He was genuinely curious about her presence in this mysterious village. Landon realized Norduir had been the reason the Dragon Arem refused to come any closer. While Arem was far larger than this Ice-Dragon, Norduir's age and power were such Landon knew she could have destroyed the black Dragon with ease.

The Dragon looked downward into Landon's eyes and answered, "It is a tale, to be sure. I will tell you, Prince Landon, with as heavy a heart as a Dragon may have."

She lifted her head, looking away into the mountain peaks and said, "More than six-hundred years ago, a Dark Wizard discovered a pass through the Cargathian Mountains. The pass connected our lands to the Land of the Khans. He entered our lands searching for Dragons. My sisters and I had forbidden any of our children to fly across the mountains, into the Lands of the Khans. This wizard, though, came across in search of our daughters."

Landon could not be sure she referred to 'our lands" as the lands of the Dragons or as all the territories of man. He did not interrupt to ask.

"He made the crossing into our lands stealthily. There are no Dragons in the Lands of the Khans, but the knowledge of Dragons exists," Norduir said. "This evil wizard sought to harness the power given to us by our mother Ea. His sole intention was to steal the power of the orbs. His name was..."

"Jochi!" Landon blurted out, his excitement evident. He shrugged, embarrassed at his outburst.

"My apologies, My Lady," he offered. His cheeks reddened.

"Accepted, young Prince. You are correct. The Dark Wizard's name was Jochi. I understand the black Dragon has given you some knowledge of our past. I do not know whether to be thankful or offended."

Landon listened silently. He was aware of the hidden threat made by Norduir toward the Dragon Arem. *"I must be careful,"* he thought. He did not want Norduir, who might someday escape, to seek out and kill Arem. Landon did not question how Norduir knew of Arem. The power of the original Titan was unequalled in the world.

He walked silently, hoping she would continue. She did saying, "Using his dark magic, Jochi enthralled many of the younger dragons in order to steal their orbs. Originally, most of this had gone unnoticed by my sisters and me. The enslavement of our daughters soon caught our attention, though.

"It was Pahaida who first encountered this warlock from across the mountains. She joined battle immediately and was defeated, though not easily. She fled into the Pyraddine Forests seeking refuge with Bosque and hoping to heal her wounds. Jochi grew more brazen as his power grew. He enslaved more Dragons and stole more orbs.

"Once healed, Pahaida joined forces with Bosque hoping their combined strength would be enough to vanquish Jochi. Once again, the powerful mage was victorious.

"The two had followed their hearts instead of their heads. My sisters avoided seeking me out because of their misguided anger towards me. In doing so, their reckless efforts almost led to their destruction."

Norduir paused, thinking about her sisters and added, "I must admit I almost refused their pleas, but changed my mind when I realized three of my orbs had been stolen. Jochi sent one of my daughters to enter my lair and steal my orbs. In my rage, I helped track down the wizard and the battle was joined. He had grown very powerful, buoyed by the knowledge gained from our orbs.

"It was the most ferocious battle in the history of the world. We three Titans were gravely, though not mortally, wounded. Yet, with the blessing of Ea, we maimed the Dark Wizard. We vanquished Jochi in the field of battle. He abandoned the Dragons he had enslaved and fled back across the mountains, without any of the orbs.

"Though wounded, Pahaida used her might to close the mountain pass once and for all. My sisters returned to their lairs, seeking shelter to recover from their wounds. I though…I followed one of my lost orbs here. Or, so I thought. The trail left by Jochi led to Mfiri. I should have realized the trickery afoot. He was a wicked, little thing, not of the human race. He was a danger to our race and a danger to the world.

"I now know three orbs went with Jochi into the Lands of the Khans. He was gravely injured during our battle, though I do not know if mortally. If any of his descendants gained his knowledge of our orbs, they remain a danger to the world and the Dragon Race is in peril. My only hope is he died from his wounds before unlocking the power of my orbs. Yet, I fear his return and suspect he has begun frantically searching in the Lands of the Khans for the babe destined to be born a King. Jochi, or his offspring, cannot rule the Khanates, but if he finds a warrior powerful enough to unite the clans, they could become an overwhelming military force.

"I did not realize the orb I sought was not here. I used all of my powers to try to enter this accursed place. I tried to fly into Mfiri from above only to be repulsed. I froze the wall of fog. Then I tried to fly through it, but I was repulsed. I used every ounce of magic to cast spells. Nothing gained me access. It was all in vain. I could not enter Mfiri.

"Finally, I found the one entrance into Mfiri. A giant bird-like creature, with the face of a woman, met me. Before meeting her, I assumed there was nothing larger than the three Titans of Ea. The universe is always full of surprises. The creature towered above me. She showed no fear of me, even laughing at my threats. She agreed to let me enter Mfiri, but only on her own terms.

"I had not realized she literally wanted to devour me. And then, she laid me onto the ground, a Dragon egg."

"You mean as an orb," Landon corrected.

Norduir chuckled, "Ah, yes. I had forgotten Meeha broke the Covenant of Ea. She gave your House the hidden knowledge of the Dragon race."

"Yes, I plopped onto the ground. Laid as an orb and rolled into Mfiri. While the number of years it takes to hatch and grow has been shortened by the magic of this place, I spent many years first as an orb, and then many years as an egg, and then many years as a hatchling. Luckily, the creature had placed me in the middle of the pathway. This prevented the residents of Mfiri from scooping me up and having me for breakfast."

The Dragon spoke sternly, her voice rumbling with power, "I have been in this accursed place, without any way to escape, for six-hundred years. The magic of Mfiri has kept me from growing any larger. Try as I might, I cannot use my powers to escape. I am a prisoner in Mfiri."

Landon listened with fascination, Norduir, the original Titan, held prisoner in Mfiri, the most damned place on the planet. If the power of Norduir could not help the mighty Dragon escape, Landon feared what it meant for his own fate.

"My Lady, I know why you are a prisoner in Mfiri," Landon stated matter-of-factly. He watched to see Norduir's response. Landon had listened carefully to her words. He hoped he could offer her some solace.

"Please elaborate, Prince Landon."

"You came to Mfiri on a quest to recover one of your orbs. Gamayun told me the rules of Mfiri. Only Mfiri can let you out of Mfiri. The only chance of escape is through completing your quest successfully. By doing so, Mfiri may choose to release you. At least, this is what I suspect," he explained.

The white Dragon listened attentively to Landon's explanation. She seemed intrigued.

He was convinced Norduir must find her orb in order to escape. He told her, "Also, you are incorrect about your orbs. One of them is here, though it is not in Mfiri. It is held at the gate by Gamayun the guardian." He watched the anger boil up in Norduir. The Dragon tilted its head to the sky and breathed an ice-blue flame that extended more than thirty feet into the air above her. The flames looked hot; though Landon knew, they were ice-cold. They would instantly freeze anything they might touch.

"Are your certain of this?" the Titan asked. The deep, resonating voice thundered loudly.

He nodded, "I did not suspect it until I heard your explanation. When I met her at the bridge, she hid something beneath one of her wings. It glowed softly. It reminded me of the orbs I have seen…in another place." His explanation trailed off. Landon did not wish to put Arem in more danger.

"Be at peace, My Prince. I have no anger, nor ill will toward Captain Arem. If I had wanted to, I could have killed him, even from within the confines of Mfiri. It would have only taken a word from my lips," Norduir proclaimed.

Landon exhaled softly. He had been holding his breath. The most powerful Titan in the history of the Dragon race knew of his quest and knew of Captain Arem.

Is it possible? With one word? Landon remembered Norduir's assertion about a Dragon and honesty. He was sure she spoke the truth. He was happy she decided Captain Arem was not a threat. He hated to bring up more bad news, but felt he should do so out of obligation to the Titan. Landon continued, "I feel a necessity to tell you the fate of your daughter Norfuir." Landon explained the feat of Chardon I, who had defeated Norfuir in battle. It was hard to imagine it had been six-hundred years ago. Landon knew why Norduir had not come to revenge the death of her daughter. He expected rage from the Titan, but there was none.

"Norfuir's demise saddens me to be sure. Yet, I cannot hold the House of Gheldari responsible. My sister chose well when she chose to break the Covenant of the Dragon Race," the Dragon said. "She did so out of a misplaced anger towards me. Yet, I can sense something in you that is honorable and courageous. Yes, Bosque has chosen well."

Her words confused Landon, "My Lady, it was not your sister Bosque, but her daughter Meeha."

Norduir responded, "Yes. It may have been Meeha. However, no Dragon would make such a decision without the approval of one of the three daughters of Ea. If Meeha was the messenger, Bosque would have given her approval. I am happy she chose your House."

Landon blushed at the compliment paid by Norduir. The most powerful Dragon in the world walked beside him, a prisoner. He was aware she honored him by doing so. Landon could see the flicker of a campfire up ahead. The sun had settled behind the mountain peaks and darkness was at hand. The whiteness of the Dragon stood out in the starlight. Landon could see the ice-blue eyes even in the pitch of night.

"I am on a quest, too, My Queen," Landon said. "Yet, I make a promise to you. If successful, I will someday return and free you from your prison. I will never break my oath, as long as I am living." He waited for the Titan to respond.

The two were less than one-hundred yards away from the campfire. It burned brightly in the night. He turned to say something again, but the Dragon had gone. He could not remember when she had turned away. He did not know how long he had walked alone. Landon hoped she heard his oath. He had not made it lightly.

The campfire burned brightly on the far end of a fifty-meter wide flattened area beneath a large, stone archway. The large gateway, with brown stone abutments, had been hand-laid and mortared with care. The arch ring, also made of stone, was more than twenty feet across.

Landon was thankful for the heat and the light coming from the campfire. He looked up confused by the constellation of stars above. None of them looked familiar.

Beyond the fire, the obsidian pathway continued up into the mountains, though it branched off into five different directions, each pathway trailing upward and away into the peaks.

Exhausted, Landon sat down and crossed his legs. He lifted his hands feeling relieved by the warmth. The fire, at least, was something welcoming in Mfiri. He listened to the quietness of the night in solitude. Once or twice, Landon fell asleep sitting up. His chin came to rest on his chest.

The third time this happened, Landon lifted his head. His eyes snapped open. Just outside the gate, only a few feet away, sat a rider on a horse.

A NIGHT WITH THE HORSEMEN

LANDON HELD HIS BREATH, HOPING THE GIANT RED-skinned warrior sitting astride the crimson-colored war-horse was only a figment of his imagination. For a few seconds he thought he might still be asleep, though each time he blinked the warrior and the stallion remained standing silently before him.

"*Am I asleep or awake?*" he asked himself. The exhaustion he felt was real. "*Was this behemoth real, too?*"

Landon had mistakenly taken the massive brute looming before him for a creature out of legend. Standing before the stone archway, the giant creature waited silently, watching Landon with intensity. Landon's mind played its trick, making him think the creature had the torso of a man and the body of a horse. The beast, staring silently at him, from across the flames, looked almost as tall as Gamayun.

After his eyes adjusted, he realized he had been incorrect. "*Fear will cause mistakes. And I cannot afford to make mistakes.*"

In his dreariness, Landon had mistaken the two of them for a mythical creature he had read about when a child. In his tales of other lands, he had read about a beast called a Centaur. It would not have surprised him to find this type of monster residing in Mfiri, but the warrior before him was just a man riding a horse. He was a giant of a man, to be sure, but still a man. Landon blinked one more time trying to drive the fatigue from his eyes. The warrior and his steed remained motionless.

Both the man and the horse were stained blood red. The massive, red stallion snorted into the cold, night air, giant billows of steam floating around its face, masking the large, dark eyes from Landon's sight.

Frozen in terror the moment the warrior appeared, Landon was also too exhausted to move. The Prince did not have the energy to stand and run or to stand and fight. Landon decided to wait for the warrior to make the first move.

Thus far, everything in Mfiri had changed his perception of what he knew about the world. He was beginning to despise this quest, forced on him by his sister and the Dragon Arem.

He hated Mfiri. It was a dreadful place. If he ever made it out, he swore an oath as future king he would be reticent about all he witnessed. He would make decisions for the betterment of his subjects. *"No one will suffer in a place like Mfiri,"* he promised. *"This place is maddening. It is Hell!"* If he had wondered about the dangers still facing him he could see one of them before him. He sat quietly, waiting for the mounted warrior to speak.

The flames of the campfire flickered brightly, casting long shadows behind the rider and the ruby-colored steed. The shadows bounced up and away, disappearing into the rocky outcroppings. The man had not spoken, but continued to sit high in the saddle staring at Landon. The warrior's eyes scanned the nearby houses for danger. He was wary and on edge, making him dangerous. Across his broad back, the warrior had slung a large, double-edged battle axe.

"That axe has seen battle. And just recently," Landon thought. He could see fresh blood on the worn metal of the axe-head.

The warrior wore a sheathed sword at his side. It lay across his left thigh, easily within reach. A leather helmet, with a dark metal band, covered his head. Upward facing ivory fangs had been mounted on the outside of the helmet, just above his brow. The man was broad chested and muscular. His strapping arms rippled with muscles when he leaned in and whispered quietly to his horse. Wearing the skin of a black wolf draped over both of his shoulders, his trimmed leather breeches rested at his thighs. His red-stained legs were muscular. Landon wondered about the dark-red war paint, thinking it might be blood. The man was powerful and dangerous.

Without standing, Landon gestured toward the campfire with his left-hand. He nodded to the warrior. Neither had spoken. Silence hung in the air. Periodically, the horse snorted loudly, breaking the silence. Landon studied the two of them with fascination. The horse was massive, at least ten hands taller than any horse he had ever seen. Its red-stained haunches were muscular and rippled in the campfire light. It was a Warhorse; the long scars on its sides proof. This horse had known battle and carried almost as many scars on its frame as the warrior carried across his chest and arms.

The warrior hesitated for a few more seconds. He slowly dismounted. Standing, he was almost as tall as the horse. He released the reins of the stallion and walked over to the campfire. The fighter scanned the area around them before stopping just on the other side of the fire. Landon had not moved and remained sitting with his legs crossed. Both hands rested on his thighs. His embarrassment about being naked had long since dissipated. He looked up into the dark, brown eyes. Long, black hair thickly braided stretched down past the warrior's shoulders. This was a fighting man, ready for combat if needed.

Slowly, without taking his eyes off Landon's face, the warrior unslung his battle axe and held the handle in both hands. The downward pointed axe-blade dripped with fresh blood. He opened his mouth and smiled at Landon, his pearl-white teeth glistening in the light. The eyes were wide and a look of glee shone on his features. Without a sound, the warrior raised the battle-axe high above his head. He stepped closer to the campfire and with one sweeping arc brought it down with force to smash into Landon's skull. The blow would have split Landon's head into two. His brains would have been crushed. Death would have been instantaneous. Landon did not flinch. His eyes remained locked onto the warrior's eyes.

The blade of the battle-axe stopped less than a fraction of an inch from Landon's forehead. He did not flinch. The warrior's muscular arms lifted the axe away from his face. He looked back to his horse nodding with pleasure. The horse whinnied in response and walked closer to the warmth of the campfire. The red-skinned warrior moved to the other side of the campfire, sat down, and nodded with admiration to Landon.

Landon returned the nod.

"How did you know I would not kill you?" the Warrior demanded. His voice strong and commanding. He too sat cross-legged. He gingerly placed the battle-axe across his thighs, cradling it the way a mother cradles her babe, his left thumb slowly caressing the blood-covered blade. He looked to Landon for a response. Releasing the axe, the warrior lifted both hands and warmed them by the fire. Landon looked at the deep callouses across the palms. The man waited silently. It was a full-minute before Landon answered him.

"I did not know you would not kill me, great warrior," the Prince responded. His voice did not waiver. Landon, too exhausted to move, did not tell this to the fighter sitting before him. "If you were here to kill me, you might have killed me. Though, I might have taken your axe and used it to crush in your skull, instead." Landon, shaking on the inside, was proud of his response.

"Well spoken," the painted man retorted. He looked to Landon and asked, "Why do you have no clothes?" He glanced downward at Landon and then returned his gaze to Landon's eyes.

"It is a tale not worth telling," Landon responded. He watched as the man stood and returned to his horse, reaching into the well-worn saddle-bag and pulling out a pair of breeches. He brought them back to the fire and tossed them over to Landon.

"Those will not fit me, warrior," Landon started to say. The man was at least a foot taller than Landon. He doubted anything the warrior wore would fit him.

"Be at ease, young King. I took these from a man I killed three nights hence," the warrior responded. The moment the warrior tossed Landon the cloth trousers, he turned and walked back over to the horse. He reached into his saddlebag retrieving a pouch of water. By the time he had returned, Landon had put on the pants and sat again cross-legged in front of the campfire. The pants fit perfectly. He was grateful to have them and said as much to the warrior.

"I must admit, I doubted the Guardian's words when I first laid eyes on you, lad. I mean no offense." He looked at Landon and continued, "When I battled my way into this accursed village she told me I would find the only man capable of besting me in one-on-one combat. If neither of us killed the other, I was to tell him my story. If he finds me worthy, he will point out the pathway that will lead me to my destiny."

The man gestured with his thumb over his shoulder, "One of the five pathways before us is safe for me to follow. Only one. The other four will end in my death."

"When you battled your way in?" Landon asked.

The warrior ignored Landon's question. He said, "When I found you sitting here naked, I must admit for the first time in my life I was afraid. I found a naked warrior sitting quietly before me. You sat without a weapon. Yet, you battled your way into Mfiri by defeating the Guardian. I have never been bested in one-on-one combat. When the guardian challenged me to enter Mfiri the way I entered the world, I unslung my battle axe and charged. We entered combat on the bridge, battling back and forth for more than an hour. She was relentless. Her talons sharp as my axe and twice as strong. The nicks on the blade are from the Guardian's unbreakable claws." He paused, continuing to size up Landon.

"Slowly, with my muscles nearing the end of their reserves, I forced her backward and off the bridge. My horse followed and we made it onto the blackened pathway."

Landon listened in awe. He had entered Mfiri only after Gamayun swallowed him and had birthed him onto the ground. This red-painted warrior, and his similarly adorned horse, had entered Mfiri by defeating Gamayun in battle.

"I would have liked to have witnessed their battle," Landon thought. He decided it best not to mention the manner in which he had entered Mfiri.

"Before entering the village, the Guardian warned me I must seek out the greatest swordsman on this side of the Cargathian Mountains. Only he can determine if I am worthy to continue on with my quest." He turned and pointed to the paths leading in different directions up into the mountains. "As I have already said, one of them offers me a chance to fulfill my destiny. Yet only one will do so. The other four offer nothing, but peril."

Landon held his breath. He looked past the warrior at the blackened paths leading into the darkness and up the mountains. They twisted back and forth, winding their way up higher into the peaks. He waited for the warrior to continue.

The man said, "When I arrived here and spied you sitting, cross-legged and naked, fear found its way into my heart. You must be a powerful warrior to gain access to this place without a weapon. What say you?" The man fell into silence, waiting for his words to have an effect.

Landon ignored the warrior's request for an answer. He asked, "What is it you seek through the Mountains?"

The man waited a few seconds before responding, "My brothers and I seek a passageway into the Lands of the Khans. War is coming. A powerful Khan will soon be born. He will attempt to unite the Lands into one, hoping to increase his strength and wield the bloodthirsty warriors to conquer the world. To do this takes cunning and power. His efforts have not gone unnoticed by the four of us. We would like to join him and help lead his armies into battle. Whenever there are armies in combat, the four of us are not far behind. Oftentimes, we arrive before the armies and slay all those on the field."

"He is overly confident of their abilities. Slaying whole armies with just four warriors. Impossible!"

The warrior started to continue, but paused to listen to some far away wolves howling into the night. Smiling, the Warrior said, "Ah. Now there are some wolves not afraid to howl." The warrior leaned his head back and howled loudly into the cold night air. "Oooowwwwww." He smiled at Landon, tilting his head to listen to the response of the far away wolves. Enjoying the sounds, he waited for the howling to stop before continuing.

"The Guardian warned me, sternly. She shrieked at me that only you will decide whether I am worthy to continue on my quest. She challenged me to tell you my story and let fate, and you, decide if I shall continue." He waited, once again, for Landon to respond.

Landon lifted both of his hands, placing them closer to the warmth of the fire. He looked deep into the flames, took a deep breath, and exhaled. He said quietly, but firmly, "Warrior, tell me your story." When the warrior began to speak, Landon could see his words play out as images in the flames.

Adeban of the Red Horse

"My name is Adeban and I am the twelfth son born unto my mother a little more than a century ago. I was born into this world in the midst of a fierce battle between two of the most ferocious clans which populate the Eastern Steppes. My clan had settled for a month near the base of the Cargathian Mountains, hoping to prepare for the Great Gathering. The Ngali clan, which was the clan of my father and mother, had more than three-hundred warriors and a strong chief. One of the Ngali clan's rivals was the Ngeti clan, a clan with less warriors, but widely known for their savagery.

Once every year, the clans will put aside our differences. Our chieftains gather the men of the clans together to plan a raid into the neighboring regions, and launch brutal attacks on the smaller, less defended villages of the frontier. Our goal is always adventure and our prize always is plunder. Hundreds of clans unite each year creating a sizeable army and menace villages far to the West, or far to the South.

Our lands, the Eastern Steppes, have never been domesticated and never will be. There are hundreds of thousands of untamed clansmen riding unbridled across the Steppes. We live life on the edge of the wilderness, closer in temperament to the animals that populate our forests than to the civilized men of the neighboring countries. We are a feral people, wild and untamed.

During the Great Gathering, the chiefs of each clan hold counsel and temporarily elect one chieftain to lead the raids. Once the issue of leadership is settled, the men ride forth to savage the civilized countries. The viciousness of these bloodthirsty raids is unparalleled in their savagery. The warriors, of the Eastern Steppes, are proud of our fighting prowess and believe we are equal in stature and abilities to the barbaric warriors who reside in the Lands of the Khans. We are the unrivaled in our ability to ride horses into battle. We have no equal when it comes to the skill of combat. Life in the Steppes requires the people to be harsh and rugged in order to survive. All young men, before the age of eleven, have killed wild boars with nothing more than a sharpened knife and their bare hands. Those who cannot do so are killed and eaten by the boars. These children, quickly forgotten, are unworthy to live as warriors among the clans.

The annual raids are grim and murderous. Many warriors do not return. They live on as martyrs, their exploits celebrated around our fires. Our people drink to the spirits of those killed in battle with pride. We live for the song of battle and the tales of glory sung by our families every evening.

Within a week of the warriors riding off to the south, the women of our village were attacked by another clan. They had been in the midst of breaking down our camps since we do not often stay in one place very long. My clan is nomadic. They were preparing to follow the great herds of elk which migrate across the grassy plains of the Steppes. With the men of the village gone, the women, the elderly men, and the children remained unguarded, though each of the women in our clan is as ferocious in battle as our men. What they may lack in strength, the women make up for in tenacity and courage. Rather than flee into the nearby woods, the women unsheathed their swords, shrieked loudly, and ran headlong into combat. They refused to shrink from the coming brutality.

One of the clans, the Ngeti, had refused to unite with the other clans for the raid. Our chief should have been suspicious. Instead, the warriors of the Ngeti launched a surprise attack on us. In the pre-dawn hours, hundreds of painted warriors rode out of the woods, wildly driving their horses through our temporary village. They had forgone the offer of plunder with the united clans in order to take their own plunder from our clan. Along with the stolen resources, they hoped to take most of my clan as slaves. The slaves would not be for them, but would be driven south and sold to the nobles and merchants of nearby nations. While the peoples of the Steppes keep no slaves, it has not prevented the clans from profiting from the slave trade. It is a hypocritical state of affairs, but such is life on the Steppes.

My mother, pregnant and near birth, was one of those who ran headlong into battle. She met the first screaming warrior who rode in upon a horse. He charged her, hoping to run her down with his steed. She side-stepped the horse, dropped to one knee, and lopped off both of the animal's front legs with the swipe of her blade. The moment the horse collapsed to the ground my mother leaped upon the man running her sword through his heart. Without hesitation, she charged the next warrior with the intent of taking his life, also.

Though the battle was fierce, ultimately the women were no match against the strength and the number of warriors of the Ngeti clan. Many in our clan were slain. This included all of the elderly men and those women deemed too old to be of any use. The children, with their hands bound tightly, were tethered to the surviving women of our clan.

My mother, though, refused to surrender. She continued to fight with the intensity of a wounded, mountain lion. Cornered, with her back against the trunk of a giant oak tree, she turned to face the four warriors who came to take her life. She kept them at bay with the flashing of her blade, impressing them with her courage. Retreating backward a step, they paused with their attack. One warrior stepped forward to offer a warm place near his hearth if my mother would surrender. She would, of course, have to sacrifice me once I was borne. Her response was to separate the man's body from his head.

The remaining three warriors pounced on her, driving their swords into her body. She was able to mortally wound one more before she succumbed. One of the attacking warriors sliced her stomach and I came spilling out onto the ground. My mother continued fighting, even with her entrails hanging from her body. When she finally died, my mother collapsed into a pile on top of me. The men who slew her took her sword and the other items of worth. They left her lying in a pool of her own blood, gasping for life. Her blood drenched my body, forever staining my skin the color you see before you now. The warriors had not seen me spill out onto the ground. If they had seen me, I would have been scooped up and joyfully fed to their hounds.

I, Adeban, was new to life. I had been borne into battle, covered in blood. The instinct to survive passed on to me, though I was only minutes old. I lay quietly beneath my mother's corpse, warmed by her body, and sheltered from our enemies. I did not cry. I did not make a sound.

Conflict between warriors is always a gruesome prospect. It does not matter if it is in the streets of a tiny village or on a field of battle between two great armies. So is what follows. Once the fighting is finished, after the armies have fled the field, the wolves will come. These bloodthirsty animals feed upon the carcasses of wounded and slain men. Hundreds of them scoured the remains of what was left of my people and the fallen warriors of the Ngeti. There were four wolves feeding on the remains of my mother. They pulled her body in four different directions. Eventually, the body of my mother pulled away from mine. Uncovered, I did not cry out, though I cannot say why I did not. But I did move. One of the wolves, a she-wolf, noticed me and snatched me up in her fangs. She ran away with me in her jaws, carrying me for more than a mile to her den.

When she dropped me onto the floor of her cave her two pups came out to feed. The female wolf had already left the cave in order to give the two pups the opportunity to practice their hunting skills and to eventually feed on me. They did not get to do either, though. Instead, I fed on them.

Even as an infant I knew I must fight to survive. I gouged out the eyes of the first pup. It yelped in pain backing away quickly. In doing so, it backed into the second pup, which had been unaware of my attack. Angrily, the second pup attacked the blinded pup. While the two were locked in their tussle I picked up a sharp stick, crawled over to them, and stabbed the both of them through the heart. By the time the she-wolf returned her two pups were dead. I was all that remained alive in the den. Instead of killing me, the she-wolf adopted me. For the next five years, I, Adeban of the Ngali clan, ran with, hunted for, trained alongside, and killed with a wolf pack of the Eastern Steppes. My power and strength grew, as did my wildness. Eventually, the Alpha male, fearing my strangeness, asserted his power and strength and drove me from the den. He was not strong enough to kill me. He had been right to do so. In another few years I would have challenged his dominance and would have taken over the pack.

In my early years I wandered the lands. I slept alone in the trees, sought refuge in nearby caves, and lived off the land. Initially, I was a thief, but never a beggar. In the dead of night I would sneak into the huts of the clans stealing food and clothing. Before dawn I would retreat and hide. I was wild and untamed. I had forgotten I was born of man. I was as wild as a wolf.

THE EIGHTH LION

One day, when I was ten years old, I heard a magnificent sound. It was the clash of steel and the screams of war. I climbed to the top of a nearby hill watching in fascination while two sizable bands of warriors fought for supremacy. I was transfixed with the sights of battle and enthralled when hearing the sounds of war. Once the battle was over and the armies had retreated, I entered the field and stole a sword from a wounded soldier. When he protested, I drove the sword through his body. He did not protest again.

Emboldened by my actions, I ran around the field of battle slaying all the wounded men. Some of them had been mortally wounded, others only slightly so, and some had not been wounded at all. They had feigned wounds hoping to avoid the battle. I slew them all with an exultant cry and glee in my heart. I especially enjoyed striking down the ones who feigned their wounds.

I did not realize the leader of the victorious clan had returned with his counselors to survey the field. He watched in silence while I was running amok across the bloody field. I was feverish and wild. One of the warriors raised his hands to give the order to have me killed. The chief, intrigued by my actions, ordered him to hold. Instead of killing me for my discretions, the great Chief adopted me into his family. It was only later I found out I was adopted by the Chief of the Ngeti clan. I lived in his household, raised as his son, and trained daily in the skills of battle and the art of war. I would not have been angry to know he had been one of the three warriors responsible for killing my mother and the others in my clan. Such is life on the Steppes.

In the first years, as his son, I was sent to do what I had already done when the carnage ended. Whenever a battle ended, and the two sides retreated, my sword and I were released. I would cover the entire field of battle killing those who had been wounded in battle. Knowledge of my purpose soon flooded the ranks of warriors of the Ngeti. All of the warriors, when wounded in battle, used all of their powers to leave the field. They knew the son of the chief, the son with the red-stained skin would slay any who remained. Additionally, I trained in horseback riding, sword fighting, and the use of a bow and arrows. It seemed my strength and agility increased tenfold in those first few years. I grew taller and more powerful.

In one of my first battles I slew thirty-two men. The warriors of the Ngeti clan were awed by my strength and ferocity. I was a red-skinned warrior with the strength of a bear. It was by accident the battle-axe became my weapon of choice. I had been locked in one-on-one combat with a large, giant warrior from another clan. His strength was greater than mine, though I countered his strength with my tenacity. The man knocked my blade from my hands and raised his axe far above his head for the deathblow. Instead of bounding away, I closed with him, locking my hands around his massive neck. He had been expecting me, in my youth, to cower rather than attack. He dropped the axe and locked his fingers onto my neck. We stood, face to face, each trying to squeeze the life out of the other. Our eyes bulged. Our veins popped. My youth and vitality won the day. The warrior collapsed to the ground dazed and confused. I grabbed his battle axe, swung it high in the air, and brought it down to crush in his skull. It was at that moment the power of the battle-axe won me over. It has been my weapon of choice since that day.

My father honored me by giving me this amulet I wear around my neck. The two wolves facing each other are brothers, yet will fight to the death with each other if necessary.

For ten years I followed the lead of my father, the Chief of the Ngeti clan. Whenever a conflict arose I was the first to lead the others into battle. When the battle was over I continued to go into the field to kill those who were too wounded to leave of their own accord. My hunger for war was never satiated. There were numerous battles. There were a few in which I was the only one who survived. I hungered for combat and fed on War! In my youth, when there were no battles to be fought, I often left the Steppes to fight as a mercenary. I fought both for and against the clans of the Steppes. I fought both for and against the armies of the Sultan of the south. And I fought for and against the armies of O'ndar in the West. I longed for War more than I longed for life.

During my young life, I rose in the ranks of my father's warriors. Eventually, my father's other sons became jealous of my exploits. When a nearby clan threatened my father's domains his other sons led a group of warriors, which included me, in an attack. We decimated the clan without mercy.

When the attack was over three of my father's sons ambushed me. I killed two of the three in my rage. They caught me off guard, though, and were able to strike a mortal blow. The one surviving brother left me on the field of battle, to die a slow death in the mid-day heat. Blood trickled down my face flowing into my eyes. It had been a good life. One in which a warrior could be proud to have been a part. I lay silently, waiting for death. I did not pray. I did not cry out, though pain wracked my body. Darkness had just started to sweep over the field of battle, which meant the wolves would soon follow. Though near death, I prayed for a wolf to come close enough so I might slay it.

Suddenly, a brilliant light illuminated the starlit sky. A Spirit, surrounded in light and clothed in a golden silk robe, floated down to me. She looked into my eyes and spoke to me softly.

Greetings Great Warrior. I am Igami, whose sole purpose is to maintain a Balance required in this world. I have always been and will always be. Since the beginning of time there has been a need for the Four, who must ride their steeds across the plains of battle, at the first sign of the coming of war. The Four, who stand in judgment on the field of combat, offering a lesson that humans refuse to learn. The Four must always be present whenever there is blood to be spilled and where the Fate of man hangs in the balance.

Great Warrior, Igami and the world requires your service. The world is once again in need of a Warrior; the one who will always lead the Four. Events have come to pass which require me to seek you out. I have been searching all the lands to find the one worthy of the Red Horse. You are that warrior! Do you accept the offer set before you?

Without hesitation I answered in the affirmative. I tried to stand, but my wounds were too great. Leaning down, Igami struck me across the face with her riding whip. With a blinding flash my past flooded into me. I could see the attack by the Ngeti clan. I could see my adopted father. He was the warrior who sliced my mother's belly spilling me onto the ground. I could see the she-wolf that adopted me. Within a few seconds my entire life had been revealed to me. I knew I was a son of the Ngali clan, a group of ferocious tribesmen of the Eastern Steppes.

The blinding flash occurred once more. The Spirit Igami disappeared, replaced with the Red Stallion. My wounds were miraculously healed.

I leaped, up screaming with fury, and mounted the fiery-red steed. I galloped across the battlefield trampling the bodies of the fallen warriors. We left a trail of flames in our first ride. Finally, I had found my true purpose. Since that day, I have led thousands of men into battle, always being the first to charge headlong into each melee. I will always be the first into War."

~

Landon listened, fascinated. The behemoth of a man sat quietly, staring into the flames. His taut muscles rippled in the light. The flames flickered back and forth casting shadows as massive as the man who sat cross-legged before him. The crimson horse remained a few feet behind the warrior, Adeban. It had moved closer to the campfire for warmth. It might have moved closer to listen to Adeban's story. Landon could not be sure the reason.

Adeban lifted his eyes from the fire looking into Landon's eyes. He said, "Young King, I am always the first of the Four to arrive. My true brothers are never far behind. We ride our horses across these lands executing our purposes without prejudice, but always with pride. I arrived in this accursed land with the goal of crossing the Cargathian Mountains in order to lead the armies of the one of the Khans. War is coming, it cannot be averted. Only by your word, though, will I find my way through the mountains. One of the paths will lead me to Glory. The others will lead me to my death. Thus, decreed by the Guardian, only you can decide if I am worthy of the Red Stallion. If not, Igami will search the lands again for another. Thus the cycle will always continue."

He paused and then asked, "Great King, which of the five paths before us is the path which will lead me to my destiny?" Landon could see the whiteness of Adeban's eyes. They widened with expectation. The warrior grew restless. He was ready to be on the move and on his way.

Landon responded without hesitation, "You are a warrior most worthy to continue on with your purpose. Before I answer, though, I must ask an oath from you before I allow you to continue on your way."

"Name the oath," Adeban said gravely. He glared at Landon with wildness in his eyes. The warrior, steadfast in his resolve to follow the path leading him into the Lands of the Khans, waited stoically.

"I ask for your allegiance. Nothing more. Nothing less," Landon said.

"You shall have it, Great King. I swear before my brothers, who are yet to follow, and all considered Holy. I, who am the twelfth son of my mother and father, the one born of the Ngali clan of the Eastern Steppes, adopted by the She-Wolf, and then by Chief of the Ngeti clan. I am honored I was chosen to ride the Red Stallion into war by the Spirit Igami. If you send me on the correct path so I may fulfill my destiny, I offer my allegiance to you forever. It is an oath I shall never break."

Landon smiled inwardly. He said, "Go, Great Warrior. Follow the fourth path laid before us to your destiny." He watched while Adeban mounted the Red Stallion. The horse snorted once more into the cold, night air as if to thank Landon for his assistance. Adeban reached beneath his shirt, removing an amulet with two wolves from the leather string. He smiled and tossed it to Landon.

"Wear it with honor and pride, young King. Every clan living in the Eastern Steppes knows the story of Adeban, the Rider of the Red Horse."

Before turning away, Adeban saluted Prince Landon. He said loudly, "*Invictus Maneo! Ego Invicte, Malis!*" He then kicked his heels into the horse's sides. The red war horse turned and trotted out beneath the stone archway. It galloped quickly up the fourth pathway, winding its way up and into the Cargathian Mountains.

Landon watched silently for a few seconds and whispered, "Yes, Horseman, you remain unvanquished." He had been surprised to hear Adeban utter the phrase using an ancient language, especially given his upbringing on the wild, Eastern Steppes. Landon was well-versed in it, but had assumed it was a language reserved only for nobility. Once again, Mfiri held a surprise for him.

He turned back to the gate. The second horseman had arrived.

The arrival of the second horsemen surprised Landon because he recognized the man sitting astride the ivory-colored mare. Landon looked at the large, barrel chested rider with disbelief. Without thinking, he stood, kneeled quickly, and said aloud, "My Liege."

He had seen the man's image often enough in a painting hung in his father's castle. The clothing, the weaponry, and the sculptured features were the same. Depicted in the painting close to a thousand years ago, in person the man held the vitality captured by the artist who had done the painting.

The horse was massive, standing like a beacon against the backdrop of darkness. Its fiery, red eyes were wild with abandon. It's snorting, also sent the breath billowing into the cold night air, though the wisps of steam could not hide the red eyes, no matter how thick.

Slowly, the rider dismounted and walked closer to the fire. The man exuded strength and vigor. He was a powerful warrior.

"I do not know whether I would fear Adeban or him more in battle?" Landon thought.

"Do we know each other? I feel we should," the Horseman asked. Landon's actions had intrigued him.

"Yes, my Lord. I am Prince Landon, heir to the throne of O'ndar. You are one of my ancestors, the first King of our House. You are the first Conqueror, Gheldari, Ghardenne's father." Landon stood up and looked into Gheldari's brown eyes. The man stood at least four hands taller. His bare, muscular chest held the strap of a sword and its sheath, strapped diagonally across his chest. Gheldari preferred to carry his sword on his back. It had been the old style, which had ceased long ago to be the preferred manner for warriors to carry swords.

"You would be one of my great, great, grandfathers, many times removed," Landon said. The excitement at meeting Gheldari was evident in his smile.

"I remember that name, from a long time ago," the second Horseman whispered. The man muttered to himself, speaking louder afterwards. "It was from a time when I was young and wild. In those days I had gathered the splintered coastal tribes and welded them into a nation. Yet, before I could enjoy the fruits of our exploits I was…" he paused a few seconds before continuing, "poisoned by my brothers." Gheldari turned and spat on the ground. "I should have known to be wary, but came to believe I was infallible. It was my destiny to conquer the world. Little did I know that my belief would become my reality!"

THE EIGHTH LION

"Poisoned by my brothers!" he repeated, spitting once again on the ground in agitation.

Landon thought, *"He would slay them all if were they here at this moment."* He had read many times about Gheldari's strength. One of his many legends included slaying a full-grown grizzly bear armed only with a knife.

Landon watched the man's eyes. His face contorted into anger at the mention of his brothers. Landon remembered the writings of Pelinnedes in the Brief History of Dragons. Gheldari the Conqueror, standing proudly before him nine-hundred years after his death, had been considered one of the greatest military tacticians who had ever lived. He was a wild, untamed chieftain. Gheldari was a general whose armies were never defeated in battle. His exploits led to the creation of the greatest nation in the world, with the mightiest army.

"I thought it was the mightiest," Landon thought.

"May we come closer to the fire, young King?" Gheldari asked with a deference required when speaking to one's superior.

Grabbing the White Horse by its reins, Gheldari moved closer to the fire. He gestured, asking Landon's permission to sit. Landon nodded his approval, before moving to the other side of the campfire.

"I thank you for your kindness, My Lord," Gheldari said. "In return, I would like to offer you something." He stood, went over to his saddlebags, took something out, and returned. It was a shirt. Long-sleeved and blue, the cotton shirt looked comfortable. Gheldari tossed it over the fire into Landon's hands.

Landon thanked him and put the shirt on. It fit perfectly. It was nice to be clothed. His feet were bare, but the fire kept the cold at bay.

"How long has it been? Since Ghardenne...," Gheldari asked nervously.

"A little less than a thousand years, My Lord," Landon responded.

The chieftain, beaming with pride, said, "I am happy to hear my son lived. I am surprised he was not executed by one of my brothers. I am also pleased to get a chance to meet you, young King. I would rather avoid referring to you as grandson, if that is okay."

Landon ignored the final part of Gheldari's statement and responded quickly, "I am no King, Master Gheldari. I am a prince. My father,

Ghardenne XVI is the King of O'ndar. You had originally named our country Chondar."

Gheldari laughed aloud, "I know we have business, you and I, but would you please tell me the story of our House. A thousand years. It seems like yesterday." It made Landon happy to see him laugh.

Landon spent more than an hour re-telling the tale of Pelinnedes and Ghardenne I. He included the exploits of Ghardenne the VII, who became Chardon I. Gheldari listened without interruption, enthralled with the exploits of his descendants.

"The cup-bearer? I had an intuition about him. My counselors thought him a fool. The moment he offered to go speak with the Dragon I knew he carried a mark of destiny. It was brash, to be sure," he agreed. "But, it was a mark of bravery. I must admit, I might have taken the Dragon up on her offer to become King, had I been in his place. Yet, without his efforts, the House of Gheldari would not have survived for a thousand years.

Landon finished his tale, stopping periodically to answer Gheldari's questions. He left nothing out. He included the purpose of his quest and his recent exploits. He had chosen to keep this hidden from Adeban, the rider of the Red Horse, but he felt Gheldari could be trusted.

"I thank you for the History lesson, Prince Landon. I too am on a quest. I came to Mfiri hoping to find the pass that will lead me safely across the Cargathian Mountains into the Lands of the Khans. My brothers and I must fulfill our purpose. I must admit, though, leading a horde of warriors for the eventual Lord of the Khans makes me afraid for our world.

"I believe he plans to build an Empire and ravage our lands. I can tell you from personal experience these tasks are no easy matter. I have been tasked by the Guardian of this village to ask for your assistance when choosing the correct path. One will help me fulfill my destiny, while the others will end in my death.

"But first, I am required to tell you my story, though you may know most of it. If you deem me worthy, I ask permission to be on my way."

Landon lifted his hands to the warmth of the fire looking deeply into the flames. He said quietly, but firmly, "Gheldari, tell me your story." When the warrior began to speak, Landon could see his words play out as images in the flames.

Abadi of the White Horse

Landon listened patiently, though he knew almost as much as Gheldari about his past. The lessons of the House of Gheldari were required of all Noble children, especially the Prince and Princess. Landon was startled to hear Gheldari refer to himself as Abadi. He noticed Landon's puzzled expression and responded.

"When visited by the Spirit Igami, I shed my previous life like a snake sheds its skin. I left Gheldari behind to become Abadi, rider of the White Horse. Both men are one and the same."

Landon understood, nodding for him to continue. Abadi finished his tale, including the moment he awakened after having been poisoned. He had been locked in a burial tomb in total darkness, with his sword placed across his chest, ready for battle in the afterlife. When the offer to ride the White Horse came, he did not hesitate. Thus, Gheldari the Conqueror became Abadi the Conqueror, the second Horseman.

Abadi finished his tale and stood up, anxious to be on his way. Landon stood with him and stuck his right hand out. The two shook hands. The first King of the House of Ghardenne and the future King of the House of Ghardenne stood together quietly for a few seconds.

"I thank you, Great Lord," Landon stated with conviction. This was a moment he would never forget.

"I thank you, too, Great King," Abadi responded. "You have the mark of destiny upon you. I look forward to seeing the path you choose." He turned, leaped up, and sat astride the White Horse. Abadi looked down to Prince Landon and said, sternly, "If the Khans do unite, be warned they are not men in the natural sense. They are warriors, all of them, skilled in dealing death in the way a chef is skilled in the art of cooking. The Khan will eventually look westward, hoping to conquer the Known World. Be warned. O'ndar, if standing alone, will be overwhelmed. The Southern nations and the tribes of the Eastern Steppes, unless united, will be obliterated. Humans, caught up in a whirlwind of death and destruction, will disappear forever. Something needs to be done to prevent this. The history of man may come to an end, should the Khans breach the mountains and lay waste to our nations."

Landon paused for a few seconds, saying, "You are the most worthy man I have ever met." "Though you will never need my permission for anything, I will play out my part and give it to you." He smiled with affection at the man. Landon pointed to the five paths just beyond the stone archway.

"You have been and always will be the first true King. Your actions allowed your son to become King. But, all who came after acknowledge you as the first. Therefore, you must take the first path."

Abadi nodded his thanks to Landon, "As one of the Four, I must ride behind my brother as War is waged. Yet, I have my own part to play. I must always ride with those who wish to conquer. Be warned, Prince. If the Khan is successful a day of reckoning will come to our lands. I hope you are strong enough to bear the weight of the world. The fate of the House of Gheldari and the fate of the world may rest with you. Remember, O'ndar is not powerful enough to stand against the coming tide. Be warned. *Bellum omnium contra omnes.*"

Landon nodded he understood. Abadi had warned him to be wary of the coming of the war against all wars. It was close at hand. *"The end of the world."*

Before Landon could respond, Abadi turned his horse and galloped through the opening of the first path. The White Horse disappeared, swallowed quickly by the darkness.

～

Landon smelled the arrival of the third horseman five minutes before his arrival. A stench of decay permeated the air around the campfire. The odor forced Landon to cover his mouth. He almost vomited.

Landon watched the arrival of the third horseman with fascination. The withered looking young man rode atop a Black Horse, the steed almost as malnourished as the rider. The horse plodded along slowly, each step taken in slow motion. The large eyes downcast, its ears drooping sadly.

THE EIGHTH LION

Both rider and horse were in no hurry to get to the stone archway. Eventually, they halted beneath the gate, both gaunt and pale. Landon noticed the leprous scabs covering the man's body. The rider's skin hung loosely. Landon could see his ribs. Without dismounting, the man reached into his saddlebag, pulled out an apple and tossed it over to Landon. The fruit landed with a dull thud, rolled a few inches, and stopped at Landon's right foot.

The rider gestured at the apple with his hands, encouraging Landon to eat. The apple was wrinkled and crusted. The tail end of a few worms squirmed in the holes dotting the skin. The brown bodies wriggling as they tried to burrow further into the apple.

Landon looked up into the eyes of the rider of the ebony horse. His stomach growled. It had been two days since he had eaten. The apple looked rotten to the core. Filled with worms it had been thrown by the hand of a man covered with leprosy.

Landon's mind screamed at him to avoid eating the apple. It was most likely poisoned, if not diseased. His body though, demanded something to eat. Slowly, without taking his eyes off the rider, Landon leaned forward and picked up the apple. He brought it to his mouth and took a bite.

"It's delicious," he thought. Ravenous with hunger, he tore into the apple and devoured it in less than a minute, eating so quickly saliva dripped from his mouth onto the ground.

The rider of the Black Horse smiled, his taut cheekbones glistening in the firelight. Slowly, he reached into his bags and pulled out a pair of brown leather boots. He tossed the boots to Landon, gesturing for him to put them on. They fit perfectly.

The rider dismounted the horse, ambling slowly over to the fire. He sat down and waited for Landon to speak.

"I thank you for the food," Landon said. He had eaten the entire apple, including the core. He wished he had ten more to eat.

The sunken eyes of the rider bore into Landon, "How did you know the apple was not poisonous? How did you know I am not contagious?" His crusted scabs stretched along the man's jawline when he spoke. The scabs were dark and purple. The man looked tired.

Landon answered honestly, "I did not know for sure, though I must admit I had my doubts. Yet, I know you too are on a quest. If you are of the same mind as your brothers then you need my help." He tried not to stare at the scabs. "If this were the case, it would not benefit you to poison me or infect me with disease. Hungry, I took a gamble I might not have otherwise taken."

The man said, "It is good you have met my two brothers. One of them always insists on leading the way. I have witnessed them battle for hours, sword and battle-axe blazing in the sun. Many times the clang of steel-on-steel ringing loudly into the night. Neither combatant besting the other. Yet, I must follow, as I am always destined to do."

Landon looked away from the man and up to his horse. The ribs of the animal spoke of years of malnourishment. He pitied the animal and considered offering to put it out of its misery. Instead, he looked back to the rider waiting for him to say more.

With effort, the pale man said, "I am quite sure, by now, you know my purpose. I am tasked to tell you my story. The guardian of this village let me pass without trying to stop me. She told me the rules as I passed; being sure to lean away, fearful I might infect her."

He chuckled to himself, "My brothers are prideful. They both are powerful and deadly with all manner of weapons. Yet, even the guardian of Mfiri fears me more than either of them."

"I must admit, "Landon responded. "I too had a similar reaction. I apologize if I offended."

"No need to apologize, young Prince. I would expect nothing less the first time someone lays eyes on me. May I tell you my story? No need to dispense with niceties."

Landon lifted his hands to the warmth of the fire and looked deep into the flames. He said quietly, but firmly, "Please." When the warrior began to speak, Landon could see his words play out as images in the flames.

∽

THE EIGHTH LION

Arksaerop of the Black Horse

"I find it easier to start at the end rather than at the beginning. I am Arksaerop, rider of the Black Horse, the one who follows two of my brothers and the one who will always precede the fourth. I have been the rider of the Black Horse for as many years as I can remember. It has been hundreds if not thousands of years.

I am from a land unknown to those who live in this hemisphere. I was born into a small, agrarian village called Aenat. Far before my birth, leprosy had infected all of the villagers. Though the disease decimated many of the families, there were survivors. The disease, for as many years of our history as anyone could remember, always has been a part of the history of Aenat.

When I was born, my father and mother rejoiced for the first time in many years. It was a time for celebration. It had been a difficult life for them, scratching out an existence as best they could, oftentimes barely having enough to survive. They rejoiced since many of us with this disease succumb to its ravages, while still in the womb. There were no more than four or five other children, of various ages, in the village when I was born. Many of the more than two-hundred villagers were unable to have children of their own. I was the first child born in more than ten years. By the time I reached the age of ten the other children had died from malnourishment or disease. After my birth, there were no other children born in Aenat.

Leprosy can be highly contagious, yet most often it is passed only from father and mother to child. Others are safe from the disease. Yet, because of the scabs and the scars others fear those of us afflicted with the disease. My people were scorned. The history of my people includes us driven from our homes in the dead of night, escorted away by force. Armed soldiers, ordered by their lords to rid the land of the accursed villagers of Aenat, drove us into exile.

When I was a small child my face and body was pock marked with scabs and scars, similar to those that covered the bodies of my parents. My ancestors were doubly cursed. We were plagued by nature and harangued by mankind. My people were harassed relentlessly every time we attempted to settle in an area. The men, women, and children of Aenat were forced to travel hundreds, if not thousands of miles, before finally settling in a land far away from others. The land was not pristine, but it was enough to offer a home free from persecution. Finally, away from the civilization of man, our people rebuilt the village of Aenat. Lest you think finding a place to call home would be the end of our suffering, remember the scars on my body. Leprosy is one of the scourges of mankind. It is not the only one.

My ancestors persevered through the pain, through the trials and tribulations of everything life threw at us.

Throughout our history, Aenat has battled locust swarms. The insects devoured all of our crops and decimated our lives. The swarms would drop from the skies and sweep across the plains. The size of the swarms and the number of locusts were such they would block the sun from our view. Daylight became night whenever locusts were on the move. My father once told me locusts would only swarm once every seven years, though I am witness to at least six different seasons in which they consumed our crops.

Yearly, though, our huts were in danger from the prairie fires started by lightning strikes during the many storms. Every few years the flames caught us unaware, burning our huts to the ground. Rather than complain, the villagers would work slowly and methodically to rebuild. Life in Aenat was too demanding to contemplate our miserable lives. We did not have time to feel sorry for ourselves. We did not have time to think about the fairness or unfairness of our situation. My people marched on with the struggle to survive in the face of unspeakable conditions.

During years of drought, massive dust storms rolled across the land blanketing our homes and suffocating the weakest among us. Men, women, and the few children still alive slept at night only to awaken in the morning covered with a layer of dust a few inches thick. It is a wonder anyone survived.

Yet, we continued our daily fight to survive. Plagued by hardships that would have brought the hardiest to their knees the villagers of Aenat refused to surrender. The natural tendency of humans to survive drove us to continue. Time took its toll, though. Eventually, there were three villagers remaining. I was one of the three. We moved into one home and worked from sun up until sundown trying to raise crops for our survival.

My mother and father had long before faded away from my life and I was alone. My father had been killed in front of me by a black bear. The giant beast had come for me, expecting to find an easy meal. Instead, my father removed his knife from its sheath, shoved me aside, and fought the animal as ferociously as he could. I watched in horror as he drove his knife into the side of the bear, over and over. Its claws scraped along his body. Large fangs sank into his neck. Finally, the exertions from the battle wore the two of them down and my father and the bear died. Rather than mourn my father, the remaining villagers, including my mother, feasted on the bear that evening. Life went on. Our existence depended on our continuing the struggle.

After my father died my sanity fled and my mind became twisted. I became resentful of men and jealous of my lot in life. I hated the world. When the next locust swarms came I refused to flee into the hut with my two companions. Instead I walked outside and stood facing the swarm. In previous years it would take more than three hours before the massive cloud of locusts flew past our home.

This time was different. I did not cower in the hut in fear. I met them with glee. I opened my mouth and allowed them to fly inside. They did. I chomped down on the unlucky locusts. I enjoyed hearing the crunching of their bodies. Thus, I was nourished by the bodies of one of the plagues of mankind. I did not do this out of madness, though. I did it out of hatred. I had developed a hatred for every living thing.

Less than a year later, the three of us became stricken with an unknown disease and my two feverish companions died. They had ranted loudly into the early morning hours until the fever took them. The two of them died within a day, but I lay in my bed fighting with all of my might. My anger at my treatment by mankind, and my anger at having lived such a hard life drove me forward. I refused to succumb. I had overcome natural plagues and disease before. I felt my mind and body would allow me to do so again.

As I stated before, I do not know how many years ago I was born, but I have been Arksaerop of the Black Horse for so many years I almost know nothing else of my past.

The disease ravaged my mind. I burned with fever and must have been mumbling and yelling like a stark-raving lunatic. I felt life slipping away, like a slow thread being pulled through a needle. Yet, moments before death overtook me, a spirit appeared before me."

"Igami?" Landon asked. He raised a hand in apology for interrupting Arksaerop.

Arksaerop acknowledged the apology and responded, "Absolutely." He paused, regathered his thoughts and blurted out.

"Exactly!" Arksaerop's eyes shone with ferocity. "It was Igami. She stood over my feverish form looking to me with pity."

"She greeted me by name. *Greetings Arksaerop of Aenat. Be at peace and do not suffer any longer.* Igami waved her long, slender hand above my body. The fever disappeared. My joints no longer ached. The scabs, these thick crusty lesions that had caused me pain all of my life no longer hurt. I stood and quickly kneeled to her.

Rise Arksaerop. There is never any need to kneel to Igami. I serve a higher purpose and a higher power, which I now ask you to do. You have been tested all of your life with the worst plagues and diseases afflicting humans. You have a hatred of mankind and thus have a purpose to serve. Mankind has never learned the true meaning of life and most likely never will. They have tortured you and your people and the time for revenge is at hand. The Black Horse is in need of a rider. Do you accept my offer?

I was ecstatic. I had cursed mankind all my life. I was angered by my afflictions. I was angrier about the treatment of my people by other men. I blamed those who did not have to suffer from the pain of disease. I blamed those who did not have to feel the pains of hunger from starvation. Igami had chosen me because of this hatred. I leaped to my feet. Immediately, I accepted.

When Igami disappeared I left the hut and found the Black Horse waiting for me. Since that day, I ride with my brothers across the lands. We teach and re-teach the lesson that has never been learned by man and most likely never will be."

Landon let the final words hang in the air for more than a minute before responding. He had listened attentively to the rider of the Black Horse, at first having pity. Yet, the more Arksaerop spoke, the pity turned to admiration and then to respect. The man had experienced more pain than any other person he had ever met. The deep, purple scars crossed the rider's face and neck disappearing beneath the shirt. Landon imagined his torso held more scabs.

Finally, Landon spoke, his voice self-assured. He spoke with firmness, asking "May I offer some observations?" He waited until Arksaerop nodded in agreement.

"You were not chosen to be the rider of the Black Horse based on your hatred of mankind. You have a right to hate others, of this I think we would both agree. It is not right for you or your people to have been persecuted. I am saddened. You have had to live a hard life. Yet, I believe your anger has twisted your understanding of why you were chosen to be one of the four.

"You were chosen because you are the best of what mankind may become. Adversity can be overcome, you are proof of this. Your people were afflicted with a disease causing others to shun them out of ignorance. They drove you from your homes and your lands. Rather than surrender, your people persevered.

"When afflicted by nature you refused to capitulate. You are the epitome of the best of man's spirit. You have been chosen because you persevered in the face of adversity."

"Why do you believe this?" Arksaerop asked. He had become so cynical of his purpose Landon's words shocked him to his core. Landon saw the awakening in his eyes when he looked at his purpose from a different perspective.

"*Fac fortia et patere*," Landon offered. Unlike the other two horsemen, Arksaerop did not understand the ancient phrase. "Do brave deeds and endure," Landon translated.

"Your life has been one of brave deeds and you have had to endure. I will elaborate." Landon paused, gathered his thoughts, and then continued.

"I will use myself as an example in my response," Landon said. "Before leaving O'ndar, my world was small, my life was uneventful. The biggest fear I had involved when I might be required to become king and rule other men. I lived a pampered life. The demands of being king would change all of this so I fought, passively, against this possibility. Because of the quest I am on to save my mother, my belief has changed. My whole understanding of the world has forced me to re-examine what it is I thought I knew. I have learned from the adversity and have grown from a Prince into a King."

Landon added, "*Non sum quails eram.* I am not such as I was." He looked deeply into Arksaerop's eyes hoping to gauge whether or not the rider understood his meaning.

Landon continued, "Mankind does not know what it does not know. In my life as a Prince I lived a sheltered life. Yet, it did not mean the outside world did not exist. As we expand our understanding of the world, looking outside of our own existence, humankind must always learn to adapt and learn to survive. Just as you did. Otherwise, there will always be a need for the four." Landon was proud of himself. His thoughts had reached a new nexus. The pieces of the puzzle were starting to fall together as his mind grasped an understanding of all of the events from the last few days.

"Though you are angry, I would say to you, be at Peace, my brother. Just as I must be at peace with Captain Arem, even though my emotions demand I be angry." A new revelation had come to him the moment he began to speak to Arksaerop about why he believed Igami had chosen the rider.

"Captain Arem did not tell me all that I need to know. The orbs have given him the ability to see into the future. It is a power, few Dragons master." Landon proclaimed. "The Dragon refused to tell me all of the possibilities the orbs have shown him."

Landon stood, walked a few feet away from the fire, turned and walked back to Arksaerop.

"Arem has seen the destruction of the human race as a real possibility. He also saw something more and is frightened by its possibility. There is one more thing which all Dragons fear. I did not say it to my sister, though I suspected. Now, after having met the first three riders, I know the destruction of man also means the destruction of life. It also means the destruction of the Dragon Race."

The Prince stood above the rider. Arksaerop remained sitting. He added, "Arem sent me here because he fears the end of time is at hand. The destruction of the Dragon Race and the destruction of the Human Race are interlocked. He did not wish to put the burden on my shoulders, knowing its weight would be too much to carry."

Landon's voice rose to a new level, "I know now I must follow the adage, *Praesis ut prosis ne ut imperes.* I must lead in order to serve, not in order to rule. Do you understand? I have changed as a person in the few days since I left O'ndar."

"Enough about me. My burdens are not yours to carry. Arksaerop, you are the rider of the Black Horse because you are the best of what humankind has to offer. I have grown as a man and will no longer complain about things life throws at me. I will always attack each of them with a ferocity knowing you attacked yours with a vengeance. From what I can tell, three of the four riders were once human. Though I doubt the fourth will be the same. I thank you for your story and thank you for your tenacity, a quality which I can only hope to emulate. Go now. Go join the Khan who is working to unite those beings living on the other side of the Cargathian Mountains. If I am to prepare this world for the coming Armageddon, I must not make any errors in judgement. Arem was right to hide this from me. Until I met you I do not believe I would have had enough will-power to meet the challenges head on. Yet now, though I know one misstep may mean the end of the world, I am prepared to meet the challenge face-to-face. If the warriors from the Land of the Khans unite and invade our world we are all doomed unless we stand together. Human and Dragon alike are doomed to extinction."

"Para bellum," he smiled at Arksaerop. "Prepare for war."

Landon reached down, offered his hand to Arksaerop, and pulled the rider to his feet.

"Take the fifth pathway, the one furthest to the right, up into the mountains. Go in peace and go with conviction. You are more than worthy of your purpose," Landon said honestly.

Arksaerop accepted Landon's offer of a hand up with admiration and thanks. The Prince had not cowered away from his presence. He had eaten the apple offered by the rider, unafraid of what it meant. *"This*

Prince has the mark of destiny!" he thought. He mounted the Black Horse without a word and rode it up into the mountains.

~

Nameless Rider of the Pale Horse

The pre-dawn hours were upon him, yet Landon knew in order to continue his quest he must meet with the final rider. Given what he had learned about himself, and the other riders, this was the one rider he was afraid to meet.

The cold air around the campfire announced the arrival of the Pale Horse. The flames burned brightly, yet even with the flames, the air felt much colder. Without looking up at the stone archway, Landon spoke, "I would offer you the warmth of the fire, but I am not sure it is something you prefer."

The dark rider sat, unmoving atop the Pale Horse. The man's long black hair stuck out from beneath the blackened helmet covering his head. His body was encased in black. Heavy, leather boots, black leather pants, a black chain-mail shirt. The rider was large and muscular. Landon could see his darkened eyes through the visor. They too were pitch-black. His arms rippled with muscles. A large broadsword sheathed at his side, the length of the blade equal to Landon's height.

Without dismounting, the rider responded to Landon, "I watched you with my father when you first entered Mfiri." His voice was deep and commanding. "We stood at the ramparts of our castle watching your passage. I thought the Children of the Night would make you their meal. Yet, you made it through the village and came close to my father's castle. It was then I demanded my father allow me to ride out to retrieve you. I wanted to bring you dead or alive into our castle and hold you prisoner. It would have been fun to see how the world got on without you in it. My father refused to allow me to do so."

Landon started to respond, but was cut short by the snorting of the horse. The Pale Horse pawed with its right hoof at the ground. It snorted harshly. The brown eyes glared at Landon with hatred. The rider reached down with his right hand and patted the horse.

"Easy Khloros. Easy old friend," he said calmly, looking into Landon's eyes.

"He wants me to kill you," the rider spoke. He laughed loudly and patted the horse again.

"Is that what you will do?" Landon asked. *"Why would the horse want me dead?"*

"I am ambivalent about your death, Prince Landon. Whether it happens right now, a minute from now, an hour from now, a day, a month, a year, or ten, it matters not. I am called across the mountains to represent my father once more. Are you waiting for my story?"

Landon rose and spoke matter-of-factly, "There is no need for your story, My Lord. It is well known. And you do not need my permission. While the other three riders needed my advice to guide them onto the correct path, you do not. I wish you well and admit I hope never to meet you again. Though, if I do, I hope it's far into the future." He bowed to the rider.

The rider did not return the salute. He turned the Pale Horse and spurred its sides, taking the second pathway up into the mountains.

The moment the rider of Khloros disappeared, Landon left the comfort of the fire and moved over to the stoned-archway. He looked at the five pathways before him. Dawn was coming. The light of day started to peak above the mountaintops. Mfiri had been a gloomy place. He hoped he would never see it again. Each pathway, chosen to allow the four Horsemen to fulfill their destiny, led in different directions. Now, looking at the remaining pathway, Landon felt a tugging at his heart. He knew it was his destiny to follow this pathway, even if it meant he was going to his doom. He began his journey a child and now walked up the mountainside a man. Landon could feel the difference in his heart and his attitude.

Landon yelled loudly at the top of his lungs, *"Ducuint volentum fata, nolentem trahunt."* He felt confident of his purpose now. He yelled the phrase once more, "Fates lead the willing, yet drag the unwilling." His voice echoed up into the mountains.

"I go now to fulfill my purpose," he said aloud. "It is my path. Whether or not it will end in my death we shall soon see." Landon exhaled. Without looking back into the gloomy village he began walking up the third, obsidian-lined pathway, into the mountains.

SEVEN LIONS

THE HOUR LONG WALK UP THE MOUNTAINS TOOK LANDON along jagged outcroppings and beside steep- ravines. Mfiri's dreariness faded away with each step Landon. The dreariness of the journey though, had not. His heart, weighed heavy with the pressure of preventing the coming apocalypse. He did not know if he would be up to the task, but the fate of humankind required he push such thoughts aside. When he had started the quest, hoping to save his sister he had no idea the fate of the world hung in the balance.

Landon looked at the glass-smooth obsidian pathway and again wondered, *"Who has maintained this place?"* Someone had done so with precision and care, working diligently to keep the darkened pathway free of falling rocks and dirt. It was in pristine condition, immaculate, as if it had been recently constructed.

"It could be magic?" he thought. Landon had considered the possibility that Mfiri, with its Guardian and the other creatures within, had been created by a dark magic. It was a sinister place.

Landon followed the winding pathway, the sight of the mountaintops a relief. He expected more surprises, but nothing happened. Bright sunlight cascaded through higher mountain peaks, driving away some of the coolness of the previous night. Landon spotted a doorway at the end of the trail, but it wound back and forth a few times, skirting craggy boulders, before he made it to the large, wooden door.

He stopped and looked around. The door offered an opening, fitting neatly into the rocky mountainside. Landon looked for a doorknob, but could not find one.

Landon stood, hands on hips, perplexed. *"The pathway ends here. I am quite certain I must enter. But how?"* he wondered. He sat down in front of the doorway to think it through. *"I am tired. I need to rest."*

Rather than spend any more time thinking about the doorway, Landon lay down and looked up into the sunny sky, eventually falling into a deep sleep. After a few hours, he woke up refreshed. The rest had done him some good.

He walked back over to the door and looked at it more closely, feeling around the edges. There was no way to open the door.

The rectangular door had been covered by a thick layer of dust. He moved closer, reached high above his head with his right hand and wiped away some of it away. The words *offendit consumentur* appeared.

Laughing like a child discovering something new, Landon reached up and used both hands to wipe away the dust. It took a few minutes, but when he finished the dust on the doorway was gone, replaced by a passage stenciled onto the door in gold lettering.

Landon stepped away and read aloud.

"Et faciem regis interaverit absque septum."

"Et offer nominibus suis vacat vobis, lieberum."

"Bis deinde offendit consumentur."

"Deorum nutu per approabiana."

"Nomen eorum vera sunt et vere liberabo te."

Some of the words were a little different from the ancient, scholarly language taught to him by his tutors. Yet, he was sure he could translate it correctly.

Landon stepped forward, put one of his forefingers on the letters and said aloud, "He who enters is required to face the seven. Offer their names and then you are free. Beware. Offend them twice and you will be consumed. The gods nod in approval. Name them true and truly free you are."

"It is a warning and a test at the same time. I must name the seven without offending them. If they are offended, I will be eaten." Gamayun's warning about 'once inside the bellies of the seven there he would remain' flashed into his mind.

"It is a test, to be sure, but it does not help me figure out how to enter," he said. Landon stepped away once again and read the passage once more.

"It cannot be that easy," he said aloud, almost laughing. Landon shrugged his shoulders once again, stepped over to the door, and knocked. *Once, twice, three times. Then four. Then five. Then six.* He paused and *then seven*. The moment his fist struck the door the seventh time it swung inward silently, opening barely enough for Landon to enter sideways. He did so without looking back. Again, the door moved without warning, closing softly behind him.

~

Landon waited to give his eyes time to adjust to the darkness, but was startled when a small torch, mounted on the wall to his left, burst into flame. A few seconds later a second torch, followed by many more, did the same. The burning torches burned brightly, illuminating an empty hallway. The rock walls were smooth. The obsidian floor glistened in the torchlight.

Landon walked to the other end of the long hallway, stopping in front of a black, metal door. The door was no more than six feet tall with the word *Unus* stamped on the middle in large, black letters.

"One," Landon whispered. He reached up with his right hand, knocked once, and waited.

The door opened, slowly. He stepped through, waiting for it to shut behind him. This time, the door did not shut on its own. The well-lit room brought a gasp out of him. He reached back to shut the door behind him without taking his eyes off the large animal lying a few feet away. The rotund feline, its entire body covered with circular black spots, lounged lazily on a large, rectangular cushion. Its coat was sun-dried yellow. The cat's rounded face, with its big, yellow eyes gave it an almost childish quality. It was longer than Landon was tall.

The body of the big cat was fat and plump. Oddly enough, the spotted legs were long and thin. If the animal had been slender, Landon would have recognized it immediately. It belonged to the family of cats that ranged some of the lands far across the ocean.

Landon walked over to the animal slowly, waiting patiently for it to notice him. It did not seem impressed with his presence and lay on its back, with all four paws facing upward. The cat made no effort to move. It yawned widely, the long, ivory fangs menacing.

"Welcome," a female voice purred. "I have not welcomed a visitor to our cave for a very long time." It rolled toward him, stopping on its side. The cat's rounded belly protruded a few feet, making it look pregnant. Landon's realized his original impression was wrong. The large cat was just fat and lazy. It made no effort to leap up and attack Landon. He was not surprised, given its plumpness.

"This cat looks too heavy to even stand on its own legs," he thought.

"I thank you for your kindness for allowing me to enter your home, safely," Landon responded.

The cat licked her lips, the yellow eyes had turning serious. She said, "Humans are foolish. Do not take my kindness as weakness, young man. Make no assumptions about your safety. That is still to be determined." The cat rolled onto its back once more, this time keeping both eyes on him. It tried to stretch its front legs, but the effort required too much energy. It stopped trying, yawning instead. The long, black eyelashes blinked at him a few times, its belly still protruding.

Landon stopped walking. *"I do not know all the rules to this game. I need to be wary."* He thought. He looked around the room, noticing the bones of many animals scattered along its entire length. Landon looked at the burning torches, trying to decide if they could be used as a weapon, if needed.

The cat yawned once more, its big, saucer eyes watching Landon with more curiosity than hunger. He hoped this was a good sign.

The cat purred loudly and said, "Do not fear Prince. I have just fed. I am too tired to chase another human around this room. The last one squealed and begged for mercy. Do not worry, I ate him quickly." It chuckled softly.

Landon looked at the bones, *"Could they be human?"* he wondered.

The yellow-haired cat continued, "Please sit and chat with me a while. Maybe, by then, my food will have digested and I will be able to accommodate you inside my belly." It yawned again. The eyes drooped slowly, and then the animal began to purr. It had fallen asleep.

Landon sat down making sure to keep a safe distance. He quickly tired of watching the sleeping feline, stood up to look around, and decided to quietly pick up the scattered bones. He opened the first door and placed them in the other room. Shutting the door softly, he returned to his original spot, sat down, and waited for the cat to awaken. Nearly half an hour later, it stirred. It yawned slowly keeping its eyes closed. A few minutes later it rolled onto its side and stared into Landon's face.

The big cat yawned again before speaking, "You have been busy, young Prince. Why did you clean my room?"

Landon answered honestly, "When I was younger, my father told me to always make use of idle time. Being young and brash, I did not always listen to his advice. He tried to instill in me the importance of a hard day's work. I had not valued his advice until recently. You were asleep. I did not wish to disturb your rest, so I kept myself busy."

Her whiskers perked up, pleased with Landon's response. She tried to sit up, grew tired of the effort, and lay back down on the cushion once more. She responded, "I thank you for your industriousness. In return, you may come closer to shake my paw, without fear." She blinked at him one more time and smiled appreciatively.

Landon walked over to the cat, leaning in to shake its paw. The retracted claws sprung out, grabbing Landon. Razor sharp, they sliced into his left forearm.

The moment the claws dug into his arm Landon jerked backward falling away from the cat. The claws raked along his arm, slicing him from the elbow to the wrist. He yanked his arm away, a stabbing pain shooting along it. Blood oozed from the gashes dripping onto the floor. Landon looked up into the big, yellow eyes shocked. He pressed on the bleeding wounds with the other shirtsleeve, feeling dizzy at seeing the blood soak through the material.

The cat had not moved off the cushion, when it tried to take advantage of Landon's trusting nature. Landon cursed himself for not being more wary. He had trusted the animal, almost becoming snared in its claws.

"I took your kindness as a weakness," Landon said angrily. He stood and moved a few steps away from the cat. "It is a lesson well-learned."

Landon lifted his left arm to assess the damage. "And a painful one I might add."

The rounded face smiled pleased, "I am sorry human. I admit I planned to eat you the moment you walked into my den. However, I have changed my mind. Instead, since you will not come any closer to me, I will allow you to guess my names. If you do, you may continue. If you fail, you will remain locked in this room with me for eternity or until I eat you."

Landon thought about everything that had happened since he had entered the big cat's den. He had developed an appreciation for the danger facing him, and he finally understood the rules of the game. Smiling with a sarcastic look on his face, Landon said, "I offer you two names, one for who you are and the other for what you represent. You are the Cheetah, an exotic and a majestic animal from a faraway land. Each of us carries a name, but we also have our nature. Because of your nature, I also name you Sloth."

The Cheetah smiled at Landon. Landon had expected her to be angry at being named sloth since it meant the same as lazy. He was surprised when she said, "You may continue on your journey. Be aware, though, some of my sisters will not take kindly to you. While I enjoyed having you pick up my mess, the others may take offense. I would remember this if you value your life."

Landon nodded thanks to the Cheetah. He stepped around, making sure to keep away from the plush cushion. Walking to the next door at far end of the room, Landon leaned in to study the wording. The words *Duo et Tria* had been intricately stamped into the center of the metal in the same fashion as the first. Landon reached up and knocked two times, paused, and then knocked once more.

∼

The moment the door swung inward and he had stepped into another well-lit room, Landon's confidence drained. This time, he was met by two nearly identical big cats. Unlike the plump Cheetah, these two cats were thick and muscular. Each cat sat facing him, watching with a feline intensity that caused the hairs on his neck to stand on end. The possibility of death became a reality. If the fat, lazy Cheetah had been capable of inflicting the long gashes in his forearm, these cats were capable of doing much worse.

He had recognized the Cheetah from some drawings in a book given to him many years ago. It had been brought to Landon, across the ocean from a faraway land. When he was younger, the pictures of the exotic animals had spurred his imagination.

The two cats, sitting majestically on large velvet, green cushions, were spotted, but the spot patterns differed from the Cheetah. Landon had mistaken them for being identical. The closer he looked, the more the differences became apparent.

The golden-yellow haired cat on the right was leaner in body, though not by much. Its head was less wide, though its mouth was larger. When it spoke, Landon could see its fangs were longer.

The burnt-orange coat belonged to the more muscular cat on the left. It's thick neck exuded a graceful power.

The spots on both their coats reminded Landon of tiny paw prints. The Cheetah's spots had been circular, while the spots on these cats were not. The tiny, paw-like spots ran the entire length of their bodies. It was as if a tiny kitten had dipped its paws in black paint and had walked back and forth, imprinting them with its design.

Landon decided it best to take some type of action, rather than wait for either to pounce. He stepped over to them, watching both cats yawn, simultaneously.

"I was mistaken if I thought I understood this challenge completely. When I entered I thought them identical, yet they are not," he thought. Landon stopped less than a foot away from the two and sat down, crossing his legs. It took a few minutes for his breathing to return to normal, but his heart continued to race with fear.

The yellow-haired cat spoke first, "Human. I admit I became upset knowing my sister would be the first to see you. She is usually luckier than I am and gets to eat those who come through her den. It always makes me angry. I was afraid she would coax you closer to her and snatch you up in her claws. I am very relieved you made it," Landon was not fooled by the velvety softness in her voice. "Now though, I am afraid my other sister," she gestured with her head to the orange-haired cat next to her, "might get the larger share. You are meaty and look rather tasty."

"*I promised myself never to be surprised, again,*" Landon thought, his mind reeling. He tried to stay focused.

"Hush," the orange cat said, keeping her eyes on Landon, the bright, green eyes flashing at him suggestively. "He is a handsome one, is he not? It has been so long since a handsome human has visited us." Her voice was soft and smooth.

The yellow-colored cat's facial features flashed angrily. She looked to her right, glaring at the orange-coated cat and said, "Do you always have to do that? It angers me to see you flirting with our visitor. Could you please stop, just this once."

"I saw the twinkle in your eye, human. Do you favor my sister over me?"

Landon panicked. *"Offend them twice and be devoured."* The words of warning, carved into the oaken door rang in his head. Here were two big cats. At first glance, both appeared identical. Yet, after watching them and listening to them it was clear they were very different.

Landon sat quietly, looking from one cat to the other. Suddenly, the warmth of the torches and the stress of the moment made the room feel ten degrees warmer. Beads of sweat trickled slowly down his forehead.

He glanced once more at the cat on the left. She smiled, winked at him with her right eye, and gently blew a kiss.

The yellow cat missed the winking, but could not miss the blown kiss. The moment her sister raised her right paw to her mouth and blew the kiss, she became infuriated. Landon was confused about why she had not pounced on him since she was clearly angry. *"I have not offended her,"* he thought. *"She has no reason, yet, to be offended. Remain calm. Do not react to either of them."*

Landon needed to name them correctly, and quickly. Either of them could pounce at any moment, using their razor sharp claws to take his life with ease. While the Cheetah had been fat and slow, these two felines were muscular and dangerous. The orange-haired cat was more concerned with desire for his attention, than she was with wanting to eat him. Her flirtations burned with sensuality, not hatred. Her orange-coat looked soft and luxurious. The black, paw-like prints on her coat were unique from her sister. They had tiny spots within the spots. The difference drew his attention in a pleasing way.

Landon thought about the descriptions of all the wild cats he had read about when a child. Pieces of the chapters about the big cats of the world began coming back to him. He was quite sure he knew her now. The orange-colored coat had been helpful.

The yellow-coated cat, though, was more difficult. Her features were less stocky, but not quite lean. She was muscular and the power in her features apparent. He was sure she too was one of the big cats in his book. Yet to name her correctly required a little more thought. Failure to do both might offend either cat. He did not intend to become dinner for either of them.

The two cats continued to argue, berating each other without any regard for Landon's presence. Without making eye contact, Landon stood and walked deliberately between the two of them. He passed them unmolested, stopping at the next door. The two continued to argue with each other, both unaware he had already covered the distance of the room and was poised to move on.

Landon looked back to the previous doorway, still refusing to make eye contact with either of them. Landon was certain these two cats had always been in competition with each other. Whenever one was near the other was not far behind.

"I name the two of you," he started. Startled, the two cats stood, turned their bodies to face him, and sat back down on the cushions. "Both of you are exotic and beautiful, powerful and majestic."

He pointed to the orange-haired cat. Without looking into her eyes, Landon said, "You are the Jaguar, ruler of the jungles in which you reside. I also name you for your nature, for you are Lust." He continued. "And you are Leopard, the apex predator of the lands from which you came. I also name you for your Nature, for you are Envy. I must admit at first glance the two of you look very similar. Yet, upon further reflection, I know you to be quite distinct. Though, whenever one of you is nearby, the other will always soon follow."

Landon turned back to the next door. He waited a few seconds for a pounce from either cat. He expected it to happen the moment he tried to leave. It did not come. Landon knocked five times, and pushed open the next doorway. The words *Quaterni Quinique* had been stamped into the metal surface.

~

The next room was the longest, more than one-hundred feet long, with white walls and a white floor. Wall-length mirrors had been mounted on the two longer walls. This den, similar to the one housing the Jaguar and the Leopard, also housed two large cats, though these two cats were identical in every way.

The moment he had turned into the room Landon felt as if his blood had frozen in his veins. Two massive, albino Tigers met him at the door, standing just a few feet inside the room.

Each snow-white Tiger had long, white whiskers. The Tiger stripes, though a shade darker, were white. Landon knew them to be Tigers, the large cats so distinct they could not be confused with any other wild cats of the world. Landon had always felt that Tigers were the most intriguing of the big cats. He was curious, though, about their color, having never seen an albino before.

The mirrors, each mounted opposite of the other, made Landon feel as if the room housed a thousand albino Tigers.

The Tigers stood almost as tall as the Prince, their large, red eyes menacing. The power of these two animals intimidated Landon to the point he almost passed out in fear. Instinct told him not to sit, and not to look away. He felt he needed to maintain their stare, though it was difficult to do since fear had crept back into his heart.

"Finally," Both of the Tigers spoke in unison. "It has been far too long since someone has made it past our three sisters. Welcome!" Both spoke softly, their gaze intense. When he had first entered the den of the seven, Landon had wished he had a sword. Against the strength and power of the two tigers, a blade would have been useless. They would have been unstoppable.

He looked at their paws, knowing they could bring a quick death if the Tigers so desired. He hoped, if they killed him, they would not toy with him. He wanted them to make it quick before they began to eat him.

"I do not want to be alive when they start to feed," Landon thought. Landon held his breath for a few seconds, startled to hear whimpering behind him. Landon looked back to see a row of wooden cages, stacked ten high. Most of the cages held a tiny puppy, though there were a few empty ones.

He looked at the puppies and then back to the Tigers, noticing both had fresh blood on their mouths. The albino Tigers smiled in unison, revealing long fangs stained with fresh blood.

On one level, Landon was happy to learn the two Tigers had already fed. It meant they were less likely to be hungry. But, he had cared for puppies when a child. The Huntsman of the Palace had brought a litter of puppies to Landon and Lyssa, offering each a puppy of their choosing. Placed in his care, his puppy Bandit had grown into a loyal dog. Each evening, when he sat down to supper in the castle, his dog sat beneath his feet. Bandit waited patiently for the scraps he always snuck under the table.

Caring for Bandit had been one of the things that had taught him to care for others. Looking at the puppies, hearing their whining, and then looking at the blood-red stains on the Tiger's faces infuriated Landon. His blood boiled red hot. Lyssa had warned him when he was younger that his temper would someday get the best of him. He did not care at this moment. It did not matter to Landon if his life was forfeit.

Landon used his anger to inflate his courage. He completely understood the law of nature. Every organism, whether plant, animal, human, or dragon, needed to feed. Yet, the idea of puppies locked in a cage, to eaten by these two Tigers, filled him with resolve. Without saying a word, Landon began to walk to the cages.

The two Tigers, their fierce red eyes glaring at him, leapt in front of him. They swiped at him with their massive paws knocking him to the floor. Luckily, both Tigers kept their claws retracted. Had they not, Landon was sure he would have suffered a mortal blow.

He rolled onto his back, dazed. He looked up into four, red eyes boring into his own. The eyes of the Tigers were boiling with ferocity.

"What do you think you are doing?" the Tigers asked, once again in unison. The anger in their voices terrified Landon. He waited a few seconds trying to gather his wits.

"I am saving the puppies," he yelled. He attempted to sit up. Instead, both Tigers placed a massive paw on his chest forcing him back to the ground. This time, though, the Tigers extended their claws. The heavy paws held Landon down while the points of each claw dug deep into his chest. Landon did not try to fight against the strength of the two Tigers. He knew there would be no point. He lay on his back waiting for the inevitable to come.

"Why would you do such a thing?" they asked him. "We find it very offensive for you to try to take our supper. They are ours and we will not share."

Offend them twice, Landon knew the end had come. They would devour him. In trying to save the puppies, he had offended the two Tigers.

"I have offended the two of you and am sorry," Landon said. "I know the punishment for offending twice. Please make it quick and painless, if it is possible." Landon turned his head to the right and shut his eyes. He waited for one of the two beasts to clamp down on his throat with their long fangs. Nothing happened.

"We are offended," both Tigers, intoned. "Yet, we are one and the same so the offense is only the first." They lifted their paws off his chest, allowing him to sit up. He took a few breaths and then stood. The Tigers had placed themselves between Landon and the whining puppies.

Before either could speak, Landon blurted out, "While you are both exotic and majestic in nature, I name you both Tigers. In addition, since you are both one and the same I name you both for who you are. Your nature makes the both of you Greed. It also makes the both of you Gluttony. You are the one sin with two names."

The front paws of both Tigers retracted. They said, "You have offended once, do not do so again. You may pass, young Prince. If you attempt to take what is mine you will not make it out of this room alive."

Landon felt saddened, hearing the puppies whine once more. Though it tore at his heart, he turned, walked to the next-door, and looked to find the number stamped into the black, metal door. He was surprised to see more than a number. *Sextus leonis* had been stamped into the metal.

Landon whispered to himself, "The Sixth Lion." He knocked six times and opened the door.

~

The attacking Mountain Lion caught Landon completely unaware. Knocked to the floor by the weight of the cat, Landon did not have time to react. The Puma had been waiting above the door for him to enter. The moment he shut the door and turned, Landon had been surprised to find the well-lit room empty. Before he could look around to find it, the Mountain Lion leaped onto his back and knocked him to the floor. Clamping down tightly onto his shoulder and neck, the cat effortlessly lifted Landon off the floor and began to carry him across the room. Landon tried to roll over to defend himself, but was powerless. The Cougar's fangs punctured his shoulder, digging into the area attached to the neck. The pain was excruciating. Landon felt as if a thousand needles had been jabbed into his neck and shoulder. Landon could not tell if it was fear or the fangs of the cat that paralyzed him.

The catamount picked up Landon and effortlessly dragged him for more than a hundred feet to the next door. It released him, dropping him to the floor. The Cougar used one of its paws to roll Landon over and look into his face.

The large, brown eyes bore into Landon. The cat snarled in anger.

"And now you will die human. Did you truly believe you would survive the seven? Do you have any last words before I kill and devour your lifeless remains?" The loathing, visible on the Cougar's face, pierced Landon's soul. This cat harbored a sense of hatred unknown by the other cats. This cat could not be reasoned with. Landon was sure his life was about to be snatched away from him. He had one chance.

The pain in his neck and shoulders was intense. He lifted both hands and pressed them against the neck of the cat, straining with all of his power to keep it from leaning in to bite him on the face. Landon spoke quickly with conviction, though his words came out in almost a whisper, during the struggle.

"You are an exotic and a majestic cat. I name you Puma for your grace and because of your nature I name you Wrath, for your visceral anger." Before he passed out, Landon looked into the green eyes hoping for a reprieve.

Landon did not know how much time had passed before he woke up. He was on his back, though he was still in the room housing the Puma. The big cat had moved back to the doorway at the other end of the room. Landon could see it perched above the doorway, waiting for another victim. It did not look in his direction any longer.

He sat up slowly, his body aching all over. The wounds had caked with dried blood. The puddle of blood around him had congealed and thickened. Landon stood, his knees almost buckling. He leaned on the door for support. It took a few minutes for his eyes to adjust. Leaning back away from the door, Landon could read the carving. *Septum* had been stamped into the metal door, though this lettering was different from the previous ones. It had been stamped and then painted with gold.

Landon whispered to himself, "The last one." He held out hope he would survive this next challenge and find the room containing his mother's soul.

This time, Landon did not shut the door until he was sure nothing was perched above him. Once he was confident he would not be pounced on again from above, Landon stepped into the room and shut the door behind him. He kept his eyes on the room ahead of him.

The whitish fur of the next big cat was speckled with black spots across its torso. This large cat sat upon a golden throne that had been placed in the middle of the room. It rested comfortably on a golden cushion. Large, grey eyes studied Landon intently.

"Welcome, human," the big cat said. Landon looked at its tail, the spots much larger than those on the cat's body. Its thick tail trailed up the back of the throne, hanging lightly over the back. This cat was much larger than the other big cats Landon had met. It matched the size of the two Tigers put together. Its broad paws well suited for the surrounding mountains.

The cat reminded Landon of the snow-lion he had met on his way to Mfiri. He doubted two small rocks, let alone an unarmed boy could scare this one away.

"Why do I still think of myself as a boy?" Landon felt he had gone through enough to call himself a man. Yet, he did not think it was up to him to decide. *"Because I am still a boy,"* He thought. His journey had changed his outlook on life. He knew things were never going to be the same, ever again. Landon's efforts and his experiences with death, which included meeting death himself, had changed him.

"Will these changes be enough?" He doubted whether it would be enough to save Lyssa, to save his mother, to save O'ndar, or to save the world. Each task seemed as daunting as the next.

"I thank you for allowing me to enter without attacking me," Landon said. His mind and body teetered on the edge. The pain in his neck was intense. The exhaustion almost caused him to collapse. If this cat chose to attack, he did not feel he would survive.

"My apologies for the behavior of my sisters, young man. They are uncivilized, to be sure. I have come to realize, as their Queen, I am the only one of the seven with any manners." When she looked into Landon's eyes, he was startled to see they were green.

"Moments ago they were grey." Landon nodded at the cat. Her whitish-colored fur was splendid.

"So you do not plan on eating me?" Landon asked. He held out hope the worst was behind him. The big cat's response reminded him he needed to stay focus.

"I did not say that," she said, her grey eyes bore into his with a ferocity reminding him of the wildness of the cat he had met in the mountains. That cat had been on the hunt and had planned to eat him if it had caught him unaware.

"Duly noted," Landon responded. He noticed the eyes had changed once again. They were grey. This cat was not what it seemed. He decided to go on the offensive, rather than wait.

"Is it okay for me to offer a compliment?" Landon asked. The green-eyed cat nodded in response.

"You are the most exotic, the most beautiful, and seem to be the most powerful of all of your sisters. I stand in the presence of greatness." Landon watched the effects of his compliments on the grey-furred cat. Her features softened, and she smiled both inwardly and outwardly.

"It pleases me to hear you say this," she responded. She motioned for Landon to come closer to her throne.

Moving forward, Landon offered again, "Your sisters pale in comparison to you, my Lady." Landon stopped, kneeled on one knee, and continued. He watched her face. The twinkle in her eyes, both which flashed from green to grey and back to green, meant his compliments were having the desired effect.

"If I were going to be eaten by any of the seven, it would be an honor for it to be you," Landon continued. He was now less than five feet away from the Golden Throne. The big cat was thrilled and did not hold back her happiness.

"I have often demanded I should be the first to meet visitors. Yet, I am denied that opportunity, though it should be rightfully mine." She looked at Landon nodding. Landon noticed her claws extending slowly. It had not taken long for him to figure her out. He knew the cat for who and what she was. He knew her true names.

Rather than waiting for her to pounce, Landon spoke quickly, "You are both exotic and majestic. I name you for the Snow Leopard, capable of living in the wildest terrain known to man. I also name you for your nature, which is Pride."

Anger flashed across the Snow Leopard's face. She had been caught off-guard by Landon's compliments. It was clear she had planned on attacking and eating him before he could offer her names. The claws retracted. The false Queen of the Seven said somberly, "You may pass, human."

Landon walked over to the next door, though instead of black metal, it was solid gold. The golden door reminded him of the wooden door at the entrance to the mountain, both covered in a thick layer of dust. It must have been a long time since anyone had made it this far. Landon reached up and wiped the dust away from the door. He stepped away from the door to read the words that appeared.

Landon's eyes widened. He had told himself nothing would ever surprise him again. The golden door, though, offered up one more surprise. He looked at the words imprinted into the surface of the door and spoke the words loudly, *"Leo Quoque Ocavus."*

"The Eighth Lion."

THE EIGHTH LION

LANDON SHUDDERED, AGAIN, OPENING THE DOOR TO THE den of the eighth lion with trepidation. The pitch-black room made him cautious about entering.

The numbness in his left forearm had spread to his entire arm. The blood, mostly dried, had soaked through the blue sleeve of his shirt.

Landon's chest ached. The puncture wounds, from the Tiger claws, had not bled nearly as much. His chest felt like a sharp knife had stabbed him in six different places, though these wounds, while painful, were nothing compared to the gaping holes in his shoulder and back. These wounds continued to bleed, profusely. Landon's neck throbbed, having stiffened, considerably. The burning sensation continued to spread throughout his upper torso, the puncture wounds making it difficult to turn his head.

Landon looked back over his shoulder to the Snow Leopard. She crouched on the golden throne, ready to pounce. Drops of saliva dripped onto the marbled floor in front of her. The moment she leaped, Landon stepped forward into the pitch-dark room. Her body struck the closing door with a thud.

"*That was close. Hesitating almost cost me my life,*" he thought.

Landon waited, listening to the silence in the darkened room. He could hear his labored breathing, nothing more.

A flash of blinding light forced Landon to shut his eyes. He opened them, slightly, hoping they would adjust to the brilliant light infusing the room. Landon looked up startled. Seven other Landons stared back at him from seven wall-length mirrors mounted on the eight-sided room.

A sleek, jet-black alley cat sat on the floor, in the middle of the room, looking at Landon. Its deep, blue eyes bore into him with an intensity that forced him to look away. Landon walked over to the cat, his body going rigid.

"They did not move, with me," he thought. The revelation that his reflections had not moved with him was shocking.

Landon stopped beside the black cat, looked down, and waited. Nothing happened. He looked up, again surprised. Each of his reflections had the same black cat sitting directly in front of them, staring back at Landon. The cat near Landon sat beside him, watching him intently.

A deep, resonating voice, full of command and power, demanded, "Who is it that stands in the den of the Eighth Lion?" Landon looked around for the owner of the voice, but the room was empty.

Landon and his seven reflections answered, in unison, "I am Prince Landon. Heir to the throne of the House of Gheldari." Landon held his breath, frightened. He had heard seven voices.

The booming voice demanded, "Which one of you is the true Prince?" The cat purred softly. Its blue eyes watching without judgement.

The first reflection stepped to the edge of the mirror and yelled, "I am Prince Landon, Heir to the throne of House of Gheldari." He crossed his arms in defiance, glaring.

The second reflection stepped forward, with the same answer, followed by the third, the fourth, and the fifth. When the seventh reflection finished, all the reflections stood behind their black cat, arms crossed, waiting.

Landon looked down at the blue-eyed, alley cat and said, "We are all Prince Landon. I carry the other seven with me, a reminder that I am only human."

The light in the room faded, returning to darkness. Landon waited, afraid of what might happen in the darkness.

The deep-voice returned, warning Landon, "Human, I will offer you a warning, one which I advise you to heed with diligence. You are standing inside the den of the Eighth Lion, the eldest and most powerful of all the lions. I am the true King of the lions. You named Snow Leopard wisely, recognizing her as a false Queen. Her Pride would not allow her to present herself in any other fashion.

"You have made it to the final room, but I will not be as kind to you as my sisters. I demand more than they ever could. I hold you more accountable than they ever would. I will not allow you to leave unless I deem you worthy. Do you understand?" The cat did not wait for Landon to respond.

The light faded in slowly, the mirrors had disappeared, replaced by eight walls. Landon looked back over his shoulder to see the metal door. It was still there.

Someone had placed a long wooden table, in front of him, less than ten feet away. The black house cat sat quietly, on top, looking at him with those deep blue eyes. Four torches, mounted on the four walls behind him, burned brightly, the flames flickering back and forth. The four walls in front of him each held a wooden door, resembling the original doorway into the mountain.

He had not expected any more challenges, after having barely survived the Seven, though the black cat was less threatening than the previous seven.

"Greetings, Young Prince," the cat stared. The voice, now soft and silky reminded him of Gamayun. She lifted her ebony tail high into the air and stretched her back. Tiny claws gripped the top of the wooden table fiercely, holding its body in place. Once she finished, she turned around two times, sat back down, and looked intently into Landon's eyes.

The cat's entire body was midnight black. Her deep, blue eyes hypnotic, forcing Landon to look away every few seconds. *"I do not need to be hypnotized. Not when I have come this far."*

Landon tried to join the cat at the table, but was repelled backward a step by an invisible barrier. "What?" he exclaimed. He tried once more, forced backward once more. Frustrated, he looked at the black cat and asked, "Why do you prevent me from joining you at the table?"

The cat responded, "Before we begin, I offer you the opportunity to exit the den of the eighth lion safely. If you choose to continue and you fail to offer my true name, the penalty will be death. I will devour you. I will look into your eyes and into your soul while I eat you alive. You will scream in agony, begging for mercy. I will ignore your pleas. Yet, if you leave now, you avoid this possibility."

"How do you choose to go forward? Leave now without penalty or remain and offer your life as sacrifice, should you fail."

Landon muttered under his breath. He thought, *"The most powerful?"* This cat looked to be no more menacing than the alley cats that frequented the halls in his father's castle. He had terrorized them when he was younger. It had become almost ritualistic, until one of the kitchen servants explained they helped keep the rodent population in check. Afterwards, he let the cats roam in peace.

"I need to kick this cat across the room, if I can get to it."

He started to offer as much, but reminded himself that nothing in Mfiri was as it seems. He decided it wise to accept the small, house cat at its word.

Having survived the seven lions, Landon was sorely tempted to take her offer. The frustration of having another challenge set before him was almost too much to bear. Though the Eighth Lion was only a cat, he was frustrated about having another challenge set before him. His gut instinct told him there was danger before him, though the cat sat demurely, on the wooden table.

"Gamayun did not mention an Eighth Lion. Why not? Did she know of the Eighth Lion? When I watched the Sergeant and the Private dispatched on their mission, Qui Oto had not mentioned an Eighth Lion, either. How did neither of them know of its presence?"

Landon scanned the room once more, looking at the rows of jars sitting behind and to the left of the cat. There were two items, behind the cat, to its right. He could not identify them.

The cat smiled at him, waiting patiently on the edge of the table for his response. The temptation pulled at him like a magnet. A stabbing pain in his neck and back reminded him about everything he had gone through on this quest.

"This is the room," he thought. *"I can see the jars, hundreds of them. One of them holds my mother's soul.*

"It has to be here. Qui Oto had the soldiers deliver it for safe-keeping. What was it she said to them?" "Your master wishes you to know these are

THE EIGHTH LION

for the Seven." Qui Oto had chosen wisely. The Seven were dangerous Guardians. They were just as dangerous, if not more so, than Gamayun.

"I will stay and accept your challenge," Landon said, sternly. He had come too far to give up. He would not be able to face Lyssa if he quit.

Landon locked his gaze onto the cat's face, staring into her blue eyes. He did not avert his gaze. It was time he met this challenge with conviction. Landon felt he had become a worthy adversary for the Eighth Lion.

"Is he my adversary?" he asked himself.

His acceptance of her challenge made her happy. She said, "Excellent. It gets so boring when humans choose to leave safely. Most of them reach my den with their spirit broken. Do not be fooled, though. I have never allowed anyone to leave. I wait for them to turn away and then pounce on them. I always eat those who shy away from destiny."

The cat's words angered Landon. He did not fear this cat the way he had feared the others. He pushed his pride aside though, aware it was a deadly sin. Pride had been the downfall of many a King and many an empire.

"You have passed the first test, having the courage to remain in the presence of The Eighth Lion. My next test requires honesty and self-reflection. I want you to tell me the lessons you have learned from meeting the Seven. Be warned, it is difficult for humans to open their souls, exposing their weaknesses and their fears. If I feel you have not been completely honest, I will eat you."

Landon thought about everything he had experienced since opening the first wooden door. He thought back to the words on the door. He thought about way he felt when he first entered the lair of the seven lions. He knew his mind had stretched to its limits. Emotionally exhausted, Landon had thought numerous times about quitting. The physical exertion of trekking through the mountains had worn him down. The deep gashes on his forearm, inflicted by the Cheetah had begun to take its toll. The claws of the albino Tigers had punctured his chest. He had been overwhelmed with sadness when forced to leave the whimpering puppies. The pain inflicted by the Puma named Wrath had pushed him to the limits of his abilities. He had had been through extreme emotional and physical anguish, barely coming through with his life.

The dried blood on his neck and back were proof. Landon, fearful of answering, knew the cat would not wait too much longer. He swallowed convulsively and spoke, hoping with conviction.

His voice waivered with nervousness, as he began, "I have learned to expect the unexpected even when the unexpected is expected. Life is always full of surprises. Some surprises are beautiful, to be met with happiness and joy. Some surprises are hideous and evil, to be met with ferocity, needing to be stamped out. I must admit I have not decided how I feel about the Seven Lions. I do not know how I feel about you, the Eighth." He did not like the cat's expression, finding the blue eyes difficult to read and interpret. He continued.

"I have learned it is important to know more about the world. The World, when viewed as a whole, is a living, breathing organism. It will not be constrained by our beliefs, some of which are misguided, self-serving, and pretentious. I have learned we do not mold the world. It molds us. The universe sets the rules. Our beliefs are an unconscious attempt to make sense of things that our minds cannot truly comprehend. These beliefs become an attempt to constrain the world in order to make sense of the unknown. We attempt to set our rules hoping it means we control our surroundings. This is a false assumption. Humans know some of the rules and are ignorant of the others. I have learned things are not always as they seem. You are proof of this."

The black cat nodded in acknowledgement. It waited for Landon to continue.

"As a Prince, I always believed I was born to rule. I wrongly believed ruling meant I would get to set the rules. As a child, I believed the rules should always benefit me. If I wanted a toy or someone to play with all I had to do was cry."

"Interestingly enough, I was always careful to avoid these tantrums, whenever my father was around. Somehow, without knowing, I realized my father set my rules. It confused me to watch him set the rules, knowing some of them did not benefit him directly. After meeting the Seven, it makes more sense to me now. I was naïve about my role in the world and the role of the world in the larger scheme of things. I have not been born to rule. I had only been born into the House of a ruler." Landon kept his pride in check, though he felt enlightened to understand this about himself. Speaking the words helped enhance his understanding of everything he had gone through.

"As I grew, I mistakenly believed in my ability to lead, solely based on having been born into my father's house. I know this to be a false assumption. Recent events have helped me to grow both spiritually and physically. I do believe I was born to lead, though not because I am a Prince. I was born to lead because I am growing into an enlightened man. Someday, I might even become as enlightened as my father, the King, though I doubt this will ever be the case."

"I have also learned what it means to lead. Leading other men does not always mean ruling them. Though, it sometimes does.

"I have learned to have courage, even when I am cowardly. A difficult lesson to learn. I have learned to be modest, even when full of pride. I have learned to be honest, even when tempted to lie. As a Prince, I grew up expecting others to show me charity. I expected the guards to play with me when I was bored. I expected the servants to serve me when I was hungry. I expected the jesters to make me laugh, when I felt I needed to laugh. I expected all of this, having been born a Prince.

"Recent experiences have taught me to temper my emotions with prudence. I have learned I need to be caring. I need to show charity, especially for those less fortunate.

"Finally, even though I have learned many things, I also know I will break every one of these lessons, primarily out of impulse, or self-preservation, or fear. I am a human and am full of faults. Even though I will falter, I shall not fall. Once knocked down, I shall rise with conviction and tenacity. I shall stand again, with the goal of looking upward into the stars. I will declare I am alive, I will declare I am always learning from my mistakes, and I will recognize I am a part of something far larger than myself." Landon paused. He could feel the anger and frustration building once again. Most of it came from having to expose his weaknesses to this blue-eyed, black haired cat.

"I have learned my anger sometimes gets the best of me, just as it is at this moment. Though I wish to strike out and attack you because of my embarrassment and my fear, I have learned I do not know all the rules set before me. I have learned it is best to temper my anger in order to continue to grow as a person and in order to stay alive.

"I have also learned I have come too far to abandon my efforts to save my sister, my mother, my country, and hopefully the world." Landon raised his voice, but kept from yelling. "Therefore, if the lessons I have learned do not meet your approval, it is time to be done with this charade and commence with the festivities. I am ready for the fate to which I am destined."

Prince Landon placed his hands on his hips and looked across the room to the ebony cat sitting on the wooden table. He stood silently, waiting for judgement. After a few seconds, he decided he could wait no longer and took a few steps forward, moving closer to the table. This time he was not repelled.

He looked down at the cat, shocked by its next words, "Would you scratch me behind the ears?" He remembered the Cheetah's efforts to snare him and hesitated.

Landon asked, "Would you truly like me to scratch you behind the ears?" The black cat responded by turning its back to him. He used his left hand and gently scratched the cat's ears. Landon smiled. It was pleasant to hear the cat purr with pleasure. When finished, he lowered his hand and waited until the cat turned back to face him.

Landon looked to the right of the table at the rows of glass jars. There were too many to count. They were of all sizes, shapes, and colors. *"How many are there?"* Landon started to count, but stopped.

"There are two-hundred sixty-seven jars," the ebony cat intoned. "She has sent two-hundred sixty-seven souls for my sisters and I to guard."

He turned to his left to look at the other items on the table, letting out a loud gasp. He asked, "Is it possible?" His body shook with excitement. Placed on the back edge of the table, a milky-white sword and a green-feathered shield beckoned to his soul.

"Can it be true? Do you guard the stolen sword and shield of the House of Gheldari? These are the most precious treasures of our House, both stolen hundreds of years ago from Chardon I after his battle with the Dragon Norfuir. The sword *Wynde Ryder* and the green-feathered shield were gifts from Meeha, the third daughter of Bosque. She was the protector of our House and to her we owe our history and our lives," Landon looked to his hands, shaking with nervousness.

THE EIGHTH LION

Finding both items on a table in the den of the unknown Eighth Lion staggered him. He wanted to reach up and grab the sword and the shield. The power offered by these weapons was incalculable. Even though he was just a Prince, the sword called out to his soul. As the heir to the throne, he would not be able to harness the strength of the sword. It could only truly serve the King of O'ndar. His father was the true owner of both. Yet, the magnetism he felt tugging on him was difficult to resist.

Landon fought the urge to reach up and grab the sword. It belonged to his House. For a fleeting second he was tempted to raise the sword and use it to slay the lions. He envisioned himself retracing his steps through Mfiri. He could slay the Children of the Night. With *Wynde Ryder* and the Emerald Shield in his hands, he would never fear to step off the obsidian pathway. He would go and meet Gamayun and challenge her to combat. Even Norduir, with all her strength and power, seemed less intimidating. Sorely tempted, Landon tore his eyes away and looked back to the black cat.

"I understand temptation, when it is placed before me. I understand all the demands it places on a person's mind," he said.

The cat offered, "In exchange for the kindness offered when you scratched my ears, I make you an offer, once again Prince Landon. You may take the sword and the shield and exit one of the four doors on the other side of the room. It is an offer I make honestly. There is no trickery, this I swear."

Landon felt as if he would burst with joy. His heart beat faster, resonating throughout his body. To return the fabled sword and shield to his father would make him a national hero. He would return to O'ndar celebrated throughout the land. His father would look at Landon the way Landon had always looked at his father, with pride and admiration. Landon looked at the jars once more. Each contained the soul of a person, one of them his mother. Landon's emotions battled for supremacy. This was the most difficult decision he ever had to make.

"*I wish my father were here. He would help me make the decision and then I would know it would be the right one.*" Landon's mind raced back and forth with the possibilities. Finally, after a few minutes, he took a deep breath, turned to the face the black cat, and said, "I must admit, I do not know which choice is the best. Before I decide, may I ask a question?"

The ebony cat looked at Landon and responded, "Of course." He thought the cat smiled at him, once more, but this time the smile did not anger him.

Landon asked, "I need advice. My father is not here to offer assistance. I would like to make a wise decision, therefore, I would ask for your help. What do you advise me to do?" He almost stopped himself from asking, afraid he would not like the answer.

The cat stood once more and without hesitation said to Landon, "I advise you take the jar."

Landon asked, "Could I ask why you advise this?" He waited, wondering if it would refuse to explain.

"The sword and the shield are not for you. They are here, waiting for another. He shall be along shortly." The cat turned and gestured to four doors at the back of the room.

"Another person to see the Seven? I mean the Eight." Landon's mind searched frantically for an explanation. If *Wynde Ryder* and its shield were not meant for a son of the House of Gheldari, who else was meant to possess them?

Landon looked up at the four, wooden doors wondering who would be coming through one of the doors shortly. *"Is my father coming through this door?"* Ghardenne was the true owner of the sword and the shield. As the ruler of O'ndar and the descendent of Gheldari and his son Gherdenne, his father was the only one who could wield the sword and access the power it held. There could be no other person to whom *Wynde Ryder* and the emerald shield owed allegiance.

The cat refused to offer any more. Landon did not ask for it to elaborate.

"I will take the jar," Landon said. His shoulders sagging, he turned away from that side of the table hoping to temper the temptation. Landon walked over to the jars and began looking carefully at all of them. Within a few minutes, he located the jar that Qui Oto had used to store Lenali's soul. He held it up to his face, studying it closely. The greenish liquid was still there. Landon was sure this was the container.

THE EIGHTH LION

"You have made a wise choice, Prince," the black cat said. Its voice grew deeper. Landon turned to look, but leaped away, startled. The cat had jumped down lightly off the wooden table. In the blink of an eye, the tiny house cat transformed into a massive, black lion. Its thick, black mane framed its deep-set, blue eyes. The soft voice was now deep and resonating. The massive paws were far larger than Landon's hands. The claws had quickly retracted, but Landon had seen them. He was convinced they could slice him open with ease.

"Most humans would not have been able to withstand the temptation placed before you Prince Landon. You have made a wise choice." The Lion moved closer, its blue eyes meeting his evenly. Powerful muscles rippled in the torchlight. Landon held no fear of the Lion, though he knew it could end his life with one swipe of its paws. Fear had left him long ago, most-likely the moment Gamayun had swallowed him whole, birthing him out onto the cold, hard ground in Mfiri. He had told himself to expect the unexpected, even when the unexpected was expected. The ebony-colored Eighth Lion, powerful and majestic with deep, blue eyes, was the perfect example of this motto.

The Lion waited a few seconds and then said to Landon, "Look at the four doors before us." He watched Landon turn to look at the wooden doors, each door identical to the others. The doors were plain, holding no lettering or phrases. There were no warnings offered.

Landon waited patiently for the Eighth Lion to continue, "Choose correctly and you will leave safely. If you choose incorrectly, you will have to start at the beginning, meeting with Cheetah, who you accurately named Sloth. But before you choose, you must offer me my true name."

Landon did not hesitate in his response, "Before I name you and choose the door, may I ask one last question?" He had already surmised the name of the Eighth Lion, but hoped his question and the Lion's answer would solidify his guess. The black Lion responded.

"Of course."

"Which door would you advise I choose?" Landon asked.

The Lion smiled at Landon pleased, "I advise you take the middle door, Young Prince." Landon nodded his thanks.

Landon began, *"Tam pulchra es, et sublimis. Monstravero tibi Regis vicit leo de mundo."*

The Lion smiled. Landon had said, "You are both beautiful and majestic. I name you Lion, the true King of the World." He waited only seconds before continuing.

"Et etiam propter naturam nominis tui et offerre tibi in qua mundi. Tu fidem. Tu fidem."

The Lion responded to Landon's words, its voice resonating pleasantly, "You may go in Peace, Young Prince. The journey before you will be more difficult than the one behind. That is always the case. When opening the door, say aloud where you would like to go. The door will take you there."

Holding the jar tightly in his hand, Landon walked over to the middle door. He did not hesitate.

Landon did not fear this Lion, if anything, he was sure he knew the nature of this Lion was the same as his. The Dragon Arem had drawn Landon across the Celestial Plane because of this nature. The Dragon had withheld the true reason behind his quest.

Yes, saving Princess Lenali was important. Arem had seen into the future and all its possibilities. His assessment included one possible future, which avoided the coming Apocalypse.

Lyssa did not know the entire scheme. His sister had agreed with Captain Arem about the importance of putting Landon on this path. She understood Landon's nature, holding faith in him.

He resented the burden Captain Arem had placed on him, though he understood the Dragon's reasons. The fate of millions of lives were in his hands, and on his shoulders. The fate of the Dragon Race was the same as that of the Human Race. Whatever happened to one would happen to the other.

Like it or not, the two of them had placed their faith in Landon, even though he doubted his own abilities. He decided it was time to have faith in himself. If they could do it, so could he.

He opened the door and looked into the quiet darkness. Landon no longer feared the unknown. If anything, he welcomed the next challenge.

"Take me to the Cave of the Dragon Arem," Landon spoke the words loudly, with courage.

He stepped forward bravely, into the awaiting darkness.

EPILOGUE

THE QUEEN REPLACED THE LID AND PLACED HER HANDS on the side of Ghardenne's face. She caressed him softly, watching his chest rise and fall. Once, twice, and then no more.

The Queen leaned in closely to his face, her dark eyes looking into his, and whispered. "Do not worry, My Love, this will all be over soon."